ALSO, BY R.W. MARCUS

The Fate of Tomorrow: Tales of the Annigan Cycle
Book One

Shadow of the Twilight Lands: Tales of the Annigan Cycle
Book Two

Whispers from Nocturn: Tales of the Annigan Cycle
Book Three

R.W. Marcus

AGENTS *of the* VOID

A Tale of the Annigan Cycle
in Three Acts

BOOK FOUR

R.W. MARCUS

LAUGHING BIRD PUBLISHING
GALAX, VA USA

Agents of the Void

Published by Laughing Bird Publications
Galax, Virginia USA

Visit us on the web!
https://AnniganCycle.com

Front and back cover design by SelfPubBookCovers
https://SelfPubBookCovers.com

Laughing Bird Publications® is a registered trademark of Mark W. Phillips

Manufactured in the United States of America
10 9 8 7 6 5 4 3 2

First Printing, 2020
Revised Second Printing 2023
ISBN 978-1-7320211-5-0

R.W. Marcus

Dedicated to the memory of
Edgar Rice Burroughs…
with a wink and a nod to
Philip José Farmer &
Quentin Tarantino

CONTENTS

ACKNOWLEDGEMENTS

As always, my initial thanks go out to my partner in crime Cheryl Pepper for both sharing and putting up with the writer's life with all that entails.

To my good friend, critique partner and all-around muse Mark Phillips for always being there with an encouraging word or an idea to nudge my twisted tale to the next level.

Big time thanks go out to my outstanding beta readers; Lynn Marie Firehammer, Dave (Too Drunk To Fuck) Holman, Tom Lancraft and Chris Breton. They especially stepped up on this project by spotting storyline issues early on, so they were easy to fix.

Finally, my sincere appreciation to Laughing Bird Publishing for believing in this endeavor enough to pick up the baton mid-series and run with it.

WELCOME TO THE ANNIGAN

This mostly aquatic planet travels in a geosynchronous orbit around a small yellow sun. It's set far enough back in the solar system's Goldilocks Zone it maintains an atmosphere conducive to a wide variety of life.

Sentient creatures, terrestrial, marine or amphibious, share a hyper-fertility devoid of genetic boundaries. Any sentient creature may mate with any other and produce offspring.

Lumina basks in perpetual sunlight on one side of the Annigan. Humans dwell alongside many other sentient races thriving across its various continents and island chains. The fertility enriching rays of the sun, and the warmth of the Shallow Sea, support a vibrant and rich ecosystem.

Although life is abundant there, Lumina is hardly a serene place as you will see. Millennia of feuds, ruthless ambition and individual hatreds forged a fragile peace, barely sustained under the rule of the Great Houses.

Because of the incredible diversity of sentient creatures, all races, genders and hybrids in Lumina enjoy social equality, judging each as an individual based upon their own merits. Beneath the veneer of peace, however, dwells a hotbed of totalitarian torture, raider uprisings and a constant escalating cold war between the Great Houses.

Nocturn, languishes in constant darkness on the other side of the Annigan. Only moonlight, starlight and bioluminescence illuminates the land of endless night. Without the warming rays of the sun, Nocturn's oceans froze over, but constant geothermal activity heats the land masses, creating a temperate and misty terrain teeming with exotic and predatory sentient races.

Imperialistic cat people rule aboveground and hive nations of humanoid mantises swarm beneath the surface. In the Ocean Deep, a race of sentient octopoids dwell in vast underwater cities worshiping the ancient ones of the abyss. You are predator or prey in Nocturn's despotic societies.

The Twilight Lands reside at the fringes of the Annigan and remain in a constant gloaming. Here, warm and cold air currents clash, generating a perpetually stormy climate.

Ruled by the amphibian Bailian race, the Twilight Lands serve as a neutral zone for cultures from every corner of the Annigan. Many encounter the other races for the first time, and like the weather, their clashes can prove tempestuous.

Only the sun of Lumina keeps back the nocturnal predators of the dark side. Legends tell of a prophesied great eclipse stripping away all boundaries and igniting an apocalyptic war. Until then…

…these are the tales from the Annigan Cycle.

R.W. Marcus

The Annigan labors
To right itself.
Form and balance
Dark and light
Picking up pieces,
An arduous task.
Best left to those
Prepared for a fight

ACT ONE

The Na-Kab Factor

T he air was thick and cloying. Its sour, peppery essence clung to the hairs along short snouts and caused noses to twitch.

They were getting close.

Creeping silently along the ceiling, two Ash-Ta of Clan Molossi cautiously made their way through the sprawling complex of wide passages which comprised the Do-Tarr's Southern Hive. The passages were luxuriously wide, averaging fifty feet across and twenty feet tall. The walls, though not roughhewn, had a course texture ideal for the Ash-Ta to latch on. Up ahead, a junction branched out into perfect right angles, which complimented the precise rectangular tunnel they now navigated.

Pausing, the humanoid bat creature's long sharp ears fluttered, searching for any sound of Do-Tarr presence. Both knew discovery by the insect peoples meant a painful death being systematically dismembered and eaten.

These Clan Molossi Ash-Ta, unlike the other four clans, were experts at raiding the Do-Tarr hives and the queen's precious nectar. It was an ironic symbiosis that the natural foodstuff of the insect nation enhanced the clan's inherent camouflaging ability, which made detection by their natural

1

enemies difficult. Their homes, which were in the nearby jagged peaks of the Spine of the World, bordered the Nectar rich chambers of both the great northern and southern Do-Tarr hives. This proximity made escape easy if they made it out.

Hearing nothing, the duo silently approached the intersection, nervously chanting back-and-forth their mantra in their people's undetectable, high frequency language.

"I am Molossi, no ward can stop me," the lead always began.

"I am Molossi, no trap can catch me." the second always replied.

And so it went, back-and-forth.

"I am Molossi, no barrier can hold me."

"I am Molossi, invisible and relentless."

At the tunnel's crossroads, both peered anxiously in all directions, sniffing furiously. Catching the distinct odor of Do-Tarr nectar, they cautiously followed the trail to the left.

"This is strange, brother," one nervously said. "Where are the work details?"

"Do not dismay," the other replied. "Rejoice our task is easier."

They continued along quickly for another two hundred yards until they heard the telltale clacking of exoskeletal feet against stone. Both froze, flattening out against the ceiling and extending their wings outward, hugging the stone to limit their profile. The insect race perceived mostly by motion and vibration. Only a direct sighting would betray their presence.

They watched motionlessly. On the tunnel floor, twenty feet below, six mantis creatures scurried down the passage. Three carried long-handled mining hammers while the others gripped wide, flat shovels with both hands. Their humanoid torsos sat atop insectoid bodies. The eyes in their mantid shaped heads betrayed no emotion while they passed.

The bat creature's hearts pounded when the last Do-Tarr in the line paused and looked around warily. Time seemed to stand still as it concentrated for any errant vibration in the rocks. Sensing nothing, it raced off after its work mates.

Taking a moment to compose themselves, they proceeded guardedly onward. After another two hundred yards, the smell of the queen's nectar was almost overwhelming. Peering around the next corner, they saw the tunnel narrow to just over five feet square. Clogging the opening was a greenish brown viscous substance.

"This is it, brother," one said, trembling in excitement. "A most potent store!"

They descended from the ceiling and stepped up to the gooey barrier. Both sniffed it curiously up and down before one slowly reached out and touched the surface. The sticky material clung to his hand when he drew it back, forming a long, dripping tendril.

Seeing it caused no harm, he plunged his entire hand into the slimy portal. There was a deep sucking sound as he parted it. The air that escaped was warm and pungent, causing both Ash-Ta to trade appreciative glances.

Hearing nothing from beyond, he peered into the opening, then pushed his head and upper body through the mucky portal. When his slime covered torso reemerged, he was smiling. With an enthusiastic affirmative nod, both bat creatures crawled through.

The room was twenty feet square. The same gelatinous material covered the walls and ceiling. On the far wall was a similar opening. Hanging from the ceiling throughout the entire area were teardrop shaped sacks. Each was approximately six inches in diameter, tapering up to a slender thread attached to the ceiling and covered in ooze. While similar, no two were the same size.

Being in such proximity to the oppressive odor of the Do-Tarr queens essence caused both Ash-Ta's breath to become ragged. Their eyes watered and widened at the treasure trove in the form of dangling liquid filled sacks. Moving between the forest of hanging orbs, they continued to sniff, furiously searching for the ones containing the freshest liquid.

In the far corner they lingered and circled a slightly larger sphere which dangled by itself. Its surface was more textured, and a buttery musk replaced the sour overtones of the other nectar sacks.

"We have found it!" one said, wings fluttering in exhilaration, "but the smell is different."

The other nodded, his eyes trailing upward to where it attached to the slime covered ceiling, then returned to the dripping bag.

"Royal jelly," he said, authoritatively.

His partner looked mystified. "This was our mission all along!"

Nodding silently, he reached out towards the mailable surface and looked over at his companion. "Are you ready my brother?"

Swallowing nervously, he also nodded. Both launched themselves simultaneously towards the roof using short wing flaps. One grabbed the tendrilled base of the royal jelly sack and, with a single swipe of its claw, sliced it off where it connected.

Instantaneously, a piercing shriek thundered through the hive when the queen felt her hive's life blood severed. A multitude of wailing voices soon joined the lone screech as the word spread instantly throughout the hive.

With the alarm now sounded the other bat creature began indiscriminately severing the neighboring nectar sacks allowing them to fall to the floor. With each slash, another shriek reverberated through the tunnels. A blaring clamor joined the cacophony when thousands of Do-Tarr echoed their enraged queen.

Holding his prize aloft, the Ash-Ta swept his wings outward and launched himself at the opening. Folding them back at the last instant, he quickly disappeared through the portal.

Now alone, the remaining Molossi kept up his assault on the hive's nectar reserves, practicing a tried-and-true strategy between the ancient enemies. Once the Do-Tarr arrived on the scene, the emphasis would be on salvaging what they could from the floor, allowing the agile, unarmed bat creature to escape behind his partner.

When the first of the humanoid mantis arrived, the Ash-Ta thieves bolted for the orifice they came through. Just as every time in the past, none followed after them, because they fixated on saving what they could of the hive's precious life blood. They flew as fast as the corridors would allow, hearts pounding with excitement.

Entering the intersection, the lead Ash-Ta banked hard to the right, following his original path. His eyes widened in horror and surprise to find the corridor before him filled with angry Do-Tarr. They covered the floor and rushed along the walls and ceilings at him, leaving a tiny opening in the dead center of the hallway.

Realizing he was moving too fast to change course, the swiftly gliding Ash-Ta gave a powerful pump of his wings increasing velocity, then folded them back and aimed for his only opening towards freedom. Tightly clutching the sack, he could see the skies of Nocturn through the opening ahead.

The trailing Molossi watched his partner nearing the exit. Excitement raced through him at the thought of another successful raid. He was about to give out a victory squeal when a Do-Tarr hand latched onto his leg, wrenching him to a halt. His bag of nectar flew open when they wrested it from his hands. The viscous liquid drenched both captor and pursuant when the fleshy sack toppled to the floor.

The Ash-Ta felt a jolt of energy from the liquid when it coated and soaked into his skin. Now free of his burden, he performed an inverted barrel roll, yanking himself free.

Despite the searing pain in his ankle, he felt a profound sense of hope and relief when he saw his companion taking flight out of the hive. His relief was short lived, when the mantis creature, also invigorated by the spilled nectar, latched onto his back. Its weight propelled the Ash-Ta uncontrollably forward. He screamed out in agony as he felt the Do-Tarr's mandibles bite into his right-wing joint, severing the pinion at its base.

Now completely off balance, both creatures spun out of control, crashing into the wall and landing on the floor of the corridor. A throng of Do-Tarr immediately set upon the stunned man-bat. They gruffly spun him onto his back, gnawing through his leg and arm joints, rendering him immobile.

Laying a dozen feet from freedom, the fresh air from the outside caressed his fur, starkly contrasting the hard exoskeletons rubbing against him as the mantis creatures swarmed his helpless body. The spilled nectar heightened his senses, amplifying the anguish. He eagerly anticipated being rended apart just to end it all. Instead, he sensed himself being lifted by several of the insectoid creatures and carried away from the opening, deep into the hive.

Peering out as far as the searing pain would allow, he noted a substantial rise in the humidity when they entered an enormous rectangular cavern. Off to his left, a loud plopping sound caught his attention. To his horror, he witnessed the large thorax of the queen discharging a foot-long larva in a rush of thick, yellowish green fluid. It tumbled down into a pool of the liquid where it joined a writhing sea of maggot children.

Halting abruptly at the pool's edge, the Do-Tarr workers summarily threw the helpless Ash-Ta into the visceral pond. The liquid was only several inches deep, and he felt his spine shatter with a loud crunch from the impact against the hidden stone floor beneath.

Now, as he lay there unable to move, but intensely aware of every sensation, he felt the slimy undulations of the Do-Tarr larva crawling onto him, eagerly devouring his nectar-soaked skin. He cried out in despair as tiny jaws ripped away little bits of flesh, realizing, at this rate, his death would take many agonizing cycles.

With his partner's high frequency screams of pain still ringing in his ears, the lead Ash-Ta swept out into the cool, star filled Nocturn skies. He banked eastward, fleeing towards the Rovina Region's savannahs in the Land of Mists, instead of his usual route back home to The Spine of the World.

This bounty was beyond the scope and understanding of his clansmen. It would fetch a handsome price from his waiting buyer.

Okawa watched Joc' Valdur drop the letter on his desk with an irritated huff and settle back in his chair. She thought her boss looked more like an artist than a diplomat, with his shoulder-length black hair and scraggly beard, but his youthful features appeared weary and troubled.

"This does not bode well," he said, grimly. "It appears Queen Shula is reluctant to send any more emissaries to our fair city until we can guarantee their safety."

The notoriously calm Valdurian envoy to Zor stared over his wide desk at the faces of his top security operative and Cha-Rod seated across from him. "And I really can't say that I blame her. I need not tell you that this really puts a kink in our plans of an Etheria trade agreement with Immor-Onn. We need those Etheria crystals."

Okawa leaned forward, placing her forearms on to his desk. "Boss, as far as the Bailian queen is concerned, I'm sure you can make the argument that Demetrius and I were the target of Stryder, not her ambassador. She and her party were unfortunately in the wrong place at the wrong time. It was an isolated incident."

"Not much solace in that argument," Joc' said, shaking his head.

Okawa sat back with a frustrated sigh.

The elder Bailian lowered his head sorrowfully. His thick handlebar mustache twitched nervously against his pale blue skin and his large almond-shaped eyes sank in melancholy.

"Ambassador, I take full responsibility," Cha-Rod said. "Ambassador Ar' Sut and her party were in my charge to protect. I failed them and my queen."

Okawa's eyes narrowed in curiosity as Joc's lips tightened. He normally never exhibited frustration in front of anyone but her.

"I disagree with your assessment." Joc' said, decisively. By every report I've read, you acted in exemplary fashion against overwhelming odds."

Cha-Rod looked up and weakly smiled. "Thank you sir, however I'm certain the members of my order would disagree."

A curtain of uncertainty descended on Joc's face. "Surely you're not required to take your own life or anything drastic like that?"

Cha-Rod leaned back and peered around the elegant but sparsely furnished office all the while keeping his sadly pleasant exterior. "No, you're thinking of an outdated practice of my people."

"Well that's good..."

The Bailian returned his gaze to his host and shook his head. "No, nowadays my people would want to kill me themselves."

The Valdurian ambassador was aghast. "What?!"

8

"Yes," Cha-Rod said, grimly. "According to the edicts of my order I should return to Immor-Onn and face a Capability Contingent."

"And that would include?"

"Literally running a gauntlet," Cha-Rod said, somberly. "It would require me to pay for my failure and the embarrassment to our order's reputation."

The silent, shocked expressions staring at him prompted the Bailian to continue. "This would not just be a test of my competency. My gauntlet wouldn't include younger Bojo-Vat, former students who might want a go at me for being too hard on them. No, only my peers would form this gauntlet."

The master stick fighter paused and stared into space with a resolved expression. "At my age, that *is* a death sentence."

Okawa turned with a look of disgust. "You mean to tell me that people you've known most of your life, people you've trained and lived among would willingly beat you to death?"

Cha-Rod shrugged helplessly. "It is our way."

A moment of grim realization gave the two humans pause. Seeing their apprehension, Cha-Rod shook his head.

"Don't worry," he said, "I agree with your evaluation, the unfortunate death of our ambassador was completely out of my hands. I have no intention of returning just to die for the sake of some inflexible regulation."

This admission caused an immediate sense of relief in Joc' and Okawa.

The Bojo-Vat master cleared his throat. "So, I offer my services to you, if you'll have me."

The head Valdurian had already made his mind up when Okawa chimed in, "Boss, he's pretty handy with that walking stick."

Joc' smiled confidently at the Bailian. "Oh, I've familiarized myself with the provenance of Master Cha-Rod.

I imagine he's pretty handy with more than just walking sticks."

Okawa shot her superior a questioning look when the elderly stick fighter modestly lowered his head.

Joc' nodded in appreciation. "Your direct lineage in the order of Bojo-Vat goes back almost a thousand grands."

Cha-Rod looked back up. The ends of his thick mustache turned upwards in a shy smile.

"My father," he said, "my father's father and beyond all served the order with distinction. I would be the first to dishonor my line. Fortunately, I have no children to pass on the shame."

"You have nothing to be ashamed of," Joc' said, definitively. "To allow your talent and experience to vanish in an act of vain repercussion is insane."

Reaching across the desk Joc' offered his hand.

"Welcome aboard."

Okawa silently observed the poignant scene with a touch of impatience.

"Okay," she sighed redirecting the conversation, "what do we do about the person who caused all of this? What are we to do about Stryder Aramos?"

The fat butcher's pockmarked features lit up with pride making the thick mustache covering his mouth resemble a caterpillar crossing his face.

"Here you go Peli," he beamed as pudgy fingers rolled the fresh raw sausage in a sheet of thick brown paper and handed it to Peligro. "Just the way you like it."

The Aramos agent nodded appreciatively, watching whiffs of steam rise from the bag when it contacted the cold air. They blended harmoniously with the ever-present aroma of garlic and basil drifting out from the small cooking hut in congested central Rophan.

"You always take care of me, Choppy," Peligro said, reaching for his coins.

The delighted butcher wiped his bloody hands on his apron before holding both of them out. Seeing the extra copper coin, Choppy gave a happy sigh.

"Ah Peli, you give me too much again."

"You deserve it, Choppy," Peligro said, backing onto Canolog Street. "How about some lamb tomorrow?"

"You got it!" the butcher said, returning to the relative warmth of the rear of his shop.

With dinner and breakfast firmly under one arm, Peligro set off southward as the turine in the harbor rang ten bells.

Kan's starting soon, he fretted. *Hope Sonja's is still open.*

Pulling his coat tighter with his free hand, he continued down the crowded street. As always, he kept to the west side of the wide central avenue which connected the city from the docks to the palace.

The west side was the poorer inner-city, and all along the route he caught the various whiffs of evening meals being prepared. The delicious smells coming from outdoor grills to attract customers made his stomach grumble. He smiled watching two EEtah arguing with a fish monger about the puny size of his catch on display.

On the eastern side of the road was the more affluent merchant track. To the practical agent, the merchants were all right; a little haughtier, more expensive. The inner-city folk were more genuine, and he loved rewarding their appreciative attention.

Picking up his pace, Peligro nervously pushed through the crowd. He visibly relaxed when he saw Mz. Sonya at her bread stand just ahead.

11

I wouldn't turn that down, Peligro assessed to himself, watching the attractive proprietor in an animated conversation with a Picean. The fishman's gill flaps fluttered furiously over his ears as he translated Sonja's negotiations.

When she saw Peligro approach she stopped, placed her hands on her hips and gave a flirtatious smile. The Picean, detecting an exit opportunity, excused himself and disappeared into the crowd.

They stared at each other briefly, smiles playing at both their lips. Not breaking eye contact, the older raven-haired beauty reached over and grabbed a single loaf resting on the far end of the counter. The stale, tubular bread made a dull clunk when she placed it on the counter in front of him. Shaking her head, she swept her arm across several baskets filled with loaves of various sizes.

"My husband makes bread fresh every day. You want day old and you pay the same as fresh?" Sonja said, with a deep confused shrug.

Peligro chuckled, enchanted by an earthy sensuousness even her plain black dress couldn't conceal. He winked, dropped two copper coins on the counter, and picked up the hardened roll.

"A taste of home," he said, before joining the crowd flowing southward towards the wealthy Bogor Tract, home to the royal palace and city's elite.

Peligro followed the winding artery through the city. His stomach grumbled and he could practically smell the sausage in his hands roasting.

His apartment wasn't far. He had specifically chosen it for its third story overlook and central location. It was perfect for monitoring things in the Eldorian capital for House Aramos.

His cover as an oyster broker on the docks was solid. It allowed him to leave for long periods without raising suspicions and also provided information on comings and goings in the city, as did his morning and evening walks to and from work.

After a long two grands on assignment here in the Eldorian capital of Rophan, it was the little things that kept him going. Like stale bread. Peligro tapped on it as he walked. *Well, it ain't Kemeny bread, but it's close.*

Passing the last bend in the road before his place, the Aramos agent froze. People streamed around his six-foot frame while he stared upward across the street to a second-story balcony.

An orange sheet lay draped on the railing to dry.

This was the only signal the deep operatives of the Aramos Black Talons, known as Wraiths, ever received. It was definitely a message, most likely an assignment.

Peligro proceeded past the row of buildings with the orange sheet and then changed to the other side of the street. Slipping in behind a row of shops, he ran his hand up and down the jam of the second rear door until he heard the telltale click.

A small hatch gave way, and he retrieved a medium sized envelope. Examining its plain exterior, the Aramos Wraith nodded acceptance and slid it in his coat.

Several stops punctuated the remaining short trip home. He greeted people on both the street and along the three flights of stairs to his modest apartment.

The two-room dwelling was chilly. Peligro set the envelope, sausage, and bread roll down on the single table and kept his coat on as he made a fire. He skewered the sausages for roasting and glanced at the letter on the table.

I'll eat first, he decided. *No point in ruining my appetite.*

As the fire crackled and the room filled with warmth, Peligro stripped down to his underclothes. He stared at the envelope's plain covering with each pass by the table. Finally, curiosity got the best of him and he pulled the paper sheath open. Inside he found a folded piece of paper and two spice notes worth twenty thousand secor in Aramos commodities.

Peligro whistled softly, examining the sizeable sum of money. *This is gonna be big*, he assessed, then looking over at the folded orders. *I better eat first.*

Taking a big bite of the succulent sausage and chewy stale bread, the Wraith broke the seal and opened the letter. His eyes widened as he read his assignment.

First, I put Shom Eldor on the throne and now they want me to kill a dangerously rogue Stryder Aramos. Peligro sighed. *Oh well, orders are orders.*

Going over to the hearth the agent dropped the secret instructions into the flames, then returned to his makeshift dinner.

At least I'm heading home to Aris this time. I can finally get a decent meal, if I live.

Kai never really understood intellectual types. She boringly scanned the bookshelf lined walls before returning her attention to Senior Pisar Tysonn de Ovara of the newly formed Bailian Institute of Arts and Letters. He shook his head in frustration.

The small book fit easily in his hand. The plain leather binding was smooth to the touch. Holding it open before him, he tapped on the pages filled with minuscule script.

"I've spent the last several lunas studying this thing, and I have come to a conclusion," the scribe said, with an air of authority.

Kai's eyes widened, and she leaned in expectantly. "What is it?"

Tysonn leaned back. His youthful features betrayed an academically questioning look when he swept back his long brown hair.

"I have no idea."

Kai's face fell as her shoulders slumped. "What?"

"I've seen nothing like this before," the young man said, turning the pages and pointed at the script. "I can speak, read and write just about every known language on the Annigan, Including a bunch of *really* weird dialects."

Tysonn closed the book with a thud.

"I mean, I can guess, but that doesn't mean I'm right."

Kai gave a bemused look. "The queen paid a lot of money to lure you away from the University of Marassa. I'm betting your opinion is worth listening to."

The young human blushed slightly at the compliment. He opened the book to a random page and passionately ran his hands over the text.

"Okay," he said, "its initial appearance is like a book of poetry. Multi-line groupings, artfully arranged."

Tysonn glanced over at Kai who acknowledged she understood. He continued shuffling through the pages.

"What's baffling about these various groupings is how they are composed of only two characters."

"I've seen these characters written in blood at a murder scene," she said.

The pisar paused. "You say you acquired this book from the apartment of the late Tiikeri Finance Minister?"

Kai managed a slight affirmative nod as she stared outward. She could still see the body of little Sied with his throat cut and the blood runes dripping down the wall. Her throat tightened, and she forced herself back to the conversation.

Tysonn set the book down on the desk in front of him. "My guess is that it's a grimoire or religious text."

Kai's intense stare shifted from infinity, to the book, then finally back to the scribe.

"I mean there's only two characters," the young man reasoned, "it's obviously some sort of code. We can break it. We just don't have the right staff here."

The assassin's demeanor softened with the pisar's more positive approach.

"I need to get this to my colleagues back at the University of Marassa," he said.

"You need to take that to Zor?" Kai confirmed.

"Yes."

The Bailian spymaster hesitated. "You realize that the Tiikeri empire is in the opposite direction of where you want to take it?"

An amused smirk crossed the scribes youthful face. "You want me to just waltz on over to the Land of Mists with this?"

Kai gave a frustrated chortle. "All right, all right, but you were the whiz kid of the Language Arts Department back there. If you can't figure it out, what makes you so sure the others can?"

"A valid concern," the pisar acknowledged. "But there we'll have more trained eyes on it. Like I said, we don't have the staff."

Kai nodded in acceptance. "I'll get with the queen and arrange secure transportation. The people over at House Valdur are trying to get back in her good graces. I'm sure they can send an airship."

Tysonn swallowed nervously. "Airship?"

"You got something against flying?"

"Well, uh, I guess not."

"Good because a trip by water would take way too long."

Kai then gave a sly smile at the scribe. "Are you sure there's not an ulterior motive for the trip?"

Tysonn returned the grin. "I must admit there's a certain young lady in Zor I'd like to pay a visit to. However, the people I will probably consort with the most will be considerably older and much more, oh shall we say sober?"

Kai chuckled lecherously. "Don't worry, we'll get you laid. You just find out what the damn book says."

Hunger clawed at Drucilla's stomach as she watched the moon dip past the dim orb of the sun in the western sky. It unceremoniously descended below the horizon, leaving the capital of the Bailian empire in a dusky twilight. The chilly wind rustling her fur and clattering wind chimes were a constant reminder of how she despised this place.

Then there were the cravings.

She had held them off for as long as she could. Once again, the cultured Avion inside her attempted to tame the wild Ash-Ta body and the appetite accompanying it. Drucilla had been able to contain her gruesome hunger for over three lunas before the urges for blood and fresh flesh overwhelmed her. She could not deny the yearning, despite her revulsion of it.

This moonless, she was certain the animal would prevail.

With a flutter of her leathery wings, she launched herself into the skies over Immor-Onn. The city was her new hunting grounds. She was through hiding on the fringes of the city, feeding on farm and wild animals. Tonight, she would dine.

Down below, she could see the streets beneath their clear crystal coverings. The blue skinned Bailians were making their way back to their dwellings and the orange glow of crystals appeared in the windows like a flickering tapestry of light. She gave a dour sigh.

This was so different from her yearning for the sun-drenched skies of Lumina. She mused how darkly ironic this

17

longing was, since her new body from Nocturn couldn't even handle the constant sunlight of that side of the world. The notion she could not escape from this trap forced a sneer.

Slipping gracefully around the snowflake shaped spires of the city's thin, graceful architecture, she made her way to the dock area with its many bars and eating establishments.

Silently landing in an alley off the main road, she folded back her wings under a black, medium length cape. She had acquired her simple tunic from her last kill. It was ill fitting but concealed enough of her animalistic appearance so she could move about in the city unnoticed. Her beautifully symmetrical face resembled a human hybrid, as did all of her Ash-Ta Desmodus Clan.

She moved amongst the thinning, mostly Bailian crowd. The charred smell of cooking meat, from the food vendors lining the wide avenue, repulsed her. She recalled how, in her prior life as an Avion, she too indulged in roasted foods. Now, through waves of self loathing, the throng of passing sentients whetted her ravenous appetite.

Heart pounding with anticipation, she stepped off to the side of the street to calm herself. Hunger could make any creature act rashly, and an impetuous kill would bring about unwanted attention.

She breathed deeply until the impulse to attack the nearest creature receded, replaced by waves of guilt and shame. This struggle raged within her every time she contemplated killing anything more than an animal. Perhaps a drink would calm her nerves.

Across the street, groups of human sailors went in and out of a large pub. The sign hanging out front read:

Dan Ton's Cantina

The queen drinks here

No one took notice when she stepped into the warm, boisterous interior. A Calden naval vessel must have just come into port. Rowdy sailors filled the large room. They laughed and carried on with the Bailian prostitutes roaming amongst the tables.

Finding a small booth near the corner by the bar, she sat and buried her face in her hands, trying to control the overstimulation of her surroundings. There were two serving wenches working the floor. One would be along soon.

"May I join you?" a friendly voice said, in perfect En'Sul, cutting through the clamor and her concentration.

Swallowing hard, she composed herself and looked up. A handsome young human smiled down at her, dressed in the uniform of a junior Calden Navy officer. His high cheekbones accentuated his broad grin and blue eyes danced beneath a short strawberry blond head of close-cropped hair.

She forced a conciliatory smile and gracefully showed the chair next to her.

"Please," she replied in Common.

There was a brief look of surprise at not being rejected, before the grin returned and he took his seat.

"Allow me to introduce myself," he said, switching to the common tongue and extending his hand. "Lieutenant Dolos de Oris."

"Drucilla," she replied demurely, shaking his hand.

The server arriving at their table interrupted the introductions.

"Please, allow me to buy you a drink," he offered. "It's the least I can do for you allowing me to share your table."

With two tankards of ale ordered, the handsome officer returned his attention to the exotic looking female beside him.

"So, something tells me you're not from around here," he said, attempting to get the conversation started.

"I'm not," Drucilla said, shaking her head. "I only arrived recently."

Dolos chuckled. "Yeah, me too. We just finished an Innaca run and now my ship the *Gahinan* is on permanent assignment here. So where are you from?"

A maudlin look crossed Drucilla's face. "Originally from Goya, but I've been around."

"I knew you looked human," he said, in cheerful recognition. "Along with something else..."

Drucilla nodded coyly but remained silent.

"Must be hard making friends traveling around like that," Dolos said, changing the subject.

"It gets pretty lonely," she admitted, taking a drink.

"Yeah, I know what you mean," the Calden officer replied. "Shipboard duty can get pretty lonely too. I mean you've got the rest of the crew, but being a junior officer, the enlisted don't want to associate with you and the top brass keep to themselves. I'm stuck in the middle of a social wasteland. Even if I am the newest Brightstar recipient."

Drucilla glanced down to see the new pin on his chest amongst his other ribbons. The star and swan stood out and marked him as a master sailor. The young man showed obvious pride in achieving the coveted rank. She considered how in her prior life as an Avion, this would have impressed her. Now, predatory hunger overpowered any feelings of admiration for him or shame within herself.

Dolos summoned his courage and leaned forward.

"Hey, it's really noisy in here," he said. "What do you say I get us a bottle and we find a quieter location where we can talk?"

She stared at him for a moment while the animal and Avion factions of her psyche battled for control. When hunger finally eroded her ethics, she reluctantly nodded.

"Sure," she said, softly.

They left the cantina and wandered down to the rocky shore just south of the harbor entrance. They passed under graceful yet precise stonework, which seemed to glitter in the glow of the ever-present crystals.

"This really is a beautiful city," Dolos commented.

"I guess."

Drucilla's unenthusiastic reply garnered a curious look from the sailor, and she quickly caught herself before he had time to question her.

"The Black Pearl Revolution almost destroyed the city a few grands ago," she said, in a more congenial tone. "The Do-Tarr rebuilt it to the queen's specifications. Otherwise it would be square and plain. The bugs are great builders, but lack imagination."

They took shelter from the winds of the moonless in a partially enclosed circle of boulders found amidst the jagged rocks dotting the pebbly beach. Settling down on a large flat boulder in the center, they stared out at the crashing waves.

"The weather here will take some getting used to," he said, turning his attention to the bottle.

"It did for me," Drucilla said, gazing mournfully out at the turbulent sea.

Out of the corner of her eye she watched Dolos examine the bottle, and she longed for this to be over. The banality of small talk about the weather irritated her, and she felt savage impulses rising.

Placing the bottle between his legs on the rock, Dolos softly grunted while he wrestled with an obstinate cap and the wires holding it in place.

"I can tell you one thing I've discovered since arriving…" Drucilla began, while watching the Calden officer struggle with the container.

"What's that?" Dolos asked, half listening, bent over and staring intently at the reluctant stopper.

In an abrupt fluid motion, the Ash-Ta grabbed the back of the naval officer's head and drove it down savagely onto the neck of the bottle. The long, thin glass spout pierced through the eye and plunged into the brain. Taken by surprise, Dolos had no time to even cry out. He died instantly and toppled face first onto the pebbly shore with the liquor bottle still perversely jutting from the front of his face.

Drucilla watched the bottle shatter and the liquid spill out before she completed her thought.

"...meat not tainted by fear and adrenalin tastes sweetest."

She leaped upon her immobile prey, and the crashing surf covered the sounds of shredding clothes and flesh.

The Bailian lovers walked along the shore with their arms around each other. The wind whipped their long black hair about, tangling it with their partners. He was a full head taller than her and she rested her slightly elongated head on his narrow shoulder. They had taken advantage of a break in her family's festivities they had been attending. The weather wasn't too windy for a romantic walk on the beach.

She leaned in for a kiss, batting her large almond-shaped eyes before cocking her head quizzically.

The adolescent male gave a perplexed grin. "I thought you said I was a good kisser."

"You *are* silly!" she said, now fully looking around. "Do you hear that?"

"Hear what?"

"I don't know, it sounds like a woman crying. Come on."

Leading her amorous companion by the hand, she followed the distressed sound. As they approached the stone circle, she could see a woman sitting on the ground at the water's edge, facing away from them and out to sea. Both could now hear the racking sobs coming from her while she rocked back-and-forth with her head in her hands.

"Hello, are you all right?" the young Bailian female said, stepping forward.

The woman ignored the question and continued her doleful wailing.

"Is there anything we can do?" the man said, coming up behind his partner.

Drawing closer, the female noticed the waves turning a ghastly shade of red as they receded back into the ocean.

"I think she might be hurt," the young Bailian female speculated with concern.

"Are you all right?" the male said, while they cautiously entered the stone circle.

Both lurched to a standstill, frozen in shock and disgust. Drucilla knelt beside a partially eaten body. She had ripped its chest cavity open and stripped the flesh from its limbs down to the bone. Gore pooled around her. The crimson tide carried the chewed up and strewn about entrails out to sea.

The Ash-Ta bounded to her feet. She spun to face them, bloody foam spraying from her mouth and hands. Paralyzed by terror, both Bailians shrieked at the top of their lungs.

Drucilla hissed viciously. She bared multiple rows of needle-sharp teeth, before unfolding her wings and rocketing out of sight.

The light from the recent moonrise glittered off the icy slush lapping the shore of the south-western Land of Mists. A lone Singa sat atop a small island of wide flat stones nestled into the expansive white sand beach. The mane of the man-lion fluttered in the morning breeze while he stared out at the distant ice flows of the Frozen Sea.

Behind him, over a row of low dunes, the tops of the Rovina Plane grasslands swayed above the constant layer of mist from which the continent derived its name.

Looking skyward, the Singa sniffed the breeze and gazed westward. The hint of a smile crossed his face when he reached between the rocks and retrieved a small wooden box. Placing it on the surface of the rock in front of him, he casually got to his feet and adjusted his opulent robe.

He could hear the beating of the wings before he saw the lone Ash-Ta come into view. It rapidly approached, swooping and diving in its races' distinct, erratic flight pattern.

The Singa trader prided himself on his relationship with the elusive and savage bat creatures from The Spine of the World. There were only a few of the clans that possessed the mental ability to engage in rudimentary commerce. Lengthy and dangerous trial and error discerned this. Once he separated the animal from the sentient, it took him a long time to gain their trust and discover their needs.

He smiled as the Ash-Ta drew closer. The fluttering of the leathery pinions kicked up a small cloud of sand when the four-foot-tall humanoid bat landed on the rocks in front of the man-lion. Both stared at each other for a moment until each broke out in amicable smiles.

"It is good to see you again Midlari," the man-bat said, in broken Singa.

Midlari nodded appreciatively. "And you, my winged friend."

Eying the tear shaped sack in the Ash-Ta's hands, Midlari's smile widened. "I take it you were successful?"

The Molossi handed the sack to the very receptive Singa.

"I acquired this at the cost of one of my clansmen's life."

"I am sorry for your loss," Midlari said, acknowledging the solemnity of the statement. "Their sacrifice honors this transaction. The reputation of the Molossi is undeniable. No others move with such impunity amongst the bug hives."

The Ash-Ta grinned broadly at the compliment. "I am Molossi, no ward can stop me."

The Singa returned the smile and nodded down at the box which rested between the two.

"And this will ensure you will become the greatest raider your people have ever known."

The man-bat's eyes widened in excitement when he reached down and picked up the carton. Holding it up to his face he opened it and inhaled deeply. Looking back up, he nodded in satisfaction.

"Ghrana," he said, breathlessly.

"Pure Tiikeri pheromone, just as ordered my friend," the Singa cajoled. "This will render you invisible and invincible to the bugs. Your people will speak your name throughout the ages."

The Ash-Ta all but panted in exhilaration. "With the reputation this provides me, leader of my clan is finally within my reach!"

"Well deserved," the Singa praised.

Closing and lowering the box, the man-bat involuntarily clicked out a statement of gratitude in its own language before catching himself and returning to the Singa tongue.

"You've earned your reputation as well, Midlari," it squeaked. "You can find anything."

The Singa bowed slightly at the compliment. "I'm glad we could make a mutually beneficial exchange."

"It was good trading with you Midlari, farewell," the Ash-Ta said, before unfolding its wings and taking off.

The Singa watched the man-bat ascend. While it climbed into the moonlit sky with its prize, he set the sack down and reached once more between the rocks. This time, he pulled out a fully loaded large crossbow and casually examined the bolts thick shaft and multi-barbed tip.

Nodding in satisfaction, he aimed it at the retreating Ash-Ta and fired. The missile plunged into the creature's groin and lodged out the back of its neck with such force that it jolted the bat's body a full ten feet. Midlari watched the impaled Ash-Ta plummet into the icy waters and disappear.

Sighing, he lowered the weapon, picked up his treasure, and padded through the sand into the mist covered savannahs.

Pootar stood erect peeking over the tops of the gently waving grasslands of the Rovina Region in the Land of Mists. About thirty yards away, he caught sight of his mate and eldest son doing the same on each side of him.

He couldn't help feeling a sense of pride in the way his family coordinated their hunting expeditions. Over the various cycles he had honed them into an effective tracking team. His beloved clan were the envy of every other family of Duma cheetahs, because they were never without food.

This time, however, they were out of their element, for they rarely hunted so close to shore. However, a large prairie elk had become separated from its herd and was a potentially easy meal. Off to their left he could see its antlers poking above the mist and grass tops.

One sniff told him Singa's had marked the area just beyond. They were precariously close to the Gronn Singa Pride territory. If their prey ventured beyond that boundary, the hunt would become extremely dangerous.

Poaching was a serious offense to the Singa lion peoples. If caught by the female hunters, the cost would be fatal. Poachers feared Female Singa's for a reason, their cunning, and relentlessness was matched only by their savagery.

He had witnessed firsthand their vicious nature. A party of three had killed his uncle when he was young. He and his father barely escaped when they took the full-grown cheetah-man down and ripped out his throat.

Female Singa's didn't just kill poachers, they made an example of them by defiling their corpses. While he and his father fled, he could hear their orgasmic howls as they rubbed their vaginas on him, marking the body with their spray before devouring his genitals.

From just to his right, the sound of voices drifting off the beach caused both hunter and prey to turn in surprise. The skittish elk snorted in panic and bolted in the other direction.

Pootar saw the disappointment in his family's faces while they watched in dismay. The six-pointed horns swept across the grass tops and disappeared into Singa territory. Sighing in frustration, his mate and son looked to him for guidance.

With their prey now out of reach, curiosity overcame any regrets of failure. The Duma leader slipped below the mist and cautiously moved towards the shore to discover the nature of the disturbance.

Slipping up to the grasses edge he stopped and listened. He heard two voices talking. His family joined him moments later, and they all peered out onto the southern shore of the Rovina coastline. The moon had recently risen casting a bright yellow illumination off the powder white sand. A breeze swept down the coast from the east which kept the thick fog just offshore.

Pootar cocked his head in confusion. Midlari, the Singa trader, stood on the beach in front of three strange looking bipeds. The merchant was famous across the whole Rovina region for his elaborate crossing tributes allowing him to travel virtually anywhere.

Dumas had never encountered humans before. Pootar stared in wonder at the strange looking hairless bipeds. Midlari was talking to one in a long black robe and cowl. The other two stood silently beside each other at a distance.

He could catch snippets of the conversation above the wind. It astounded him he could understand what they were saying. It was as if the words appeared in his head.

"Isn't that Midlari?" the mate whispered.

Pootar nodded.

"What's he doing traveling alone?" she wondered aloud in a hushed voice. "Doesn't he normally pass with a small caravan?"

The Duma patriarch remained silent. He watched the famous Singa trader kneel before the mysterious figure. In his hand he carried a medium sized sack which looked like it held liquid. Midlari bowed his head and offered it to the mysterious figure before him.

"Father, what's going on?" his son blurted out.

Pootar shushed him and strained to hear the conversation. When the cowled figure accepted the bag, he overheard "a job well done," emanating from under the hood.

The figure then pulled back his cowl. He was bald with bulbous eyes and small markings all across his head, face and neck.

Slowly and deliberately he raised his other arm. Pootar could see the long solitary nail on the hairless hand when it appeared from under the cloak and he cast a puzzled look at his family.

Only one claw, he thought, *how strange.*

Reaching down, the figure appeared to be tracing something on the Singa's forehead while saying something about "his reward."

"Father, what's he doing?!" his son cried out in shrilled surprise.

Pootar reached out and swatted at the young cheetah.

"I told you to..."

Any chance of stealth vanished with the youth's outcry. All those on the shore now looked in their direction. Pootar pulled back in alarm when he saw the eyes of the two solitary humans glowing red.

"Run!" he commanded in a panic, spinning to escape.

The order came too late.

One of the human figures opened his mouth. The inside of its maw started glowing with the same red ferocity as its eyes. With a sudden, bright flash, a long tendril of fire burst out. It arced across the ten yards of beach blasting into the grass with a minor explosion, igniting the area.

Pootar had never experienced fire of this intensity before. He screeched and leapt into the air as the rest of his family bolted through the field, fur burning like running fireballs setting the grasslands alight.

When Pootar landed on the beach, he found himself miraculously still alive. Survival instinct kicked in and he bolted on all fours to the nearby ocean.

Once he bound into the water a fresh wave of agony enveloped him as the magical fire, unnaturally hot and unstoppable, boiled the surrounding water. He thrashed about in a panic, both burning, and boiling alive. With a last shriek the Duma patriarch sank beneath the bubbling orange water. The aquatic inferno finally subsided, leaving a bubbling pool of oily ash floating on the surface.

The fire on the prairie raged for a short while before consuming the bodies of the family. Once the inferno finally burned out, it left only two smoldering mawl skeletons in its wake.

With a gentle turn of the wheel, Demetrius guided the *Drakin* in a silent eastern passage over the individual island chains comprising the greater Goyan Islands. Down below, the Otoman Group of islands signaled their departure from the Shallow Sea as they crossed over into the Ocean Deep. The airship's cabin interior tensely reflected its silent trek.

"You can quit sulking anytime now Demetrius," Okawa said, with a touch of impatience.

The pilot had been silent since their sudden departure from Zor a mere deci ago. Demetrius scowled and kept his eyes forward looking out the windshield.

"What was that pep talk you gave me a little while ago?" he asked. "You know, the one about speaking freely and we're all on the same side!"

Okawa sighed. "Demetrius, this is a secure operation. That means, it's secret. I can't discuss the nature of the secure ops until after departure."

Demetrius's demeanor slowly softened. "So, we're headed to Immor-Onn, huh?"

Okawa relaxed and gave a weak smile. "Yeah, and we need to get there fast."

The pilot nodded in recognition. "And that's where I come in."

"You invented the whole skirting the upwinds thing," the Valdurian said, with a tilt of her head.

Demetrius was still a touch perturbed at his exclusion. "So now that you can talk, what's up?"

"We were commissioned to pick up a scribe with a book and then transport them safely to the University."

For the first time since take off, Demetrius looked over at Okawa.

"Let me get this straight," the airship captain quizzically began. "They, whoever they are, called a secure operation for a scribe and a book?"

"More the book," Okawa replied. "The scribe's just tagging along."

"With all this secrecy that must be some book?" Demetrius probed.

The Valdurian agent's eyes bore into Demetrius. "You remember those two runes that Stryder Aramos used?"

"The creepy ones written in blood?"

Okawa nodded somberly. "Those runes make up the entire book. The locals got the book off the late Tiikeri Finance Minister."

Demetrius blinked in astonishment. "The entire book is written in just those two runes?"

Okawa kept her serious expression and silently nodded.

"This operation has a duel purpose," she added. "Joc' Valdur is doing this favor for the Bailian queen to smooth things over for House Valdur's part in allowing their ambassador to get killed."

Demetrius gave a knowing chuckle. "I was there, remember?"

"Anyway, House Valdur needs Etheria crystals and Immor-Onn and the Bailian Empire is the distribution point. We need ambassadors and a good relationship. So, this is a kind of diplomatic mission too."

With a loud exhale the pilot stared back out into the cloud bank they were entering. Sensing the pilot remained slightly upset, Okawa reached out with uncertainty and gently touched his arm.

"Demetrius, I keep calling on you because I know what you can do and I trust you. In my business, that means a lot."

Demetrius gazed down at the woman's hand resting tenderly on his shoulder, then followed the arm back to a warm smile.

"We may find ourselves hip deep in trouble, but we're in this together," she said, reassuringly. "I'm not willingly keeping you in the dark. I realize my ass is in your hands and I will not jeopardize that."

An awkward silence descended on the cabin. Demetrius blushed and lowered his head snickering like an amused preteen. Okawa stopped and gave a confused look when she leaned back.

"What?"

Demetrius peeked over at her between giggles.

"You said your… you know, rear end was in my hands."

The seasoned Valdurian operative gave an amused grin and shook her head remembering Demetrius never used profanity.

"You are annoyingly charming."

Demetrius cocked his head. "Why, thank you, I think."

Okawa chuckled confidently. "Well, you are the only man to see me naked and live."

The pilot stared out the windshield with a mischievous grin. "That you know of..."

Okawa lowered her head suppressing a smile.

"Hold on," Demetrius said, pulling back on the controls. "We're headed upstairs."

Zau swatted away an annoying drop of water that dangled on the tip of her snout. Sighing heavily, she gazed around the main Zorian baths and its naked, mostly human patrons. The massive pool just about filled the busy room and whiffs of steam gently trailed off the surface of the water.

"So, we're just supposed to sit here and marinade?" Zau asked, looking around at the water's reflection off the smooth marble walls and high vaulted ceiling.

Mal was leaning in the chest high water with her back resting against the wall of the pool. The Spice Rat lazily opened her eyes and glanced over at the humanoid lioness.

"Will you fucking relax?" she asked.

The Singa's gaze followed two naked attendants while they walked past carrying stacks of fluffy towels. The petite human females tittered quietly, engaged in a private conversation as they passed.

"How can I relax sitting in a stone pond with a bunch of humans?" Zau asked. "All these hairless bodies give me the creeps."

"Because it's the way they do business in this part of the Annigan," Mal said, closing her eyes again. "*You've* got the Agora Den over in the Land of Mists. *We've* got the baths."

"This isn't so bad," Zaad said, swirling his hands in the clear liquid which only rose to the nine-foot-tall humanoid shark's waist. "It's a little warm though."

"Yeah, well you're used to the water, I'm not." The Singa countered.

"A bath isn't gonna kill you," Mal said, keeping her eyes closed and head back. "The both of you were smelling a little ripe."

The lioness inwardly shuddered at the stench of soaps and oils, rolling her eyes in frustrated acceptance.

"So, who exactly are we meeting?" the Singa asked.

"The Amarenian ambassador should be along any time now," Mal said, nonchalantly.

A look of perplexed amusement crossed Zau's face. "So how is it a woman in your particular line of work comes to know a foreign ambassador?"

"I was kinda wondering the same thing myself Captain," the EEtah added.

The Spice Rat finally stood and opened her eyes.

"It's a long story," she said, pulling her wet hair back. "but the gist of it is, the previous crew and I helped them out a grand ago."

Zau gave a greedy smile. "I trust they took care of you?"

Mal grinned, mischievously raising her eyebrows. "We all did okay. Besides some land, they also awarded me full Amarenian citizenship and a title."

The Singa's face wrinkled in surprise. "Really, what title?"

"Valorous Sister," Mal said, in a playfully haughty tone.

"Valorous huh," Zaad said, impressed. "Sorry I missed that one. It sounds like you kicked ass!"

"You remember the fucking bitch with the zombies back in Immor-Onn?"

The EEtah chuckled. "Yeah, they tasted like shit."

"Well in the corn fields of Amarenia is where we first ran into her fucking handiwork."

Zau was genuinely curious. "And now the Amarenians want to hire us?"

"That's what she said," Mal confirmed. "She also said something about the job paying well."

"I heard that!" Zaad enthusiastically trumpeted.

"If it pays well, it will probably be dangerous," Zau said, wryly.

"Well, they don't hire us to attend tea parties," Mal said.

"Now there's something you don't see every day," Zau said, appearing perplexed.

All followed her line of sight to see a naked ambassador Alosus and Sareeta headed their way. The two brunettes could not have appeared more different. The ambassador was a diminutive five-foot-three with delicate features. Her posture was regal, and she carried herself with an air of authority.

Sareeta, her seneschal, and bodyguard stood six feet tall and towered over Alosus. She had a confident, domineering stride which caused her large breasts to bounce. However, it was her sizable penis swaying in front of her that never failed to attract attention.

"Male and female parts on the big one," the Singa curiously noted.

"You see it all the time in Amarenia," Mal said, acknowledging the two's approach. "They're called Hill Sisters and they're bad ass."

The Amarenian duo slipped into the pool beside Mal.

"Valorous," Alosus greeted with a smile.

34

"Esteemed," Mal returned the greeting.

"I see you have new friends," the ambassador said, eyeing the Singa and EEtah.

"Yeah, the others took a break and decided to do something else. As for me, I gotta ship to keep in the air."

The ambassador grinned at the explanation. "And your sword wielding lover?"

Mal's face fell slightly.

"He's off teaching school" she said, with a touch of sadness.

Sensing a touchy topic, the Amarenian dignitary changed the subject and after the introductions, got right down to business.

"I understand your ship now has Flavian capabilities?"

Mal jerked a thumb at Zau. "Not my ship, my navigator."

The ambassador smiled demurely at the correction and nodded at Zau.

"We would like to enlist your services to locate someone and bring them back home."

"We?" Mal asked, with a curious tilt of her head.

Alosus organized her explanation. "The Taia-Dor chapter of the Amarenian Archery Academy has raised a substantial amount of money and petitioned our queen for permission to hire you. The queen granted the request and has charged me with delivering the offer."

"Taia-Dor, that name sounds familiar," Mal said, searching her recollection.

"It should," the ambassador said, with a resolute nod, "from your involvement with Wostera, Grand Bowmistress of Taia-Dor awhile back."

Mal brightened at the reminder. "She only had the one Flavian arrow!"

"Yes," Alosus confirmed.

"Last I saw her she followed a crazy ass insect mage into the Middle Realms because he stole her arrow."

Mal abruptly paused when the realization set in. "You want us to *find* Wostera?"

"Yes."

"In the *Middle Realms?*"

"Yes."

"And bring her *back?*" Mal shook her head in disbelief.

"How much does it pay?" Zau interrupted.

"We are prepared to offer you ten thousand Amarenian Volas."

Mal's face soured. "I'm not even sure how much that is, and the Middle Realms is a fucking big, dangerous place!"

The lioness's mind raced listening to the conversation. Her captain had a point in noting the peril of the Middle Realms vast uncharted expanses between the various planes of existence, but Zau had an idea.

"I think I can find her." Zau said, cutting in on the negotiations.

All attention turned to the Singa.

"How?" the Spice Rat asked in disbelief.

"Anything passing through the Middle Realms leaves a trail," Zau said, with authority. "The arrow is the key. All we have to do is follow the Flavian arrow's trail."

This left Mal at a complete loss for words.

"Then you'll take the job?" Alosus asked hesitantly.

Mal's attention vacillated between Zau and Alosus.

"I really think I can do it," Zau assured.

"All right ambassador," Mal agreed reluctantly, "but you gotta sweeten the deal. I really don't share my navigator's optimism and I think this will end up a much bigger thing. It could easily turn into a shit show of epic proportions."

"What did you have in mind Captain?" Alosus asked, maintaining a pleasant neutral demeanor.

The Spice Rat smiled avariciously. "I know House Valdur is building an air station in your capital City of Mostas."

"Hardly a secret," the Amarenian admitted.

"I want a permanent slip reserved for the *Haraka* with all port fees and taxes permanently waived."

"I will have to get Queen Omara's permission," Alosus said, "and that might take a few cycles."

"You know how to get a hold of me," the Spice Rat said, with a jovial nod.

Without further conversation or pleasantries, the ambassador and Hill Sister slipped out of the pool. Watching the mismatched pair exit the baths, Mal leaned in to Zau.

"So, you really think you can find this person?"

"I really do Captain."

An unexpected, broad smile exploded across Mal's face.

"Captain?"

"Think about it, we'll be the team known for delivering the goods inter-dimensionally." Mal grew even more excited postulating on the possibilities. "If we pull this off, we will have upped our reputation, as well as the amount we can charge for virtually *any* job!"

"If we live through it, Captain," Zaad pragmatically said. "After all, we are talking about the Middle Realms."

Mal leaned back and closed her eyes once again, relaxing in the warm water.

"Yeah," she said, "like I said before, they don't fucking hire us for tea parties."

Stryder Aramos could see the glow and feel the heat from their bodies through the thick mist. The clacking of their mandibles echoed upward from the small depression on the side of Mount Natal and into the star filled Nocturn sky. Red, round eyes set atop elongated mantid skulls peered above the fog.

Fifty Na-Kab, the last of their insectoid race, cautiously approached a naked Stryder Aramos. He levitated a few inches off the ground and slowly spun in the air. As they drew menacingly closer, Stryder could see their humanoid torsos set atop insectoid lower bodies covered in scaly plates. A reddish glow betrayed their fiery interiors where the exoskeletal sheets connected.

They hissed malevolently and surrounded the dark cleric. The Herald of Pa-Waga's arrogance faded as the five-foot-tall mantis creatures encircled ever closer, sniffing and hissing furiously. He winced when the penis shaped talon barbs of their long stinger tails waved dangerously close.

Pa-Waga be praised, he nervously repeated over and over in his head. *Pa-Waga protect me, for I serve a mighty god!*

He nervously recoiled when one of the oozing phalluses, obscenely bloated with boiling seed, came within inches of his face.

Pa-Waga protect me, he repeated, his lower lip trembled slightly.

Stryder was well aware of the consequences if stung. Any place the talon stinger penetrated, deposited an embryo which rapidly developed into a monstrous mutant fire bug. After a short gestation period, it would erupt from his body, resulting in a horrific death.

I serve a mighty god!

"Fleshy one," they hissed, while lunging, retreated, and shuffling rapidly on eight legs.

In a placating gesture, he held aloft the bag of royal jelly, which had already claimed five lives.

"Have… Have I not fulfilled my part of the bargain?" he stammered.

Stryder stopped in mid spin and hovered in place when a huge Na-Kab stepped out of the mist. He stood a foot taller than the rest and possessed a thick, muscular human torso.

The insect people cleared a path as the larger Na-Kab slowly approached, the muscles of his chiseled torso rippling when he walked. A thin trail of smoldering red drool oozed from the corners of his narrow, mandible flanked mouth.

Stryder bowed his head slightly and visibly trembled when he ceremoniously offered the bag to the insect sovereign.

"King Krol," he greeted apprehensively, "the royal jelly as promised."

The Na-Kab ruler studied the bag then assessed the human warily.

"This is only half of the pact fleshy one!" Krol growled, snatching the royal jelly. "You must provide a proper new location for the hive before our bargain is complete."

The human kept his meekly respectful demeanor.

"Great king," he said, "rest assured your help in my glorious endeavor will be well rewarded."

The Na-Kab king sneered. "We shall see."

He then motioned to the crowd behind him. A single insectoid stepped up to his side.

"This is the Chosen One," Krol proclaimed, handing it the bag.

His dark beady eyes then returned to the human.

"You aligned yourself with the Chosen One," he stated definitively. "You *also* will drink with him!"

The command deeply concerned an already skittish Stryder. There was no telling what might happen if he ingested secretions from a race so alien from his own. This was not part of their agreement.

The former quartermaster nervously eyed the plump sack of royal jelly. These fire breathing insects were an integral part of his plan. At any moment they could obliterate him with a single fiery breath. Refusal was not an option.

"Of course," he said, in a feeble attempt to sound honored.

The chosen Na-Kab opened the bag and drank. After emptying most of the contents he handed the remaining royal jelly to Stryder.

Holding the open container, the human faltered when the chosen Na-Kab suddenly screeched out in agony, grabbing his stomach, and doubling over. His mantid features racked with pain and large smoldering boils erupted on his chest. He cried out again, in seemingly unbearable torment, causing Stryder to wince in pain at the high-pitched wailing.

The plates on the creature's thorax separated with a cracking sound while its body mass increased. Stryder looked on in horror as the beleaguered Na-Kab clutched at its throat, its legs twitching. The eight appendages then folded up beneath him and it dropped to the ground and rolled into a ball. His long tail curled around him and the glow between the plates of his exoskeleton dimmed. An orange fluid then oozed from in-between the separated plates and covered its entire body in a thick, rubbery cocoon as the creature now lay silent and motionless.

Stryder stood frozen in shock, his face a mask of dread and uncertainty. Krol noticed the human's hesitation.

"Drink," it demanded.

Stryder found himself unable to move or take his eyes off the spectacle he had just witnessed. The Na-Kab king then waved his penis shaped barbed tail inches from Stryder's face. A smoldering drop of orange semen seeped from the tip of the talon barb and dripped onto the ground at his feet.

"Your choice fleshy one," King Krol snarled ominously. "You can drink from the queen's nectar… or from mine!"

There was now no turning back. Before he could think about it or recant, Stryder quickly lifted the sack to his lips.

I serve a mighty god, he repeated to himself, gulping down the nectar.

To his immediate surprise, the oily fluid had only a mild peppery taste. When the liquid hit the back of his throat it began to burn, growing increasingly hotter as it traveled down his throat.

Still levitating just above the ground, his torso suddenly began convulsing. His mouth dropped open and his eyelids fluttered wildly when the sack fell from his hand and toppled to the ground. He remembered hearing the clicking of mandibles before everything went black.

When Stryder's eyes opened, he was standing on a vast sea of gold coins and gems. The glittering hoard stretched out as far as he could see against a solid black backdrop and sky. In the distance he could make out a large building rising from the bed of treasure.

Checking himself over he appeared to be unharmed and totally naked. Seeing nothing else around and with nothing to do, he made off for the structure. When he was halfway to the edifice, he squinted at the strange shape, trying to discern any detail.

This isn't a typical shaped building, he thought, when, to his right, the sea of coins and gems stirred and parted. A head of golden blonde hair ascended from amidst the expanse of treasure. He gasped in recognition when he saw the two blue diamond berets on either side of the head.

Stryder stared, mouth agape, as the naked figure of his late wife, Duri Eldor, rose smiling at him. Speechless, he looked her up and down. She was as beautiful as ever, with her delicate facial features, hourglass figure, and perfectly shaped breasts. Her eyes carried the same sad look they always did, however now they were black and featureless instead of sparkling blue. She began walking towards him with a much more confident, brazen gate than he had remembered her having.

"Hello dear husband," she greeted, stepping up to him.

"Duri," he gasped, "you're dead!"

"Am I?"

"I was at your funeral!"

Duri said nothing but gave a sinister smile.

"What are you doing here?" Stryder asked, bewildered.

She held the cunning grin. "The question, dear husband, is, what are *you* doing here?"

After a moment of uneasy silence, Duri extended her hands and gestured around her.

"Is this not everything you ever desired?"

Stryder peered around at the seemingly endless ocean of wealth surrounding them.

"What was it you said to my father?" she asked. "'What's real to me is a ship's hold and my cut of it. Everything else is bullshit.'"

This stunned Stryder. Those were the very words he had spoken in anger at her funeral.

"Duri... I... how..."

"That was right before you abandoned our children to be raised in the streets," she said, cutting him off, her tone turning ominous.

She glanced back at the object in the distance before returning her attention to him with a disturbing gaze.

"Your quest is almost complete dear husband," she said, in a hauntingly distant voice which seemed to echo in his head.

"But you must make a final sacrifice," Duri continued in the same ghostly echo, while reaching down and cupping his penis and testicles. "You must surrender something before you can be reborn to your chosen destiny."

Her hands were ice cold on his genitals and the dark cleric felt a sense of unease sweeping over him. In a slow deliberate motion, all the while holding his gaze, she pulled off his penis and held it up before him.

His eyes grew wide with shock. He looked down at his groin, astounded to see there was nothing there but smooth skin, not even a wound, and yet he felt no pain. He cried out at his wife who laughed and held his castrated flaccid member before her.

"You can now pursue the fate you have always desired," she said, in a mockingly joyous tone. "Go!"

While she continued to laugh, Stryder screamed in panic and bolted towards the object in the distance. He ran as fast as he could. Behind him, he heard her unrelenting echoing laughter over his ragged breathing. While Stryder kept up his terrified sprinting through the treasure horde, he felt coins and gems cut into the soles of his bare feet. He left a trail of bloody footprints across the carpet of wealth.

When he drew closer to the enigmatic object, he finally realized it was not a building at all, but what appeared to be an immense statue of a humanoid Black Jaguar seated on a golden throne and buried up to its ankles in the sea of riches.

When Stryder couldn't run any longer, he approached the gigantic idol at a labored walk, staring upward in awe. The seated figure rose at least a hundred feet tall and, instead of looking outward as with most monuments, it appeared to be staring directly at him.

Immediately, wave after wave of overwhelming power and insatiable avarice swept over Stryder. The pungent odor of ammonia filled the air as he cowered before the manifestation of Pa-Waga.

Stryder gasped when the figure moved. He remained frozen in place, mouth agape, while it stood up. The sea of wealth rustled around its feet and shifted as it wordlessly stepped towards him. Reaching down, it picked up the paralyzed human and brought him up to its face.

Stryder's mouth remained fixed in a silent scream as Pa-Waga smiled and opened its wide jaws. He could feel its warm breath coursing over him and the lack of odor surprised him. In a single fluid motion, the Jaguar god popped the startled cleric into its mouth and snapped its jaws shut. The once and future Herald of Pa-Waga descended into a curtain of darkness.

Stryder's eyes opened with a start. He was back in the Land of Mists facing the Na-Kab. He started laughing maniacally, levitating higher into the air with the presence of Pa-Waga coursing through him.

His ecstasy came with joyous illumination. Past attempts to bring about his lord and the subsequent new age of prosperity had been unnecessary. He burned with the revelation that *he* was the true manifestation of his lord in this world.

The runes, which had multiplied covering his entire body, strobed and radiated brightly. The insect people watched in amazement while his genitals receded into his groin leaving no trace of their prior existence. His eyelids peeled back and disappeared, revealing round and black eyes, devoid of any features. Bursts of blue energy erupted from the runes inscribed in the palms of his outstretched hands.

When he slowly descended, the Na-Kab turned their concerned attentions to their prone hive mate. Its cocoon undulated while the entombed chosen one continued its metamorphosis.

"He is changing," Stryder said, his voice now deeper and boasting more natural volume. "Evolving into that which will be your salvation."

Stryder stared at the Na-Kab king with lifeless eyes and smiled. "Best take the savior below into the Fire Hive and be ready for the summons. Remember, separate those who will assist me."

"The Na-Kab need not remember," the king replied with a touch of indignation. "The Na-Kab never forget. As before and as agreed, Valvur and Trazar will accompany you."

"Are they capable of walking amongst their enemies without giving themselves away?" Stryder asked. "We will encounter many Tiikeri, Do-Tarr and Ash-Ta. They must be able to control themselves or all will be lost."

"Your reminder is unnecessary," Krol said, realizing Stryder was ignorant of their race's customs. "The Na-Kab always keep their word."

"We go then," Stryder proclaimed to the group, "to secure both our futures!"

The rousing approval of clicking mandibles rang through the hive and they tended to their savior, carrying him below.

The room was chilly and Rafel shivered off the damp Kan fog as he closed the door. It had been another long day. Regretfully, returning home offered no solace.

Hoyt's favorite chair was always the first thing that greeted him. It faced the fireplace and he could still see him sitting there tending the flames. It always started the same way, the profound feeling of loneliness along with the knowledge he would never see his lover again.

Rafel pulled back his hood and started across the room. A painting he had cared for hung on the wall to his right. It depicted a battle between the Annigan's deities of eternal light and everlasting darkness. He remembered succumbing to Hoyt's enthusiasm for the abstract piece with a sad chuckle. It had always been a little too dark and foreboding for his personal tastes.

Rafel choked back a sob, recalling when he first felt tempted to call upon any in a pantheon of many dark gods to bring Hoyt back. His eyes moistened when he realized he still fought that temptation.

He hung up his coat and stared at the thick wide belt hanging from an adjacent hook. Running his hand down the aged leather he could hear Hoyt ordering him to 'get the belt' in his usual low sexy voice. He could feel the tears well up in his eyes and he tore himself away from the instrument which had given him so much pleasure and pain.

He grimaced as sudden visions of Hoyt's lifeless bloody body stared upward at him from his mind's eye. Finding it difficult to breathe, he felt the tears start flowing down his cheek.

By the time he reached the bedroom he was always sobbing. He undressed and focused on the restraints on each of the four posts of his bed. Gripping one tightly, he leaned his forehead against the post and knew he would never find a love like that again. The grieving spymaster took in several large gulps of air attempting to compose himself before settling in for the evening.

He started a fire, stared absently at the flames as they grew, and then went about preparing a meal. He forced down a meager dinner of cured meat and cheese only because Zekoff had made a comment about his weight loss. Afterwards, he reached for his latest constant companion, a bottle of Cupam Whiskey.

Just as he did every night since Hoyt's death, Rafel sat naked on the animal rug they had made love on so many times in the past and warmed himself in front of the small fireplace. The liquor burned as it went down. It didn't take the pain away, it just made him numb.

Into the depths of the night he stared at the flames, drinking and crying until his eyes swelled shut and he passed out. He couldn't bear to be in his bed. Hoyt's scent on the sheets made him cry in his sleep and gave him nightmares.

He could still see the blood around his feet and the anguished look on his lover's face.

A new fountain of tears erupted when he contemplated Hoyt's last moments. He teetered a bit reaching again for the bottle, thankfully he felt the sweet release of unconsciousness nearing.

Taking a large mouthful of the amber liquid, he heard a scraping sound by the door. He wobbled and tried to focus. A folded piece of paper slid underneath.

The drunken spymaster struggled to get to his feet only to topple back to the floor. He finally crawled to the note on hands and knees. Propping himself against the wall, he unfolded the paper and strained to read it. Huffing in frustration and brushing away tears, he crawled back in front of the fire.

In his condition even with enough light it was still a challenge to read. Closing one eye the words eventually came into focus. As he read, the crying slowly ceased and his face grew hard and cold.

> *The ambassador's death was murder.*
> *It was not a robbery.*
> *The Kan has a thousand eyes.*
> *There are those who saw what happened.*
> *These are the ones you must seek.*

Rafel angrily crumpled the paper and tossed it to the floor beside him. His demeanor had transformed from grieving to vengeful.

Da-Olman knew he was being followed. The blue skinned Gila lizardman/Bailian hybrid's bulbous eyes scanned to the left and right, independently of one another. His foot-long tongue slithered out of his scaly lipless mouth flicking away an annoying clump of sand from his open nostrils.

The two Gilas had waited most of the moonrise for him to exit the lapidary compound. The moment he entered the hard-packed sand streets of the Asero-He oasis, they trailed at a discreet distance.

A sandstorm blew in during the moonless, fueled by gale force winds whipping down from the Os-Oni Mountains to the north, sweeping across the Dark Waste Desert and blocking out the starry Nocturn sky. Now, drifts of sand piled against the sides of buildings and gritty particles seemed in everything.

He stopped in front of an apothecary's shop and studied the reflection in the front window. Not caring about the window display, he looked past his blue green face, through the passing crowds of Gila lizard folk, Bailians and those like himself, the many hybrids such unions produced. The same two Gilas stood across the street, staring at him.

Casually unbuttoning all but one button on his floor length duster jacket, he started off again down the busy street. He knew they wouldn't try anything in public.

Asero-He was the largest and most cosmopolitan in the Dark Waste Desert. It was also the closest to the Plains of Taka-Vir, placing it just over the cusp of the Lumina/Nocturn border in the Twilight Lands. This isolated nomadic camp grew into a boom town of civilization when it became renown as a conduit for Etheria crystals from the mysterious far flung oases of Nocturn.

The Etheriat gem trader knew the large population almost guaranteed someone could witness any act of violence at any time. Making a quick, unexpected right turn into an alley shortcut to his workshop, he could hear the padded footsteps behind him.

"Da' Olman," someone called out.

The Etheriat mage pulled at the last button, opening his coat, and kept walking.

"Da' Olman!" the other's voice reverberated down the narrow passage. "We would like a word with you!"

Realizing he could probably not outrun them, he sighed, stopped, and turned towards his pursuers. The two large Gilas were easily a full head taller than him.

"And what can I do for you two?" he said, wearily.

"The love powder you sold our boss stopped working," one said, sneering and stepping aggressively forward. "His betrothed left him and he's very angry."

Da' Olman's brow furrowed in surprise. "I made no claim how long it would last. And you really can't blame her, can you? Your boss is fat, ugly, and totally unpleasant to be around. I mean, that's why he needed the powder in the first place."

"He wants his money back," the other declared, stepping up next to his companion.

"Sorry, I have a strict no refund policy," the mage said, his face sadly resigned. "Besides, my product worked. I can't help it if your employer's social ineptitude can't keep a mate."

The lizard thugs stepped forward menacingly. "We're here to get it back, one way or the other."

Da' Olman gave a nervous smile and held up his hands in a placating gesture. "Now, now, there's no need for any of that."

The Etheriat reached inside his coat.

"I have something that I just know will make him happy," he said, retrieving a small glass globe containing a glittery orange powder.

"He wants no more of your crappy powders," one thug growled, stepping forward and closing the distance.

"He wants his money back!" the other thug roared, staying in step with his partner.

"That's unfortunate," the Etheriat said, with a pout.

The henchmen lunged forward and Da' Olman threw the object at the wall nearest them. He immediately spun, covered his ears, and sprinted for the other end of the narrow back road.

The explosion was deafening when the globe shattered against the brick wall. Rays from the flash filled the alley behind him, along with the screams of the Gila thugs. Their scaly flesh melted off their faces and their clothing fused to their bodies.

Da' Olman slowed to a walk when he reached the street and turned left. He ignored the curious onlookers peering past him into the recesses of the backstreet.

It was a short walk to his shop. He grew furious when he pulled on the double wooden doors only to find them locked.

Why are we closed? he incredulously thought. *These are business hours! If my two worthless employees are back in the workshop huffing ubar dust...*

He unlocked the doors and stormed into the store front. The room was unoccupied. The gems and powders lining the walls appeared undisturbed. He could hear voices coming from the room directly behind the counter.

"Why are we not open for business?!" he roared entering the workshop.

The sight that greeted the irate Etheriat caused him to freeze in shock. Three tall bipeds, the likes he had never seen before, stood on one side of the room. He had heard about humans, but these three barely met the description. Two towering men stood motionless off to the side, their eyes glowing an eerie red. The other, though not as tall as his companions, displayed a much more ominous appearance. He had pulled the cowl of his robe back revealing a bald head covered in small glowing scars. His solid black, lidless eyes, devoid of emotion, seemed to stare right through Da' Olman's soul.

Kneeling before this strange biped was Mazadoor, one of the Etheriat's two employees. The robed figure's hand rested gently on the employee's head and he whispered to him. Blood stained the back of Mazadoor's collar, pooling around two marks carved on either side of the base of his skull.

Da' Olman found it even more disturbing they had propped the corpse of Delavec, his other worker, against the wall on the other side of the workbench. They had cut his throat and crimson drenched the front of his garment.

Intricate patterns of "*X*" and "*I*" covered the floor in front of him, penned in the young Gila's own blood.

The three strangers stared at Da' Olman when he entered. Stryder looked up and gave a thin, sinister smile.

"Ah, just who I was looking for," he said, removing his hand from the young Gila's head.

Da' Olman reached inside his coat but stopped when one of the two silent figures opened his mouth revealing its fiery red interior.

"Sudden moves like that make my friends very nervous," Stryder said, calmly. "Besides Da' Olman, I make you a very lucrative offer."

The Etheriat appeared genuinely perplexed. "Do I know you?"

Keeping the unnerving smile, Stryder gestured towards the body in the corner and the glyph covered floor.

"No," he said, "but the sacred numbers have told me everything about you."

Da' Olman stared suspiciously at the scarred face.

"Have they now?"

"You are a very *special* gem dealer," Stryder said, with certainty, "one might say unscrupulous."

"Here now!" the Etheriat protested.

"Oh, I make no judgments," Stryder assured, "and my Lord Pa-Waga, condones such profitable actions. Allow me to introduce myself. I am Stryder, Herald of Pa-Waga.

"You see, my lord has noticed that even though you still have strong contacts, your list of powerful enemies also grows. Perhaps a foreign endeavor in service to my god— let's call it a missionary trip—will allow you to line your pockets while things settle down here."

"I can't just pick up and leave," the crystal mage insisted. "I have an operation to run."

"This young man will be capable of running the day-to-day operations here," Stryder declared, assisting the kneeling Gila to his feet.

Da' Olman eyed his worker skeptically. The young lizardman's face now carried a serene and self-assured smile.

"I have shown him the prosperous ways of my Lord Pa-Waga and he is more than willing," Stryder said, confidently. "You will still be in contact with your sources here, as we will need a substantial amount of the special crystals you are known to deal in."

Stryder's smile broadened when he saw the greedy look sweep across Da' Olman's face.

"Substantial amounts of Etheria, huh?" the Etheriat asked. "You know that won't be cheap?"

"Money is not an object," Stryder announced, "and the reward shall vastly exceed the expense."

The Etheriat's skepticism cracked.

"What about him?" Da' Olman asked, indicating the body in the corner.

"Young Mazadoor, here, should be more than capable of cleaning up of this mess. We need to leave soon as possible."

"And I get a cut of the Etheria ordered?" the gem merchant asked.

Stryder chuckled. "Of course, of course."

Da' Olman's face erupted into a satisfied smile, ignoring the growing stench of ammonia.

"You got a deal," he agreed, giving a last glance at his dead worker staring blankly into space. "Delavec was probably stealing from me, anyway."

The bed creaked and moaned while Mal tossed about restlessly. The sound of Zaad snoring across the room and the glow of Zau's map made sleep impossible.

Mal knew they had the money for independent quarters, but she discovered long ago once they accepted a job, it payed to keep as much of the crew together as possible. On more than one occasion a quick trip was necessary and having everyone together was just easier to manage.

She gave an annoyed sigh when she heard the grand turine in the Zorian harbor ring twenty bells. The Kan and the chance for sleep slipped away.

"Oy," Zau lamented in frustration.

The projected multi-dimensional globe vanished, and the room dimmed. The lioness lowered her eye patch, sat back, and gave a disheartened sigh.

Hearing the Singa huff in frustration, the airship captain rolled over and propped herself up on an elbow.

"It's a fucking job isn't it?" Mal tried to keep her tone calm and supportive, despite her sleep deprivation.

Zau gave an ironic chuckle. "Its so tedious."

Mal remained silent, debating trying to fall back asleep.

Her navigator continued, "Did you know that there are fish on this side of the world that have natural Flavian abilities?"

"I've heard about them," Mal answered. "I just thought it was local superstitions."

"Oh yeah, I mean they're small and their Flavian signatures are brief, about the same size as an arrow, but they're all over the place…" Zau caught herself beginning to rant and blushed slightly.

"Sorry Captain, I don't mean to complain," she apologized. "Working with this eye of mine can be a blessing and a curse."

"What are you sorry about?" Mal asked, rolling onto her back. "From what I can see, that's a pretty neat trick you've got going on under that patch."

Zau smirked in reflection. "Yeah, well my advice is to be careful if you're ever in the Dark Waste. Don't casually offer to trade any of your body parts for knowledge. Something might just take you up on it."

The Singa suddenly went quiet, briefly reminiscing about her tutelage under Master Garak in the Buried City of Nof-Saloom and the Flavian mysteries he had shown her there. She smiled nostalgically rubbing her eyepatch, thinking about the price she paid to learn them.

"Thanks Captain," she sincerely said, "I appreciate your having my back on this. I mean, I got you into this."

"No," Mal said, chuckling, "the Amarenians got us into this. You just went along with it."

"Fair enough, I know we've got a lot riding on this, though."

The Spice Rat nonchalantly shrugged. "There's always a lot riding on any of the shit we try."

"I just want you to know," Zau said, "I won't let you down,"

"Fuck, I know that!"

The lioness suppressed an appreciative giggle by placing a hand over her mouth, nodding at the sleeping EEtah. Mal waved her hand dismissively.

"Unless it's the sound of impending combat or dolphin sex," Mal said, "he's not waking up."

Zau shook her head in surprise. "Dolphin sex?"

The airship captain shrugged. "It gets him off."

The Singa playfully rolled her eyes. "Everybody's got something that gets them going."

Mal propped herself up on both elbows. "Speaking of which, what made you want to tag along with us?"

Zau stared contemplatively for an instant. "I had to get out of Tiikeri land and you looked like my best bet."

"Not fond of the tigers, are we?" Mal said, sitting up and crossing her legs.

"Is there a stronger word than hate?" Zau sneered.

"Oh, this I gotta hear," she said, patting a spot on the bed beside her.

Zau smile sadly when she joined her captain. She took a deep breath and stared down at her hands folded in her lap.

"A rival pride kidnapped and sold me to the Tiikeri slavers when I was very young." The lioness noticed Mal's look of shock. "It's a common practice, Captain. Anyway, I was young and their special breeding center was the highest bidder for me."

"Breeding center?"

"The Kharry Institute," Zau proclaimed with faux condescension. "Sounds impressive, right? They experiment on breeding different pure races to produce useful mongrel hybrids. In my case, a powerful Yagur raped me multiple times. They wanted me to give birth to a Worrg."

Mal's brow furrowed. "Yagur, Worrg?"

"Yagurs are the Jaguar people from the great northern forest in the Land of Mists. They're natural shamans. The Tiikeri use them for most of their magic. Worrgs are mongrels that can see remotely through a specific, sometimes multiple animal's eyes. The perfect spy."

Mal gave a silent whistle. "Fuck!"

"Yeah, well I got pregnant. I was so pissed off I had to do something about it."

"It didn't sound like you had a whole lotta fucking options," Mal said, growing angry.

"I would not be a breeder for those bastards. Luckily, they didn't treat me like most of their slaves. Training is brutal for your average mongrel slave. They claim they have to break 'the wild streak' out of them. I was lucky because producing a Worrg is a delicate process. They fed me well and mostly didn't harass me.

"I had noticed an enormous growth of Tandy flowers in the garden. One moonless I slipped out of my room and ate them all. The flowers did the trick. I left their aborted abomination laying in the middle of the floor of my room and got away."

"The Tiikeri didn't attempt to recapture you?" Mal asked.

"Sure," Zau confirmed. "Losing me was a real setback for them. Not to mention a major embarrassment for my guards. All throughout the Dasos region there's a network of Mawl slaves which aid and shelter those who dare to escape."

Zau gave a forlorn frown. "A lot of my brothers and sisters in bondage helped me. Some paid the ultimate price for their support. The Tiikeri are especially cruel to abettors."

The Spice Rat nodded grimly with a newfound respect for her navigator.

"I made it to Shun-Dra," Zau continued. "The place was awful but at least I was safe. I got into a few misadventures there and with Twitch's help managed to get along fine."

"You know Twitch?!"

"Everybody knows Twitch."

Both smiled at the coincidence.

"So," Mal said, turning serious again, "you still think you can pull this off?"

Zau gave a confident yet frustrated nod. "I really do."

"Okay, show me what you got."

Zau lifted her eye patch and the blue multi-dimensional globe projected between them, hovering above the sheets.

"Here we have the Annigan," she said.

The hologram projected the ghostly glowing continents of the world. As before, twinkles of Flavian activity danced across its surface.

"Now let's survey from another view," the navigator said.

She reached out to the top and bottom of the spectral globe and brought her hands together, collapsing the orb into a flattened sphere shape.

"Okay, so now we're looking at it from the side as a plane inside the Middle Realms," she explained. "These Middle Realms connect all the known planes in the multiverse."

Mal stared in amazement when it exhibited the Flavian activity by displaying vertical eruptions across the top and bottom of the orb's compressed surface.

"This gives me a better view when I go in close, like this…" Zau pulled her hands apart from side to side and the view homed in on details of specific areas. "But like I said, it's tedious. The arrow's Flavian signature is slight. I'm not even done searching the Goyan continent."

Mal stared intently at the small glowing bars flaring from both of the sphere's surfaces.

"Goya, huh?" An idea came to her. "Can you bring up Amarenia?"

"Sure," Zau confirmed, brushing her hands to the left, which swept the floating spectral map eastward.

"Just west of the lower mountain range," Mal qualified, her mind racing.

The Singa rotated the map into the proper position. As before, both surfaces came alive in tiny eruptions.

"Orb fish," Mal said, shaking her head.

The lioness moved her hand across the considerable minuscule activity.

"They must use their Flavian abilities to escape danger and sneak up on food," she said. "I mean they don't teleport very far and they stick to their own plane but…"

"It creates clutter." Mal finished her sentence.

"Yes, it's a lot to sort through… Hello!" the Singa suddenly blurted, bolting forward in surprise.

A small blip suddenly traveled upward a little further than those surrounding it. It then plummeted back downward through the horizontal orb, plunging out the bottom and continuing onward out of sight.

"What?" Mal said, unsure what she had just witnessed.

"There it is again!" The Singa pointed at the ephemeral line in space pursuing the same course.

"Something small just pierced the veil of the Corporeal Reach then returned to another plane. All we have to do is follow it."

"The Corpor… what?" Mal asked, confused.

"The Corporeal Reach is the plane we occupy," Zau explained. "We share the multiverse with at least seventeen other dimensional planes all connected by the Middle Realms—this space between dimensions is dangerous and unpredictable, not to mention vast."

Zau was ready when the blip occurred again. She moved her hands upward and followed the phantom line as it intersected another section directly below it. Then she stopped, looked up, and gazed in satisfaction at Mal.

"It returned to the Pasture Plane, Captain," she said. "I think we've found her."

"Pasture Plane?" Mal cocked her head.

Zau exhaled, collecting her thoughts. The Singa then projected the map once again over the bed.

"Okay," she began, "each one of the known plains have a certain characteristic."

She adjusted her hands until the side view of multiple orb spheres appeared. A pulsing network of small blue dots erupted between various planes, connecting and intersecting with other planes.

"This is a map of the known multiverse," Zau clarified, "and these blue lights flaring up and linking planes represent the active usage of Flavian portals."

"Busy place!" Mal noted in awe.

"You have no idea," Zau warned.

She then pointed a furry finger at one plane.

"We're here," she stated confidently, "the Corporeal Reach."

She then pointed to another.

"This is the Endless Ocean Plane."

Her finger indicated another.

"And that's the Great Desert Plane."

She then showed them all.

"Each of these is a destination of a creature's essence or soul when they die here on our plane."

"What does it all mean?" Mal asked, glaring at the map.

Zau shrugged, lowering her eyepatch and the holographic atlas faded.

"My first guess is it's some cosmic punishment and reward system," she suggested. "I only know how it works, not why."

The two sat staring at each other in silence for a moment until Mal snapped out of her quandary and perked up. She slapped her knees in celebration.

"Good job!" she said. "We sail at the lifting of the Kan."

"Captain, one thing, how did you know to look in Amarenia?"

"I remembered my old navigator mentioning that in the Middle Realms things moved like water, with currents, eddies, and rip tides. The battle where she lost the arrow took place in Amarenia. It was just a hunch."

The Singa sighed and nodded. "Impressive, well, I guess that's our destination."

The moon dropped behind the skyline of Immor-Onn leaving only the weak rays of the sun in the far western sky for illumination. Winter winds, which had buffeted the city, were waning as the season passed. The political winds, on the other hand, were nothing less than palpable.

Kai had seen the reports. Something had killed and devoured a Calden naval officer his first day in port. Eyewitnesses stated it was some kind of bat creature. This immediately struck down any hope Kai might have had about Drucilla's return to society.

Kai was genuinely torn. She always held an absolute sense of love and duty to her adopted city and sovereign, but she couldn't dismiss her feelings for Drucilla—or her nagging guilt over being the one who created her condition.

This, however, was a full-blown diplomatic crisis which ascended all the way to the top. The incident even made her beloved monarch nervous, and whenever the queen got nervous, Kai got to work.

The one-armed assassin slipped through the shadows of the city's ever shrinking Available Regions. At the rate displaced citizens were now returning, they would fill the regions within two grands. For now. the vacant structures remained a refuge for the city's undesirables and various criminal elements.

She made her way undetected around the squatter's sporadic lone campfires and bandit gangs. Her destination lay in the far western area of the region. This group of remote buildings butted up against a steep cliff face. Because of its unappealing location, it would probably be the last occupied with repatriated citizens. Its edifices were cold and dark, seemingly devoid of all life. The locals called it 'The Deep.'

The low light of the moonless didn't prove a problem for Kai. She deftly slipped through the building's long shadows. Her sense of smell guided her tonight.

Her nose twitched when she approached a large warehouse type building. She smelled Drucilla was close.

Making her way around to the front of the building she detected another scent, also close, human body odor. She barely had time to assess the stench before a powerful set of arms grabbed her from the shadows. A cackle came from the darkness and they pulled her towards the offensive smell.

"We got us a pretty one!"

The rising crackle of energy from Kai drowned out the grunts of approval around her. A phantasmal blade materialized from her left arm stump and bathed the immediate area in a shimmering blue light. She could now make out the three men surrounding her.

She turned towards her attacker and slashed upward with the glowing blue sword. The spectral blade sputtered and flashed, entering between his legs, and easily traveling up through his body, severing the man cleanly in half. Without even a chance to cry out, the two halves fell to the ground and showered everyone in blood.

Kai brought the blade down on the next mugger. Its glowing tip raked across his upper torso, and with an anguished cry, he also dropped in two pieces beside his severed companion.

The glow of the blade now illuminated one shocked, remaining face spattered with his friend's body fluids. With a cry of panic, the ruffian sprinted away.

The assassin gave a frustrated sigh, the altercation had robbed her of any chance at stealth. Continuing to follow her nose, she cautiously entered the cavernous structure.

Once inside the massive single room, she examined the bare walls and wide structural beams supporting high ceilings. The distinct stench of bat guano, which led her here, fully assaulted her olfactory senses, and she winced in revulsion at the rank odor.

On the floor near the center of the room a small patch of mushrooms grew from a pile of waste. She approached the fungi while keeping a constant vigil on the rafters above. She tested the guanos consistency with the toe of her boot. It was fresh. She then scrutinized the network of support structures in the ceiling above her.

"Dru," Kai called out, "I'm pretty sure you can hear me. I just want to talk."

Silence followed the trailing echo of her voice.

"You don't have to live like this."

Once again no reply.

"I can help you, *please* let me help you!"

Kai's eyes might have been playing tricks on her, but she thought she could make out the dark outline of something

61

peering out from the shadows in the rafters at the far side of the room.

"We can work this out," she pleaded.

After a few moments of silence, Kai sadly turned to go. She lowered her head, overwhelmed by the feelings sweeping over her, both sadness at being rejected and a sense of failure in her duty to protect society from this threat.

"All right, I'll go," she said, in a disheartened tone. "I've left you two meals on the east side of the building. If you hurry, one's even still alive."

Kai had only taken a few steps when she heard the fluttering of wings. Drucilla dropped to the ground between her and the door. She hissed through rows of exposed teeth, but she made no motion to attack.

The queen's spymaster also made no aggressive moves. The two eyed each other warily.

"I... I still love you," Kai whispered.

The Ash-Ta briefly dropped her malevolent demeanor and stared forlornly at her former lover. The anger quickly returned. She hissed again, before racing out the door and into the moonless sky.

At first, Mezulari thought he was being robbed when the two large men stepped in front of him. He knew it was something else, however, when they slipped the bag over his head from behind and dragged him away.

"Unhand me!" were the only words he said before being knocked unconscious.

When the young man came to, he groaned at the aching knot on the back of his head. He could see nothing through the bag but realized he was now naked and bound to a low, uncomfortable stool with a donut shaped seat. His lips quivered and his body's frantic trembling caused the legs to rattle on the cold stone floor.

In a rapid, fluid motion someone yanked the bag off from behind. He violently winced at the intense light assaulting his eyes. The blinding light illuminated the room on either side of him with the radiance of mid-day. The room appeared stark and empty from his limited view.

His heart was pounding wildly and over the ringing in his ears he heard an effeminate male voice call out from beyond the light.

"Hello Agent Mezulari, I thought we might have a brief chat."

The young man struggled futility against his restraints which bound his extremities to the short legs of the stool.

"Chat!" he cried out. "Who are you?! What is the meaning of this?!"

The disembodied voice continued in a calm, almost friendly tone, "I told you, we, well, you need to talk to me."

"I don't know what you're talking about!"

"Now Agent Mezulari, I think you might have *some* idea."

The young man was sweating profusely and his eyes swept from side to side in a panic.

"I'm not an agent!" he insisted. "I'm just a courier for House Aramos."

"And in particular?"

The courier hesitated before answering, "The Imperial Bank of Zor."

"You see, *now* we're getting somewhere," the voice cajoled. "A little while ago Stryder Aramos ordered an executive withdrawal of forty thousand secors. Because it was an executive withdrawal, they didn't need to list a payee. The withdrawal itself, however, is on record. You took possession of that money, Agent Mezulari. You and your security detachment delivered that money to the Free City of Tannimore in the Doldrums. Let's talk about that trip, shall we?"

Mezulari rapidly shook his head. "Couriers may not discuss assignments."

There was a moment of intense silence which seemed like an eternity to the bound young man.

"Agent Mezulari, do you like being a courier?"

"Um, uh, I guess, sure."

"And I imagine you would like to continue on in that capacity?"

The threat was obvious.

"Um, I, I…"

The terrified courier abruptly halted his ramblings when a lone figure stepped into the light and approached him.

"Agent Mezulari we can handle this one of two ways."

The figure stopped directly in front of the quaking man who peered meekly upward, finally able to see his interrogator. Captain Rafel's long black hair and mustache framed his pasty white skin and sunken eyes from beneath the cowl of a dark robe. His slender, bone white hands brushed the raven curls from his face and he smiled at his captive.

"You tell me what I want to know and I release you," Rafel offered. "All of this, will be our little secret."

The delicate featured inquisitor knelt in front of Mezulari at eye level.

"Or you will force me to resort to more extreme measures," he threatened.

The Aramos youth swallowed hard. He stared into cold dispassionate eyes while his captor continued.

"But rest assured," Rafel said, "you *will* tell me what I want to know."

"What… what do you want to know?" he asked, panicking.

"Very simple really," Rafel said.

64

The inquisitor reached under the seat of the stool and fondled the young man's scrotum. Mezulari glanced down in wide-eyed dread when he felt the Captain's hands gently cupping and caressing his balls.

"Only one simple question, who did you deliver the money to?"

"I mean, I…"

The young man winced when Rafel's grip tightened.

"We don't have all day Agent Mezulari."

With that admonishment the spymaster savagely twisted the courier's manhood. Mezulari screamed and pitched forward. Rafel easily caught him and pushed him back. Releasing his grip, the Zorian gave him a questioning look.

"The temple of Orad," the bound figure gasped. "We took it to the Temple of Orad!"

Rafel stared blankly at the young man contemplating the information he had just heard—Orad is the goddess of death and patron saint to The Hand of the Wind assassin's guild.

So, it wasn't a robbery, it wasn't even a simple murder, it was an assassination.

Rising to his feet, he looked down at the injured and frightened courier. "Very well, I'm glad we had this little talk. Remember Agent Mezulari, we never met and this conversation never happened."

Panting in pain and fear the young Aramos courier watched the robed man casually walk away and disappear back behind the light.

Harper Aramos, unlike most of his extended family, was not an especially ruthless man. Most counts described him average in almost every way, except for his sense of loyalty. Because of this admirable trait, they chose Harper to be caregiver for his uncle and family patriarch Talon Aramos, who'd succumbed to a stroke two grands ago. Unfortunately, being the most senior Aramos, it also put him in charge of the branch of the Imperial Bank of Zor in the Aramos capital City of Aris, a job he was wholly unprepared and unqualified for.

As the Kan fog swept around the multiple ornate buildings and extensive well-manicured grounds of the royal palace, the young Aramos stood staring out the open window into the murky mist. Fighting back a wave of panic, he frowned and took another healthy swig from the mug in his hand. The liquor warmed him from the dampness which clung to his tunic and short brown hair. It did little to ease the overwhelming feeling of being a total failure.

"Close the window and come to bed," came a feminine voice from behind.

Taking one more sip he closed the window and forced a smile at his wife, Soless.

"Let me check on Uncle and Talliana then I'll be right along."

"Don't be too long," she said, in a weary, resigned voice before falling back onto her pillow.

Harper stepped out into the wide hallway and started towards his uncle's bedchamber. Passing a small alcove, he thought he detected movement from within its recesses.

"You look troubled Harper," came a familiar voice from the darkness.

Spinning towards the sound, he gasped when Stryder stepped out into the hall. He had not seen his cousin in several grands and he appeared just as he had remembered him. His slicked back, jet-black hair and cruel smile beneath a thin mustache, set off his handsome features. Something surreal about his appearance gave the encounter an inviting, dream like quality. All he could do was stand transfixed, mouth agape, while his younger cousin approached.

"Stryder!" he gasped. "They said you had disappeared."

The former quartermaster silently put his arms around Harper's waist. Stryder pulled him close and looked lustfully into his eyes, before leaning in for a kiss.

Harper quickly glanced around, he flashed back to memories of their younger days. How they concealed their dark family secret sneaking into each other's rooms. Satisfied they were alone, he fell into his cousin's embrace with a deep passionate kiss.

When they broke, Stryder stepped back and smiled.

"I have become reborn."

Harper reached up and gently touched his cousin's lips.

"Well, some things you haven't forgotten," he said, shyly.

The shock wore off. Harper looked his cousin up and down.

"How do you do it?" he asked. "You look the same, maybe even younger? What do you *mean* reborn? *Where have you been?* Because of your disappearance they assigned head quartermaster to my brother, Cowen."

"He is an excellent choice."

"So?" Harper asked, exasperated.

"I've been to the far side of the Annigan, cousin," he said, his eyes growing wide with excitement. "I have been shown many wonders."

"Do you wish to see your father?" Harper offered nervously. "I was just going to check on him."

Stryder shook his head. "There will be time enough for father. Right now, no one can know of my return. I'm traveling with three others and we'll need private lodging."

"Of course," Harper said, his voice betraying uncertainty. "The outer gardener's quarters is empty and... Stryder, what's going on?"

A sly smile crossed Stryder's glamoured face. "I can't share the details, but if I'm successful, it will bring in a new era of riches and prosperity."

The older cousins face fell. "I could use some prosperity right about now."

Stryder watched his cousin bow his head in embarrassment.

"So, I was right, something troubles you."

Harper gazed meekly back up. "It's the bank."

"What of it?"

"It's not doing well," he admitted. "Ever since uncle Talon's stroke, I've tried to keep things running but, apparently, I'm no banker. If things get much worse the Zorian Monetary Council will step in and take over. I'll be disgraced."

Stryder placed a reassuring hand on his cousin's shoulder.

"Do not worry about money, cousin," he said. "My god has the power to rain prosperity down upon you."

Harper gave a sad chuckle. "That would be some trick."

"Oh, it's no trick. I've seen it myself." Stryder's eyes danced with enthusiasm. "I've experienced his power!"

"What are you talking about?"

"I serve Pa-Waga, a mighty god! A god that wants us to prosper. All you must do is accept him and believe. Power and riches shall follow as soon as you receive his mark."

Harper shook his head in bewilderment and leaned his shoulder on the wall. He could feel the textured plaster through his thin night shirt. His mind raced while he watched his younger cousin grow more animated.

"Stryder, where is this coming from?" he asked. "You've never been religious."

"As I told you, I have witnessed many wonders, and they have transformed me."

"Transformed? What are you talking about? You look the same as you always have."

Stryder took several steps back, dropped his arms to his side and opened his hands palms out.

"Behold," he said.

Stryder's palms glowed blue, and he slowly rose into the air. Once ascended, his appearance shimmered as the glamor faded. Harper's face froze in shock and he backed away, the textured wall now scraping his upper arm.

A naked Stryder hovered a foot off the floor. Patterns of intricate scars covered an entirely chalk white body, which showed no discernible genitalia. His eyes grew round and black like a shark, with no irises or pupils. A small row of binary scars stretched horizontally across both upper and lower lips, glowing blue when he spoke.

"I am Pa-Waga manifest! Soon all will feel my reach!"

Shock and fear gradually faded while Harper stared at Stryder's glowing mouth, replaced by a growing sense of longing. He pushed away from the wall and drew closer.

"Pa-Waga will bestow substantial power and riches on you, cousin," Stryder preached. "All you must do is receive his mark, *my* mark."

From back down the hall, Soless' voice called from behind their bedroom door, "Harper, are you talking with someone?"

"Just talking to myself dear," he placated.

Harper broke into a profuse sweat. He watched Stryder slowly lower himself to the floor and assume his prior appearance. Although he no longer had a beautiful cock and scars covered his body, Harper found his cousin sexier than ever. He wanted to taste him, please him, serve him. If this was religion, he was born again.

"I will return the same time next Kan," the dark cleric promised, before his tone grew serious. "Make sure no one approaches the garden house, not even you. Think about what I have offered. I serve a mighty and prosperous god."

Golden waist-high tallgrass swayed gently in the breeze as far as the eye could see. Slowly, a circle fifty feet in diameter swirled. From the middle of the grassy cyclone blue lightning began erupting into the gray featureless sky. When the spinning hurricane of tallgrass stalks reached its zenith, the *Haraka*, accompanied by several azure bolts, shot out of the void and into the skies over the Pasture Plane of the Middle Realms.

A startled cry rang out in the airship's cabin when the craft raced upwards. Mal gripped the dashboard tightly.

"Why is arrival always such a bitch?!" the Spice Rat asked, staring wide-eyed at the alien expanse.

"We're literally being spit from the Middle Realms," Zau said, deftly spinning the ship's wheel.

The airship did a wide arc downward and leveled off fifty feet above the grasslands below. Mal surveyed the seemingly endless sea of waving flora.

"Talk about a lot of nothing," she said.

"Don't be fooled, Captain," Zau cautioned. "There's a lot going on down there."

The Singa no sooner spoke when on their starboard side, a small cyclone formed in the tallgrass. More bolts of blue lightning materialized, followed by two large buffalo leaping out of the void. They tumbled on the prairie upon landing, but quickly scrambled up and ran off.

"Whoa, what the fuck?!"

"They must have just died back in the Corporeal Reach," Zau said, watching the beasts lumber off. "Their spirit bodies have just returned home."

"So, beings just show up here when they die?" Mal asked, genuinely curious.

"Only if their spirits identify with the pastoral nature of this plane," the lioness explained. "For them, this is paradise. To others, especially sentients who don't identify with the rural, this could be a place of punishment."

Zaad joined Mal side at the windshield.

"I know this would be an awful place for me to end up," he said. "No water, now *that's* torture."

"Oh, I'm sure there's water around here somewhere," Zau countered. "There's just not going to be any large bodies."

She lifted her eye patch and projected the holographic multi-dimensional globe. Mal noted the different topography.

"Okay, it looks like the signal is about thirty degrees off to port," she reported, altering course. "Unfortunately, Captain, that portal dropped us quite a distance away."

"Hey, whatta ya know," Zaad said, in amazement, pointing to a small stand of trees on the horizon. "There is more than grass around here."

Zau nodded and was about to respond when she noticed a rustle in the tall grass directly below the *Haraka*. A coiled form erupted from the ground cover with a loud hiss. When it struck, it rocked the craft, sending the man-shark toppling to the deck.

"Holy fuck!" Mal howled.

Zau rapidly spun the wheel to avoid the tail of a giant snake, longer than the ship, being repelled off the Ukko wood and back into the air.

Any comforting thoughts about impunity and safety were fleeting. The Singa gasped when two short wings unfolded from the upper portion of its serpentine body. A collar of blueish feathers extended, and it banked around the airship, hissing furiously.

"Flying egg sack slippery," everyone heard from the creature as it circled menacingly.

"That's no dumb animal," Mal said, watching the winged serpent stalk her airship.

"How is it we can understand it?" Zau asked, spinning the wheel again.

"The same way we communicate with you," Mal answered. "Zaad and I have Etheria crystals, talking stones on us."

"That's good, right?" the Singa asked.

Mal stared out the windshield frantically looking for the beast.

"It works both ways," she answered. "If we understand it, it can understand us."

Effortlessly circling the escaping craft, they could hear it slithering across the top of the ship. Zau followed the dragging sound trailing across the sides of the *Haraka*.

"Captain, it's attempting to entangle us." Zau said, breathlessly.

"Don't let it get ahold of us!" Mal yelled.

"Hold on to something!" the lioness warned, yanking back on the flaps and violently spinning the wheel.

The airship lurched upward and hard off to starboard, dislodging the winged beast off the hull. It squealed in frustration sweeping directly in front of the craft.

"Make for that stand of trees!" Mal ordered. "We can't outmaneuver it. Maybe we can tangle it up."

Keeping an erratic flight path, the airship barreled towards the dozen trees towering above the golden grasslands. The creature easily kept up with the fleeing craft. Several times it attempted to strike out, but the naturally repellent properties of the Ukko wood hull repulsed it. A shriek of exasperation filled the air with each failed strike.

While the grouping of trees drew ever closer, Mal could make out what appeared to be three large tan colored sacks hanging from the top branches of the middle tree. In between all the surrounding trees was a network of thin white ropes crisscrossing each other in a haphazard lattice network.

"I don't fucking like the looks of that," Mal said.

"It kinda looks like those Cevot spider webs back in the mountains," Zau noted.

"Too much like them," the Spice Rat replied, rubbing her chin. "Be ready to pull up at the last-minute and we can skim the tops of those trees."

"Uh, Captain," the Singa said, her voice laced with uncertainty. "I just learned how to fly one of these things. I'm not sure if I can pull off anything too tricky."

"On my command just pull the nose up," Mal said, confidently, "and ready both ballista pods."

"I don't know how to do that!" the Singa wailed.

Zaad got up and stepped over to the ships wheel.

"These two levers right here," the EEtah said.

He pointed down at two short handles resting at the base of a T shaped slot. Reaching down, he pushed both levers to the center of where the slots converged.

"Okay, they're ready," he announced. "To fire, you pull the lever to the left. To reload, slide it to the right, then back to the middle and you're ready to fire again."

The lioness nodded nervously, then focused back on the ship's trajectory.

"Coming up now, get ready," Mal said, holding up a finger, "and... now!"

The *Haraka* veered rapidly upward towards the treetops, skimming the webbing. When it approached the underside of the canopy, the rear lower tail fin clipped the outer edges of the web. It sliced into several of the cords and caught, spinning the craft so it now faced the complete opposite direction, before becoming ensnared in the sticky restraints.

The creature too became trapped in its close pursuit. The trio now faced the tangled serpent, watching it furiously screech and flap its wings. Its panicked undulations only further entrapped it.

"Shoot it!" Mal shouted.

Zau looked skeptically at the levers. Choosing one, she pulled it to the left. One of the three-foot-long ballista bolts shot out in front of the airship with a loud thump. It sailed past its target to the right.

"Fuck, it missed!" Mal spat.

"We can't adjust the ship to aim," Zaad said, "but the other pod should be in the right position."

The EEtah reached past the overwhelmed pilot and fired the second round. The projectile plunged into the creature's upper body between the wings. It roared in pain, but continued straining against the webbing, ignoring the protruding bolt.

"That's one tough fucker," the Spice Rat said. "Hit him again."

Zaad shifted the lever and loaded another round, when Mal detected movement from out of the treetops.

"Hold that shot!" Mal ordered.

She watched an arachnid creature, with a humanoid female's torso atop a spider's body, race down the web. It stopped short of the struggling snake and began shooting streams of silk from an orifice at the end of her thorax, coating the creature's frantically flapping wings. Each ropy white blast restricted the beast's movements until only a small area just below the head remained exposed.

The spider woman then scurried atop the mummified body and leaned over the struggling creature. She parted her sensuous black lips and opened her mouth to an unnaturally immense to make room for two long protruding curved fangs. Without hesitation she sunk them into the snake's neck through the small opening. Slowly, the struggling diminished and she resumed shooting silk until she encased the entire body.

Once satisfied she had subdued the snake, the spider woman ran quickly across the web to the *Haraka*. Both parties stared curiously at each other through the windshield.

Her torso was mostly humanoid, with areas of hard black exoskeleton spanning up her back forming a loose-fitting head covering which stretched out into mandibles on either side of her head. The shell continued down her arms stopping just before her hands. In front it reached upward to a point between two firm human looking breasts with large black nipples. There was a bright red hourglass shape adorning her abdomen just before where the human and spider bodies joined.

Cocking her head inquisitively to the side she studied the three beings through the glass. Mal noted her face was perfectly symmetrical with sensuous black lips and a delicate nose. The texture of her skin dimpled from her cheeks upward across the top of her hairless head and ridged resembling a carnival mask. Two sultry, almond-shaped, solid black eyes accentuated four smaller round eyes on her forehead.

"You help protect my children, thank you," she said, before disappearing from view underneath the craft.

Moments later they felt the jolt when the spider woman picked the airship off the web. Zaad wisely took a seat while she carried the ship down the web and set it on the ground just outside the perimeter of the trees.

"Wow, she's really something!" the EEtah swooned.

"Easy there, big fella," Mal admonished, getting to her feet. "We all just met."

Zau stared in astonishment as the airship captain made her way to the side hatch.

"Uh... Mal?" she asked, skeptically. "What exactly do you think you're doing?"

Mal gave an amused look at the tone of her navigator's question while reaching for the lever.

"She helped us out," she said. "The least we can do is to be friendly."

"Are you crazy?" the lioness asked, in a startled voice. "I can have us airborne and out of here in no time!"

Mal threw the bar, breaking the door's seal and flashed a sarcastic smile.

"Where's your sense of adventure?"

Zaad slipped Bowbreaker onto his back when he saw Mal step out into the tallgrass.

"Let's go see what the lady has to say," he said, following his captain out. "Besides, there's something very arousing about her."

Zau huffed, "That's okay, I think I'll stay put for at least a little while."

The ground below Mal's feet felt hard and dry while she waded through the thick waving stalks. The strands crunched under her weight giving off a pleasant earthy smell. Looking up into the trees she could see the spider woman removing the sacks from the limb and placing them beside the encased giant snake on the web itself.

When the humanoid spider saw the Spice Rat on the ground beside the ship, she scurried off the web and over to her.

"I'm Kumo," she said, staring in awe as a beguiled Zaad approached. "Thanking you again, Madu stalk my children since I laid egg sacks."

"Hey, my name is Mal and the big walking fish here is Zaad," Mal said. "I take it this 'Madu' you're referring to is the big ass flying snake."

"Yes," Kumo answered, "now he will feed my children when they hatch, giving me chance to escape."

"Escape?" Zaad asked, perplexed.

"When the children hatch, they swarm, they eat anything near them," Kumo explained.

Mal was aghast. "Even their own mother?"

"Even one another," the creature said, smiling sadly. "Land supports few of our kind."

"And what kind is that?" Mal asked, curiously.

"We are Makari, there can only be so many of us."

"What a shame," Zaad cooed.

Mal rolled her eyes. "You must excuse my friend. He's normally not like this, unless you're a dolphin."

Kumo looked up at the EEtah and gave a sultry smile.

"Not his fault, friend Mal," she said, apologetically. "I have same effect, all males, every race, and species."

"Really?" Mal chuckled, giving the man-shark an amused side glance.

"We encountered peoples much the same as you in the mountains back in our home called Cevots." Zaad said, unable to take his eyes off her. "Not nearly as beautiful though."

"We seeded many races throughout the void," the Makari said. "Your race is also spreading. Two just arrived. One coming home. A female traveler followed him though."

This immediately got the Spice Rat's attention. "You saw them?!"

Kumo pointed to the horizon behind them. "They settled over there."

Mal and Zaad exchanged excited glances.

"Looks like Zau's map was right," the EEtah said, optimistically.

"Sure does," Mal confirmed. "Okay, let's see if we can wrap up this brief run and get paid. Kumo, it was good meeting you. Thanks for taking care of the Madu and..."

Several loud popping sounds rising up on the web interrupted the airship captain's farewell. Kumo gave a panicked look up to see one sack had broken open in several locations. Miniature Makari spider creatures, about a foot tall, poured out onto the web. Almost on cue, the two other sacks erupted.

Some newborns began attacking each other. The rest overran the cocooned snake and began sucking up the rapidly liquefying body.

"The children!" Kumo said. "We cannot stay!"

"Come with us!" Zaad eagerly proposed.

Mal watched the spider woman glance hesitantly back-and-forth between her and the EEtah. When she saw a flood of the young Makari swarming down the web towards them, the Spice Rat quickly nodded her acceptance.

"Let's get the fuck outta here before we all end up as breakfast."

The bed was wide and comfortable. Peligro lay back with his hands behind his head and watched the Kan fog slowly rise outside the nearby window.

Nothing like traveling first class, the Aramos agent reflected, gazing around his opulent cabin. *The damn thing's big enough to throw a party in.*

He admitted this trip would be a brief one and boarded the luxury yacht a short while ago at mid-day from the Eldorian capital City of Rophan. The trip to the Aramos capital City of Aris was just a few islands over in the Goyodan Chain and should only take two cycles.

It really didn't matter to Peligro. Unless ordered differently, he always traveled first class. Not only did it compliment his cover as a successful oyster broker, the Aramos Wraith realized any assignment might be his last, so he afforded himself the small modicum of luxury.

If this wasn't his biggest mission, it was right up there near the top. Killing Stryder Aramos wouldn't be easy. He will be difficult to locate and well protected.

He also traveled unarmed. Oyster brokers didn't really carry weapons. He would purchase whatever armaments he needed once on location as usual, based on the situation.

First things first, he strategized, *find Stryder Aramos.*

The grumbling in his stomach coincided perfectly with the knock on his cabin door, ending his mental planning session. Dinner had arrived. Smiling in anticipation Peligro bounded off the bed for the door. He loved the food on these trips and, like the room, spared no expense.

He opened the door. A young cabin maid greeted him, carrying a covered platter. The fear in her eyes revealed she was not alone. Three scowling large men with short stubbly hair and crew uniforms stood behind her. One held a dagger to her back.

They shoved her into Peligro—sending the surprised agent staggering backward and the platter of food clattering to the floor—before storming into the stateroom. The two unarmed ruffians lunged at Peligro while the one with the knife quickly slit the cabin maid's throat. She toppled to the floor on top of the overturned platter of food. Her blood mixed with the juices from Peligro's medium rare steak.

The first thug to reach him charged wildly. Stepping to the side, Peligro caught the ruffian's arm and, using his momentum, flipped him over the bed. He crashed headfirst into the wall.

The next attacker opened his arms wide to grapple him into a bear hug. A short front kick to the stomach doubled him over, allowing the Aramos agent to concentrate on the most dangerous assailant, the one with the knife.

The armed thug stepped over the body of the girl he murdered brandishing his bloody dagger. Peligro rushed him. The mugger swung his knife. Peligro felt the sting of steel slice his forearm when the blade ripped through the sleeve of his shirt. The slash left only a flesh wound and adrenalin surged through him.

Peligro grabbed the attacker's knife hand by the wrist and redirected the blade away from him. He shoved his hand against his assailant's chin and, driving forward, smashed him backwards into the door.

The criminal stiffened when the coat hook mounted on the back of the door penetrated the base of his skull. A shocked look froze across his face as a ribbon of blood streamed from his mouth. Dropping the knife, he hung there, pinned to the door like a macabre garment.

Peligro leapt to the ground diving for the knife. He just about reached it when a savage kick to the ribs propelled him several feet away from the blade.

"Rich fuck!" the assailant snarled, delivering another blow. "Where's the gold?"

Peligro cried out in pain when two more kicks landed. When he tried for a third, Peligro grabbed his foot and violently wrenched it to the side. The ankle shattered with a loud crack and the thief screamed in agony falling beside the wounded agent.

The only threat remaining climbed out from the far side of the bed where he had landed. He was rubbing the bump on his concussed forehead when he noticed Peligro rising to his knees and rushed him. In one fluid motion Peligro scooped the dagger up from the floor and hurled it at the attacker. It plunged into the knot on his forehead, halting him in his tracks. A sheet of blood streamed from the swollen wound, highlighting the man's astounded expression in a ghastly shade of red.

The final thug still alive writhed on the floor, screaming in pain over his broken ankle. Peligro rose to his feet. The Aramos Wraith calmly walked over and watched him squirm. Tears streamed down the mugger's face and he clutched his shattered appendage.

Peligro sneered and put the sole of his boot against the thief's throat.

"Shut up!" he spat.

He drove the boot downward viciously. Frantic gurgling replaced the thug's screams of trauma when it crushed his windpipe.

Peligro grabbed a towel from a freshly delivered stack resting in a nearby chair. He tossed the remaining linens on the floor and sat down by them. After bandaging his wounded forearm, he began wrapping his bruised ribs when a handful of security guards rushed in followed by the captain of the luxury yacht.

"What's the meaning of this?!" the captain bellowed, causing his thick handlebar mustache to tremble.

Peligro calmly looked up at them and then at the dead bodies surrounding him.

"Robbery," he said, calmly, keeping pressure on his cut. "Looks like some of your cabin boys wanted an extra tip out of me."

The captain inspected the grizzly scene and gestured for his men to stand down.

"This woman has served me for years," he reported, shaking his head, "but these men are not part of my crew."

His demeanor became contrite when he turned back to the wounded Aramos agent, one of his best customers.

"Si Peligro," he said, "please accept my deepest apologies for this unfortunate incident. Let's get that arm looked at."

Peligro lifted the towel wrapped limb and shook his head examining it.

"I'll be okay," he coolly assured. "What I really need, is another room, another dinner, and another bottle of whisky."

The bedchamber held a distinct chill despite the crackling fireplace. The smell of disease and slow death tainted the room's ornate opulence. Harper Aramos leaned over the prone body of his beloved Uncle Talon and wiped away a trickle of drool which had escaped the corner of his mouth. Luckily, he caught the yellow tinted fluid before it added another stain to the expensive Awan cotton sheets.

He contemplated the absurdity of the once powerful house patriarch and towering bank magnate now reduced to a semi-catatonic state. It almost seemed fitting that the health of the patriarch failed along with the institution he ran for so many years with ruthless precision.

He found comfort in the memory of how, unlike his father, Uncle Talon had always been there for Harper, guiding him with a firm yet loving hand.

"Uncle," he whispered, leaning in close. "There's someone here to see you."

Talon Aramos' tired, confused eyes fluttered open focusing on his nephew and care giver. He babbled something unintelligible and weakly waved his hand. Harper turned to the nurse who stood dutifully by the door.

"Please give us some privacy," he requested.

The purple robed clerria nodded and quickly exited, closing the door behind her as she left. A magically glamoured Stryder stepped over to the bed and pulled back his cowl.

"Hello father," he said, softly.

The patriarch's shriveled face brightened at the sound of his son's voice and the left corner of his mouth pulled upward in a weak, twitching, distorted smile. As quickly as his happy acknowledgment appeared, it faded, and Talon Aramos descended into his prior non-responsive state.

Harper looked pained and questioningly stared over at his dominant cousin. Stryder nodded grimly at him and placed a hand on his shoulder.

"The greatest rewards require the greatest sacrifice," he said, stepping away to the foot of the bed.

The elder Aramos cousin stared down at the failing family head, lingering while he weighed what he knew he must do. Tears streamed down the young man's face and he choked back a sob grabbing a nearby pillow.

Slowly he positioned the cushion over Talon's face and pressed down hard. The old man thrashed from side to side and his arms flailed from under the bed sheets while the primal part of his brain fought for oxygen. His much stronger young nephew kept up his relentless pressure until the limbs went still.

Behind him Stryder had assumed his true form. Holding his barbed finger aloft he panted in excitement. When Harper finally stood up, he wept openly at the lifeless body of his favorite uncle. He didn't feel the needle-sharp tip carving a single X and I on either side of his spine at the base of his skull. The trickle of blood running down the back of his neck and staining his collar caused the fledgling Aramos to peer inquisitively at Stryder.

The dark cleric nodded in satisfaction. "A true sacrifice never fails."

Demetrius knew well the symptoms. Pisar Tysonn's face went flush, and he appeared on the verge of throwing up, but there was nothing the pilot could do about it. He watched the scholar pull back his long brown hair and stare down at his lap avoiding the sight of clouds rushing past.

"First time flying, Pisar?" Okawa asked, trying to distract the nauseated scribe.

Tysonn gave a pained nod but remained silent while keeping his attention away from the window.

Poor kid, Demetrius thought, *just his luck that the first flight he takes has him skirting the upper atmosphere.*

"Yeah, first time's always the roughest," Demetrius said, guiding the *Drakin* downward from the Annigan's upper atmosphere to the eastern Goyan coast. "If you're gonna get sick, do us all a favor and don't do it on your package. There's a vomit bag next to your seat."

Tysonn nodded again, noting the small, metal box chained to his wrist. Another steep bank of the airship brought a groan from the passenger and the *Drakin* dropped beneath the clouds above the bustling City of Zor.

Despite the upper cloud deck, the weather cleared over the metropolis. Demetrius could make out the wide variety of buildings sprawling all the way from the Northern and Southern Docks, along the beachheads, to the gilded suburbs of Shimol and Tuath Plat in the foothills. An enormous, sun bleached basin of forums and baths dominated the base of the cityscape. The immense structure of Air Station Three jutted out from the mountainside above it all.

"You're missing a splendid view," Demetrius said, piloting the craft towards the cavernous entrance of the air station.

"That's okay," the Pisar assured, not lifting his head. "How soon before we get there?"

The sunlight fading as they entered the air station answered the scribe's question. The young man finally looked up and took in his surroundings with a relieved sigh.

All about the massive chamber were parked airships of various sizes in neat rows. The area was abuzz with activity as the crafts were being loaded and unloaded with cargo and mostly human passengers. All around them ships lifted off and landed in precise order, all guided by a team of animated air bosses.

"Hey, they're directing us into the military hangar," Demetrius noted watching the air boss flag him to a slightly smaller chamber to his left.

Okawa calmly watched Demetrius steer the ship through an opening flanked by EEtah sentries.

"Given our passenger and cargo," she said, "I'm not surprised."

Demetrius glanced over and smiled at her insight. He then caught himself momentarily distracted by her alluring presence. The voice of the air station controller calling out directions broke the spell and Demetrius deftly maneuvered the ship towards slip number five.

A Sunal EEtah security guard stood attentively by the air dock with a traditional Udon harpoon lashed to his back. The imposing man-shark's twelve-foot frame towered over the mostly human flight crews milling about him.

"Looks like your babysitter is waiting," Demetrius noted, settling into an oversized landing area normally designed for a larger military craft.

Releasing the door Okawa stood and faced the peaked looking scribe. She gave him a moment to compose himself while the EEtah positioned his imposing frame just beyond the open side hatch.

"Okay, Pisar," she said, "this is where we part ways."

Tysonn weakly nodded, finally able to stand without fear of retching. Demetrius also stood up and almost collided with Okawa in the close quarters when she attempted to pass.

When he brushed up against her, reflexes kicked in and she reached out and gently gripped him by both upper arms. A tingle shot through the pilot's body when their eyes met, and both smiled. The encounter was brief, but Demetrius noticed his heart beating faster.

Once the moment passed, Okawa reassuringly patted his arms and looked away nervously. Pushing a lock of hair from her forehead, she glanced quickly back up at Demetrius who had not taken his eyes off her.

"Well I better…" she stammered pointing to the open hatch.

"Yeah," Demetrius blurted in agreement, snapping out of his amorous trance.

He sighed heavily while watching her shapely butt saunter down the ramp after Tysonn and out onto the flight deck. Demetrius shook his head to clear it and then went down his mental checklist for securing his ship. He had just about finished when he gave a startled jump upon noticing Okawa standing back in the doorway gazing at him with an enraptured look.

"Oh, hello! That didn't take long. I'm almost done," he noted, before returning to inspecting the control panel.

Okawa blushed slightly at being caught staring.

"Pisar Tysonn's someone else's problem now," she said. "They secured quarters for him on the university grounds."

"Well, all right," Demetrius said, standing up, "we're all set here."

"So, do you always check things over after every flight?" Okawa asked, awkwardly glancing around the cabin.

"Yep, I like to be ready in a moments notice," Demetrius answered, suggestively.

Okawa returned a provocative grin.

"I'll keep that in mind," she said.

"Is this the part where I'm annoyingly charming?" Demetrius asked, with a lascivious smirk.

The Valdurian couldn't contain her grin. She averted her gaze downward.

"No, just charming."

There was a brief silence as Demetrius was unsure how to respond to the compliment.

"Anyway…" Okawa said, breaking the tongue-tied situation and turning to go.

"Hey," Demetrius finally spoke up, fighting to overcome the severe dryness in his mouth.

Okawa stopped before exiting the craft and turned.

"So, you maybe want to get a drink?" he stammered nervously, examining her captivating profile.

The pilot held his breath in anticipation as the moment stretched into an eternity. He breathed a sigh of relief when the corners of her mouth turned upwards into a broad smile which lit up her face.

"Sure."

It pleased Jo-Rakk that the population of the Bailian capital of Immor-Onn were growing accustomed to the sight of mawls traveling about the city. He was also grateful that his peoples had been so warmly welcomed by the blue skinned humanoids and, because of this, trade currently flourished between the two cultures.

The Tiikeri ambassador had gotten word that a large transport ship arrived with the rising moon. They informed him a special representative arrived with that ship and awaited him with urgent business.

The seven-foot-tall white tiger moved rapidly through the busy halls of the palace nodding aloof greetings to those he passed. He stopped at the door of one of the many meeting rooms and, without knocking, promptly entered.

It surprised Jo-Rakk to see a young female Singa, in a brown cape with the hood pulled down, standing beside the lone table. On her back she carried a full-sized fighting staff.

"I am ambassador Jo-Rakk," he began in a patronizing tone. "Is there something I can do for you?"

Ignoring the elitist Tiikeri's greeting, the Singa reached into an inner cape pocket and retrieved a small multi page booklet.

"My name is unimportant," she said, flatly, handing the papers to Jo-Rakk. "My orders."

The Tiikeri's eyes swept suspiciously over the Singa while he accepted the bound leaflets. He opened the cover and slowly turned the blank pages, sniffing each one for their invisible message. All the while he kept his eyes on the mawl. A begrudging acceptance registered on the ambassador's face with each page he turned. The olfactory message in orders concerned the missing Tiikeri finance minister, Ma-Tah.

Quite frankly, Jo-Rakk was glad to be rid of him. He resented this impertinent mawl for even bringing his name up again. When he reached the last page, he snapped the pamphlet shut and thrust it back at her. Che-At calmly accepted the book with a thin superior smile.

"And?" Jo-Rakk huffed, wishing he could back hand the smile off her face. "So what about Ma-Tah?"

"When was the last time you saw the finance minister?"

"No one has seen him for at least thirty lunas. He accompanied a small human delegation to our homeland, then returned for a short period before disappearing. We assumed he was away on some confidential errand or missing, perhaps dead."

Che-At mulled over Ambassador Jo-Rakk's statement.

"Was there anything unusual about the finance minister?" she asked.

"No one really trusted him and except for his seneschal," he answered. "No one was close to him."

"I need to see his dwelling," the Singa demanded.

The Tiikeri bristled at the lesser creature's imperious tone.

"If I could know exactly what this is about?"

"My orders were fairly clear," Che-At said, with an impatient sigh. "The minister possesses a special item which your king wants back."

"And you're here to get it?"

"At all costs ambassador," she stressed, "it cannot fall into the wrong hands."

"His apartment is empty," Jo-Rakk said, stroking his whiskers thoughtfully. "His belongings are in a secure location and I was preparing to send them back to Hai-Darr. My seneschal, Takki, personally oversaw the apartment's eviction. There was nothing out of the ordinary."

"I still need to see those belongings," the Singa said, adamantly.

"For that, I'm afraid you'll need special permission," the ambassador announced in a bored bureaucratic voice. "It could be a lengthy process."

The Singa held his eyes in her intense gaze.

"Time is a luxury I do not possess, Ambassador."

Zau stared out the side window and watched while gentle rolling hills dominated the landscape below. She piloted the *Haraka* through the blank gray skies of the Pasture Plane in the Middle Realms. Zau suspiciously observed Kumo wander the cabin and stare in wide-eyed amazement at the ship's interior.

The Makari ran her hands lovingly across the surface of the wall with a cooing sound, taking in every detail. Her hands then trailed down to the seats and back to the cargo storage area. She then made her way over to the ship's wheel and stared intently at Zau. The Singa avoided eye contact while making subtle adjustments in course and conferring with the map projecting through the spokes in front of her.

Zau resumed eyeing her suspiciously when Kumo walked past her and up to the command chairs in front of the windshield. The spider woman stood motionless watching the activity on the dashboard for a bit and then turned her attention to Mal surveying the grassy terrain beneath them.

"I've seen nothing like this," Kumo said, in a barely audible tenor. "Amazing, comfortable… feels like home."

Mal spun in her chair. "Yeah, she's something. This baby has got our asses out of many a scrape."

The Makari stared excitedly around the entire ship's interior. "Like the safety of egg sack and my birth."

The Singa diverted her gaze from the map once again and stared skeptically at the female spider.

"Yeah, well I wouldn't get too used to it," she snarked.

Kumo cocked her head quizzically, not comprehending the Singa's verbal jab. A disapproving glance from Mal sent the Singa back to her piloting duties.

"So, Captain," Zaad said, sitting forward. "What happens if we find this bowmistress, and she doesn't want to come back with us?"

Mal gave a decisive shrug. "This is a rescue mission not a kidnapping. Either way, if we find her, the Amarenians have got to pony up."

"Getting close, Captain," Zau said, watching the blip on the map grow larger.

"It sure looks like it," the Spice Rat said.

Several small buildings and an animal pen came into view on the side of a shallow indentation between hills.

"This is where the two that just arrived settled," Kumo declared.

Zau pointed to the tops of some trees peeking above the hilltops to their left.

"The signal is emanating from those trees," she said.

"Okay everyone, this is where we earn our keep," Mal announced. "Let's get over there and see what the fuck's going on."

The airship banked gently into a valley between three hills and flew at treetop level over a stand of trees. Just beyond the tree's dripline, Wostera, a statuesque woman in flowing black robes, stood with a long bow in hand.

She gracefully let an arrow fly. It soared towards a minuscule target set in the side of a far hill. The arrow struck the barely visible target dead on and then disappeared in a small blue flash. With a smooth flourish she swept her release arm out to her side and the arrow appeared in her palm with the same blue spark.

Kalaka, Itori insect mage, sat naked and cross-legged under the nearest tree with a swarm of flies buzzing about him. He peacefully gazed with a lovesick smile at the archer who took his life.

Settling gently down in the open field beside the trees, Zau cut the engines and the *Haraka* gently rested a few inches off the ground nestled in a blanket of tall, golden grass.

Kalaka rose to his feet, pointing excitedly. Wostera lowered her bow and joined him while they hurried across the field towards the airship.

Zaad climbed out of the side hatch behind Mal and Zau. The EEtah slipped Bowbreaker onto his back and glanced over at Kumo, who stood just behind the ship's wheel gazing rapturously around at the interior.

"Are you coming?"

The Makari shook her head no.

"I should stay with the ship," Kumo said, in a hauntingly serene voice.

Nodding in acceptance, the man-shark waded out into the knee-high grass. He saw his friends just ahead being warmly greeted by Wostera and Kalaka.

"I knew I recognized that ship!" Kalaka declared joyously when his eyes swept over the *Haraka*.

"You've made some improvements since I saw it last," he exclaimed, pointing to the ballista pods on the side.

He then turned to Mal and opened his arms.

"And you my friend, how are you?" he asked, and without waiting for her reply, he hugged the Spice Rat. "It's so good to see you!"

A startled Mal meekly returned the embrace while giving the approaching Wostera a quizzical look. The bowmistress returned a sad, resigned smile. She broke with Kalaka, who made his way over, wide-eyed to examine the airship. Mal enthusiastically clasped forearms with the Amarenian.

"It is good to see you Maluria," she said, with a soothing look.

"Right back at ya, Valorous," Mal said, with a knowing smirk.

Wostera appeared briefly confused following the Spice Rat's jargon.

Reaching into her pocket, Mal retrieved her Amarenian Simikort and handed it to the bowmistress. The Amarenian's face lit up examining the round green coin.

"Valorous, you well deserve this," she said, returning it.

"Aww, thanks," Mal said, blushing slightly.

"Your traveling companions are different," Wostera said.

On cue, the Spice Rat introduced Zau and Zaad before noticing her newest crew member was missing.

"Where's Kumo?" Mal asked.

"She stayed with the ship," Zaad replied nonchalantly.

Zau's disposition turned instantly suspicious. "Really?"

Wostera examined the group.

"Tell me Maluria," she asked, "where is the swordsman to whom I owe my life?"

The airship captain's face fell. Seeing Mal's reaction Wostera grew worrisome.

"He's not dead, is he?"

"No, he's fine," Mal said, sadly, shaking her head. "He's following his dream of opening his own sword school."

The older Amarenian's brow furrowed sympathetically.

"He will return to you," she confidently predicted.

The Spice Rat raised a skeptical eyebrow.

"Now that he has experienced the venturous life—and *you*—any other path will be but a diversion," Wostera said.

"Yeah, well, we'll see…" Mal murmured.

Kalaka came bounding back happily from the ship.

"It's just how I remembered it," he exclaimed, "and I really didn't have time to get this close of a look at it back in Amarenia."

"Yeah," Mal said, with a chuckle, "we were all a little busy."

"Well, I'm certainly glad to see you, but what has you traversing the multiverse?" Wostera asked.

"You," Mal said, pointing at her. "Your people want you to come home."

A brief flash of hope passed across the bowmistresses' face before turning into a serene sadness.

"Home?" Kalaka asked, disappointment clearly in his voice.

"Thank you Maluria, but I cannot leave him." Wostera sounded troubled, wiping away a lone tear.

The bowmistress gently placed her hand on the Itori's shoulder in response to Mal's intense, questioning expression.

"Never have I encountered such love and devotion from *anyone*, let alone a man," Wostera proclaimed. "He loves me, not in spite of the fact I killed him, but *because* I killed him."

"I was ready to pass and return to here," Kalaka said, gesturing at the serene pastoral setting, "but they robbed me of my crossing over and forced me to do things I never would have done in life. The two of you released me from an existence of servitude to that... that woman... For that I am truly and eternally grateful."

"You'll be happy to know she's dead now," Mal reported.

"I hope her spirit finds rest," Kalaka said, wistfully.

His mood then shifted back to jovial. Spinning to face Wostera he reached out and held her by her shoulders.

"But you *must* return with them," he graciously said. "This is my forever home now. I will *always* be here waiting for you."

The Amarenian protested when Kalaka cut her off.

"Go, return to your destiny. You still have much to accomplish. My hope is that when it is your turn to pass, you will return here, to me."

Wostera sobbed and fell into his arms.

"I don't want to leave you or this peaceful place," she choked through the tears.

"Your people need you," he assured, gently patting her back.

"But I…"

The sound of the *Haraka's* Etheria engines whirring to life cut short any further debate by the Bowmistress.

Wostera remained in Kalaka's arms, her face buried in his neck, weeping. Everyone else turned in shock to see the airship lift off. Zau felt her stomach knot up while a flash of rage swept across her.

"That BITCH!" Zau shrieked. "I knew we shouldn't have left her alone with the ship!"

The hijacked craft quickly ascended and steeply banked, circling the area. Everyone watched in stunned silence, except Zau, who kept screaming expletives at the ship now performing a series of complex rolls and loops.

Zau eyed the craft warily and turned over one seashell on her belt. Rubbing the rune on the back, she reached up pointing towards the ship. Mal gently touched her arm halting the spell. The look on the Spice Rat's face was more of interest than concern.

"Let's not damage our only fucking way outta here," she said. "Besides, if she was gonna steal the ship she'd be long gone by now."

The *Haraka* banked once again at the far end of the valley before swooping down on the group causing all to duck. It came to an abrupt stop ten feet from them and then settled to the ground.

When they started towards the airship, the side hatch dropped and Kumo appeared in the door. Her face was radiant with accomplishment.

"I Think I figured this out."

The fat tavern owner set the two drinks down on the bar with an annoyed scowl. Demetrius made sure he placed more coins than required in front of him and took possession of the two glasses. The man's heavy jowls seemed to flutter while he eyed the extra money suspiciously. In a decisive moment, he quickly swept the currency into his pudgy hand and walked away.

Handing one drink to Okawa, Demetrius flashed a mischievous smile. "I don't think he wants us here."

The Valdurian agent scanned the empty bar room and snickered. "Well we seem to be the only ones left. He probably wants to close up."

"Hey, according to the posted hours out front we've got awhile," Demetrius said, with a playful nod.

Okawa motioned towards the small stage. "Are you kidding? Even the band has gone home."

The airship pilot surveyed the instruments carefully placed in their stands.

"That's okay, they weren't very good," he said.

She gave a small snicker of agreement, sweeping back the chestnut curls which tumbled around her face, and gazed at Demetrius with a distinctly softer expression.

"Anyway," the pilot said, raising his glass, "between my piloting and your, uhh, various martial skills shall we call them, we seem to make a good team. So, here's to a good team."

Okawa caught Demetrius' gaze and held it while they gently touched glasses.

"To us."

His cheeks slightly flushed under her attentive stare and he fought to think of something to say.

"So, you didn't like the band either?"

Okawa broke from her beguiling focus and glanced back at the stage.

"Not really, the lute was constantly out of tune and the musician, if you could call him that, didn't seem to notice. The harpsichord player was just as bad and don't get me started on the singer's voice."

Demetrius gave out a whistle while he sat back. "Wow, harsh!"

The agent shrugged. "I call them as I see them."

"So, you could tell all of that from the few songs we heard?"

"Sure," she replied. "And the sad part is, the instruments were an easy fix. The singer, not so much…"

Raising a finger, she got up and walked over to the stage.

"Allow me to demonstrate."

Carefully taking the lute from its stand, she sat down on the stage, with her feet hanging over, facing the bar and a very curious Demetrius. Plucking two of the strings, she tuned and tightened their respective pegs until she nodded in satisfaction.

"See, easy fix," she said, glancing back up at Demetrius.

The airship pilot had barely enough time to acknowledge her statement before she launched into a beautifully complex melody. He sat dumbstruck watching her fingers dance across the fretboard while the other plucked and strummed the strings with virtuoso like precision.

"Hey, knock it off!" came the gruff voice of the bartender. "Leave those instruments alone!"

Okawa immediately stopped, clearly embarrassed, and returned the instrument to its stand. Demetrius applauded as she walked back to the bar.

"Where did you learn to play like that?" he asked, incredulously.

"I've been playing since I was five," she said, sitting back down next to him.

"Really?"

"They threw the term child prodigy around. I hated it."

"I'm impressed, I mean you can really play that lute."

"I can play all of them," she whispered, leaning close.

Demetrius turned towards her; their faces were only inches from each other. He swallowed nervously at her proximity.

"All of them?"

"At ten I was playing in the Dryden Orchestra," she said, in a seductive hushed tone.

Demetrius, already a bit unnerved at her subtle sensuality, sat back with a surprised expression.

"So, if you played that well," he asked. "how did you end up lurking around dangerous places for House Valdur?"

"I was eleven years old when I saw my first airship, and that was it, I was hooked," Okawa said, with a scoffing chuckle. "It really upset my parents when I announced my decision to join the Valdurian Air Service the day after my fifteenth birthday."

Demetrius huffed in agreement and took a drink.

"I know all about parental disapproval," he said. "So, are your folks still upset with you?"

The Valdurian agent stared wistfully into her drink.

"Three grands ago in the Unification War they died during the invasion attempt by House Eldor. You wanna hear the ironic part in all of it?" She didn't wait for a reply. "I was part of the Valdurian repelling force, but I couldn't save them."

"I'm so sorry," he said, reaching out and gently touching her shoulder.

Peering into his concerned stare she gave a sad smile and rested her hand on his. They briefly sat in silence. She sighed. He cleared his throat. When they both realized where their hands were, they shyly drew them back.

"So," she said, clearing her throat, "I take it your parents weren't happy about your career choice?"

"There's an understatement," Demetrius admitted. "My mom is a scribe to the mayor of my hometown of Vana and my dad is the artificer for the turine there. They expected me to follow in his footsteps. Instead, what did I end up doing? Moving merchandise from one dangerous location to another for, let's just call them sketchy clients.

Yeah, they disapprove. We haven't spoken in many grands. Which I guess isn't so bad, because my mother is cold and efficient and my father is overbearing and demeaning."

"Demetrius, that's terrible," Okawa said, taking a matronly tone. "You should reach out to them. Take it from me, you'll regret it when they're gone."

She took a quick swig from her drink.

"I regret it every day," she forlornly added.

"I tried," he said, leaning over until their shoulders touched. "On quite a few occasions and after a bunch of rejections, I just gave up."

Sighing, she leaned her shoulder firmly against his.

"Still…"

"Still nothing," he said, "between the two of them they really did a hatchet job to my confidence."

"You seem confident to me, especially in the pilot's seat."

Demetrius chuckled and gazed adoringly at her.

"Yeah, well, until recently that was the only place."

"What happened recently?" she asked, with a tilt of her head.

"You happened recently," he said, reaching out and taking her hand. "When I'm with you I feel like I can do anything."

Okawa smiled sweetly, and they both sat silently staring into each other's eyes. Slowly, as if pulled by gravity, they leaned in, both hearts racing at the impending kiss.

"We're closing!" came the gruff interruption from down the bar. "You been here too long, you gotta go!"

Both halted, lips mere inches apart. Sighing at the same time, they kept their eyes locked while they sat back. Picking up his drink Demetrius gently touched it to her glass sitting on the bar.

"To us," he softly toasted, still holding her attentive stare.

He then lifted his glass and downed the rest of the drink.

"Well, I guess tomorrow I'm back to being a flying errand boy," he said, reluctantly getting to his feet, "and you can get back on Stryder Aramos' trail."

"Just don't take any long-term jobs," she said, walking with him to the exit. "I'm going to need you."

Demetrius paused when he opened the door for her.

"Hmm, 'you *need* me,'" he said. "I kinda like the sound of that."

They could hear the howl of the wind sweeping past the nose of the *Haraka* while it raced across blank gray skies. Zau sat beside Mal in the navigator's chair, staring straight ahead with her arms crossed tightly in front of her. Now and then she would let out a frustrated huff which would take the Spice Rat's attention off the grasslands below them.

"Bitch," she spat to herself, glancing briefly back to the ships wheel.

The angry Singa could see Kumo through the spokes standing behind the wheel, deftly manipulating the ships steering device. The exhilarated smile on her face infuriated the lioness even more. Her two humanoid hands worked the large spoked wheel and her eight legs gripped the floor, giving her a stable base no matter what kind of precarious maneuver or adverse condition. She simultaneously operated the rudder, flaps, throttle and if need be, the ballista pods, with her legs.

When the Singa huffed again even louder, Mal finally grew fed up with her navigator's tantrum.

"Will you knock it the fuck off," the Spice Rat said, "you never fucking enjoyed piloting, anyway. You should be happy. Besides, she's a natural."

Mal could see Zau's eyes shift her way. Assessing the captain's admonishment, she begrudgingly unfolded her arms.

"Fine."

"Right now, we could use a portal." Mal said, commandingly. "So, why don't you work your magic and try to find us one."

Zau lifted her patch and the blue holographic globe projected between the two of them.

Zaad sat in his usual spot sharpening his great sword, Bowbreaker. He watched Wostera serenely kneeling just before the cargo bay, her bow, and a single arrow placed ceremoniously before her.

"Doesn't that hurt your knees?" the EEtah asked, curiously.

The bowmistress broke from her trance and smiled. "No, in fact it is comfortable and functional."

"It doesn't look very functional to me."

Before the man-shark could utter another word, Wostera was up on one knee, bow drawn in hand with the arrow nocked and aimed.

Zaad sat shocked for a moment, then suddenly rocked back in his seat pointing and laughing. "Bow lady is good!"

Grinning in satisfaction Wostera resumed her formal kneeling stance and replaced her armaments before her with regal precision.

"Why thank you, Zaad," she said.

Zau carefully examined the topography in the map displayed before her.

"Looks like we've got one ready to open about half a mile away and twenty degrees to starboard," she announced.

"You heard her, Kumo," Mal said, over her shoulder.

"Yes," the Makari replied.

"That's yes, *Captain!*" the Singa snapped.

Kumo grinned and nodded, unphased. "Yes, Captain. Thank you for correction. I'm learning."

Mal reached over and swatted the lioness on the shoulder.

"I told you to knock it off!" Mal growled. "You will have to learn to work together or we could end up regally fucked. So, get over whatever you've got going on. I need a professional crew."

The Singa scowled, then returned her attention to the map.

"Coming up on it now," she said, in a clipped tone.

"Coming up on it now, *Captain*," Kumo innocently corrected.

Mal suppressed a snicker when the Singa bristled at the correction and peered out the windshield. The tallgrass below swirled, erupting blue lightning.

"Take her down, Kumo," she ordered. "Aim for the lightning."

"Yes Captain," the pilot replied.

Her arachnid front right leg effortlessly adjusted the flaps, sending the *Haraka* into a steep dive. The sudden shift in trajectory caused anything not secured in the cabin to fly wildly about and threw Zaad violently from his seat.

At the mercy of the ship's velocity, the EEtah and his sword plunged towards the bowmistress, who still knelt serenely with eyes closed despite the surrounding chaos.

Without opening her eyes, she waved her right hand and deflected the great sword. It passed within inches of her and embedded itself in the rear cargo hatch with a thud. Her left

101

hand moved slowly in the air, pushing Zaad against the side hatch, breaking his fall and guiding him to a stop.

Kumo, who was holding on just fine, didn't realize there was a problem until she saw the reaction of her captain and navigator.

"What the fuck!" Mal screamed, fighting to stay in her chair.

Zau's projected map immediately disappeared when the Singa fell backwards, flipping over the back of her chair.

"Apology, apology!" Kumo squeaked, immediately adjusting course. "Still learning."

As gravity pulled everything back to its rightful place, the airship plummeted into the spiraling prairie and disappeared in an azure flash of energy.

The Kan fog receded and the turine in Aris harbor rang twenty-three bells. When the morning sun streamed into the bedroom window of the royal palace, Soless de Baka, wife of Harper Aramos, woke to find her husband absent from their bed and the sheets cold on his side. At her bedside, the sound of her daughter Talliana sniffling caused the regent to stir.

"Mommy, what's wrong with daddy?"

She felt her throat tighten and bolted up in bed. "What?"

"Daddy's with Unka, he has a booboo."

The raven-haired consort sprang from the bed. She shivered as the room's chill seeped through her thin nightgown. Leaning down, she stroked her daughter's face.

"Stay here, beloved," she said, before rushing down the hall.

She found the door to Talon's bedchamber open. The family patriarch lay face up in his bed. His pallid features stared vacantly at the ceiling, obviously dead.

Then she noticed her husband's body sprawled face down on the floor by the bed. Blood stained his collar red from two wounds on either side of the back of his neck.

Crying out, she rushed into the room and knelt by his side. Leaning in close, she could see he was still breathing. She shook his shoulder and tried to roll him over.

"Harper!" she cried.

Harper slowly came to with a groan. He still seemed dazed so Soless helped him sit up.

"What happened?" she asked.

"Uncle Talon died in my arms last night," he said, as if reciting the words from memory.

"What happened to your neck?"

"Mommy, is daddy okay?" asked a small voice from the door.

Both looked over to see their four-grand-old staring wide-eyed on the verge of tears.

"He's okay, dear," Soless said. "Now run and get Sluzka."

The daughter nodded and quickly ran off down the hall.

"Can you get up?" she asked, putting her hand on his back.

He nodded, and she assisted him to his feet. Just then, the head maid Sluzka, accompanied by two aides and a palace guard, rushed into the room.

"Uncle Talon died in my arms last night," Harper repeated the line to the group, gingerly rubbing the back of his neck.

Soless addressed the staff, "My husband's injuries need looking after…"

"Never mind that," Harper said, cutting her off. "We must attend to uncle's body and prepare a period of mourning."

One aide stepped forward and bowed.

"Forgive me, Imperia," he said, "but I have news from the bank!"

Harper sighed and braced himself. "What news?"

"You are needed immediately, sir," came the insufficient reply.

"What's going on?"

"Imperia, there are representatives from several large Calden fishing fleets who wish to open sizable accounts. They request your presence."

The news had a sobering effect and Harper felt a twinge of excitement rise in him. This could be the break his failing bank needed. He almost hated to get his hopes up lest they be dashed like so many times before.

"Let me get cleaned up and I'll be right down," Harper said to the aide. "Extend them every courtesy and apologize for my delay."

"Yes, Imperia," the aide replied, before hurrying away.

He turned to the other aide. "Get the Verr clerics and the royal scribe. Tend to Uncle's body, and we must let the rest of the family know.

"What about your wound, dear?" Soless asked, when Harper started for the door.

"It's nothing," he casually replied.

While the Aramos cousin made his way to the family's private baths, he was awash in mixed emotions: hope, trepidation, and a distinctive rush of exhilaration. All the while the voice of Stryder kept resonating through his head.

"*A true sacrifice never fails.*"

While Tysonn discreetly watched, he couldn't help but notice she had gained weight since he last saw her. As long as he had known her, as both fellow scholar and lover, he never considered Kasha de Tuath thin. Like her mother, she carried her weight evenly, which disguised sudden fluctuations. It especially showed itself however in her pleasantly round face framed by a short-bobbed cut of blond hair. Now, with her sitting hunched over her cluttered desk, the weight gain was obvious.

Keeping her attention on the papers in front of her, she absentmindedly reached over and picked up a half-eaten portion of Dolca Cake. She brought it to her mouth and before she could bite, she caught sight of Tysonn. The former head of the Language Arts Department and current estranged boyfriend stood in the doorway, gazing fondly.

"It's impolite to stare," she said, in a bored tone just before taking a bite.

"Keep that up and you're going to need a bigger desk," Tysonn responded. "Good thing you're beautiful."

Kasha gave a sardonic smile, then aimed a penetrating stare at Tysonn.

"Yeah," she said, "I guess I'm just trying to fill a void in my life."

The Picar dropped his head and gave a frustrated sigh.

"Are we going to go through this again?" he asked.

"No, but I can only handle being abandoned so many times before I get a little testy!"

"You weren't abandoned! I took a position that anyone in my line would have jumped at taking!"

"I suppose the Bailian women are keeping you occupied? They say they're beautiful."

Tysonn's mouth dropped open at the insinuation. Infidelity was not in him, and she knew it.

"Kas, that's not fair!" he protested. "Have I ever given you any reason to think I sleep around?!"

The now Head of the Language Arts Department yielded and held up both her hands, palms out.

"No, you're right, when you're right you're right," she said, after a calming breath. "So, what took you so long?"

Tysonn gave a perplexed head cock.

"We just arrived before the Kan," he said. "How did you even know we were coming?"

Keeping her eyes on her former scholarly partner and boss, she reached over and retrieved one of the myriad of papers littering her desk.

"This is from the Head Marassa's office," she said. "All current projects are now on hold. Whatever you've got, they ordered the entire Language Arts Department to assist. I was expecting you two cycles ago."

"Unforeseen circumstances detained us, Kas," he said, curtly.

Kasha stared down at the small oblong box chained to his arm and her face went grim. When she looked back up, Cha-Rod had stepped in the room behind him.

"Important and confidential, I take it?" Kasha asked, returning her gaze to the box.

Tysonn's face scrunched. "Someone apparently thinks so."

Her gaze then shifted to the older Bailian, and she addressed him in fluent En-Sul.

"Hello sir, I am Kasha," she said. "Welcome to Zor and the University of Marassa."

"You speak my language well, young lady," the Bo-Jo Vat master responded, pleasantly startled. "I am Cha-Rod."

"My guard," Tysonn interjected in En-Sul.

"Actually, I'm here to protect the book," the Bailian confided.

Kasha snickered when Tysonn gave a subtle scowl.

"I speak your tongue because my current project is a poly-dictionary from your language to Amarenian and Yassett," She said, before turning her attention to Tysonn. "That is until this little sidetrack…"

Tysonn shook his head in disbelief.

"Kas, you're acting like this was my idea!"

"Wasn't it?"

"Well, kind of…"

Kasha sighed and shook her head. "All right, let's see it."

Tysonn set the case on her desk and Cha-Rod produced two keys, one released the chain from around the scribe's wrist and the other opened the box. Reaching in, he delicately lifted the tome and set it on her desk.

Picking it up, she examined the small book from all angles before opening it. Slowly turning the pages, the look on her face appeared more and more puzzled.

"I've seen nothing like this," she said, returning to the common tongue.

"From all accounts it's Tiikeri in nature," Tysonn said, watching her scrutinize the tiny glyphs, "and various combinations of these runes written in blood have been present at several murder scenes."

"I've witnessed this," Cha-Rod interjected, "over in the valley of chains."

Kasha closed the book with a plop and glared at the two.

"I'm betting it's a grimoire," she said, "but we need to be sure. Besides my people, I think we should reach out to the school of magic and get one of their runeists involved. I'll also order the staff to make a copy for our archives."

"I don't think that's a very good idea," Tysonn said, with trepidation. "I mean, given it *is* a grimoire like you suspect."

Kasha tossed Tysonn an irritated glance while she set the book back down on her desk.

"Look Ty," she said, "you're the one who decided to up and go work for the Bailians. This is my department now. When you're right, you're right, but now you're wrong!"

Kai could see the Ash-Ta's wings fluttering up ahead in the reflected starlight. Drucilla was quickly making her way just above the crystal covered streets of Immor-Onn, towards the towering spires of the Avion ambassador's suites. The one-armed spymaster and Priestess of Orad leapt from one crystalline shaped rooftop to the other, easily keeping up with the humanoid bat's erratic flight pattern.

Kai paused under cover of a wide eave and allowed herself a congratulatory smile when she saw Drucilla hovering around the balcony of her brother Julius. *Eventually she always comes home to big brother…*

Dak was trying with all his might not to yawn. It was getting late and Julius was well into one of his frequent, painfully long diatribes. Down feathers fluttered upward from his wings every time they shuddered in frustration or elation—emotions which could occur within moments of each other.

The towering EEtah and Seneschal to the Avion Ambassador of House Pyre to Immor-Onn stood dutifully while the mad Avion paced wildly, banging his fist into his palm. Suddenly he would stop, raise a single finger in jubilation and revel in his deductive powers.

Beyond the recurrent pattern of Julius' pacing, Dak detected movement on the balcony. When he could make out Drucilla's face in the glass doors he sighed. *This could be a long night.*

"Uhh, sir?"

"… and if they think they can get away with it, well, I tell you, no sir…"

"Lord Julius!?"

"… I would give them a proper thrashing. They've obviously never tasted the business end of a Kel whip…

"LORD JULIUS!"

"Huh, eh, what?"

The EEtah nodded towards the glass doors leading to the balcony behind him. Jerking about, sending more down feathers into the air, Julius' demeanor changed again to that of a loving brother when he saw his sister the Ash-Ta.

He grimaced slightly when he saw the bottom of her beautiful face stained in dried crimson. Her pleading eyes peered from the blackness while she tapped on the glass.

"Dear Drucilla," he rejoiced, rushing to the doors and opening them.

She fell into his arms, weeping uncontrollably. Dak couldn't help but notice the regal Avion wincing with obvious tactile discomfort and aversion to the smell. Drucilla, lost in consuming grief, remained oblivious to her brother's discomfort. In a gallant effort of consoling, he awkwardly patted her back.

"There, there, now," he consoled. "How can I help?"

"I don't know what to do," she moaned between racking sobs.

Julius held her out at arm's length.

"Come, tell me about it," he said, leading her into the room.

"I've done it again, I couldn't help it. The hunger."

"I heard about it," the Avion said, in a paternal voice. "It's caused quite the scene at the palace."

The Ash-Ta's sobs subsided into sniffles while she brushed away the tears.

"I loathe this body Kai forced me into," she said, "with its barbaric needs. I have no where left to turn. Self-pity wearies me but I lack the resolve to kill myself."

"We'll think of something," Julius soothed, "but you've got to keep a low profile until this ruckus subsides."

109

"That won't help!" Drucilla lamented. "In another few cycles the hunger will rise again. I can only fight it for so long. What scares me the most is that as the hunger grows, I don't want to fight it. I'm almost aroused at the anticipation. When I finally feed, the pain goes away. It's the only time I truly have a sense of silence and peace and... comfort."

The Ash-Ta's reflection turned painfully inward. "Then, when I'm through, the feeling of guilt and loathing comes back tenfold."

"If the hunger is inevitable, perhaps all you need to change is your diet," Julius said, to calm his distraught sister.

Drucilla shook her head. "I survived on animal flesh for too long, hiding in the woods on the periphery of the city. Don't ask me to go back to that!"

"I would never suggest such a thing," the Avion said, with a conciliatory smile, "but perhaps if you directed your culinary choices at the more nefarious elements of the city? Thinking of it as more of a public service?"

The Ash-Ta paused and assessed her brother's proposition. "I... I don't know. I mean, I don't want to kill at all."

"Well, it's something to think about until we can find a remedy to your situation."

While the anguish slowly subsided, she gave her brother a wary glance.

"There's more."

"Oh?"

"Several lunas ago, two of Clan Molossi's marauders approached me," she confessed.

"Two of Clan Who?"

"An Ash-Ta clan whose territory borders the Land of Mists. Molossi marauders are renowned for their ability to raid Do-Tarr hives."

"What in the name of the gods did they want with you, and how did they know where to find you?"

Drucilla gave a sad, knowing chuckle. "The Ash-Ta have spies everywhere. They sought me out because of my unique make up of an Avion inhabiting an Ash-Ta body."

"What could they possibly want with you?"

"They were certain they had located the Do-Tarr queen's private nectar reserves for the Southern Hive. The Molossi are skilled raiders, but this raid was especially dangerous because it was deep within the hive. They also believed it to contain royal jelly. Enough to make us fabulously rich. They wanted me to join their crew because I'm naturally invisible to the bugs."

At the mention of royal jelly, Julius reeled where he stood. Waves of murky visions clouded his mind. Opaque glimpses of bug-like creatures briefly swept across his consciousness, taking command of his senses as they passed.

"Julius?" Drucilla said, when her brother briefly teetered out of balance.

Dak noticed his master swaying and started for him. Suddenly he doubled over and started falling forward, just as Dak made it to his side. The EEtah steadied him when Julius bolted back upright, his eyes wide in astonishment.

"Giant bugs," he gasped. "GIANT BUGS! BEWARE THE FLAMES! EMBRACE THE FIRE! BEWARE THE FLAMES! EMBRACE THE FIRE!"

Dak caught him just when his eyes rolled back and he went limp in his arms.

"Lord Julius, are you all right?"

The Avion ambassador shook his head and slowly regained his feet.

"I'm fine," he muttered.

Julius then straightened his clothing, cleared his throat, and gazed around at two concerned faces as if nothing had happened.

"Now, where were we?" he asked. "Oh yes, the royal jelly proposition! I take it you said no?"

Sneering in contempt, Drucilla turned away.

"I avoid mirrors because I can't stand the sight of myself as an Ash-Ta," she confessed. "The thought of being around them, working with them, their smell, their disgusting habits. *Of course*, I said no."

She stepped back, shuddering at the thought.

"Speaking of hygiene," Julius said, scanning her sullied appearance. "How about we make your general deportment more presentable? Come now, let's get you cleaned up."

Drucilla shot him a mortified look, tears welling up. She shook her head and rushed for the balcony doors.

"Drucilla!" he pleaded, following her.

Julius stepped out onto the balcony just in time to watch her take flight into the moonless skies of the Twilight Lands. He watched until she flew out of sight closing the double doors and turned to Dak, who was busy picking up feathers from the floor.

"I can't quite put my finger on it, but there's something very haunting about her news."

Che-At slipped through the shadows of the moonless in Immor-Onn. She knew well this was the time where most of the inhabitants of the shining jewel of the east stayed safely indoors. Realizing she would stand out, the Singa kept to side streets, making her way to the city's twin harbors, Fall-Arak and Rilli-On. She had barely avoided detection twice by shop keepers closing up and heading home. Buffeted by high winds and rain, she climbed up on the massive cave structures housing the wharfs. The effects of a late winter gale swept through the caverns. The inclement weather had brought commerce to a virtual standstill.

With a casual inspection she passed the obvious passenger docks of Fall-Arak and stealthily entered the crate littered docks of Rilli-On Harbor.

A lone EEtah marine guarded the last pair of enormous doors along the far north cave wall. He stoically faced the storm. The fury of the weather plastered his soaked green jumpsuit to his muscular frame and water streamed from his thick arms holding a full-sized loaded crossbow.

She ducked behind a large shipping crate when a bolt of lightning struck just beyond the cave's mouth and an instant clap of thunder echoed off the cavern walls. The lightning's brief flashes lit up the storm-tossed sea.

The marine sentry winced at the sudden, intense brightness. When the illumination subsided, Che-At bolted for the temporarily blinded EEtah. With extraordinary speed and precision, three blows from her staff toppled the oblivious man-shark to the deck, unconscious. The fury of the storm masked the dull thud of his falling body.

She examined the simple hanging lock which bound the two doors. Raising her staff and bringing the end forcefully down on the lock, sent it clattering to the deck beside the prone EEtah. After peering around and making sure the sound drew no one's attention, the lioness opened one door just wide enough to slip through and disappeared inside.

The interior was dark, and she retrieved a small orange gem from inside her cape. Tapping it on the inner doorjamb produced a bright orange light which illuminated the room.

Rows of crates, stacked in individual piles, filled an enormous area with a high ceiling. They had labeled each wooden container, marking destination and status. The Singa moved rapidly down each isle reading the labels. She halted when she recognized Ma-Tah's last reported address stenciled on the side.

Not wasting any time, Che-At set the glowing gem down and slammed the tip of her staff in at an angle, striking the lip of the crate's lid. It penetrated the wood with a sharp crack. Bearing down on the other end of the staff, she pried the top open.

The Singa agent sighed in frustration when she held the light above the open container. The book she sought wasn't in the late Tiikeri finance minister's belongings.

Not bothering to replace the lid, Che-At extinguished the light and quickly made her way back to the door. She could see the motionless EEtah laying where he fell and heard the storm still raging.

When she stepped out and closed the door, something bathed the area behind her in blue light, casting her shadow across the surface before her. Spinning with a hiss, she deftly swept her staff in front of her body, readying it.

Four Bailians and an EEtah, dressed in the green jumpsuits of the Valdurian marines, surrounded her in a semi-circle. All four of the native blue-skinned guards trained their crossbows on her. A diminutive human female in a cloak stood silently off to the side, a glowing blue sword jutting from beneath her cape.

"Drop your weapon!" the EEtah ordered in a menacing growl.

Che-At hesitated for a moment. Her eyes darted across the confronting sentients. The EEtah sergeant saw her assessing her chances.

"Don't even think about it," he said. "You'll be dead before you make your first move."

"I am an agent of the Tiikeri empire," she defiantly spat. "You have what is ours and I am here to retrieve it."

"Yeah, well that's gonna have to wait," the EEtah said, confidently. "You're under arrest for attacking a city guard and breaking into a secure warehouse. Drop your weapon NOW!"

Without warning, the Singa launched herself into the air to the height of the Bailians heads. Lashing out with her staff, she caught one of the Bailian marines on the side of the head and he dropped. The other three marines released crossbow bolts in unison. Two missed completely, burying themselves in the wooden doors. Che-At's spinning staff, humming in cyclonic deadly arcs, deflected the one with judicious aim.

Kai stood calmly watching the altercation. She noted the Singa deflected the missile away from any living targets on purpose.

She's good!

Che-At landed, swept her staff low to the ground and caught two of the three remaining Bailian's on the ankles, sweeping them off their feet. When the staff revolved back around, she planted one end on the ground and used it like a vaulting pole to deliver a punishing assisted jumping kick. The blow struck the blue skinned marine square in the chest while he attempted to draw his short sword and catapulted him six feet away onto his back.

The EEtah sergeant prepared to lunge when the area behind the Singa agent became blindingly backlit in blue. He froze in place when he saw Kai standing directly behind the marauding lioness. Her arm, extending from beneath her cape, had transformed into a glowing, ghostly blue sword, pointed directly at the back of Che-At's neck.

The Singa froze when she felt the tingle of energy coursing across the hairs on her neck and head.

"Such discipline and skill," Kai lamented with a sigh. "I'd hate to waste all those cycles of training over such a comparatively minor offense. Then there's the whole international incident thing."

Che-At cautiously weighed her options, watching the marines climb to their feet. Eyes narrowing, her face fell in resignation knowing they had her and she tossed her staff to the deck with a scowl.

They were immediately upon her, gruffly spinning her around and binding her hands behind her. One of the Bailians kneeled over the prone guard, trying to revive him.

"You have no right to detain me," she protested while they led her away. "I am a sovereign citizen of the Tiikeri Empire!"

"Maybe so," the EEtah sergeant countered, "but as far as I'm concerned, you're just another criminal."

Kai retracted her glowing blade and watched while the Bailian revived the EEtah sentry. She felt sorry for him. This was a huge disgrace for an Outer Clan EEtah, which could result in a demotion and shame amongst his peers.

In the distance, she heard the outraged Singa screaming over the storm's tempest as they dragged her off, demanding to see the Tiikeri ambassador.

Not a bad idea, she thought.

Without a word, she started off towards the diplomatic compound near the palace.

I think it's time I had a conversation with my old friend Jo-Rakk and then maybe the queen.

The Tiikeri had insisted on the prime seat next to Demetrius. As usual, the newly appointed ambassador to the High Holy City of Zor got what he wanted. Settling in and securing himself, he gave a rare, excited look over his shoulder to his bodyguard.

The imposing orange tiger guardian sat directly behind the human pilot, just in case. A fawn colored mongrel seated behind the ambassador secured her messenger bag and gave her boss a placating smile.

The hairless mongrel in the yellow tunic who was the sole occupant in the last row of seats, especially drew Demetrius' attention. Her pale, angular face stared straight ahead, and she said nothing. More than anything, her stark, wrinkled features unsettled the airship pilot, and he fought to keep a professional demeanor.

When the *Drakin* lifted off from the central courtyard of the Tiikeri capital City of Hai-Darr, the crowd gathering to witness the wondrous craft erupted in cheers and applause.

"Hey, looks like you're getting quite the sendoff Ambassador Za-Tar," Demetrius said, noting the pleased look on the white tiger's face.

"It is just that I receive this honor," he said, in a smug, superior tone.

"It is just," the bodyguard and aide responded in unison.

Demetrius noted the hairless mawl in the back had not recited the sycophantic chant. *No matter the race, the royal types love to get their egos stroked.* Demetrius thought, maneuvering the *Drakin* upward through the canyons of unadorned bamboo architecture.

When the airship climbed into the moonlight filled skies of the Land of Mists, the pilot gave a satisfied grin watching all his passengers except the hairless mawl stare out the window marveling at their first taste of flight. Down below, the rooftops of the circular walled city gave way to lush countryside and eventually dense multi-colored rain forests.

Pulling back on the flaps, the craft ascended through a cloud bank into the clear skies dominated by a bright full moon which almost drowned out the sea of stars overhead.

A collective gasp passed through the mawls gazing at the illuminating orb in an entirely new way, but a deep guttural hacking sound from the back of the craft doused the elated mood. All faced the back of the cabin to witness the hairless mongrel vomiting on the deck.

"I apologize for my Worrg," Za-Tar said. "The breed's constitution is delicate by nature, but her skills are even more specific. Unfortunately, she is susceptible to almost any change in her condition."

The Worrg now sat back upright, staring like before, as if nothing had happened.

"Things are gonna change a *whole* lot more, I'm afraid," Demetrius said, with a good-natured smirk. "I'm about to take us upstairs."

Just when the airship pilot was about to pull back on the flaps again, the Worrg set off a high pitch yowl and her eyes rolled up in her head.

Demetrius sighed. "She's not getting sick again, is she?"

Za-Tar shook his head, listening intently to the series of yowled Tiikeri phrases. She finally passed out when she finished and her head slumped against her chest. Demetrius had picked up enough words to know that plans had suddenly changed.

"I'm afraid we must take a bit of a detour," the Tiikeri ambassador said, his voice betraying a touch of irritation.

Demetrius leveled the craft off. "Oh?"

"Make your best time to Immor-Onn," Za-Tar ordered. "We're taking on another passenger."

The rocky coast of Taia-Dor was a perfect example of the monumental stone formations stretching across the continent's entire northern shore. These starkly beautiful edifices broke suddenly from the land and stretched out into the sea until the continental shelf abruptly dropped off to the ocean floor.

Reflections of the rising moon glittered off the turbulent waters of the northeastern Ocean Deep, churning around the massive granite formations rising defiantly from the surrounding white caps. Tendrils of blue lightning crackled and merged with the glistening sea foam in the center of an immense stone archway. Gradually the bolts of electricity built until they filled the gap, leaping wildly between the stone confines. At the height of the electrical agitation, the *Haraka* spit out from the center of the archway and flew into the moonlit skies over Amarenia.

Mal heaved a deep sigh of relief, assessing both her navigator and pilot. "Not bad you two. It's amazing the shit that can get done when you work together."

Zau, seated next to her, cast a cynical glance at the back-handed compliment.

"Thank you, Captain," Kumo naively said, beaming from behind the wheel.

Mal surveyed the coastline below them. "All right, if I'm not mistaken, the City of Taia is just a little way to the east."

Wostera gracefully rose from her kneeling position in the ship's rear and moved to the command chairs.

"Captain," she began, in a calm but sorrowful tone, "with your permission, I would like to travel with you for a while."

Mal gazed up at the stately older woman in surprise.

"Um, why?" she asked.

"In the martial arts of my people we have a tradition called So'Gen," she explained. "It is a sort of martial pilgrimage, a required quest one takes in order to achieve the rank of Mistress. Once she achieves that rank, tradition requires she takes another So'Gen pilgrimage at some point in the Mistress' life."

"And this is that point?" Mal asked, skeptically.

"Existing on that other plane taught me that the Middle Realms are where I can truly test myself. Also, I need the distraction."

Mal gave her a sardonic look. "I would think you've had your fill of the Middle Realms."

The bowmistress' smile was almost condescending. "I would return as a traveler, not as one trapped."

"That's one less split in any profits," Zau said, greedily.

The Amarenian peered down at the Singa with a patronizing raise of an eyebrow before returning her attention to the captain.

"I require no share in whatever spoils or fees you may receive," she said, placidly. "This is a spiritual journey meant to test me. Outside of my basic needs, remuneration would only be counterproductive to this undertaking."

Mal sat staring contemplatively at the human female, assessing her sincerity. Finally, the Spice Rat gave a resigned shrug.

"Sure, why not," she agreed, "We could always use another set of hands and eyes. Besides, it's your ass."

"Thank you, Captain," the bowmistress said, sincerely. "We will however need to petition the queen."

"You just got back," Mal asked. "Do you think she'll go for it?"

"With your help," Wostera replied.

"Me?!"

"They rarely deny the requests of two Valorous Sisters," Wostera said, confidently.

"Oh, yeah," Mal smirked, "I keep forgetting I've got some pull around these parts."

"I don't know about all this," Zau said, skeptically.

"Bow lady should stay!" Zaad piped up from his seat. "I like her."

Wostera gave a shy grin at the compliment. "Thank you Zaad."

"Well, I guess that settles it," Mal proclaimed. "Kumo, turn this baby around, we're going to Mostas."

Zau shook her head in frustration at being outvoted.

"Besides," Mal added, "I want to get a peek at the progress of the air station going up there, and our private slip. Then there's also the matter of collecting our ten thousand Amarenian Volas."

At the mention of payment, the Singa's mood noticeably softened.

"Now we're talking!"

Upon receiving word of his father's death, Bartol Aramos caught the first available ship to the family's ancestral home; the City of Aris.

He did not travel alone.

Following the now elder Aramos down the gangplank was his aide Sandor, and twenty of the elite Aramos Black Talons. After procuring several wagons and affixing his standard, Bartol Aramos led the procession from the docks to the Baka Sector of the city along the waterfront. All throughout the congested capital, crowds parted when they saw the royal Aramos banner waving, allowing the procession to pass quickly along the busy streets.

The cavalcade of three wagons came to a halt outside of the Aris branch of the Imperial Bank of Zor. Bartol eyed the structure suspiciously while the Black Talons scrambled off the wagons. Its outer facade resembled a smaller version of its parent company—a stately two-story building with a course of wide stairs leading up to a large, pillared landing and two ornate wooden doors. Unlike the bank in Zor, this contained an ostentatious bronze placard above the doors comprising two symbols: an "*X*" and an "*I*."

Standing on either side of the entrance were two EEtah sentries of the Zorod Sunal. The twelve-foot-tall, specially trained guards effortlessly slid the Yudon harpoons off their backs and readied them, watching the Aramos special forces approach the steps.

"That's close enough!" one of the EEtahs spat when the Black Talon's climbed the stairs.

"Stand down!" Bartol ordered, rising from his seat. "These men are with me. In fact, I will not require your services during my visit. Please feel free to take a break."

The EEtah eyed the brash human with misgivings. The portly man talked and dressed like a royal, and he even carried the royal Aramos banner. However, the guard had never seen him before, *and this was a bank*. He decided to err on the side of caution.

"We only take orders from Master Harper!"

The Aramos special forces began steadily climbing the stairs, hands on the hilts of their sickle swords. Defiantly, the EEtahs advanced to the edge of the landing, harpoons pointed forward.

"I told you to halt!" the EEtah bellowed at the advancing troops.

"And I told you to stand down," Bartol replied, with an insolent sneer. "I am the new sovereign of House Aramos. You *will* obey me!"

The Black Talons almost reached the top of the stairs, when the doors to the bank flew open and Harper Aramos swept out onto the landing.

"Barra, Chawea, stand down!" he abruptly ordered.

Harper rushed to meet the oncoming soldiers but stopped in surprise when he saw his cousin climbing down off the front wagon.

"Bartol!" he cried out, waving excitedly, and wading down the stairs through the crowd of armed men.

Bartol pushed past his aides to greet his cousin, undeterred by the potentially hostile crowd. The Black Talons, being a savvy special forces unit, detected no threat and let him pass. Harper embraced his cousin's corpulent frame in an enthusiastic warm hug, which Bartol apprehensively returned.

"You've arrived early for the funeral," Harper said, when they separated.

"Yes," Bartol confirmed, nervously stroking his eyebrow. "However, I was hoping we might have a word in private."

"Of course," the head banker exclaimed, guiding Bartol towards the stairs.

The black tunicked forces followed the two men up the steps. Half fanned out in front of the financial institution while the others followed the Aramos cousins inside.

Bartol noted the interior was considerably more spacious than the exterior led him to assume. The ceilings were high. To his right was a conference room with a long table in the middle. To the left was the massively thick round vault door. Straight before him, a wide stairway led up to several smaller meeting rooms.

Harper led Bartol into one of the smaller offices and closed the door.

"What can I do for you, cousin, at this time of grief?" Harper asked, sincerely.

Bartol began playing with his eyebrow again.

"I'll come straight to the point," he said, in a clipped tone. "As my father's oldest son, I claim my right to the throne of House Aramos."

There was a brief silence, as if the weight of the words expressed held back time.

"Thank the gods!" Harper erupted in joy.

He then reached over and gave a very stunned Bartol another heartfelt hug.

"This news makes you happy?"

Harper gave a short, loud laugh.

"Did you expect me to fight you for it?"

"Well…"

"Ahh, that's what the manpower was for. Just in case I had become a little too enamored with the power."

A slightly embarrassed Bartol lowered his head when a broad smile lit up his face.

"I'm no politician," Harper admitted, placing a hand on his relative's shoulder. "Besides, I'm just now turning the bank around. This is where I must focus my attention. I want to keep the legacy of my beloved uncle alive. Naturally, you are the logical one to assume the position of family patriarch, especially now that Stryder has disappeared."

"Yes, I've read the reports," Bartol said, his tone much friendlier than before. "Bringing in those Calden fishing fleet accounts was an astute move."

Harper blushed at the compliment.

"The timing was right."

"You mentioned Stryder," the new patriarch said, in a probing tone. "You two used to be close. Have you seen anything of him?"

Harper shook his head and lied, "I haven't seen your brother in quite a few grands."

"Rumors say some malevolent entity from Nocturn possesses him now," Bartol said.

"I've heard nothing," the Aramos banker reiterated.

"Well, no matter," Bartol said, in a boisterous voice. "We've got things under control here. We'll wait for an official notification after father's funeral. And I agree with your assessment. You are much more needed here. There will also be a place for you as my economic adviser on the royal council."

"Thank you, cousin, I'm honored."

"I think this is the dawn of a new era of prosperity for our noble house!"

Harper chuckled knowingly. "I agree your majesty."

"Well, I guess I can release that detachment of Black Talons."

"Actually, I probably could use them…"

Bartol gave a quizzical look. "Elite soldiers as bank guards?"

"Actually, I've got an extensive project about to begin," Harper said, with a devious undertone, "but I'll probably only need half of them."

The senior Aramos gave a questioning look, then quickly abandoned the notion.

"As long as you make the family money and it doesn't start a war, don't burden me with the details," he said.

Everyone in the lobby visibly relaxed when the two Aramos cousins emerged from their private meeting with smiles and affectionate banter.

"Half of your force can return to duty," Bartol said to one of the older Black Talons. "I hereby now assign the ones in this room to The Imperial Bank of Zor under the supervision of my cousin Harper."

The plump patriarch puffed out his chest, bathing in the thought of almost unlimited authority.

"You will obey him as you would me!" he announced.

All ten elite troops positioned strategically around the room came to attention and saluted with the right hand, fist facing outward, brought smartly to the temple. Bartol spun to face his family and first council member. Reaching out with both hands he grabbed Harper's shoulders in an outburst of unity.

"I've got a good feeling about this," he said, optimistically.

Harper gave a sly smile. "As do I."

In an instant the sovereign's face turned solemn.

"Those two EEtah guards…"

"Yes?"

"Get rid of them."

"What?!"

"You heard me," Bartol demanded. "Terminate their contracts and replace them."

Harper was aghast.

"But… But surely you must realize, they didn't know you. They were just doing their jobs! If we end their contract and ask for a replacement, that would be an insurmountable stain on their reputation. They may never work again."

A firm, uncaring glance from Bartol caused Harper to slump down in concession.

"Yes, of course, your majesty."

Kai was not happy. The five-foot four brunette looked up and scowled at the seven-foot tall Tiikeri. The mismatched pair were waiting together on the windy flight deck of Air Station East in Immor-Onn. In front of them, beside the appointed slip, the female Singa, Che-At stood suppressing a gloating grin.

"I wouldn't take it personally," Jo-Rakk said, in a conciliatory tone. "Both our orders came straight from the top, my king and your queen."

"We caught the bitch red handed," Kai said, her voice laced with frustration. "Do we punish her? No. We let her go and give her a free airship ride. I mean we didn't even get a name out of her!"

"Neither did I, but I think you need to keep this in perspective," the Tiikeri said, securing the front of his robe which was about to blow open. "It wasn't murder or espionage. She broke into a warehouse."

"I don't know which I hate worse," Kai said, continuing to stare at the Singa, "the fact that we have to let her go, or that smirk I want to carve off her face."

"I just want this entire dreary episode over with," Jo-Rakk's tone dripped of elitism.

Kai knew firsthand the disdain the Tiikeri felt about the other mawl races.

"Thankfully, your wait won't be long," Kai said.

She motioned towards the *Drakin* sweeping into the military hangar and settling into the slip next to them.

The side hatch immediately opened and ambassador Za-Tar along with his aide stepped out. Che-At silently passed them with a blank expression while she boarded. Za-Tar watched with a disdainful stare until the Singa disappeared inside and then turned back to Jo-Rakk.

"Ambassador," he said, with a slight nod.

"Ambassador," Jo-Rakk replied. "Well, she's your problem now, or should I say, the good people of Zor's."

"Ambassador I share your exasperation," Za-Tar said, with resolve. "This diversion has cost me in time!"

The two Tiikeri nobles stared defiantly at one another.

"Well," Jo-Rakk said, "I won't detain you any longer, Ambassador. I wish you well on your new assignment."

With the obvious dismissal, Za-Tar gave an amused leer before quickly returning to the ship. The *Drakin* promptly lifted off and sped out into the sky just now being lit by the rising moon.

Once in the air, Za-Tar finally addressed the mysterious passenger who now occupied the seat next to the Worrg.

"May I see your original orders?"

Che-At stared at the ambassador assessing his demand. Reluctantly she reached into her cape and handed it over.

"I see they've changed," he said, upon his olfactory inspection and returning the small booklet. "I take it you feel whatever the finance minister lost is in Zor?"

The Singa gave the Tiikeri a bored expression.

"Ambassador, while I appreciate the ride," she said. "I cannot speak about my mission."

An awkward silence descended on the cabin. It was obvious the Singa would say nothing more.

"I see," Za-Tar calmly replied before focusing his attention back out the windshield.

"Okay everyone get ready," Demetrius said, cheerfully, breaking the uncomfortable silence. "We're behind schedule, so I'm taking us upstairs."

The jail in the High Holy City of Zor is located in the rows of buildings surrounding the infamous Justice Square. The structure is relatively small given the size of the city. Its two dozen jail cells briefly host a constantly rotating wave of sentients just prior to the city's swift retribution against them. Justice Square always carries out these various forms of punishment in full view of the public via the many gruesome instruments littering the square's common area.

Captain Rafel became a common sight in the courtyard, mostly shuttling between the various barristers' offices and the city guard's headquarters. This morning, shortly after the lifting of the Kan, he strode purposefully on the short trek from the spacious double doors of the Zorian Guards headquarters to the stark, barred entrance of the city's jail.

The grizzled old guard, just inside the thick iron bars, nodded when he saw the Zorian spymaster, and scratched his three-day stubble.

"Mornin' Captain," he said, turning the key and the heavy door swung open with a loud creak.

"Good morning, Ramsey," Rafel replied. "How's your mother?"

The captain entered, looking around the tight quarters. The old guard closed and locked the door behind him.

"Mean as ever," he answered. "I gotta' feelin' the old bitch ain't never gonna die."

Rafel snickered. He'd known the seasoned guard since he'd traveled to Zor from the tiny village of Corab many years ago. He rode in the same caravan as Colonel Zekoff. All this time, Ramsey had always taken care of his mother, even to the point of never marrying.

"Where is he?" Rafel asked, peering down the row of cells.

"Last one on the right," Ramsey said, with a tilt of his head. "They brought him in during the Kan. He was trying to steal a wagon full of wine. He's been askin' fer ya all morning."

The spymaster nodded his thanks and strolled down the short corridor. He stopped at the designated location and peered through the bars into the six by eight-foot enclosure.

A solitary naked man seated against the wall occupied the empty room hugging his folded legs in front of him. He was small and wiry with a head of thick unkempt brown hair. A life on the street had left deep furrows in his pockmarked face, making a guess at his age all but impossible.

"Three Fingered Jak," Rafel greeted, hands on his hips, "I figured you'd have learned your lesson by now, for sure."

The nude man looked up at Rafel and chuckled.

"The wagon was just sitting there, no guards, no one around," he said, with a sad smirk. "You'd think they'd pass a law against folks being so stupid."

"I doubt that will happen," Rafel mused.

"Yeah," the thief agreed, his voice trailing off.

"This is your third offense," the spymaster noted. "I'm no judge, but I'm betting they cut off the entire hand this time."

Jak held up his right hand and stared wistfully at the two missing fingers.

"I don't think you want that to happen."

Rafel gave the thief an intrigued stare. "What do you want Jak?"

"I want you to open the door and let me out."

"I'll bet."

"Yeah, but this time, I think the bet's a solid one."

Rafel couldn't contain his amusement.

"Oh really?"

The thief stood up and stepped over to the bars. Looking cautiously down the hall, he motioned the Zerian officer to come closer. The spymaster grimaced at the stench when he leaned in.

"I got some information I'm pretty sure you're gonna find useful."

"I'm all ears," Rafel said, moving closer.

Jak gave a knowing chuckle. "No, no, no. I gotta have some assurances."

"My friend, you are in no position to demand anything."

"Even if it has something to do with the death of Hoyt Eldor?" Jak asked, with a manipulative smile. "That's *Ambassador* Eldor if I'm not mistaken."

Rafel froze. His pulse quickened and throat went dry. He locked his gaze on the grimy reprobate in front of him.

"What about him?" he choked out.

Jak's grin widened. "So, that's something that might interest you?"

Rafel leaned forward, his face contorted into a malevolent sneer that rocked the hardened thief.

"If you are playing me," he warned, "this game of yours will cost you more than just your right hand!"

Jak recoiled, holding up his hands. "Hey, hey, hey, I don't want no trouble. What I got is real!"

Rafel calmed himself. "All right, if what you say is true, I *am* interested. But in order for me to open this door and inflict you on the citizens of our fair city, I'm going to need something more."

Jak's eyes narrowed. "Like what?"

The Zorian officer quickly made sure the adjacent cell was empty. "You work for me now."

The thief's faced hardened. "I ain't no fucking snitch!"

"And exactly what do you call this?" Rafel asked, with genuine amusement.

"I'm saving my ass and helping yours!"

"That is exactly what I'm proposing," the spymaster said, his serene voice carrying a hardened edge. "Let me assure you, the day-to-day escapades of you and your friends are of no concern to me. It's the big things that keep me up at night. Like say, the killing of a foreign ambassador."

Jak swallowed hard at Rafel's intensity.

"I need eyes on the ground in the Seven Sisters." Rafel let the words sink in. "You could be those eyes and still keep your day job. Or, the full weight of the law, plus a little extra could come down on you, *today*."

The thief quickly weighed his options. "Okay, okay, deal."

"Now, you were saying?"

Jak cleared his throat and nervously looked around. "I saw!"

"Saw what?"

"The ambassador, the night he died."

"And?"

"I was up on the roof over the alley that night."

Rafel gave a questioning look. "What were you doing up on the roof that Kan?" Jak's stupefied glance at the irrelevant question allowed the spymaster to catch himself. "Sorry, go on."

"He was being dragged through the alley. I think he was already dead."

This revelation caused Rafel's stomach to tighten.

Unaware of his stories effect, the thief continued, "One person, fairly small, set him by the alley entrance. Then…"

"Yes?"

"Then they cut on the body, mostly hands, and throat."

Rafel was fighting hard to keep his composure as he felt his face flush and form a sheen of sweat.

"Did you see who it was?"

Jak shook his head. "No, they were small but really powerful. They muscled around the ambassador's body like it was nothing. What makes it even stranger…"

Rafel's inquisitive gaze prompted the thief to continue while he licked his lips nervously.

"… is they only had one arm."

Stryder Aramos was proving to be the ultimate hard target. Intelligence placed the former quartermaster in House Aramos' ancestral home, but it was up to Peligro to find him, and Aris was a big city which straddled a wide river. After securing a small room in the densely populated Cibiya sector, just off the docks, he staked out the bank first. The pub across the street was the perfect spot.

Ordering a tankard of ale from a table by the front window, he prepared to settle into surveillance, his least favorite part of the job. Waiting never sat well with the Aramos Wraith, but he had to locate his target before purchasing the necessary weaponry for the assignment.

When the turine finally rang eight bells, he realized he had been there most of the day with nothing to show for it except a slightly intoxicated glow. He was just about to settle up and leave, when he saw three security guards he recognized exit the bank and linger on the wide landing. They wore the familiar tunics of the Black Talons and peered cautiously about practicing textbook security procedures.

Placing several coins on the counter, he downed the rest of his drink without taking his eyes off of his former comrades in arms. *Ruta, Brule, and Rigmor, what are they doing here?*

His confusion compounded when the doors opened again and a detail of eight Black Talons' security guards emerged surrounding the two men. He identified one of them as Harper Aramos.

The other was Stryder Aramos.

He knew, and previously worked with, all the Talons. *There's at least half of Acer Squad in that detail.*

Ruta, Brule, and Rigmor descended to the street in time to meet two private passenger coaches and a sizable open-top wagon. All the wagons bore the Aramos standard.

The Aramos nobility climbed into separate private coaches and the Talons piled into the wagon. They wasted no time in setting off north towards the river.

The good thing about being in a major city is the streets were always alive. Peligro bounded out the door and had no problem hailing a passing two-person coach. He easily followed the ostentatious procession when they turned and continued east on the city's main artery through the riverfront Baka Sector.

When they arrived at the bridge leading to the elite Aramos Sector, Peligro knew it was the end of the line for him. The two city guards on the other side of the river kept all but the most preeminent of society out.

Peligro directed the driver to pull up by the waterway and hopped out. Once the coach sped off, he positioned himself beside a large tree and withdrew a small spyglass from his jacket.

After checking to be sure no one could see him, he extended the spyglass and followed the caravan entering the distinctly sparser populated section of the city.

While he watched, the coach he assumed carried Harper Aramos, peeled off from the group and headed for the Royal Palace. The massive castle dominated this restricted sector of the city.

Stryder's coach and the following wagon full of Black Talons continued on into the region until Peligro lost sight of them heading towards the rear of the royal grounds.

He absentmindedly collapsed the spyglass, deep in thought. Elite troops used as common bodyguards were rare. Even though he didn't see where they went, they would be easy to locate.

At least now he knew where to find his target.

Demetrius watched the Tiikeri shield their eyes when the *Drakin* dropped from the upper atmosphere into the bustling metropolis of Zor. Thankfully for the Nocturn natives, clouds blanketed the normally sunny skies above the High Holy City, due to a lingering late winter storm.

"There's a great optics shop in town," Demetrius said, noting the mawls discomfort. "You all will need dark glasses to operate in the constant sun."

"Thank you, Captain," Za-Tar said, squinting at the entrance of Air Station Three looming just ahead.

The ambassador then once again addressed the mysterious Singa in the back row, "Seeing how you are here representing the Tiikeri empire, I trust you will check in with me frequently?"

This caused Che-At to smile slyly. "Ambassador, if I'm successful I'll be gone before there would be any time to 'check in.'"

The Tiikeri scowled at the insolent answer. "Look, whoever you are, I may not know your name or mission because I'm not supposed to, but I *do* know the tasks *your kind* are assigned. Keep in mind that whatever actions you take in this city, I will ultimately be the one who must answer for them."

The Singa kept her composure during the condescending rebuke. "I will try to keep that in mind, Ambassador."

"See that you do," he said, turning back around. "It is just!"

"It is just," his aide and bodyguard both repeated.

"Okay," Demetrius chirped, interrupting the tense exchange, "we're here."

The pilot gently settled the airship into its slip. A welcoming committee of three human officials dressed in traditional yellow bureaucratic robes stood next to the landing pad.

The ambassador's party quickly disembarked once the side hatch dropped. Demetrius let out a sigh of relief. He noted, through the windshield, the Singa didn't engage with any of the humans and hastily made her way to the exit alone.

After conducting his usual post-flight inspection, he was off to the forum. He found Okawa's office in the Valdurian diplomatic sector next to Joc' Valdur's office. Giving a respectful knock on the open door, Demetrius entered her cramped quarters.

Just a small desk with two chairs sat against the far wall and a floor-to-ceiling pigeonhole sorting rack stuffed with papers covered the wall to the left. He noticed a large map of Lumina and Nocturn hanging on the other wall. Red pins dotted its surface and Okawa gazed at it with another pin in hand.

"You know, that map of Nocturn isn't entirely correct," he said.

"It's the best we've got," Okawa said, not looking away. "I thought I told you not to take any long-term jobs."

"Huh? All I heard was that you needed me," Demetrius said, playfully, stepping close behind her. "What's going on?"

The Valdurian gave a wry smile at the excuse and motioned to a piece of paper on her desk.

"We intercepted a secret dispatch from an Aramos agent code named, Needle," she said, returning her attention back to the map. "It states they located the target, and the operation is proceeding. I'm pretty sure they've spotted Stryder Aramos."

"Mmm," Demetrius murmured.

He ever so slightly pressed his body against her back while looking over her shoulder. Okawa closed her eyes for a moment and sighed inwardly when she felt his breath on her neck. She smiled lustfully when she sensed him sniffing her hair and she leaned back into him.

"I've got a feeling we will be traveling companions again," Demetrius softly said, placing his hands on her hips and his mouth by her ear. "So where are we off to this time?"

A shiver coursed through Okawa when his lips passed close to her ear. Catching herself, she pushed away from the distraction and back up to the large wall map. She cleared her throat and stuck the pin on the southern tip of Vakai Island in the Goyodan Chain.

"Aris," she answered.

Demetrius took a deep breath, tried to slow his heart back down, and studied the location.

"Well, it's a short run," he said, picking up the paper and staring curiously at the coded message. "You do realize this city doesn't have an Air Station?"

"Yeah, House Aramos and Valdur have talks scheduled for later this quinte on that very subject," Okawa answered, in a husky voice, struggling to remain composed—which grew harder with each encounter with Demetrius. "For now, I'm having a spot on the docks reserved for us."

"When do we leave?" he asked.

Okawa silently raised an amused eyebrow.

"I know... I know... immediately, right?" he said, chuckling at the obvious answer.

"It would put us there right before the Kan," Okawa calculated.

"So, what about this 'Needle' character?" Demetrius asked, with a touch of concern.

"It looks like we're not the only ones looking for Lord Aramos," Okawa said, grabbing her shoulder bag. "Let's go."

As promised the trip was short. The Aramos home City of Aris loomed on the horizon just as the Kan fog rose from the Shallow Sea.

"Am I putting her down on the docks?" Demetrius asked, beginning a shallow descent.

Okawa grabbed her ghost suit and headed toward the rear of the craft.

"No," she answered. "I've got a sneaking suspicion that our elusive Lord Aramos might hide in plain sight. Bank around and come in low on the east side of the river. Drop me outside the palace grounds. Right now, I've got to get changed. No peeking!"

Demetrius tapped the side of his round blue glasses which allowed him to see through clothing and grinned mischievously.

"I've already seen you naked, remember?"

"Yeah, yeah," Okawa playfully scolded. "Eyes forward fly-boy!"

"Yes ma'am!"

"So, what was the job you just finished?" the agent asked, slipping out of her green jumpsuit.

"I was bringing the Tiikeri ambassador and his party to Zor," the pilot said, passing low over the Vakai river. "I had to make a last-minute stop in Immor-Onn to pick up this female Singa. From what I could gather, the ambassador wasn't too happy. They tossed the word 'mission' around, but the Singa stayed tight lipped. They didn't even know her name."

"Interesting," Okawa said, donning her skin-tight, gray bodysuit. "Wait, you speak Tiikeri?"

"Not well," Demetrius admitted, watching the Kan fog rising steadily. "I could only make out snippets of the conversation."

"Did you let the Zorians know?"

"Yeah," Demetrius confirmed. "I tracked down Rafel. That's why I was late. Hey, is it just me, or has that guy changed?"

"It's not just you."

"I mean, lately he's been kinda grim," the pilot said, watching the river to his left disappear into billowy gray mist. "I don't know, I guess he just lost his lover, but it's something more. He seems more... more driven."

Okawa returned to her seat and Demetrius' gaze swept across the voluptuous brunette. As before, the blue Etheria laced glass saw through the skin-tight outfit. This time, he didn't turn away blushing.

"Still liking what I'm seeing," he said, with an appreciative nod.

Now, it was the Valdurian agent's turn to blush. She reached out and playfully placed a gentle tap on the tip of his nose with her forefinger.

Leaning over, her lips ever so gently brushed his ear whispering, "I'm glad."

The two now stared directly into each other's eyes and their gazes lingered. Demetrius felt the beginnings of an erection as his pulse quickened and his hands became slick on the wheel.

By now, fog engulfed the airship. Sensing the opaque curtain outside the *Drakin,* the pilot skittishly looked away and lowered his orange Etheria lenses. As soon as he lowered the umber glass, the heat signatures of all the objects and creatures below them appeared.

"All right, here we are," Demetrius said, when the outline of the palace loomed in the distance.

Okawa dropped her orange lenses and scanned the area.

"Over there," she said, pointing to a small stand of trees just off the palace grounds.

The ship hovered a few inches above the ground and the side hatch dropped open.

"Okay, don't wait up," Okawa said, making for the door.

"Wait, don't you want me to hang around and wait for your signal, you know, like normal?" asked a bewildered Demetrius.

Okawa stopped halfway out the hatch. Touched by the innocent question she put her hand over his on the wheel and shook her head.

"No, park this thing on the far western dock," she answered. "I want it seen there. I'm just going to have a look around. Don't worry, I'll make it back to you."

"You better," Demetrius blurted out. "I mean... I..."

"Don't worry," she assured with a confident smile.

Before Demetrius could respond she disappeared into the fog. He watched her orange silhouette sprint across the grounds when he lifted off and headed for the docks.

The grand turine ringing twelve bells in the Zorian harbor didn't fully awakened Tysonn. His bed was soft and cozy just as he remembered it. The familiar peeling bells made him bob just close enough to the surface of sleep to enjoy the feel of the comforting linens against his skin.

He grumbled something unintelligible rolling over to snuggle next to Kasha's warmth, only to find her sheets cold and empty to the touch. When his knee slipped into the cold, wet spot from their amorous evening, the master linguist sat up and looked around the darkened room.

"Kas?"

When she didn't reply, Tysonn got up. Shivering, he quickly slipped on a robe. After several passes through the small apartment, he stopped at the window and parted the curtains.

The entire area was deep in the Kan and the fog shrouded Jezik Square in the University of Marassa. Tysonn could make out the central gardens enclosed by its benches, but directly across the academic crossroads he could barely discern the outline of the Language Arts Building.

He gave a frustrated sigh when he saw the light on in Kasha's office, radiating as a lone beacon across the quiet, misty courtyard. Grumbling, he grabbed his keys and slipped into some shoes and a coat. With a mumbling comment about someone "being obsessive," he opened the door and stepped out into the dampness.

Pulling the coat tighter, he set out from the university dormitory over to the building dedicated to the collection and study of all languages. When Tysonn got to the double doors of the three-story building, he found them unlocked. He cautiously entered; his face shrouded in uncertainty.

The entrance hall felt eerily quiet and vacant. The dense fog diffused the light drifting through the windows and strange shadows danced across the walls. His boots clicked on the floor reverberating throughout the empty building. He stepped more thoughtfully when he realized the amount of noise being made climbing the stairs to the second landing.

Tysonn paused when he finally reached the second floor. Down the hall to his left he could see Kasha's door slightly ajar, light streaming out into the darkened hall.

Straining, he thought he heard voices coming from Kasha's office. He apprehensively started down the hall towards the mysterious midnight meeting. As he drew closer, the voices became clearer. Kasha conversed with a man who spoke in a deep beguiling baritone. Her voice was so low he couldn't make out what she was saying, but by her tone she appeared to be asking questions.

The responding male voice had a sinister, demonic quality to it and occasionally it slipped into a mysterious cadence. Now and then their voices overlapped and the hairs on the back of Tysonn's neck stood up along with the goosebumps on his forearms.

He gasped when Cha-Rod stepped from the shadows of a door's recesses right in front of him and broke his concentration. The older Bailian raised his forefinger to his lips and beckoned Tysonn over.

"They've been at it for almost a deci," Cha-Rod whispered, staring up at the much taller human.

"Who is it and what are they talking about?" Tysonn asked, in a barely audible voice.

The Bojo-Vat master shook his head. "I haven't been able to understand what they're saying."

Tysonn's puzzled expression prompted the Bailian to continue.

"I came because of the book," Cha-Rod explained. "A short while ago I awoke and found the locked container open and the book gone. Seeing the light on, I thought this the logical place to find it."

Tysonn turned his attention back at the voices emanating from the office.

"Then it appears we both have reasons to go into that room."

"Indeed," the Bailian said, lifting an eyebrow and hefting his cane.

Cha-Rod was reaching for the door when the voices abruptly stopped. Pausing, they searched each other's perplexed faces. The master stick fighter nervously rubbed the head of his cane and nodded at the cracked door.

"Nothing left to do but enter the play," he resolutely whispered.

Holding his cane directly in front of him with its green bulbous head waist-high, the Bailian stepped through the doorway of the well illuminated office. Tysonn, swallowed hard and followed behind.

Both were astounded to find Kasha unconscious, slumped across the desk, hand still gripping her favorite pen. There was no one else in the room and the temperature felt oppressively warm despite the cool weather. Just to her left, beside a small stack of papers, lay the mysterious book open about a third of the way.

"What's that smell?" Tysonn asked, wincing.

"Ammonia," Bojo-Vat master said, nostrils flaring.

Despite the pungent aroma, they quickly entered and did a more detailed inspection. Hearing Kasha snoring, Tysonn rushed over to her side.

"She's sleeping," he reported. "She seems okay."

Tysonn leaned over his sleeping girlfriend and gently rocked her shoulder.

"Kas," he gently aroused.

Cha-Rod made his way over to the desk and examined the stack of the unconscious linguist's recent writings. Below her pen hand lay a half-composed text of Yassett combined with the book's strange binary language.

After a few more soft nudges Kasha awoke with a start. She blinked and sputtered in uncertainty as she sat up, anxiously looking around.

"Ty, Cha-Rod, what are you doing here?" she asked, rubbing her eyes. "What... how did I get here?"

"You must have been sleep walking," Tysonn said. "You've been pretty consumed with this project."

"Not just walking," the Bailian added, drawing their attention to the freshly penned notes, "but writing... and talking."

Kasha looked around in a newly awakened haze genuinely bewildered.

"Yeah," Tysonn added, "we heard you speaking with someone."

Shaking her head no, she looked down at the partially written paper beneath her hand.

"I... I don't know." She set the pen down and shuffled through her papers. "I mean, It's my handwriting, and..."

Tysonn leaned forward when she lingered on a solitary page. "And what?"

She looked back up at her lover, her eyes were wide with a combination of mystery and joy.

"Ty, this is it!" she exclaimed, pointing to a series of binary combinations and her notes pertaining to them. "This is what I've been looking for!"

Tysonn relaxed a bit at the apparent positive outcome of the bizarre situation. Kasha broke into a broad grin and laughed aloud while she continued pouring over her somnambulist writings. She grew increasingly manic over the findings with each leaf examined.

"This, this is a breakthrough!" Kasha said, overwrought with excitement. "I... I don't know how it happened! It's nothing short of miraculous! This gives me... I mean us, an extraordinary start really translating this!"

"Huh, I guess the answer was right there all along, you just needed to sleep on it," Tysonn said, attempting to rationalize the incident.

"Aren't you forgetting something?" Cha-Rod asked, somberly. "We both heard two distinct voices coming from this office. You want to know what I find even *more* disturbing? Last night I locked that book in a safe I keep beside my bed and I'm the only one with the key."

Demetrius sat back in his pilot's seat, propped his feet up on the chair next to him and held his dinner before his face. He deeply inhaled its mouth-watering aroma. With a rapturous lunge, he took a bite out of the meat pie nestled between both his hands.

Immediately, his eyes and head rolled back and a content, guttural sigh escaped the sides of his mouth. Aris had the best street food, especially around the harbor. Sighing as he chewed, his fingers gently squeezed the remaining treat bringing the juices to the top.

He smiled contentedly, even though he found himself confined to quarters in the back docks while a person he was *very* fond of faced a dangerous assignment alone. The City of Aris, having no air station, parked all airships on the far western docks on the edge of the city limits. This created a solitary and tedious respite for the pilot of the *Drakin*.

However, there was the food. He chewed slowly and savored every moment. His thoughts lingering on Okawa while he stared out into the Kan fog.

The bow of a small ship overshadowed his longings. It appeared out of the fog and silently made its way his direction. Demetrius quickly reached up and extinguished the overhead light, plummeting the cabin in darkness. He put on his spectacles and flipped down the orange Etheria lens.

Peering out into the fog shrouded harbor, littered with airships of various sizes, he watched the vessel settle into a secluded slip thirty feet away. Demetrius grew genuinely curious when the crew immediately began unloading large crates of cargo onto the empty dock.

Smugglers, he confirmed in his head keeping his reposed position between seats. *A remote dock. A quick in and out. Classic!*

Sitting forward, he began chomping his food furiously when he saw a small detachment of Aramos Black Talons arrive to receive the obvious contraband. The grey tunicked soldiers went immediately to work transferring the heavy boxes into the back of a large open-top wagon.

"Hello, what's this?" he pondered aloud to himself.

Demetrius popped the rest of the treat into his mouth and watched them finish loading the crates. He smirked, while chewing the last bite, and sat back in his seat.

An elite Aramos security unit babysitting a smuggled shipment... of what?

This fully piqued the airship pilot's curiosity. They immediately set off into the city after finishing loading the wagon. Demetrius fired up the Etheria engine. The initial low purr of the orbiting crystals gave way to silence when the power core fully engaged and the *Drakin* lifted off.

Hovering well above the city's rooftops, he followed the unwitting Black Talons' heat signatures below, while they trekked eastward through the nearly empty city streets. Demetrius kept the ship down river and just above the trees, while he watched the procession get waved across the bridge into the restricted Aramos Sector.

The airship pilot sucked on a lodged piece of meat pie between his teeth while slipping across the Vakai River into the most affluent area of the city. It came as no surprise when he discovered the caravan headed towards the Royal Palace.

When they bypassed the main estate and headed towards the outer grounds, Demetrius considered the destination might be a storage area. His brow furrowed when he saw four Black Talons, along with what looked like a hybrid Gila lizardman, meet the wagons at the remote garden house. The front of the modest estate house came alive when everyone immediately began unloading the wagons under the Gila's watchful eye and direction.

Curiosity and not concern, led him to scan the nearby woods for Okawa. He located the glowing orange and yellow outline of her heat signature hiding, and no doubt witnessing the activity, amongst a stand of trees fifty feet from the garden house.

Curiosity gave way to concern, when he spotted the glow of someone, or something, closing in behind her.

The moon had just dipped in the west, cloaking the Os-Tor Forest in long shadows. Now, the main illumination for the northern Twilight Lands came from the faint sun on permanent station in the far western sky. Pounding horse hooves and rumble of wagon wheels on the forest's treacherous southern road reverberated through the trees and out into the moonless.

A large muscular Bailian with long flowing black hair sat on the buckboard and watched nervously as the darkened silhouettes of trees raced by them. He cast a concerned glance at the female seated beside him furiously driving the two-horse team.

"Al-Vee," he cried, "if you don't slow this thing down, we're never gonna make it to Immor-Onn in one piece!"

As if to emphasize his concern, the right wheel struck a partially raised tree root. The small, unseen obstruction lifted the long cart off the ground, violently jarring the riders and cargo when the whole side of the open-top wagon briefly went airborne. When it crashed back onto the road Al-Vee pulled hard on the reins, deftly manipulating the team, but not breaking stride.

"If any of the local bandit gangs get ahold of us, we won't make it there either," she said, concentrating on the bends in the road as they became visible. "We lost too much time in that last hamlet."

"I told you we should have held up there for the moonless," the male Bailian admonished.

"You are always such a worrier, Bi-Tann!" she scoffed, spurring on the horses. "No wonder you've only got three eyes on your Samboon."

Bi-Tann inadvertently peeked down at his necklace of three dried Cevot spider eyes bouncing wildly against his chest with each wagon lurch. He felt a rush of anger flush his cheeks.

"It's not my fault the overlord does not choose me for raids!" he spat, holding tightly onto his seat.

"'It's not my fault!'" she cried out mockingly. "'It's not my fault!' He doesn't choose you because you are way too…"

The horse's lower legs suddenly colliding at a full gallop into a wire suspended across the road violently interrupted the argument. The animals screamed in shock and agony when the impact shattered both their forelegs. Their heads plunged forward and crashed to the ground vaulting their hindquarters upward.

The attached wagon hurtled out of control and flipped over with a thunderous crash, landing on the side of the road near the tree line. Riders and freight sailed through the air. Their cargo of spider silk spools and small kegs of whiskey littered the roadway. Several casks had broken open. Their liquid content poured out and small streams of alcohol coursed across the hardened earth.

Al-Vee landed on her back. The force of the fall knocked the wind out of her and the back of her head collided with the road rendering her unconscious. When she came to, her

147

vision was cloudy and everything around her seemed to move in slow motion.

She was lying beside the injured horses, and their agony-racked braying filled the night air. She could make out Bi-Tann hanging motionless, impaled on a broken sapling by the side of the road. His spent lifeblood painted the thin, broken trunk a ghastly shade of crimson.

When Al-Vee tried moving she discovered her right leg broken and bent off to the side at an unnatural forty-five-degree angle. Surprisingly, the Bailian female felt no pain through the constant numbing fog. She felt her eyelids growing heavy and rested her head.

Over the sound of the horses' suffering, Al-Vee thought she heard the excited chattering of voices approaching from both sides of the road. She recognized the language as Bailian with an En-Sul dialect. She forced herself to stay conscious and watched in horror when a dozen bizarre creatures filled the crash area.

They appeared to be mostly Bailian, however they were all badly mutated. Some moved on long insectoid legs with external spines running down their backs. Others displayed bulbous compound eyes and pincer like hands. There were also several bear/mantis hybrids crawling about on four and six legs. The two-legged mutations immediately began collecting the items littering the ground and placing them onto the backs of the mutated animals.

Two creatures, with elongated skulls and ominous looking mandibles jutting out from the sides of their mouths, shuffled over to the wounded horses. Plunging their sharp protuberances into the beast's necks silenced the horses' anguished braying. Then they severed the tangled reins and dragged the carcasses off into the woods.

A creature resembling a grotesque combination of Bailian, ape, and insect scurried over to the skewered lifeless figure of Bi-Tann. Confident he was dead, he called out to someone outside Al-Vee's range of vision.

"Pity," the voice rang out in broken En-Sul. "Check the female!"

The monstrosity covered the ground quickly and hovered over the crippled Bailian. She reeled from the smell of rotting flesh on its breath and turned her face away.

"Alive," it reported.

"At least there is one to carry on my offspring," the voice proclaimed, as its owner came into view.

Al-Vee tried to scream and crawl away, but her limbs refused to move and she couldn't seem to find her voice.

The creature, she assumed was the leader, retained the body of a Bailian, but with large blazing red compound eyes which dominated each side of its face. It walked hunched over on two legs with an insectoid thorax protruding from the buttocks area. The most frightening aspect was that the tail and telson stinger at the end of the thorax resembled a barbed penis.

She recognized the beast from the stories told by the old women of the hamlet to scare the children into behaving. It was told these were the offspring of fire creatures from the Land of Mists. Some could still breathe fire like their parents.

The most horrific part of the legend claimed these offspring could impregnate any species of creature, either male or female, by penetrating them with their hideous tail. The inseminated could do nothing but serve as a womb until the abomination were born, erupting violently from the host, and killing it. These cautionary tales were always told with great relish and gruesome detail emphasizing the slow painful death.

To her utter terror, she now realized the stories were true when the creature loomed over her, its barbed phallic tail swaying. It smiled down at Al-Vee and revealed a mouth full of long, tubular fangs open at the tips.

"Mmm yes," it said, sizing her up and down greedily.

The creature reached down and tore off her simple tunic and trousers. It roughly ran its hand over her naked body and between her legs while trying to decide on pleasure or procreation.

Al-Vee's eyes widened in panic watching the tail undulate towards her. The phallic barb wept with ejaculate hovering over her stomach. Drops of boiling hot seed burned her flesh.

An ear-splitting screech from above caused all to stop. The leader quickly retracted its tail and held its hands over its ears in pain. The creatures cast about in a panic when a winged figure swooped in and grabbed one of the ape/insect hybrids. With the monster secure in its powerful talons, the humanoid bat performed an erratic turn which propelled the captured creature into the crowd of its companions knocking them to the ground.

The ones still on their feet quickly brandished crude swords and spun in circles terror-stricken. Drucilla swooped in once again and raked her talons along one's back. It dropped to the ground shrieking in agony while the others waved their weapons wildly about.

Al-Vee was now all but forgotten while the mutants struggled to engage the Ash-Ta's aerial assault. Even the leader lost interest in her. It drew its weapon and slashed in the air with both tail and sword.

Drucilla shot upward fifteen feet and let loose another piercing shriek before diving for the leader who reflexively covered his ears. She latched onto its back, opened her mouth extending multiple rows of teeth, and snapped down, biting halfway through its neck. The leader creature immediately dropped limp to the ground and stared lifelessly at the wounded Al-Vee lying beside it.

With a satisfied growl, Drucilla raised her head skyward and swallowed the bloody hunk of flesh before turning her attention to the remaining stunned creatures. Keeping her lips back and teeth bared, she shrieked again. The remaining seven mutated Bailians winced and began a nervous advance toward the crouching Ash-Ta. Drucilla snarled once again, but the beasts continued their cautious progress.

Suddenly, a small, bright, blue bolt shot out from the tree line beside them. Just before striking, the bolt materialized into a double-edged dagger and plunged into the lead figure's head. Before its body had even hit the ground, the creature right behind him suffered the same fate.

With two more of their companion's dead, the others panicked and ran. While the last one was escaping into the forest, a longer blue bolt streaked out, turned into a short spear, and impaled him to a tree.

Drucilla stopped and drew in her teeth looking around. She ignored Al-Vee trying to crawl away on her back, squirming in fear and wincing in pain. Calmly wiping the blood from her mouth, she gazed up into a nearby tree at Kai kneeling on a lower branch.

Without a word Drucilla crouched over the dead mutant leader and gnawed on his thigh. She gobbled three large mouthfuls and swallowed them greedily, shaking her throat to force them down. She slowly stopped chewing and looked up at Kai who had still not moved.

"My brother suggested I change my diet," she said, dispassionately, before ripping off another strip of raw thigh meat and stuffing it into her mouth.

Peligro could just barely make out the figure through the Kan fog. It was crouching inside a small stand of trees. Just beyond, he could see the glow of gems and hear activity outside the front of the remote garden house. When the

Aramos agent drew closer, he could see it was definitely a human, dressed in a gray ghost suit.

That's a Valdurian outfit, he pondered and silently drew his double-edged knife.

Okawa was studying the last of the crates inside the house when she heard a slight rustling of the grass behind her. With a half turn of her head, her orange Etheria laced glasses registered the large heat signature of an approaching human almost on top of her. Already in a crouch, she launched herself into the air and lashed out with a vicious kick, while reaching to draw the crossbow pistol on her hip.

Peligro partially sidestepped the blow. The blade of her foot connected with his right shoulder instead of his throat, jarring the knife from his hand. The attack spun him to his right, and he used the momentum to assist a left hook striking Okawa's weapon arm. His blow knocked the crossbow from her hand and it landed in the grass with a soft thud.

Damn that kick would have crushed my throat if it connected, Peligro assessed lunging at the mysterious gray figure.

Okawa landed and rolled forward toward the charging figure, coming up inside his attack. Her tumble connected with his legs, sending him toppling over her, landing flat on his back. However, the maneuver and impact sent the custom spectacles flying off the Valdurian's face.

Coming out of the roll, Okawa made it to her feet first and aimed a front kick at Peligro while he was still getting to his knees. The Aramos Black Talon deflected and grabbed her ankle. He wrenched it violently to the side and threw his gray suited opponent into the grass beside him.

Circling above, Demetrius watched the two heat signatures clash on the ground below. Shaking his head in disbelief he pushed the flaps forward.

"'I'm just going to have a look around,'" he said, in a mocking tone, beginning his descent. "'Don't worry, I'll make it back to you,' she said."

When the *Drakin* neared the treetops, Demetrius caught sight of the door to the garden house opening and people quickly exiting.

"Oh golly!" he exclaimed, increasing the speed and angle of the dive.

Okawa was attempting to roll away from an impending submission hold when Peligro pounced on top of her back, pinning her to the ground. When she rolled to her left and tried an elbow strike, Peligro struck her in the back of the right shoulder negating the blow. The Valdurian grunted in pain and lost most of the feeling in her right arm.

Grabbing the assaulting limb, the Aramos agent flipped Okawa over onto her back. He was about to execute a choke hold when he finally saw the face of his opponent.

"Okawa?!" he gasped, ceasing his attack, and sitting up straddling her stomach.

"Peligro?" she said, a look of confusion crossing her face.

"What in the name of the empire are you doing here?" he asked.

Flexing her hips, she bucked him off her.

"Probably the same thing as you."

Peligro shot to his feet and offered her a hand. She slowly got up, gingerly rubbing her right shoulder.

"You still got a wicked punch," she said, trying to rotate the unresponsive joint.

"I'd say the same about your kicks," he replied with an appreciative nod.

"What's going on?" Okawa queried, looking around the fog covered ground for her spectacles.

Peligro was about to respond when he saw the *Drakin* plunge from the sky and settle in a clearing near the stand of trees. The side door instantly dropped open. Demetrius appeared in the opening and gave a whistle of alarm pointing to the bushes behind them. They heard crashing foliage and approaching footsteps immediately following the whistle.

"Can you run?" Peligro asked, noting her wounded leg.

She nodded while slipping her spectacles on, but her leg buckled when she put weight on it and Peligro caught her.

"Maybe not so well," she said, wincing in pain.

"We gotta go," he said, prompting her forward with his arm around her.

They started off awkwardly hobbling toward the ship. After a few steps Peligro grabbed her and slung her over his shoulder.

Just like basic training, he thought, taking off running. He then gave a quick glance at Okawa's shapely butt in the skin-tight suit just inches from his face. *With a much better view.*

Now facing backwards, Okawa saw the first of the Black Talons break through the bushes. With her orange lenses in place, she detected several more just behind the leader.

Pulling out her crossbow pistol she rapidly fired off a bolt at the pursuers. She huffed in frustration when the projectile missed, striking a nearby tree.

"Can't you run any smoother?" she asked, anxiously.

Peligro grunted an unintelligible answer.

She was reaching for another bolt on her thigh quiver when she saw several more of the gray tunicked guards clearing the bushes. They couldn't see their targets through the fog, but ran in the general direction of the sound of the escaping duo.

Okawa, not visually encumbered by the thick mist, fired off another round. This time the six-inch long bolt found its target in the chest of the nearest guard. The force knocked him backwards into two more just behind him.

They reached the airship with the enemy twenty yards behind still obscured by the Kan. Peligro handed Okawa off to Demetrius and then spun to face the inevitable.

"What are you doing?!" she demanded incredulously. "Get in!"

"I know these guys," Peligro said, shaking his head. "I've served with them. This is my way in. Get outta here. I'll say you escaped."

Pulling out his knife the Aramos agent slashed the front of his jacket and a thin ribbon of blood appeared.

"GO!" he ordered, flinging himself to the ground.

"You don't have to tell *me* twice!" Demetrius said, closing the hatch.

As the Drakin swiftly lifted off, the pilot and the agent could see glowing blobs of heat signatures surrounding Peligro as the Black Talons took him captive.

"You wanna tell me what that was all about?" Demetrius asked, navigating the airship away from the altercation.

"That was Peligro de Aris," Okawa said flexing her shoulder as the feeling slowly returned. "He's a fixer for House Aramos *and* I'd be willing to bet he's the agent called 'Needle' we read about in that intercepted dispatch. We've worked as both allies and rivals in the past."

"What the heck was he doing here?"

The Valdurian agent shook her head. "I can only guess, but by now I'm pretty sure we're not the only ones interested in Lord Stryder Aramos."

Kai resisted grimacing at the powerful smell of ammonia which struck her immediately upon stepping across the threshold. It hung in the warm humid air and permeated the entire two-bedroom apartment. Despite her revulsion, she kept it to herself. The last thing she wanted to do was insult her old friend Jo-Rakk. However, in all her dealings with the tiger people of Nocturn, she had never gotten used to the odor of a Tiikeri den.

"She's here, sir," Takki said, closing the door behind them.

The Tiikeri ambassador to Immor-On sat with his back to the door on a low bench in front of a glowing pile of orange gems. Without turning, he extended a fur covered hand.

"Welcome," he said. "Thank you for coming so quickly, old friend. Have a seat and share the warmth with me."

"It's pretty warm in here," Kai said, pleasantly, taking a seat on the bench directly across from the man-tiger.

"Please forgive any discomfort," Jo-Rakk apologized. "It's as close as I can get to the rainforests of home."

"Yeah, as I recall it was pretty warm and muggy there too," she answered.

"How far we have come since restoring the Cub Prince," Jo-Rakk mused.

"From war hero to ambassador," Kai said, returning her gaze to the Tiikeri. "Did you ever think you would end up assigned so far away from home and in a fairly quiet job?"

"I must admit, it was a change," he said, pointing at two streaks of gray hair framing her face. "You also recently returned to us very much changed, little sister."

It was now the human's turn for sentimental deportment.

"Evolution and its cost," she said, softly, before breaking away from the small talk. "Anyway, what can I do for the Tiikeri Empire?"

"It's what I can do for you, little sister. I have information."

"You have my attention."

"It's about the Na-Kab."

Kai took a moment and searched her memory.

"Those are the fire bugs from beneath your homeland?"

"Yes," Jo-Rakk confirmed. "I'm getting reports. Something strange is happening."

"That's halfway around the world. What has the Na-Kab got to do with us?"

The Tiikeri stroked the fur under his chin. "Quite a while ago the Na-Kab lost their queen. Without a queen and her royal jelly, the hive has been slowly dying. I estimate there are less than a hundred of them left."

"Okay?" Kai said, curiously.

"After their population dwindled," he explained, "those remaining panicked. They began impregnating anything they could hoping it might produce a queen. It's quite a horrendous process. Their seed has become overly fertile I'm afraid. They can impregnate any race—*male or female.*

"The fetus then grows like an invasive parasite, developing its own womb out of any suitable internal cavity. Often the gestation alone kills the host, but by this point the fetus is strong enough to continue development in the carcass on its own, feeding off the rotting flesh and the gasses given off. If, by some miracle, the host survives the gestation period, the birth of the mutant child will eviscerate it. The newborn then feeds on the remains of the host during its infancy."

Jo-Rakk paused and gauged the repulsed look on Kai's face before continuing, "By the time the second generation of these mutants came around, the pure Na-Kab knew it was a failed experiment. Now we are seeing third and fourth generations of these hideous mutants. They travel in packs, family units if you will."

"That's all pretty disgusting but I'm still not following you," Kai asked. "What does this have to do with us?"

"My people have been able to keep their numbers in check at home," Jo-Rakk said, patiently, "but they quickly arrived on this continent and have been spreading westward. There have been recent reports of a gang of about twenty in the Os' Tor Forest just outside the city."

Kai softly gasped when the revelation hit her. "I encountered them last luna in the forest!"

157

"Oh?"

"I saw their leader, the one with the penis tail, get killed and eaten."

The Tiikeri gave a knowing nod. "That was one of the second generation. It doesn't matter. They're all dead now."

This visibly surprised the Bailian spymaster. "Wait, how?!"

"The pure Na-Kab are killing off all their mutated offspring."

"Why?"

"I don't know. What makes this even stranger is that the Na-Kab have gone abnormally quiet. There have been no reported skirmishes between my people or the Do-Tarr. No sightings *at all* for that matter, just dead mutants."

Kai silently considered the information just presented to her.

"Thanks for the ear-full," she said, standing, "but I'm still not sure how this affects us. Especially if the mutant gang outside of town is now dead."

The Tiikeri ambassador rose to his feet and shrugged. "Consider it a professional courtesy. You can't have *too* much information."

"No argument there," Kai agreed just before mischievously smiling. "Are you making up for telling the Singa the book's destination was Zor?"

Jo-Rakk's grin betrayed a touch of embarrassment.

"Caught in the chains of duty I'm afraid," he said. "No hard feelings?"

Kai shook her head. "We all have our duty old friend."

The spymaster stepped out into the cool fresh air of the diplomatic compound in Immor-Onn deep in thought. There was something disturbing about the report she had just received. The Tiikeri's words danced ominously in the back of her mind. She had a feeling this would come up again, but how?

That was the question. The answer was almost always deadly.

The *Drakin* had only traveled a short distance over the rooftops of Aris when Okawa snapped out of her contemplative trance. She had been staring silently out into the Kan fog nursing her leg since they had escaped the Aramos estate and Demetrius was growing concerned.

"So, what now?" he asked, breaking the hush that hung over the flight cabin.

"Turn this thing around," she finally said.

"What?!"

"You heard me. We're going back."

"Uh... I don't think that's a very good idea."

"Demetrius..."

"Okay, okay," the pilot said, rotating the wheel in front of him. "You realize you're wounded and outnumbered?"

"I won't engage with anyone," she said, reaching into her shoulder bag and bringing out three replacement bolts. "I just need to see what's going on down there."

"That's what you said last time," Demetrius challenged. "If I hadn't been following that shipment they might have overcome you like your friend back there."

"He's not my friend," she said, slipping the bolts into the slots running down her thigh. "And that was a solitary, unforeseen incident."

"You don't think they're gonna be on guard?"

"No," she replied definitively, "just the opposite. I'm betting they think it's over, at least for now. If they didn't kill him outright, they'll concentrate on their captive and that shipment."

The airship slipped silently over the Vakai River and into the restricted Aramos Sector. While they neared the royal estate, Okawa took a quick inventory of her shoulder bag.

The Drakin circled the grounds just above the treetops, while both pilot and agent scanned the area around the garden house for signs of movement. There appeared to be only two guards, one at the front door and one at the beginning of the road leading to the solitary building.

"Looks like you were right," Demetrius said, concentrating on the ground.

Light streamed upward from the interior of an oblong glass greenhouse attached to the main house, causing the surrounding fog to glow.

"Come in from the north and hover just above the roof of the house," she said. "I'll get out and have a peek through the greenhouse roof. Then we can leave. No one will know we were ever here."

Demetrius gave a resigned sigh and guided the craft through the fog to a spot just inches above the building's wooden roof and quietly opened the side hatch.

Okawa slipped out carefully and softly padded over to the clear greenhouse roof. The room below was abuzz with activity. They had moved aside the usual plant tables to allow room for the shipment of large crates.

Stryder stood beside the large Gila, who supervised the men unloading what appeared to be large, thick circular disks of multi-colored Etheria crystals. Two tall humans with glowing red eyes remained motionless, watching the group from a distance.

The aquamarine Etheria lens of Okawa's spectacles revealed the two humans as glamoured Na-Kab in their true form. They very much resembled the Do-Tarr mantis people. These appeared much more ominous, with large scales covering the insect portion of their body's. She could see glowing red in between where the plates touched.

At the Gila's direction, the soldiers arranged the Etheria disks into four stacked cairns. They constructed each cairn with a three-foot purple disk base, followed by two slighter clear disks, and an even smaller iridescent disk topped off with a dark green capstone.

They placed two of the cairns beside the soldiers and the other two flanked a bound and gagged human. With closer examination she recognized the captive as the assassin, Peligro.

Reaching into her messenger bag, Okawa retrieved two cone shaped pieces of rubber connected by a thick wire. Placing one cone against the glass she put the other to her ear. She could now hear them speaking.

"All right, put the amber disks on these two," Da'Olman said, indicating the cairns closest to them.

Once the Gila completed the task he inspected each cairn. When he finished, he appeared almost giddy.

"We're ready for a test," the man-lizard said, voice quivering with excitement.

"Is that necessary?" Stryder asked, with a touch of impatience in his voice.

A shocked look swept across Da'Olman's face. "You always perform a test when dealing with things of this importance. This experiment is very precise. We must be certain. After all you wouldn't want to disappoint your fiery friends. I hear they are quite unforgiving."

"Very well," Stryder said, sighing. "What do you suggest?"

An evil grin played at the corners of the Gila's mouth when he peered over at Peligro.

"He should do nicely."

The Aramos agent's eyes widened in surprise and he struggled against his bonds. The gag in his mouth muffled his protests.

"Very well," Stryder said, directing two of the Black Talons over to their former companion.

"Stand him up," Da'Olman said. "Place him directly between those two cairns."

They muscled Peligro into place. He fought to keep his balance with his feet bound.

"You should feel honored," the Gila Etheriat patronized. "You are at the vanguard of a new and wondrous process."

The captive mumbled profanities into his gag, nervously staring at the small cairns flanking him on either side.

"Ready anytime you are," Da'Olman said, glancing at Stryder.

"Get on with it," the dark cleric ordered.

Manipulating a ring on each hand so that the iridescent Aur-Quaz head gemstones faced inward, he briskly brushed his hands together.

The stones collided, sending a shower of sparks outward before the Gila. The corresponding iridescent disks forming the cairns immediately started glowing, setting off a chain reaction in the other Etheria crystals. Once all the gems were glowing, they gave off a great blue flash and then went out.

Okawa reeled from the flash but what she saw next made her gasp in horror. Peligro's groin and legs completely vanished from beneath his torso, neatly severed just above the hips, and reappeared between the cairns on the other side of the room.

His lifeless upper torso toppled to the floor preceded by an avalanche of blood and internal organs. His detached legs remained upright for a moment between the other two cairns, before teetering and falling over, spilling intestines, bowels, and fecal laced gore across the floor.

"A failure!" Stryder's disappointed voice thundered across the room.

Da'Olman's face was the exact opposite of Stryder's. He stroked the cairn next to him with a satisfied grin.

"No, no, not a failure," he said, almost out of breath. "All we need to make are slight adjustments."

A repulsed Okawa watched while the Gila directed the men to swap the iridescent disk so it rested directly on the purple cairn. They walked across Peligro's remains like stepping through a mud puddle and scraped the carnage from their shoes as they would dog shit off their heel.

"We are now ready," Da'Olman proclaimed.

The Valdurian agent leaned her entire torso over to get a better view, stunned by what she had just witnessed. Her partially open messenger bag dangled from her side and a pair of pliers dropped out, clattering noisily against the transparent roof.

Immediately all eyes in the room flashed upward.

Damn it, just damn it! Okawa chastised herself, quickly retrieving her instruments from the glass roof and shoving them into her bag. Down below, she saw everyone in the room staring up at her. She especially noted the amused smile of recognition on Stryder's face.

Sprinting towards the airship, the Valdurian could hear the doors below fly open followed by the grunting and cursing of men spilling out onto the grounds. The Black Talon soldiers cried out in astonishment when the two red eyed humans scrambled up the walls of the greenhouse, their hands and feet easily clinging to the sheer surface.

When Okawa bounded up the ramp into the *Drakin,* she saw the two humanoid mantis' scurry onto the roof. Without breaking stride, she drew her crossbow pistol and took a shot at them. Not waiting to see if the bolt struck its target, she lunged through the side hatch.

"GO!" she screamed while the door closed behind her.

The ship went airborne almost instantaneously. They performed a quick bank to the north and heard arrows pinging off the hull.

"So much for just having a look around," Demetrius said, pulling back hard on the flaps.

Both were watching the frustrated archers below continuing their futile attack, when a long streamer of fire shot past them. A stunned Demetrius swiftly veered the *Drakin* hard to port.

"What the…"

"It must be those bug creatures." Okawa said, glancing back at the roof.

The second Na-Kab opened his mouth and she could see the glowing interior.

"Here comes another one!" she warned.

"Hold on!" Demetrius said, jerking hard on the wheel.

The airship's nose abruptly arced to the right when another column of flame shot past them. The *Drakin* performed a tight loop and spiral. Leveling out, Demetrius got a look at their assailants.

"Those are Na-Kab," he said, in a startled, clipped tone. "What in the name of the gods are Na-Kab doing here?"

"I don't know, but they were pretty cozy with Stryder Aramos back there. And speaking of him…"

Two more staggered bursts of flame cut short Okawa's explanation. Demetrius swung hard to starboard and successfully avoided the first blast, only to collide with the second. The ship's windshield filled with fire, forcing both passengers to shield their eyes from the sudden flash and searing wave of heat. The glass held, but sections of the hull were now burning.

"We've been hit!" Demetrius called out.

"I thought Ukko wood didn't burn." Okawa said, her voice laced with stress.

The pilot sheered off to port avoiding the next blast before headed west out of the city. Okawa noticed another jet of flame lashing out into the Kan fog and diminishing harmlessly just behind the airship. They were now safely out of range, but the fire remained ablaze and spreading across the *Drakin's* hull.

"Uh, Demetrius..."

"I'm working on it," he said, calmly, angling the ship downward towards a small farm just outside the city. "At least we now know Na-Kab fire is one of the few things that can burn Ukko wood."

Smoke began entering the cabin by the time the airship leveled off ten feet above rows of lush grapevines. Okawa looked around worriedly as the vapors continued to increase and then over at Demetrius staring out the windshield past the flames, deep in concentration.

"This is gonna be close," he said, aiming the burning craft towards the farms water tower.

"Demetrius!" Okawa cried out.

The *Drakin* clipped the edge of the tower smashing the side spout, rocking the airship slightly when it made contact. Water started streaming from the side of the reservoir. Demetrius pulled to port and slowed the craft, executing a tight circle around the leaking water tower. They drifted beneath the flowing water and it cascaded over the ship, but the liquid seemed to have no effect on the flames.

"Not normal fire," Demetrius noted to a wide-eyed Okawa. "Gotta try something else. Hold on!"

Wrenching back on the flaps and hitting the accelerator, the airship blasted upward. Okawa watched Demetrius with anxious regard of his calm demeanor and focused concentration manipulating the controls.

The force pressed both occupants back in their seats as the Drakin rocketed upwards at full speed. Okawa swallowed hard and her ears popped while they swept through layers of clouds towards the darkened sky of the upper atmosphere.

When she noticed her breathing becoming labored, the flames across the ship's hull sputtered and died down. A feeling of light headiness swept over her when last of the fires finally extinguished. The Valdurian agent was on the verge of passing out when Demetrius finally stalled the craft and to enter a rapid but controlled descent.

"Are you okay?" Demetrius asked, when he saw Okawa rubbing her temples.

"I've got a splitting headache," she said, in a labored voice.

"Yeah, sorry about that. I had to take her up a little higher than normal to starve out those flames."

"How's the ship?" she asked, dabbing away a small nosebleed.

"Hard to say," the pilot replied. "The helm's sluggish, but she's flyable. I know we've got some damage. I just can't tell how bad it is from up here. So, I'm taking us back to Zor to get this baby looked at."

Okawa shook her head. "I've got a better idea."

"It better include fixing my ship," Demetrius said, skeptically, "because we're sure not much help to anyone like this."

"Fixing *and* upgrading," she replied confidently. "We must study the damage those fire creatures did to develop a better defense system. And while we're at it, I can think of a few additional improvements which would make this ship, and us, far more effective."

"Exactly who is the 'we' you are referring to?"

Okawa winced slightly at the remnants of her headache.

"Head towards the central mountains of Atar island."

Demetrius raised a questioning eyebrow at the suggestion of the Valdurian home island.

"We're going to Landagar," she said, sitting back. "It's time to get the experts involved."

The baths were always empty and quiet during the Kan. Rafel sat alone on a stone bench beside the giant pool watching gentle whiffs of steam rising from the water. The dim orange illumination of glowing gems cast dancing reflections up the stark white walls and high ceiling.

He needed the time to himself, to think, to plot, and to get away from the temptation of strong drink. He had long since run out of tears. Now only stomach twisting rage remained.

He scrutinized the brief message in his hand once again. His cheeks flushed and mouth twisted into a sneer. The Zorian spymaster had read it over a dozen times since its arrival by gull that afternoon. It affected him the same way with each review.

> The one-armed assassin
> Is an Orad-Sto.
> Her name is Kai.
> She is the queen's spymaster in Immor-Onn.

This, however, was no time for unbridled fury. His newly revealed adversary would prove monumentally formidable, bordering on invincible. No, this act of retribution called for calculation and cunning. For this, he needed the water with all its wisdom and council.

Rafel slowly stood and stepped over to the edge of the pool. He remained motionless for a while, staring into the warm, calm water. Then, as if hearing a call from the depths, he stepped down into the man-made lake fully clothed. The sleeves and leggings of his soaked garments billowed outward. He closed his eyes and felt the liquid surround him.

"I seek the guidance of Padi," he said, extending his arms to float on the surface.

The words reverberated off the walls of the empty baths while he gently floated on his back through the water. He concentrated on his future endeavor and any guidance which might come from beyond.

Ink from the message ran as the paper became soaked in his hands. The fateful words streamed off the page and formed a dark cloud of ink. It swirled around him and then dissolved into the watery expanse.

When Tysonn stepped out of his dormitory apartment building and into Jezik Square, he caught the fragrant scent of the Manis trees on the morning breeze. The University of Marassa was a big place, and he felt fortunate the walk was short. With the sprawling series of interconnected complexes encompassing virtually all the Kampo Plat in the City of Zor, it was easy to get lost. He remembered drawing a crude map for himself when he first arrived.

The linguist loved the fact, that at any time of day, the halls and classrooms bustled with academic industriousness. Scholars and students alike strived to make sense of their surrounding universe. In stark contrast to the rest of the campus, the Language Arts Department had been under a state of virtual lock-down for the past few cycles and it amplified his feeling of isolation. Making his way under a canopy of delicate pink spring flowers, he smiled at the thought of winter finally fading away.

Crossing the nearly empty square, he nodded his greetings to an EEtah standing guard at the entrance of the main Language Arts Department building. They had stationed the twelve-foot tall man-shark here ever since Kasha's "voices" incident several Kans ago.

A flurry of activity met him on the second floor, with various linguists and their most senior students working feverishly on their department's solitary project.

Stepping off the landing Tysonn turned left and headed for Kasha's office. He knew she would be there. It was where she spent almost every waking hour.

Her door was open, and she was speaking with a man and woman Tysonn hadn't seen before. Both wore the coveted red robes of a Senior Marassa. The woman was tall and frail with a head full of wild gray hair and the man was short and stout with a dour disposition, an intricate blue tattoo covered the crown of his bald head.

Kasha sat with the mysterious tome open in front of her. The book appeared to be the topic of discussion. Cha-Rod sat in the corner leaning forward on his cane transfixed by the conversation.

Kasha stood when she noticed him at the door.

"Ah, Ty," she said, in a staccato voice. "Come in, come in. There's two people here I want you to meet."

Tysonn examined Kasha's appearance when he first stepped into the room, having grown concerned by having seen so little of her over the past several cycles. She noticeably had lost weight. Her clothes hung loosely off her diminished frame. Puffy dark bags sagged under her sunken eyes. His nose twitched slightly when he recognized the same ammonia scent from the other night. He also realized she hadn't bathed lately.

Ignoring his observations, Tysonn smiled and reached his hand out in greetings. The bald man was closest.

"Ty this is Marassa Tohu, from the Osaya Runeists School." Kasha said, while they shook hands.

The frail, wild haired woman leaned over the desk.

"And this is Marassa Ganita of the Philosophy and Mathematics School."

"Bringing in the notables," Tysonn said, cheerfully, as her small bony hand disappeared into his.

"And this is Marassa, excuse me, *Pisar* Tysonn," Kasha continued.

"Your reputation precedes you," Ganita said, retrieving her hand. "You made quite a splash when you left. Everyone was talking."

"Oh, yes," Tohu chimed in. "So, how are the Bailian's treating you?"

Tysonn gave a satisfied chuckle. "I've got an unlimited budget and authority. Queen Shula has entrusted me to build a world class university and library in Immor-Onn. I really can't complain."

"Every Marassa's dream," Ganita said, in a wistful voice.

The comment highlighted a constant sore spot between the two linguists. Tysonn noted however that Kasha didn't flinch at the unintentional jab.

"As I was saying," Kasha briskly began, pointing at the book. "I wish I could grant you access to the original, but that would be an enormous security risk. My scribes, however, have copied just about the entire thing. You are more than welcome to work from that. It's on display in the main rectory. Besides, the copy will be much easier to read."

Kasha indicated the redundant pages of tiny binary script on the book in front of her. Both Marassa's smiled and nodded in agreement with the concession.

"I welcome any insight you can provide," Kasha said.

After they said their farewells, bowed, and left, Tysonn closed the door behind them. He gave his colleague and lover a concerned stare.

"You look like death on a biscuit," he said, anxiously. "You haven't been eating. Come on, let me buy you some breakfast?"

Kasha shook her head. "Not hungry."

"You didn't come to bed last night."

"I, I know... work," she said, staring down at the book.

"Don't you think you're pushing this a bit too hard?"

Kasha peered eerily up at Tysonn.

"I translated some of it."

He froze. Curiosity quickly overcame any concern for his partners wellbeing.

"Really?"

Her eyes held his without blinking.

"It's called the Cisla a Moc."

"Is that Tiikeri?" Tysonn asked, tilting his head quizzically.

"Yes," she confirmed. "It means numbers and power."

Tysonn's intentionally forced his interest away from Kasha's disturbing stare and on to the book.

"And it's not a grimoire like I originally thought," she said, her tone took on a direful chill.

He looked back into her ominous gaze. "What then?"

"It's a prayer book."

The fog receded into the Shallow Sea and a light rain fell on the City of Aris. *Fitting*, Harper Aramos lamented to himself, wiping away another wave of tears.

Harper caught his reflection in the polished black granite of his uncle's tomb. His eyes were puffy and his nose discolored from crying. He ran his fingertips across the chiseled epitaph.

TALON ARAMOS
48 P.A. - 3 G.A.
He Ruled With Wisdom

The funeral service long since ended. The entirety of House Aramos gathered for it. Seeing his brother Ward and cousin Donal, who had journeyed all the way from Immor-Onn, pleased him.

He had stayed away from his estranged father who still remained unhappy with the succession of power. As commander of the powerful Forsvara Guards he could be a problem in the future.

Fortunately, Uncle Cedar from the Zorian Monetary Council, and his many cousins, greeted him warmly. He hadn't seen them in many grands.

Bartol, the new family patriarch, led the procession behind the auburn robed clerics of the fire god Vurr. They carried the urn containing his favorite uncle's ashes.

Now, staring at the sealed crypt, he couldn't help but wonder what lay in store for the fragmented family. The murder left a part of Harper racked with guilt and consumed with longing for his departed uncle. The other side of his divided soul, however, felt heady with power.

He peered up and caught the reflection of Stryder walking up behind him.

"I killed him," Harper whispered, choking back a sob.

"A necessary sacrifice to secure the blessings of our lord," Stryder replied dispassionately. "Regret is for lesser men."

"Still…"

"Still nothing," Stryder said, cutting him off. "We have set the strategy in motion. Today I implement the groundwork. You must be ready with a clear head."

The dark cleric placed a hand on his cousin's shoulder.

"Within a few cycles this will be a very different world," he said. "We must be ready to take our rightful place in it."

The late-day sun beat down upon the Valley of Chains in the central Goyan Mountains. Its rays refracted off the thirty-foot-tall pillar of purple Etheria crystal jutting from the rocky ground.

A lone monk knelt in a meditative trance on a large flat boulder near the monolith. His brown robes gently rose and fell with each controlled breath. A large bell hung inside a hastily constructed tower and belfry beside him. Ever since the eclipse two quinte ago, the Four Hundredth Enclave of the Azorith Monks acquired an extra duty. They now stood watch over the area's recent Etherial addition.

In the distant Zorian Harbor, the bells of the grand turine reverberated four times through the canyons. The monk stirred. He rose to his feet to begin his final inspection of the invasive crystal outcropping before they relieved him for the Kan. Tomorrow, his watch would start all over again.

He stepped down off the boulder and felt a tingle of electricity in the air. Hairs on his arms and neck stood on end. The nearby pillar shuddered and emitted a shower of blue sparks. He shot a panicked look at the alarm bell.

The monks comprising the watch detail didn't know what to expect, but surely this qualified sounding the alarm? Decision now made; the monk took off running towards the bell when the Etherial crystal erupted.

A blinding flash of blue light, originating from the center of the jutting purple crystal knocked the monk back onto the flat boulder. His head collided with the hard surface, gashing open his forehead. Blood immediately flowed over his face and soaked his dreadlocks.

The monk rose to his knees and attempted to put pressure on the wound to stop the bleeding. He recoiled in stunned horror when the first Na-Kab drones passed through the Etherial gate. Five more of the humanoid mantis creatures arrived by the time he staggered over to the bell tower.

The monk wavered and dropped to his knees, reaching for the bell's ringer cord. Tendrils of flame erupted from two of the fire creature's mouths just as his blood-stained fingers grasped the ringer. The human screamed in agony when the inferno engulfed him and the bell tower's wooden frame.

Within moments, both his blackened corpse, and the incinerated belfry toppled to the cold stone. The scorched bell clanged against the rocks before coming to a rest several feet away.

Satisfied there were no more threats, King Krol summoned the rest of the race's remaining pure blood Na-Kab through the open portal from the Fire Hive in the Land of Mists. Lines of mantis materialized, scurrying from out of the shimmering blue field enveloping the massive shard of Etheria. In the center of the exodus, two of the drones bore the cocooned savior on their backs.

The Na-Kab vanguard rushed the valley's nearby cliff face and began frantically tunneling. They would need to construct a suitable hive before the advent of the queen.

Mal felt the audience with Queen Omaris took forever, but it pleased her when Wostera's prediction turned out to be correct. By the petition of two Valorous Sisters, the

Bowmistress of Taia-Dor was now an official crew member on the *Haraka*.

While they traveled along the circular roadways of the Amarenian capital of Mostas, it amazed the Spice Rat the amount of people that recognized the duo. From the Royal Palace westward to the construction site of Air Station Mostas, wherever they went female citizens bowed and offered their greetings.

"I think they like us," Mal said, with a touch of disbelief.

"They do not give out the title of Valorous frivolously," the Bowmistress said, just before smiling and nodding at another group of grateful inhabitants.

The airship captain chuckled. "I guess not."

They could hear the sounds of carpentry and masonry before they rounded the last ring in the city's main avenues. They were erecting Air Station Mostas, already nicknamed "Big Mo," on the western shore of Zaliv Bay near the outer reaches of the city. This project excited the Amarenians, whose laborers comprised the entire workforce. The promise of increased trade and prosperity, along with the jobs already created, made for a motivated populous.

Mal could see her ship parked on the only completed landing pad. They stacked several boxes just outside each of the *Haraka's* open rear cargo hatches. Zaad stood in front of the frame of a nearby hangar still under construction. He talked with two official looking women while workers busied themselves all around.

They had just reached the stairway leading up to the pad, when they saw Kumo rapidly exit the side hatch and climb onto the roof. Zau, in a clearly agitated state, followed the humanoid spider out of the ship. The animated lioness stood beside the craft yelling up at Kumo. Mal gave a cross between a loud sigh and a groan.

"I can only fucking imagine," she said.

The EEtah greeted them first after excusing himself from his conversation with the officials.

175

"Captain, they just gave us permission to take off," Zaad said, all but ignoring Mal and flashing a wide smile at Wostera. "Moon's almost down. If we're leaving, it better be soon."

Mal loudly cleared her throat jolting the EEtah from his stare.

"Good," she said, "let's get packed up and we're gone."

The man-shark cast a brief embarrassed look at being caught. He struggled to stop staring at Wostera and found himself gazing up at Kumo.

"Sounds like a plan, Captain," he agreed.

"What's going on over there?" Mal asked.

She had followed Zaad's line-of-sight back over her shoulder to the Singa's one-sided verbal altercation with the arachnoid pilot.

"Zau's not happy with sexy spider lady's habits," he answered.

"It sounds like you don't mind," Wostera amusedly said.

"There's a reason I was keeping those two officials away from the ship," the EEtah said, with a touch of concern. "It's nothing we haven't seen before from her, but you probably want to have a look for yourself, Captain."

Mal's eyes narrowed suspiciously at the man-shark then darted over to the *Haraka*.

"Oh, for the love of the goddess," she said, in an exasperated bluster, starting for the ship.

The Bowmistress and EEtah kept up with the Spice Rat's brisk pace approaching the parked craft.

"Zau, shut the fuck up!" the captain snapped. "Kumo, get down here."

The Singa headed toward Mal complaining with every step. Kumo scurried down the outside of the hull and into the open side hatch.

"You should see what she's done!" Zau screeched when she met Mal by the rear of the craft.

"Will you please settle down," Mal asked in a calm authoritative tone.

"Look, just look!" the Singa continued shouting, pointing at the extended rear ramp and into the cargo bay of the *Haraka*. "Go look for yourself and *then* tell me to settle down!"

"Okay, Okay," the Spice Rat said, holding her hands up in front of her. "Just fucking stop yelling."

"This is gonna get us in so much trouble," Zau said, walking beside Mal. prompting her up the ramp. "Despite the fact it's disgusting!"

"Look, there's gonna be a natural adjustment period for all of us," Mal rationalized. "Let's just…"

She froze when she entered the cargo bay.

"Oh…"

The airship captain stared with her mouth open in shock. An intricate spider web now covered the entire ceiling. Two completely cocooned humanoid shapes hung horizontally from the webbing.

"What the fuck?!" Mal shook her head in astonishment.

The Singa's tirade continued unabated. "See! This is what I'm talking about!"

Mal spun aggressively to face her navigator. "Maybe you should yell a little louder. You're not drawing enough attention to us!"

Zau caught herself with a sheepish look and went silent.

"Zaad, finish loading the cargo," Mal ordered, jerking a thumb over her shoulder. "Then for the love of the goddess get that hatch closed."

The Spice Rat collected herself and glanced around the interior of her airship.

"We're leaving as soon as we get loaded," She ordered. "Zau, get to your station and plot us a course for Zor. Kumo…"

The Makari bowed her head meekly and walked to them across the walls of the cargo hold. Zau gave her a dirty look when she passed.

"Kumo, what the fuck is all this?" Mal asked, more curious than alarmed.

"Food for trip," the spider woman said, innocently, her eyes still fixed on the floor.

Wostera stared silently at the room's recent additions. She then paused and turned to the captain when one cocoon moved slightly.

"Still alive," she mouthed.

The Spice Rat shook her head in resignation, allowing for the fact their diets were vastly different. When it came down to it, this really wasn't any worse than watching Zaad tear into a carcass for dinner.

"What were you doing on top of the ship?" Mal asked, her tone softening.

The Makari finally looked up.

"Looking over ship… Getting away from her," she said, softly, indicating Zau who now had projected and was consulting her holographic map.

The captain gave a commiserative nod. "Yeah, she can really get worked up."

Just as Zaad closed the rear cargo hatch, Zau's map flared in the cockpit, causing all to turn.

The Singa cried out, covering her eye, and looking away.

"What's going on?" Mal asked, leading the others towards the front of the vessle.

Zau had regained her composure and was studying the map when the others gathered around.

Breathing hard she pointed to a distinctive trail across the glowing continents.

"Something big just gated all the way from the Land of Mists in Nocturn to the Goyan Mountains of Lumina," the navigator announced.

Mal stared at the trail slowly fading. "Any idea what it was?"

Zau shook her head. "It was probably more than just one thing. The gate remained open for an extended period."

"Okay, well, we're headed that way," Mal noted. "Who knows? Maybe we'll run into whatever it was. Kumo, fire up the engines."

Tysonn hadn't slept well lately. Then again, everyone on the project now complained of various degrees of insomnia. What worried him was Kasha suffered the worst. Every day the studious linguist worked until she literally passed out. Even then, she entered a troubled slumber, filled with tossing and turning, stressed by mumbling incoherent diatribes.

This Kan was no different. When her head hit the desk for the third time, Tysonn finally convinced her to come to bed. His justification was the book was all but translated and she should begin gearing down. As usual, an eerie restlessness overshadowed her repose.

The turine rang twelve bells and, through a sleepy haze, Tysonn sensed no movement from Kasha's side of the bed. A quick tap on the cool sheets proved her side to be empty. He grunted in frustration thinking she had once again gotten up and gone back to work until he heard her voice and caught the faint smell of ammonia.

He sat up, shook his head, and rubbed the sleep from his eyes. In his daze, he could barely make out Kasha standing at the foot of the bed.

She spoke in Tiikeri. Repeating the same phrase.

"Kas," he said, reaching over and tapping the orange Etheria gem beside the bed. "What's going on?"

When the room filled with orange light, the scribe fell silent in shock. Kasha stood in a blue nightshirt hanging loosely on her gaunt frame. She exposed the whites of her eyes, by rolling them back in her dark, recessed sockets. Her emaciated arms hung motionless at her side. Cracked, dried lips mouthed the foreign sounding words over and over.

Tysonn rushed to the edge of the bed when he saw blood dripping from her right hand.

"Kas, you're hurt!"

She remained unresponsive, constantly repeating the same Tiikeri phrase. Standing beside her, he gently shook her shoulders.

"Kas," he implored, "come on, snap out of it!"

When there was still no reaction he looked down at her hand for the wound and felt his throat tighten. A minor cut on the wrist still openly bled. He quickly elevated the hand and applied pressure.

It was when he looked around for something he could use as a bandage he saw it. Tysonn felt his pulse quicken, and a gasp stole his breath.

Lines of "X" and "I," penned in blood covered the wall above the head of the bed. Tysonn recognized they were scrawled in Kasha's own handwriting.

The enchanted forest of Zer, which encompasses the entire island of the same name, has eyes. Between the myriad of sentient animals to the clans of Zerian Rangers occupying their respective territories, almost nothing in the magical woodland went undetected.

The Kan had just set in when Eneas and Alvah, two Zerian Rangers of the Burning Tree Clan, heard the grinding sounds of a boat sliding onto the pebbly beach. The rangers cautiously approached the tree line and the source of the sound with arrows nocked.

They peered through the dense foliage and watched a humanoid lizard leap to the shore and begin directing six humans in grey tunics. Another human in cowled black robes floated above the bow of the ship. Two motionless humanoids with glowing red eyes stood behind him. The men in tunics immediately began unloading large stone disks and placing them on the beach.

Eneas and Alvah traded questioning looks. This was highly unusual. Smugglers normally would sneak up on the island during the Kan to steal the Ukko wood, its largest vital natural resource. The various clans remained on guard for these smugglers. When the smaller Alvah raised his bow to aim. Eneas held out his hand.

"No, let's see what they are doing," he said, via sign language.

The lizard-man silently supervised the humans in robes, as they stacked the stones neatly on top of each other and built a large cairn.

"A totem?" Alvah asked.

Eneas ignored the question, remaining silent while the mysterious group completed their strange task. Then, as quickly as they arrived, they returned to the boat, and it sailed off, disappearing into the fog. From what they could tell the craft was heading west hugging the coast around the northwestern tip of the island.

Both Zerian Rangers guardedly advanced from the jungle and onto the narrow beach towards the strange stack of stones at the water's edge. Eneas and Alvah lowered their weapons and alertly circled the cairn taking in every facet.

"Not stones, crystals," Eneas said, examining the composition.

"Four different kinds," Alvah added, reaching out and touching the larger purple cairn at the base.

When the ranger's hand trailed across the Etheria crystal, it pulsed and gave off blue sparks. Before Alvah could pull his hand away, the cairn gave a quick blue flash, and the Zerian disappeared.

A stunned Eneas jumped back and looked around in a panic for his companion who had vanished. Starting to back away, he felt the pull, and he dug the heels of his bare feet into the beaches' pebbles.

An unseen force dragged the ranger across the beach. He could feel the tiny stones cutting at his feet. Unsure of what else to do, he quickly raised his bow and let an arrow fly at the mysterious object. The projectile struck the edifice, but instead of bouncing off or cracking against rock, it also disappeared into the glowing crystal cairn.

Eneas gave out a futile cry before being wrested into the pulsing blue field before him. He disappeared, swallowed into the light, leaving only deep drag marks across the rocky shore to mark his ever being there.

The corvette *Krydderi* sat motionless in the thick Kan fog with sails lowered and lights extinguished. A dozen crew members were lying quietly on the deck. They nervously watched the silhouette of a mysterious ship between them and their prize a half a mile off. If they could get to it, a large haul of stolen Ukko wood lay waiting for them on the Zerian shore.

"Do you think it's a Quartermaster's interceptor?" the first mate asked, in an anxious whisper, peering over the ships low railing.

"Nah, the shapes all wrong," Captain Horvat said, quietly, raising his spyglass. "It matters little. We're pretty well screwed. Any movement gives us away and our friends on shore aren't gonna wait forever."

Horvat winced slightly behind his spyglass when a showering spark of blue light illuminated the deck of the unknown vessel. He could now see it was about the same size as his forty-foot ship and its Ukko hull kept it hovering inches above the calm water. The sudden light came from the bow where four figures now stood. He could also make out several other people milling about the aft side of the ship.

Towers of blue lightning began discharging from the shore the moment the blue sparkles would hit the deck and fade. They erupted into the sky, building into a massive blue glow from their place of origin. A rumble started and the entire fog draped eastern sky glowed blue. It built into a crescendo whipping up the sea and tossing the *Krydderi* about like a bath toy.

Horvat fought to keep his grip as the waves pitched and rolled sending some of his crew overboard. He could see the black silhouette from the backlit Ukko craft while it amazingly remained motionless, despite the turbulent condition of the surrounding sea.

The rumbling finally reached its climax with an ear-shattering roar and the entire island of Zer erupted in a massive explosion of blue light. Captain Horvat had only the briefest of moments to wince from the flash before the immense shock wave swept outward from the explosion and blew apart the Krydderi.

Zau studied the spectral blue globe projection from her navigator's chair in the bow of the *Haraka*. Her hands spread the display and adjusted the depth of field until it showed the three-dimensional outlines of a chain of landmasses in the Shallow Sea.

"We're almost over the far eastern Goyan Islands," she reported, not removing her attention from the map. "If we maintain course at this speed, we should reach Zor by the lifting of the Kan."

Mal nodded, wearily rubbing her eyes. "Sounds good, I'm gonna try to get a little sleep before we get there."

"You might as well, Cap..."

Giant bolts of blue lightning erupted in the distant western sky interrupting Zau. A massive blue explosion followed immediately after, corresponding with an eruption of light in her holographic globe. The Singa reeled from the flash.

A rumbling shock wave violently buffeted the airship, roughly jostling everyone in the cabin about except Wostera and Kumo. The bowmistress serenely opened her eyes from her meditative stance and looked warily around. Kumo fought to gain control of the craft and Zaad frantically gripped his seat while swaying back-and-forth.

"What the fuck was that?!" Mal said.

Once the turbulence passed, Zau slowly climbed back into her navigator's chair.

"That," she gasped, frenziedly panting, "was the biggest Flavian displacement I've ever seen or felt. Something enormous just gated across the Middle Realms."

"Something that big should have left a trail anyone could follow," she said.

All eyes were on the Singa when she lifted her patch and projected the globe once more. They could plainly see the massive spot slowly fading on the surface. It left a trail which streamed off the orb and into space.

"It originated in the central western Goyan Islands," Zau said, studying the ghostly features.

"Can you be more specific?" Mal asked, following Zau's outstretched finger.

Using both hands the Singa brought the Western Spice Islands closer.

"It's this one," she said, pointing to the outline of a single large island continent. "What island is this?"

"That's the island of Zer," Mal said, nervously running her hand through her hair. "So, you're saying something big just transported out of the enchanted forest of Zer into the Middle Realms?"

"No, Captain, the entire island transported."

The Spice Rat stared blankly not entirely sure she heard correctly. "The whole fucking thing?"

Zau nodded grimly. A moment of stunned silence descended on the cabin of the *Haraka*.

"Where did it go?" Wostera finally asked, moving toward the front of the craft.

The navigator motioned with her hands and collapsed the globe into a flattened sphere. The trail coursed off the bottom of their plane and around several other spheres until it finally connected with one. Converting the new sphere into a globe, Zau sighed in recognition.

"The Great Desert Plane," she answered.

"Fog," Kumo announced from behind the wheel.

The *Haraka* crossed over the border of the Ocean Deep to the Goyan Rise. They watched out the windshield as the Kan fog of the Shallow Sea swallowed the airship.

Moments later, they all heard a doleful moaning. It seemed to come from the islands ahead. The pervasive sound drifted through the hull of the speeding craft causing everyone to peer at each other uneasily.

"It sounds like a woman crying," Zaad said.

Mal stared questioningly at her navigator "Can you follow that trail?"

Zau nodded, swiping through the spheres to plot a course.

"All right then," the Spice Rat said, "find us a portal and let's go check it out."

Before Captain Horvat opened his eyes, he felt the course pebbly beach beneath his back and the warm sun on his face. The coolness of the receding Kan fog against his wet clothes caused him to shiver. He tested moving his legs and then his arms. His body felt sore but otherwise unharmed.

When he finally sat up and looked around, he could see he was on an expanse of beach littered with his ship's debris. His clothing was in tatters and his boots gone. Rising to his feet, he stared out at the calm waters of the Shallow Sea. In the distance he could make out sails heading his way.

An omnipresent keening wafted across the beach from the islands interior and then back out to sea, all but drowning out the gentle lapping of the waves only five feet from him.

Turning inland to locate the origin of the mournful feminine wailing, the seasoned Spice Rat captain's mouth opened to scream, but nothing came out. Stumbling forward, he rubbed his eyes then looked again, but the scene had not changed. The enchanted forest of Zer had vanished.

Where once grew a lush, triple-canopy jungle, there now remained only a shallow indentation of rocky soil. The barren landscape extended up through the central mountain range, stripping away all foliage and life forms.

Horvat dropped to his knees in shock. He stared incredulously at the devastation, all the while wincing at the lamentations from beyond the mountains.

ACT TWO

Tannimore Burning

It had started deep in the Kan. Those who were awake recalled a giant tremor and the western, fog laden sky glowing blue. Buildings shuddered and unsecured items tumbled about, jolting many from their slumber.

The quaking and accompanying azure hue in the sky didn't last for long. The ubiquitous keening however, continued unabated and could be heard across the thirteen continents and island chains making up the Goyan Islands. All across Lumina's central lands, sensitives and psychics wept uncontrollably as a deep sense of despair permeated the very fabric of society.

When the sea fog receded from the High Holy City of Zor, a concerned populous now ventured outside to survey the extent of the destruction. Moving about the city, they thankfully considered the relatively minor damage. Everyone's attention now fixated on the constant lamentation carried on the winds.

With nervous glances skyward, everyone attempted to get on with the business of everyday life. However, all felt something profound had changed. Things were not right in Lumina's seat of humanity.

The Zorian High Council called for an emergency assembly. Head clerics of the major religions and Marassas from the university attended the summit. All had an opinion on the strange events which had transpired. A hail of voices echoed across the tiers of seats in the massive circular chamber. The chairman's gavel rapped loudly to restore order. It took an extended period of pounding before the voices settled.

"You may continue Learned One," the chairman said to the red robed individual standing alone in the circle below.

The attention of the attendees returned to the Head Marassa who stared upwards and around the tiered rows, addressing the crowd in a calm, authoritative voice.

"While earthquakes are not common, they have been recorded from time to time," he began. "I find no reason for panic at this juncture…"

"What about all the damn wailing going on out there?!" a panicked voice interrupted from somewhere in the audience's middle tiers.

"Ya can't get away from it," a member of the merchant's council angrily added, rising to his feet.

Immediately others began calling out, their outbursts blanketed in concern.

"There are fishing boats missing…"

"Windmills to the north of town are damaged…"

"Bodies are washing ashore to the north of the city…"

The forum descended into chaos once again.

Seated by an exit in the first tier, Kesis, High Priest of the Earth God Toma, tensely watched the frightened bickering. His headful of supple waist length tree sprigs swayed over his naked body while turning back and forth trying to follow the chaotic conversations over the chairman's frantic gaveling. He and his priests felt not only the physical aftereffects but also sensed a profound disruption in the very foundations of earth magic.

Startled cries suddenly replaced the ruckus debate when the floor rumbled and cracked. The circular stage broke apart into minuscule chunks forcing the addressing Marassa to flee. Some terrified delegates panicked and rushed for the doors screaming past Kesis who was now on his feet.

An overwhelming feeling of uneasiness swept over Kesis. The earth shaman felt what was coming. Waves of vengeful rage swept upward from the splintering floor. The Toma cleric's stomach knotted up and his hands trembled. He closed his eyes, dropped to his knees, and reverently raised his arms above his head.

Kesis watched the pulverized floor rise and take shape with a thunderous resonance. Members who didn't flee watched a column of pebble-sized marble merge with the earth below it and form into a thirty-foot-tall humanoid earth demigod rooted in the soil. It clenched its verdant fists and the plain features of its face contorted in rage. Its deep, thunderous roar replaced the earth shaking quakes of its arrival, reverberating through the forum and silencing the frightened participants.

Stunned whimpers rose when the rocky gargantuan slowly turned around and surveyed the mostly human crowd. It halted when it faced the Twelve Elders of Zor seated along the top tier in the northern stands.

"MY LADY WEEPS BECAUSE OF *YOU*!" it bellowed, pointing a jagged green finger at the quivering group of six men and six women. "YOU STOLE HER PRECIOUS FOREST AND CHILDREN!"

"Oh, great and powerful Elmos," Kesis said, head bowed. "These are not the ones responsible for the transgression."

The earth demigod glared down at the kneeling Toma cleric and scowled.

"This abominable act reeks with the stench of humanity."

"Oh Elmos, what are we to do?" Kesis reverently beseeched, prostrating himself.

189

The demi-god gave a frustrated snarl and addressed the entire forum.

"My lady Lardia is a kind, benevolent goddess," it declared. "She is incapable of revenge. That is what she has *me* for. *You* will find the ones responsible. *You* will bring them to me and *you* will see that the children of Lardia are returned."

"But great Elmos…" Kesis implored.

"You *will* do this or I shall topple this city into rubble that will return to the earth, never to be rebuilt, and your kind shall never harvest the Ukko again."

The audience sat in stunned silence while, without another word, the giant creature reverted into a formless tower of rock and soil. It teetered for a moment before crashing to the ground, showering all in a thick, choking blanket of dust.

Rising above the windy, snow-covered peaks of Atar Island, the *Drakin* pulled away from the Valdurian research station of Landagar.

"I had no idea this place was here," Demetrius said, watching a massive stationary balloon slip by the port side. The airship pilot marveled at the line of floating fortresses, tethered on either side of the remote high valley. Passing the last station, he could see through an open hangar door they were about to launch a small scout ship.

"That's the way we like it," Okawa said, studying their newly received orders. "I'm just sorry we didn't have time to get all the improvements made."

"Hey, they got the fire damage taken care of," he said. "I'm a happy guy."

The Valdurian operative smiled at the pilot's sensitive good nature.

"Are you always a glass half full kinda person?"

"Unless it comes to ordering another round of drinks," the pilot quipped.

Without looking up, Okawa chuckled and shook her head. Demetrius glanced up at a small wooden rectangle with several Etheria disks inset on the ceiling between the seats.

"The new panel up there is pretty nifty."

"It should make things a little easier for you," Okawa said, turning to the second page. "Especially the Ethericom."

"What's the range on that thing?" Demetrius asked, glancing up at the milk white disk with blue striations.

"It really doesn't have a range," Okawa explained. "You just touch it and think about with whom you want to talk. If they're near any Larimar Etheria Crystal, you can communicate. It also acts as a translator for anyone in the cabin or anywhere in the ship's vicinity."

"Slick!" the pilot complimented.

When they reached the far western edge of the mountain range Demetrius slowed the craft until it just hovered. Stretched out before them were rolling foothills, which gave way to plains, and finally the blue of the Shallow Sea.

"Okay, where to?"

Okawa stopped reading and peered up. She furrowed her brow. Her normally twinkling green eyes became mere slits and her full lips drew into a pout.

"There's been an incident at the Forum in Zor," she said, grimly. "We're to make a course towards the Island of Zer, check on things, and report back."

"The island with the Ukko wood forest," Demetrius confirmed.

"I hope so."

Demetrius scrunched his face in uncertainty.

191

"What does that mean?"

"The orders say, 'best possible speed,'" Okawa announced, holding up the two pieces of paper.

"Okay, okay," Demetrius agreed. "Hold on."

Throwing two levers and pulling back on the stick, the *Drakin* shot upward so abruptly it caused Okawa to gasp.

"Best possible speed," the pilot said, grinning.

The seasoned agent stared out at the rapidly approaching upper atmosphere and looked a bit green. Demetrius kept on smirking when the airship rocketed back downward into the skies over the Island of Zer.

"Wow that was fast," she said, after catching her breath.

"Best possible speed," he said, backing off the throttle and tossing her a mischievously raised eyebrow.

"I believe you did that on purpose!" she proclaimed, in an amused tone.

Demetrius comically feigned shock. "Me?!"

Reaching over, she caressed his cheek and gave a coy smile.

"Yes, *you*, Mister Skirting-the-Upwinds."

Demetrius returned the smile, and the two leaned in toward each other. With eyes closed and heads tilted, their lips brushed when Okawa stopped. Leaning back, she opened her eyes, her look turning inquisitive.

"Wait, what's that noise?" she asked, looking around.

Demetrius sighed in frustration, opened his eyes, and listened. "It sounds like... crying."

"*Demetrius!*" Okawa called out, staring in disbelief at the island below.

The airship was close enough now to get a good look at the landscape. Demetrius gasped in shock when he saw the hilly terrain now devoid of any life, plant or animal. The stark, barren island baking in the relentless Lumina sun resembled a desert more than a tropical isle.

"What the heck happened to the gosh darn forest?"

A stunned Okawa could only stare silently at the desolation while the sorrowful keening filled the cabin. Without taking her eyes off the spectacle on the ground, the Valdurian agent slowly reached up to the newly installed panel and found the multicolored Ethericom crystal.

"Confirmation positive, the forest is gone," she said, her tone hollow.

"Understood," came Joc' Valdur's voice in both of their heads. "We'll need a full briefing upon your return."

"Very well," she said, signing off.

Demetrius took the *Drakin* down to a low altitude and began a slow circle of the island. When the ship neared the Kerin Pass in the central mountain range, the doleful weeping grew louder.

"Over there," Okawa said, pointing to the middle of the mountainous divide.

The pilot banked the ship off to port and entered the wide ravine once known as the neutral meeting place for the many Zerian Clans. There, in the dead center of the desolate pass, stood a giant tree with all of its green foliage intact. Its limbs were drooping, and it occasionally shuddered. With each quiver, leaves tumbled to the ground. She watched them fall, noting that the ones striking the exposed roots disappeared in tiny blue sparks. The volume of the keening increased the closer they got to the arboreal aberration.

"Let's be careful," the agent advised, while rapidly approaching.

When the craft slowed, Okawa heard a sniffle and glanced over at Demetrius, who was openly weeping.

"You okay?"

Demetrius shook his head. "I... I don't know. I just feel like I'm being bombarded by wave after wave of sadness and grief. I can't seem to stop crying."

"See if you can get us closer," she said, to help him focus.

Nodding, he took the ship up. Okawa stared at the massive tree trunk while they ascended and she could swear the intricate wooden knots facing the pass formed a woman's face. The airship finally reached the tree's crown and circled.

"How in the name of the empire did this lone tree not get affected?" Okawa thought out-loud.

A tearful Demetrius shook his head and said nothing.

"All right, we've seen enough here," she said. "Let's check out the rest of the island."

When the *Drakin* exited the pass on the north side of the island, the pilot's tears slowly stopped. The craft turned east and continued along a coastline dotted with shipwrecks and debris. The scene remained much the same with the rest of the bleak land mass.

When Okawa saw what appeared to be a lone mound of stacked stones on the northwestern beach. She sat forward and pointed.

"Take her down," she asked. "I want to get a look at that."

"It sure looks out of place," the pilot noted, starting his descent.

"It also looks familiar," the Valdurian said, suspiciously.

Demetrius set the craft down on the rocky shore and both disembarked. Okawa discovered they constructed the mound from large disks of purple Etheria crystals neatly stacked on top of each other. The two warily circled the strange cairn while the waves gently lapped around its base.

Okawa suddenly stopped when a wave of recognition swept over her. She scowled, watching an ever-curious Demetrius step up for a closer look.

"Don't touch it," she snapped.

The pilot immediately raised his hands and backed away.

"I've seen these before," she announced in a resolute tone. "I'm willing to bet there are three more of these somewhere around the island."

Demetrius stared quizzically but remained silent.

"Come on, I know who's behind this," Okawa said, somberly, starting back to the ship.

Rafel's eyes narrowed, and he nodded to the five Zorian Guards flanking him in the alley. Across the narrow, refuse littered street, three humans and a Bailian were shaking down a street vendor. The old pottery merchant's eyes widened with fear while one human held him by the front of his stained shirt, shaking him violently. One of the other humans rifled through the merchant's simple cash box while the other stood look-out.

The Bailian, who was obviously the leader, stood off to the side. Rafel could hear him admonishing the terrified potter in a thick accent about being late in his protection payment, just over the sound of the mysterious weeping coursing across the city.

Rafel had to admit, Three Fingered Jak's tip paid off. He turned out to be quite the asset in the Seven Sisters slums.

The Bailian was an ex-Valdurian Marine from Immor-Onn who went by the name Stro-Bek. Larger than most of his race, his badly scarred face betrayed a violent past. Word on the street claimed he had been part of the queen's guards before having to flee in disgrace. Now in Zor, he had committed the most heinous criminal act decreed by the High Holy City, establishing a gang.

"I want the Bailian alive," he said, in a whisper, not taking his eyes off the violent scene before him.

Seeing they had their money, the man holding the shop keeper released him with a shove, sending him back into a shelf full of ceramics and knocking several to the ground. The Bailian gave out a last threat before they turned to leave.

As they stepped out into the street, three crossbow bolts found their mark with a series of rapid sequential thumps and the humans toppled to the cobblestones, gripping their wounds. Their faces betrayed surprise and shock.

Rafel led the guards out of the alley. The Bailian froze when he saw the weapons trained on him. The gangster holding the merchant's money still lived and gurgling something unintelligible. Rafel stood over him and peered down with a cold, merciless stare.

He then turned his cold-blooded glare on Stro-Bek, while casually raising his leg and driving the heel of his boot into the dying man's face. The spymaster never broke with the Bailian's eye contact while the criminal's head burst like a ripe melon, showering the street with gore.

Rafel calmly pried the stolen coins from the mutilated thug's death grip. He walked back over to the horrified merchant, gave a conciliatory smile, and placed the coins on the table. He then turned his attention back to Stro-Bek.

"Bring him," he ordered.

The guards seized the stunned Bailian and bound his hands behind him. A rapid flick of the knife shredded his clothing. Rafel tossed a noose around his neck and led him naked through the crowded streets, serving as a warning to any criminals who contemplated trying to organize.

The foreboding procession snaked across town to Judgment Square. Panic showed in Stro-Bek's eyes when he saw the variety of torture devices littering the courtyard. He then visibly relaxed when they bypassed the implements of pain and entered one of the smaller buildings. His momentary relief ended when the door slammed behind him and the bolt slid into place with a resounding clack.

The room was empty of furniture and stark. A single wide table sat in the center of the windowless room. Reeking of stale blood and bodily fluids, the tabletop was stained an ominous shade of red.

Three guards muscled him onto the table and bound him to it spread eagle. The Bailian gang leader was now looking around with wide-eyed dread.

"I... I..." Stro-Bek stammered.

Rafel shook his head and held his forefinger over his lips. Walking the length of the table, he delicately ran his hand over the nude Bailian's body. He had never seen a naked Bailian before. His gaze and fingers lingered at his corkscrew penis, which was now all but shriveled up into his groin.

Interesting, he mused to himself.

"You will have your chance to talk soon," he softly said, leaning in close to his ear. "I would suggest you make it substantive."

He nodded at one guard who left, and returned shortly after, carrying a small covered pail, and set it down next to the table.

Rafel silently acknowledged the delivery, then returned his attention to the prisoner.

"Do they call you Stro-Bek?" he asked.

The Bailian was wide-eyed in fear but remained silent. Rafel gave a weary sigh.

"Did they assign you to Queen Shula's protection detail?"

Stro-Bek locked a terrorized gaze on the Zorian spymaster, his lips tautly closed. Rafel reached down and picked up the pail by the handle, removing the top.

"I see we will have to do this the hard way," he said, just before emptying the container's contents down the length of the table about a foot from the Bailian.

The hardened criminal cried out in a panic upon seeing two dozen oval shaped creatures, each about an inch and a half in diameter. The brown vermin showed no discernible features, and fine hairs lined their edges.

"We call these little fellas, Piling," Rafel said. "They like to congregate around bone yards, or really wherever you'd find dead things."

The hairs on the Piling started fluttering wildly, adjusting to their new environment. Stro-Bek uncomfortably writhed on the table.

"Don't worry, they'll find you any moment now," the spymaster assured.

The small brown ovals began undulating slowly across the table towards the terrified Bailian.

"Ah, there we are," he said.

"You see, they love to eat dead skin," Rafel said, the creatures now mere inches from naked blue flesh. "I've been told they smell it through those cute little hairs."

Stro-Bek whimpered and unsuccessfully strained at his bonds, eyes bulging at the imminent threat crawling toward him. He cried out and flinched violently when they began crawling onto him. His cries turned into shrieks of horror and revulsion when the Pilings slowly trekked across his body.

When there was none of the expected pain, his cries died out and uncertainty consumed him. The little brown creatures gave off a gentle brushing sensation which pleasantly tingled. Rafel stepped next to the table, smiling.

"I find it highly ironic that the elite of our city find it fashionable of late to use these rather macabre little things in their beauty regiments," the spymaster said, with a shallow shrug. "They say it gives them a youthful glow."

Stro-Bek's eyes nervously darted about while the small oval creatures slowly crept across his body. He winced as one slogged its way across his forehead. When he felt one slide between his thighs, he forcefully jerked his legs against the restraints.

"How then does this relate to our situation, you might wonder?" Rafel asked. "You see, these fascinating creatures have a most *unusual* defense mechanism. Allow me to demonstrate."

Reaching over, Rafel gently placed a finger into one of the Pilings resting on Stro-Bek's abdomen. The Bailian wrenched violently upward and shrieked in pain when hundreds of minuscule hairs, once so soothing, extended into sharp points and tunneled into his flesh. Blood immediately flowed from under the tiny burrowing creature.

Rafel released his pressure on the Piling. The grinding immediately ceased and the brown oval undulated in the bloody wound. The spymaster resumed his sadistic smile.

"Now that we understand each other," he asked, "what say you and I have a chat?"

The Bailian panted heavily while the residual agony still burned in the small raw, bleeding circle on his belly. When he still refused to speak, Rafel reached over and touched a Piling on his leg and held it down. The frightened creature burrowed furiously. Once again Stro-Bek thrashed about screaming and cursing. Rafel released it after it had buried itself half an inch into the meat of his thigh.

The spymaster leaned over and peered curiously at the creature in the oozing cavity.

"It will remain there until it thinks the danger has past..."

A loud banging on the door disrupted Rafel's soliloquy. When a guard opened it, the omnipresent keening drifted inside as they passed a message through.

"Now that I have your attention," Rafel said, returning his attention to his captive. "I would like to discuss queen Shula's spymaster. I believe her name is Kai."

"Sir, it's labeled important," the guard interrupted, handing him the folded piece of paper.

The spymaster tersely snatched the note from the intimidated guard's hand and read it.

"Well, it appears our little chat must wait," he said, peering contemptuously down at the Bailian. "There seems to have been a bit of a fracas over at the forum just now."

Rafel paused in the doorway before leaving.

"Don't go anywhere, I'll be right back.

Che-At hated virtually everything about this place, but especially the smell. Humans had an odor about them and their surroundings the Singa found distasteful. The stench of the one following her was almost overwhelming. The man reeked of cooked meat and garlic, and his telltale scent had assaulted her senses everywhere she went throughout the City of Zor.

She had arrived three cycles ago and, under her cover, attempted to contact the Language Arts Department at the University of Marassa. Her story seemed reasonable enough. They had commissioned her to offer her services in developing a translation dictionary for the mawl family of languages.

She didn't count on the whole Language Department being under lockdown. Untimely as it may seem, the heightened security made her nearly certain this was where they kept the book. Unfortunately, now she was under suspicion and her odoriferous companion was never far away, always watching.

The Kan fog had rolled in several cycles ago, and by the time the grand turine in the harbor rang six bells, the cloudy dampness covered the entire city.

The Singa nonchalantly approached the Kan food vendor she had patronized her entire stay here. Initially it surprised him when she requested her skewer uncooked, but now he always had one ready for her.

Holding her breath against the affluent odor of his cooking meat, Che-At held up two fingers and then produced two silver coins, holding them aloft. The grizzled street vendor nodded and grabbed two skewers of massive chunks of red meat. As they passed, she performed a rapid, graceful exchange with the merchant without losing her pace.

She ate while she walked, moving steadily away from the Kampo Plat and the University of Marassa, which comprised most of it. After passing well into the neighboring Shimol

Plat, she stopped. The streets were nearly vacant, and she heard her pursuer step behind a nearby wall.

In a grandiose flair she stripped away the last chunk of meat, then licked the sharpened hardwood skewers clean. With a sly grin, she deftly slipped the two-foot long spikes into her cloak before continuing on.

They long ago converted most of the buildings in the city from their primitive wood beginnings, rebuilding them out of stone. Some, for whatever reason, kept their wooden, old world flair. When she reached the first clapboard structure bordering an adjacent alley, she abruptly changed course, slipping into the narrow passage.

In a single graceful motion, she leapt straight up, extended her claws, and latched onto the side of the building. Quickly shimmying up to the roof, she peered over the side. The fog was so thick she didn't see him enter the alley, but she smelled him. When she heard his rapid footsteps following her presumed path, she stood and began making her way back to the university by rooftop.

When she finally entered the university complex, the distance between buildings made it necessary to return to the ground level. Keeping to the edifice's shadows, she moved towards the Language Arts Department.

The towering form of the EEtah sentry guarding the entrance loomed just ahead, and she slipped into a recessed doorway instead. She peeked out and scanned the area. Sniffing furiously, she made an olfactory note of the EEtah's position.

A lone light burned from a window at the far end of the building on the second floor. She flanked the sentry by slipping through the tree lined Jezik Square, then flattened herself against the building just below the window. The rough stone fascia of the walls made for an easy climb, and she cautiously looked inside.

The room was well lit. An emaciated female scribbled furiously on a chalk board while talking. Occasionally, she would turn to a young human male with long brown hair pulled back into a ponytail. He folded his arms in front of him while he listened to the animated female who pointed to groupings of figures on the board.

"We're really close to a breakthrough." She heard the woman say through the glass.

"Kas, we're already done," the man said, reaching out to the female. "You really need to start backing off…"

This seemed to irritate the female who brushed away the man's hands.

"Yes, but we still don't know what it means!" she screamed, pounding on the board with her open palm. "I have to know…" her voice lowered and trailed off.

Che-At scanned the room, and she marveled at her good fortune. The book she hunted laid open on the room's solitary desk. An older Bailian sat with his back to the desk, leaning forward on his cane and following the argument. She noted he stayed within arm's length of the book and kept it in the corner of his eye at all times.

The Bailian sat up suddenly and cocked his head. He turned to the window as if he sensed something, and the two locked eyes for the briefest instant before she pulled her head back out of sight.

When he bolted from his seat, the Singa leapt to the ground. The thud of her landing alerted the EEtah. It growled, unsheathed its Yudon harpoon, and rapidly moved her way.

She sprinted in the opposite direction, disappearing into the fog, just as Cha-Rod threw open the windows and peered outward. Finding nothing, the Bailian locked the window while the EEtah's alarm whistle cut into the night.

Tysonn studied the Bailian's concerned face when Kasha returned to furiously scribbling and erasing as if nothing had happened.

"What was it?" the scribe asked, a touch of panic in his voice.

"There was someone at the window."
Tysonn began looking nervously around the room.
"Did you see who it was?" he asked.
Cha-Rod shook his head. "Only that it wasn't human."

The top of the dune exploded in a massive blast of powdered white sand and the *Haraka* burst forth into a gray featureless sky over a seemingly endless expanse of sand extending to the horizon.

"I'd like to say I'm getting used to this, but I'd be lying," Mal said, as Kumo leveled the airship off and circled.

Mal turned in her seat. "Is everybody all right?"

A round of affirmatives echoed through the cabin.

"What exactly are we looking for, Captain?" Zaad asked, getting out of his seat, and stretching.

Mal cast an inquiring glance over to Zau.

"Not sure," the Singa replied, "but whatever it is, it's immense."

"Then it shouldn't be hard to spot," the EEtah said.

Zaad made his way to the front of the ship. He paused at the ship's wheel and gave Kumo a salacious grin. She briefly met his gaze, then shyly looked away. Wostera opened her eyes and gracefully rose from her meditative kneeling position. She left her armaments on the floor and joined the EEtah at the helm.

Zau lifted her eye patch, and the globe projected out in front of her. She attentively traced a faint trail across its surface with her forefinger then pointed out the windshield.

"That way, beyond those dunes, and we're not far," she declared.

"Okay Kumo, get us there." Mal ordered.

"Yes, Captain," came the meek reply.

Everyone murmured when they saw treetops peek over the entire horizon line.

"What the fuck," Mal muttered in wonder. "Kumo take us up two hundred more feet."

The *Haraka* steadily climbed to four hundred feet rapidly approaching the arboreal anomaly. When the displaced forest finally came into full view, a collective gasp ran through the cabin.

The lush tropical greenery starkly contrasted against the barren white sand surrounding it. All across the lush vegetation were circular recesses where the trees had fallen in on themselves. Flocks of birds circled and dove above the forest canopy.

Mal blinked in disbelief. "The entire island, that's the entire fucking island!"

"What in the name of the goddess could do this?" Wostera asked.

"If it was a Flavian glitch, this could be as catastrophic as Konaleeta," Zau said, lowering her patch. "If someone or something caused it…"

"They just cornered the market on Ukko wood," Mal said, finishing the thought.

"What about the inhabitants?" Zaad asked.

"Good question," the Spice Rat acknowledged. "Take us down for a closer look, Kumo."

While the airship descended, a lone mantis figure raced along the sand just outside the forest's edge.

"So, what is this?" Zau asked, with a cock of her head.

"Kinda looks like a Do-Tarr," Zaad said, drawing closer.

The creature suddenly halted, kicking up a small cloud of sand which briefly obscured it. A strand of fire erupted from out of the sand cloud and narrowly missed the ship. They could feel its wave of intense heat from inside the cabin. The blast burned so hot, it crystallized the sand in the cloud it emanated from, causing it to rain tiny shards of glass around the lone Na-Kab.

"Holy fuck!" Mal bellowed. "Everybody grab onto something. Kumo, evasive action!"

"Yes, Captain," the Makari said, slightly more forcefully.

Mal watched the creature open its mandibles. The inside of its mouth and throat glowed red.

"Right fucking now, people!" she cried.

Zaad dove for his chair just when the *Haraka* did a sudden corkscrew turn hard to starboard and narrowly avoided another burst of flame. Kumo spread out her six legs and hung on, maneuvering the ship's wheel with her hands. Wostera continued to stand between the two command chairs, unaffected by the pitching of the craft.

The Na-Kab got off two more blasts, one of which passed within inches of the windshield as the *Haraka* performed evasive maneuvers.

"Captain, we cannot continue this," Wostera said, looking down at Mal. "eventually that thing will hit us."

"We can't use the ballistas while were fucking around in the air!" Mal yelled.

There was an eerie, yet serene calmness about the Amarenian.

"Captain, allow me," she offered.

"Allow you what?!" Mal asked, when the ship did another erratic maneuver causing her to lurch in her chair.

"Just open that side hatch," the bowmistress replied.

Wostera picked up her bow and arrow heading towards the stern of the ship.

"What the fuck are you talking about?!" Mal asked.

Kumo jerked on the wheel and the craft pitched violently again, while the windshield lit up from another near miss.

Wostera calmly walked over to the side hatch and extended her free hand. The lever operating the door moved on its own accord and the side hatch dropped. Instantly hot torrential winds filled the interior of the cabin.

"Wostera!" Mal screamed over the howling gusts.

The Amarenian stepped out of the ship and onto the side hatch, now acting as a horizontal platform.

"Captain?" Kumo shouted in confusion.

"Don't stop or we're toast," Mal said, watching the creature prepare for another blast.

The ship performed a steep barrel roll upward while Wostera stood calmly on the ramp, garments fluttering furiously, drawing her bow and aiming. The arrow struck the sand just beside the Na-Kab. It kicked up a minor explosion before disappearing in a blue spark. This caused the mantis creature to flinch, sending the next streamer of fire harmlessly in the other direction.

Her arrow reappeared in Wostera's extended hand with another blue flash. After the ship performed another quick loop, she carefully aimed again. The next fire blast coursed just below her feet. Heat waves rolled over the Amarenian, igniting the hem of her robes.

She ignored the flames and let the arrow fly. The Flavian projectile struck the Na-Kab mid thorax, causing its exoskeleton to explode. It dropped and writhed about while a shower of molten body fluids fused the surrounding sand.

A cheer went up inside the cabin and the airship resumed a stable flight path.

Out on the extended ramp, the fire traveled up Wostera's robes as she lowered her bow. The arrow returned to her hand, and she transferred it to her bow hand. Looking down at the burning garment, she extended her open hand. Concentrating deeply, she slowly closed it. When the extremity tightened into a fist, the flame gradually went out.

Wostera stepped back into the ship. Kumo closed the hatch behind her and the howling of the wind ceased, replaced by an awed silence.

"Damn, that was pretty good bow lady!" Zaad said.

Wostera smiled sweetly at the man-shark. "Thank you Zaad."

"Damn right, that *was* pretty good!" Mal said, getting to her feet. "How the fuck did you do that?"

"When aligned with the forces of the multiverse many things seemingly impossible, are not only possible, but inevitable," she said, setting down her bow and arrow on the floor precisely where they had rested before.

"That was damn good flying," Mal said, turning her attention to the Makari at the wheel.

"It sure was," Zaad chimed in with a love-struck gaze at the pilot.

A smile crossed Kumo's face, and she peered reverently downward.

"Thank you," she said, in a low, shy voice.

Mal shook her head and sighed. "Well, so much for the warm welcome. Let's get down there and see what the fuck's going on."

Kumo brought the *Haraka* down ten feet away from the Na-Kab's body and hovered inches above the soft, white ground as all but the Makari exited. The creature's blood fused the sand surrounding the still warm corpse into a solid sheet of glass. The group's feet clicked across the hard surface, walking around the dead humanoid mantis.

"Well it sure isn't a Do-Tarr," Zaad said, examining the interconnected plates of exoskeleton.

"It appears we have company," Wostera said, directing everyone's attention to the dense foliage ten yards away.

Three human males slowly emerged from behind the trees. They were nude with wild, unkempt hair and black and distinctive green geometric patterns streaking their pale bodies. They each brandished crude bows and nocked arrows in a cautious approach. The expressions on their faces conveyed a mix of fear and relief.

Mal looked up from the dead Na-Kab and watched them slowly make their way over to them.

"Maybe these people know what the fuck happened,"

Morning arrived as it always did, heralded by seventeen bells from the grand turine. The brutal interrogation had taken the entire Kan. This Bailian had been a tough one.

Rafel felt a great sense of accomplishment as he collected the Pilings off Stro-Bek's corpse. The Zorian spymaster always took great pleasure in making people talk. It thrilled him to make them break a sacred vow of secrecy, usually taken on their mother's life.

Putting away the last of the sand dollar sized creatures, he examined the remains of the Bailian's body. The Pilings had completely stripped it of skin. He marveled at the resilience of his victim. But, in the end, they all talked.

He was now in possession of information about the assassin known as Kai. Not only was she the Bailian spymaster to the queen, but the human was also a Member of the Hand of the Wind, Priestess of Orad the Air Goddess of Death, and owner of The Whispering Zephyr Inn.

As he suspected before, the task would not be easy, but he would avenge Hoyt.

The Kan rapidly approached and a state of shock and confusion spread through the Zorian Forum. Scribes, assistants, and soldiers moved in and out of offices and meeting rooms, scurrying furiously down the many hallways on some superior's errand.

Then, there was the ever-present wailing that wafted across the city. It had not abated once during the day and showed no signs of stopping.

In a side room meeting of the forum, Okawa and Demetrius stood at the head of a long, polished table addressing four grim-faced men. Zekoff and Rafel sat across from Joc' Valdur and Pierce Calden, all stared apprehensively at the duo.

"The forest and its inhabitants have disappeared," Okawa emphatically stated, "all but one tree in the middle of the island. Apparently, this is where the wailing originates."

A collective groan went up from the table at the news and its potential consequences. Zekoff reached into his jacket pocket and retrieved his pipe.

"Any idea how they accomplished this and by whom?" he asked.

Okawa leaned in on the table, her face scrunched into a scowl. "I know who, and how. Why, not so much."

"Don't be shy, Captain," Pierce Calden said, desperately.

"The *who* is our old friend, Lord Stryder Aramos," she said. "He's hooked up with some humanoid lizard who's an obvious Etheria mage. Which brings us to *how*. It appears they used combinations of large Etheria crystals to teleport the entire surface of the island to somewhere else."

"How do you know this?" Rafel asked, sitting back in his chair, obviously unconvinced.

"I witnessed it being tested in the Aramos compound several cycles ago," Okawa said, in confident defiance. "And it gets worse, he travels with two humanoid mantis creatures that can breathe fire and a security detail of nine Aramos Black Talons."

"Na-Kab," Demetrius spoke up. "They're called Na-Kab."

All attention turned to the venturesome young pilot.

"You know of these creatures?" Zekoff asked, pulling the pipe out of his mouth.

"By reputation only," Demetrius answered. "Their fire hive is under the eastern Land of Mists by Mount Natal which is an active volcano. I briefly dealt with their less fiery mantis cousins, the Do-Tarr."

"If what you say is true," Rafel asked, eyebrow raised and leaning forward in his chair, "why in the name of the gods would a lord of House Aramos *do* such a thing? It makes little sense."

Okawa's attention locked onto the doubting spymaster.

"Captain," she snapped, "this is your second time calling my observations into question. Have I given you reason to doubt my abilities?"

A tense moment passed while the two traded contentious stares. Joc' Valdur finally spoke up, attempting to break the tension.

"It doesn't really matter what the motive is, *if any*," he insisted. "The sudden lack of Ukko wood will have a *devastating* effect on Houses Calden and Valdur."

The Valdurian diplomat paused and stared inquisitively at his operative.

"You're certain Stryder Aramos is behind this?" he asked.

"I'd bet my pension on it," Okawa answered.

"That's all I need to know," Joc' said, confidently, eying the men around the table.

"What about the forest?" Pierce Calden interjected. "What about the wood? Our navy depends on that wood!"

"As does House Valdur's air service," Joc' quickly countered. "I have a feeling if we find Lord Aramos, we'll discover what happened to the wood."

"Then, we still have that beast which interrupted the forum this morning," Zekoff said, between puffing on his pipe. "What did that priest call him?"

"Elmos, sir," Rafel said, continuing to stare angrily at Okawa.

"The witness that communicated with that thing," the colonel asked, "he was a cleric of that fertility god Toma, right?"

"Uh, yes sir," the spymaster answered.

Zekoff nodded, while puffing and sending columns of evergreen scented tobacco into the air.

"Let's start there," he suggested, looking over at Joc' who gave a subtle gesture of agreement. "The Temple of Toma is located in the city's eastern agricultural fields. It is my understanding that these clerics have had a very direct hand in the interaction between the island of Zer and the rest of the Annigan for quite a few grands. A visit might be in order. If nothing else, to gain some perspective on the background of our situation."

In the distance, over the constant lamenting moan, the grand turine in the Zorian harbor struck six, announcing the beginning of the Kan. All in the room noted the sound.

"We'll visit them in the morning sir," Okawa confirmed with a nod.

"We?" Demetrius innocently questioned.

Okawa slipped him a sly, amused glance. "What? You know you were coming."

Demetrius deflated and shook his head. "I guess..."

"Okay, tomorrow," Joc' agreed, grinning at the couple's dynamic. "For now, get some rest."

He turned his attention back to Rafel and the group.

"How easy is it going to be finding Lord Aramos?"

"With Amarenia now coming into the fold," the spymaster said, with a sinister grin, "Lumina is virtually transparent to me. To the east, Immor-Onn is now also within my field of vision. If Lord Aramos surfaces, I'll know."

Zekoff tamped out his pipe and gave a satisfied sigh.

"I'm counting on you Rafel." He said, then turning to everyone else. "We all have our contacts and informants. I suggest calling on them at every level, including putting Red Division on alert, just in case things go bad."

They exited the room chatting quietly, leaving Okawa and Demetrius alone.

"So," Demetris said, stepping up to her, "it's early enough, what say we go get a bite to eat and then a drink?

Okawa gave a seductive grin and played with the collar of his shirt.

"And then?"

"Oh, we're a couple of intelligent people," he coyly replied, leaning in close. "I'm sure we can figure something out."

Okawa felt her pulse quicken when Demetrius's face drew near.

"If I didn't know better, I would swear you were about to kiss me."

"I was thinking about it."

"Maybe you should do more than think about it," she cooed.

"Third time's a charm," Demetrius said, just before the door flew open and Rafel poked his head in.

The two quickly separated. Demetris closed his eyes and dropped his head in frustration. Okawa blinked innocently at the Zorian spymaster while attempting to catch her breath.

"Captain Okawa," he said, apparently oblivious to the intimate scene. "I have a contact I was going to look in on. You might find this interesting. In the spirit of cooperation, would you like to accompany me? I could use your insight."

Now it was Okawa's turn to sigh in frustration.

"Sure, thank you Captain."

"I guess I'll take a raincheck," Demetrius said, watching the two operatives walk away.

Before closing the door, Okawa gave Demetrius an alluring smile and winked.

"Count on it."

By the time the grand turine finished ringing seven bells, the Kan fog had enveloped most of the High Holy City of Zor. Even the pealing bells couldn't drown out the constant keening carried on the wind. Kasha's eyes popped open halfway through the alarm and she bolted upright in her chair.

She was at her desk. The lone crystal lamp bathed the flat surface before her in a warm orange glow. The book was there, open at the halfway point, with her usual stack of copious notes piled beside it.

"I thought I'd let you sleep," came a friendly voice from across the room. "You've been pushing yourself pretty hard lately."

She groggily rubbed her eyes and focused on Cha-Rod sitting in a chair by the window, leaning forward on his cane. Seeing the fog outside she hastily looked around.

"What time is it?" she asked.

"It just turned seven," he replied. "Why don't we lock that thing up and let me walk you home? You could use the rest and I'm sure Tysonn will be glad to see you."

Shaking her head, she focused on the book and notes.

"I'm close," she declared, studying a line on the page. "I think I'm able to start writing in this language."

The Bailian furrowed his brow.

"Is that wise?"

"I don't see how it could hurt," Kasha said, with a glib chuckle.

The Bailian's moustache twitched nervously.

"I mean given the nature of the tome."

"Don't be silly," Kasha said, picking up a blank sheet of paper and pen. "It's just a book."

Cha-Rod watched her briefly consult the text and then hesitantly write. With the first character on the page a feeling of assertiveness swept across her and she wrote with confidence. She penned a few more lines even faster, before looking up with a satisfied smile.

"Hey, I think I'm getting this."

When her pen returned to the paper it moved with much greater fluidity. Her writing speed steadily increased until her hand flew across the page.

The Bailian's Eyes narrowed suspiciously, and he caught the faint odor of ammonia. He rose and quietly made his way over behind Kasha, glancing over her shoulder. The Bojo-Vat Master could not read the language, but one thing was obvious. The linguist furiously wrote the same line over and over.

"Kasha," he said, gently placing a hand on her shoulder.

The woman remained unresponsive while her scrawling continued on in a frantic, building pace. When she finished with one page, she reached for another.

Cha-Rod gently shook her shoulder. "Kasha!"

The head of the linguistics Department of the University of Marassa stopped, teetered and then fell unconscious over her desk.

Tysonn arrived to find her still unresponsive on a small couch with a clerria in attendance. He paused at the doorway and winced at the rooms unnatural heat and humidity. When he saw her lying there, he fought back a wave of panic. He rushed over to her side and caught the familiar, ominous scent of ammonia which had grown pungent.

Her rest appeared tormented, she tossed about mumbling fitfully in her sleep. Occasionally she would cry out slightly before dropping back into silent slumber. Moments later the scene would repeat itself.

"Is she going to be all right?" Tysonn asked.

An old woman in purple robes, dabbing her forehead, stopped and looked up at Tysonn.

"I think she'll be okay," she said. "It's probably just exhaustion."

Tysonn nodded his thanks then turned his attention to Cha-Rod.

"What happened?"

The older Bailian loudly exhaled and ran his hand across his bald head.

"She claimed to have some breakthrough," he began. "Said she could write the language. When she started, it was slow going but picked up speed. She became more and more entranced until she passed out."

"Okay, I've seen enough," Tysonn announced defiantly, pointing to the still open book. "Get that thing locked up and let's get her over to Clerria House…"

Suddenly Kasha's eyelids opened, her eyes were white and rolled back in her head. She lashed out, gripping the Clerria Marassa by the throat.

"Give it back!" she growled in a deep other worldly voice.

The old woman sputtered, eyes bulging while the grip tightened. Tysonn and Cha- Rod quickly bounded to her side and vainly pulled at her arms trying to release her from the vice-like stranglehold.

Kasha suddenly roared, shoving the clerria and both males aside like rag dolls. She rapidly rose to her feet as if pulled by an unseen force. Roaring again, she looked around the room with white, pupil-less eyes. Her gaze settled on Tysonn and then levitated over to him, feet inches from the floor.

Tysonn was just rising to his feet when she floated in front of him. When he stared into her featureless eyes a wave of fear paralyzed his limbs. Hissing furiously, Kasha's hand shot out and grabbed Tysonn by the neck. Continuing to hiss and growl, she lifted him up off the ground with one hand holding him in the air in front of her.

"Fucking thief," she spat in a deep demonic snarl. "You took what was mine!"

Tysonn choked and sputtered, his legs flailing about in the air. Desperately, he grabbed her bony arm with both hands trying to pry her away, but she held tight with a strength Tysonn had never encountered before. Slowly she brought the wide-eyed linguist directly in front of her snarling face.

"You thought you could have your fucking bitch steal my secrets!" it screamed.

Tysonn was on the verge of passing out when he heard a resounding thud from behind Kasha. Her eyes immediately snapped shut, and she released her grip. Both toppled to the floor. Tysonn looked up to see Cha-Rod standing holding his cane prepared to strike again.

Both men were breathing heavily while they stared questioningly into each other's faces. Tysonn got to his feet rubbing his neck.

"She'll need to be restrained over at Clerria House," Tysonn said, grimly, staring down at Kasha's limp form on the floor. "What in the name of the gods was she writing before this happened?"

Cha-Rod led him over to the desk and handed him the piece of paper.

"She kept writing the same line over and over. Can you translate it?"

"Well, unfortunately the actual expert on this is unconscious over there," Tysonn said, examining the lines of binary text. "The best that I can make out, it says, 'return what is mine.'"

The delicate aroma of lavender drifted upward as the silken bedsheet slowly descended towards the two naked humans seated just below. Shom Eldor watched the linens casually envelop the beautiful young woman seated beside him and mused at how his situation, in a relatively short time, had changed very much for the better.

Shom was in fact, pleasantly surprised at how smooth things were proceeding in his reign. He was now more certain than ever that getting rid of his father's inner circle of sycophants was a good idea. The people, especially the merchants, loved him because he lowered his father's crippling taxes and the poor considered him a friend because of the social programs he'd launched.

He was now finally free to attempt a little royal procreating. The apple cheeked young maiden tossed her long brown hair and mischievously smiled while the linen drifted down covering her.

An amused gasp erupted from the six formally dressed ladies-in-waiting standing at the foot of the bed when she dove at Shom. Giggling, she tackled the Eldorian sovereign and sent both of them toppling backward into an undulating pile beneath the floral printed sheets.

A very aroused Attina stood to the bed's right. While observing the lusty frolicking, she gave a self-satisfied smirk at her successful matchmaking abilities.

A thin, elderly man in yellow robes, standing directly across from the Hill Sister, huffed with elitist exasperation. He wearily eyed the bedroom sex play and tried not to stare at Attina's throbbing erection, which now tested the stitching in front of her crop pants.

"Uhh, your majesty?" he called out, loudly clearing his throat.

From the position of the sheets it was obvious Shom had mounted the eager concubine and now thrusted away with wild abandon. The pumping motion abruptly ceased at the sound of the officials croaking address. A nervous murmur coursed through the maiden's attendants when Shom's head abruptly popped out from beneath the covers and peered around.

"Sir, I hate to disturb you," the old man cajoled.

Shom broke from his full lust haze and focused on the intruding official.

"And yet still you persist!"

"I'm most sorry, sir, but we need an answer immediately,"

Without breaking his mount, the newest Eldorian Sovereign glared at his impertinent cabinet member.

"Honestly, what could be more important than propagating the Eldorian line of succession?" Shom asked, incredulously.

"Again, my apologies, sire, but the barge arrives at port within the deci."

Sighing in frustration, Shom dismounted with a wet plop and sat cross-legged eying his partner with an apologetic pout. Her glistening breasts jiggled slightly when she propped herself up on her elbows and sulked disappointedly. Shom begrudging turned his attention to his Minister of Seed, who, he realized, ironically prevented him from spreading his own seed.

"All right Meaai, what is so all-fire important that it keeps me from between this beautiful woman's thighs?"

The official shifted nervously. "Sire, it's about the excess grain."

Shom gave a frustrated huff. "Did you not get my communique?"

"Yes sire," the minister said, clearly confused, "but we failed to understand the meaning."

Shom shook his head in frustration. "I thought the meaning clear! Place all excess grain on wagons for the poor! What's so hard to understand about that?"

"The poor, sir?"

"Yes, you know," Shom said, rapidly losing his patience, "those smelly, scruffy people that seem to be everywhere, the poor!"

"But sire," Meaai asked, "you are aware we could sell back the excess and make a very handsome profit?"

Shom rolled his eyes at the minister's greedy proposal.

"Meaai, this isn't open for debate. Make it happen!"

Sensing the displeasure in his sovereign's voice the minister bowed and backed out of the room quickly.

"As you say, my sovereign."

The young king rolled his eyes watching the minister depart. "He was almost as annoying as that awful moaning on the wind. Does anybody know what that is?"

The lack of response prompted Shom to turn his attention once again to the lady seated beside him. One of her attendants now served liquor from an ornate silver tray. Taking one of the small delicate glasses, the concubine regarded her king.

"Tell me my sovereign, what is this fascination you have with the poor?" she queried, before taking a sip.

"It's really quite simple," Shom replied, removing a glass from the passing tray. "The well-fed poor are always more productive, you see. They also tend to breed more, therefore producing more poor, and a constant workforce. It really is quite a winning proposition. Hungry poor, on the other hand, have a tendency only to work under the whip. They would just as soon see our heads on Pikes or platters."

Reaching over, Shom deliberately poured the thick liquid between her breasts. He watched it run down her stomach and pool at her belly button, before spilling between her legs.

"And I, my dear, like my head exactly where it is."

With that statement, the Eldorian sovereign leaned over and delicately traced the thick brown liquid with his tongue following its trail slowly down the front of her body.

"As do I, your Majesty," the young woman giggled when Shom's head disappeared between her legs.

"Now, where were we?" Shom asked, gently licking the alcohol from the folds of her nether region.

"I believe we were going to make you a son, sire." She gasped between moans.

The Eldorian king abruptly halted his oral adoration when he heard their cries.

Gulls...

Gulls circling above the City of Rophan, dozens, perhaps hundreds of them.

Robeen de Zor never quite grew accustomed to working with idiots. Even now, every time they made one of their stupid, juvenile jokes he cringed, his fingers tightening on the pen in his hand. As harbor scribe in the Free City of Tannimore, he had hoped to work with a more educated class of people. He was wrong.

Ever since escaping the mob, in a land deal gone bad, he had ended up in the most remote and lawless locality in Lumina. The Roncell Family, who controlled the docks, had immediately put him to work doing what he did best, counting and recording things.

The job wasn't *that* bad. It afforded him lodging, food and equipment for his favorite hobby, fishing. For no matter what time of the luna, the fishing was always good.

The City of Tannimore rested in the center of a fifty-mile diameter patch of Lumina's southwestern Ocean Deep called the Doldrums. This unique spot in the Annigan carries the distinct honor of being exempt from all tides and currents of both air and water. The floating city, originally constructed from the ships of three separate marooned pirate fleets, expanded upward and outward with each passing cycle.

The city's center accommodated the central docks, beneath a massive arch connecting the windowed sterns of the two largest pirate flagships. Those towering rows of ornate windows, which overlooked the city's entrance, now housed the offices of the harbormaster. It was in these light drenched rooms where Robeen, along with three spotters, worked keeping track of the busy morning ship's traffic.

As usual Robeen sat at his harbormaster's desk facing away from the windows. This allowed for the maximum amount of illumination on the large ledger book open in front of him.

"All right, we've got a hundred fifty-foot barge stopped at the entrance," the gruff young man known as Rozzy said, peering through his spyglass. "The name on the side is, *Kreeger*."

"The *Kreeger*, check," Robeen confirmed, making a note in the ledger.

Rozzy then snickered lecherously. "Those two big bales on her deck looks *just like* the tits on the whore I had last night."

This caused the other two spotters to erupt in laughter while Robeen rolled his eyes. Peeko, a bald young man with a lazy eye standing next to Rozzy noticed Robeen didn't join in with their suggestive banter.

"Eh, look at Robeen here," Rozzy said, mockingly. "I guess he don't *like* tits!"

"Now you leave Robeen alone," scolded the large, toe-headed harbormaster on duty, teasing the much smaller, slightly effeminate scribe. "He's got different tastes than you two horndogs."

It was true. Robeen enjoyed more disciplined erotic pursuits from one of three Kinjuto Dominators which called Tannimore home. He shifted and winced in his chair whenever he accidently brushed against the welts from the caning he'd received two moonless ago.

Robeen perceived the sudden flash of blue light behind him when Rozzy glanced away in pain and lowered his glass. "Did you see that blue flash?"

"What the?" Peeko replied in shock.

"It came from the edge of the Doldrums," the harbormaster said, aiming his spyglass in the occurrence's direction. "Wait, there's something moving out there."

They turned and watched the spot on the horizon rapidly approaching.

"It's moving fast," Rozzy noted.

"Too fast for my liking," the harbormaster responded. "Best sound the alarm."

With the order given, Peeko reached over and pulled on a small red cord. Down below their station, a bell on the outside rang and two ballista ports swung into place on either side of the entrance.

While the object rushed ever closer, Robeen joined his companions at the window. All looked on in astonishment. It was not one object, but four individuals levitating and gliding just across the top of the water. A human with long black robes and glowing blue eyes appeared to lead the group, followed by a Gila hybrid and two ominous looking mantis creatures.

Both ballista operators eyed each other nervously when the group came to a halt directly in front of them. A tense moment passed before the robed figure floated slightly forward and faced the harbormaster's office.

"I am Stryder, Herald of Pa-Waga," he called out. "We will restore order and balance to this lawless place. You will announce me immediately."

The ballista operator to his right chuckled and aimed the twelve-foot bolt directly at Stryder's chest.

"Yeah," he said, "we're doing just fine without your help. Now move on!"

"My Lord will not be denied," Stryder calmly answered, giving the weapon an amused glance. "Now announce us!"

"Maybe you don't hear so good," the guard said, throwing a switch on the side of the ballista. "You and your band of freaks need to move on."

Before any could react, streamers of fire erupted from the mouths of the mantis creatures engulfing both the stations in flames. The shrill screams of the men echoed above the roaring pyre. A collective gasp of shock reverberated through the harbormaster's office. They knew well the dangers of a fire in their location.

Two fire control spouts engaged, drawing water from the reservoirs high above on the roofs. The torrent of water doused the destroyed defense stations but could not extinguish the flames. They flickered out only when there was nothing left to burn. It was too late for the ballista operators, however. Their smoking, blackened bodies had grimly fused to their now charred weapons.

Stryder's voice rose to a booming proclamation. "You will announce me and submit to my Lord or this city will be reduced to a smoldering hole in the ocean!"

Shom Eldor closed the robe around his naked body while bolting out onto the balcony of his bedchamber. Just as he suspected, a massive flock of seagulls swirled and dove around a huge circular building over near the city center. Seemingly the birds disappeared into a large opening just below the roofline only to reappear moments later.

"The commodities exchange!" Shom gasped. "Attina..."

"Your carriage?" Attina finished his thought as she quickly left the room. "Yes, sire."

Dutiful citizens getting out of the way for the Royal carriage made the ride through the streets short. Soon Attina and Shom stood in the private Eldorian balcony witnessing the chaos on the trading floor below.

Gulls squawked furiously, coursing through the air, delivering messages to the throng of traders who screamed orders to a handful of people placing large numbered markers on a board dominating the far wall. They quickly replaced the markers with each new message delivered.

The numbers were rapidly plummeting. A quick glance at the noble houses' representatives in the private balconies revealed grim faces.

"Shom, what's going on?" Attina asked, over the din of the mayhem engulfing the room.

"For some reason all the markets are in freefall," Shom replied, studying the rapidly changing board.

"What could cause that?"

"I doubt if anyone around here knows for sure," Shom said, sighing. "We need to talk to our man in Zor."

The Hill Sister winced slightly. "Uh, I hate to say this, sire, but we don't have a man in Zor."

"What!?"

"We were getting to it, sire," she explained.

"Well, whatever happened to the previous man?"

"The previous 'man' was a woman and your father had her executed."

"In the name of the gods why?"

"From all accounts I've read he was having a bad day," the seneschal reported in a stony voice.

"Yes, well father *delighted* in taking his frustrations out on the help." Shom said, returning his attention to the commodities board. "Well, it appears we're going to Zor."

The Na-Kab scurried through the dimly lit tunnels under Mount Goya with a single purpose. Their queen's time drew near. They felt it buzzing through the whole hive's collective consciousness, calling them to action.

King Krol ordered them to place the cocoon between two molten rivers of magma flowing outward from a huge bubbling lava pool. Soon, if the fleshy ones spoke the truth, they would have a new queen to go along with their new home. She would save the Na-Kab race and the Fire Hive would rise again.

The hive's excitement grew with each detected movement beneath the cocoon's leathery surface. Anticipation however slowly gave way to uneasiness. Something was wrong. The slow undulations of the queen's body turned into wild thrashing tremors.

A small orange smolder appeared and burned its way through. The small point of flame eventually became a trail slowly running down the front of the cocoon, burning it open. The creature wildly flailed and screeched. It freed itself from its containment and toppled onto the cavern floor.

The metamorphosing queen resembled one of their own, however with no arms, legs, or eyes. A long black tongue snaked around in front of its face, extending from a mouth comprising nothing more than a round hole lined with hundreds of tiny sharp teeth. A small, stunted thorax extended from the opposite end of the monstrosity. The glow from between the armored plates dimmed. The six breasts on the torso which should provide life giving nectar, hung limp and shriveled like empty water sacks. It writhed about on the floor, hissing furiously at anything near it.

The shocked Na-Kab looked on in horror when the mutated queen's thorax began making cracking sounds. The individual plates separated and thousands of long prehensile hairs peeled apart the armored thorax panels. They propelled the creature across the floor towards one of the twin rivers of fire flowing on either side. It slipped into one of the burning rivers and swam away toward the main magma pool beneath the volcano.

The hive gave out a screech of frustration and rage in unison. It echoed through the tunnels and along the valleys of the Goyan mountain range.

"Hail Stormwinds," Mal said, placing her open hand over her heart.

The three Zerian rangers visibly relaxed at the tribal greeting and continued their cautious approach. The Spice Rat realized she'd caught a break when she recognized they wore the markings of the Stormwinds Clan. She had dealt with them many times over the years during her spice runs.

"Hail stranger," the lead ranger said, with a similar hand over the heart greeting. "Many thanks for defeating this creature which plagued us since our arrival. It killed our leaders."

Mal nodded her understanding. The Zerian clans were co-ruled by a shaman and a head ranger, with them gone they were leaderless and vulnerable, especially to other more hostile clans.

"I am Vadovas," he said. "Stormwinds Clan now looks to me as leader."

"What happened?" Mal asked, after the introductions.

The rangers had seen an EEtah before, but the female Singa with an eyepatch captivated them. Mal couldn't stop staring at the once great forest, which already showed signs of turning brown and wilting, while starting to die.

"It was just after the Kan fog rose," the ranger explained. "The ground rumbled, everything went black for an instant and then we ended up here. What is this place?"

"We are on the Great Desert Plane of the Middle Realms," Zau said, eyes scanning the blank gray sky.

The perplexed look on Vadovas' face showed the woodsman didn't understand.

The Singa sadly smiled and explained, "You're a long way from home, ranger."

"Not just the tribes," Mal added, "but there are millions of other creatures that depend on this forest. If it dies, they die, so we don't have long. Where are the Jissic?"

"They have been in council since we arrived," Vadovas answered. "It is forbidden to disturb them."

"*Of course* it is forbidden," Mal said, sarcastically chuckling. "Yeah, well, we're gonna need them to rally all the clans. So disturb away, if that's what it's gonna take to get the fuck out of here.

"Zau, I know there gotta be more portals around, but we can't just go traipsing across unfamiliar and potentially hostile territory."

Her navigator lifted her eye patch, projecting the glowing blue globe in front of her, and the rangers collectively gasped. She pondered the topography of the display.

"Looks like there's a massive portal about a hundred fifty miles west of here," she said.

"That is where the Kerin Valley and Lardia used to be," Vadovas said, with a touch of dread. "It means we must pass through Iron Tongue territory."

The concern on the Rangers face was noticeable, causing Zaad and Zau to exchange puzzled glances.

"The Iron Tongue Clan practice cannibalism and a bunch of other equally nasty activities," Mal clarified.

"Perfect," Zau moaned.

"Will you fucking relax," Mal said, dismissively. "Don't forget, we can fly."

"Yeah, but we're the only ones," the Singa said, unconvinced. "The ship isn't big enough to transport everyone and everything. We gotta get them through there. So that means still having to deal with cannibals."

"And that's why we need the Jissic," the Spice Rat said, with a nod, before turning back to the Zerian Rangers, "Are they close?"

Vadovas reluctantly nodded.

"Okay then, lead on," Mal ordered. "Zaad and Wostera, you're with me. Zau, you and Kumo follow behind us in the *Haraka* just in case we run into something we can't handle.

When they started out through the bush, Mal marveled at the ranger's stealth and camouflage abilities. They could literally be standing next to you and you wouldn't know it. The Spice Rat had dealings with the Zerians frequently but had never seen them operate in their natural setting. She now knew why some called them the Invisible People.

The ironic part was anyone could hear them coming a mile away with Zaad stomping through the foliage. Stealth was hardly an EEtah's strong suit, but the dried vegetation crackling underfoot made it painfully obvious the sands of the desert lie just beneath.

They smelt the dried-up riverbed long before they encountered it. Thousands of dead fish littered the now barren rocky ground where water once flowed. The stench of rot grew overwhelming. While they walked amongst the fish carcasses, Zaad reached down, picked one up, and popped it in his mouth.

"You know, whoever did this deserves no mercy," he snarled between bites.

The riverbed eventually gave way to a large dried-up lake where the scene remained much the same. Surrounding what was once the shore, water plants withered brown and brittle with dead aquatic creatures lying everywhere. Movement beneath a massive lone tree on the other side of the lake caught their attention.

"Jissic Council," Vadovas said, pointing towards the activity. "We stay here."

"I guess this is where we test my powers of persuasion," Mal said, addressing Wostera and Zaad. "Stay behind me and keep quiet, let me do the talking. The rangers maybe the defenders of the forest, but, by the gods, the Jissic Council calls the shots."

Both nodded in agreement and they set out for the tree with Mal in the lead. When they drew nearer, the council abruptly halted their heated conversation and stared at the approaching strangers.

A large panda, with his hands laced across his ponderous belly, sat facing them with his back to the tree. An otter lay unconscious, propped against the other side of the tree. A large raccoon and hare stood erect on their hind-legs beside them leading the discussion. A golden lynx with striking black markings crouched on a low branch just above the group.

Mal assumed the topic had been about a small wicker figure standing lifelessly a few feet from them. It resembled a human child in amazing detail, with a four-foot frame constructed entirely out of branches, twigs and foliage.

"Hail Jissic," Mal greeted them, hand over heart.

"Who dares disturb the Jissic Council?" demanded the lynx, staring at them suspiciously.

"I am called Maluria. I have sailed your waters for many Kans. These are my companions. We come to offer help."

The raccoon stepped forward and made a sad face.

"Might you have some water for my friend?" he asked, indicating the otter against the tree.

Mal's heart sank when she thought about how devastating it must be on the aquatic creatures. She stepped out from under the tree's canopy and motioned for the *Haraka,* which settled to the ground twenty feet away.

"Get two large skins," Mal ordered.

Zaad nodded and trotted off towards the airship. The Spice Rat then turned her attention back to the council.

"Great Jissick," she said. "I believe we have a plan that can save the remaining creatures of your island, but it will require your assistance."

"You ask us to trust you?!" the lynx objected defiantly.

Mal gave a small shrug. "It's that, or everything around here dies. This Council must let the various clans know what is happening and get them working together or at least to stop fighting temporarily."

The wary animal turned its head in anger and shame when Zaad returned with the water skins. When the EEtah poured water on the otter it awoke immediately and became responsive.

"There is enough for all," Mal said, pointing out the second skin.

When the Jissic descended on the water skin, Zau came walking over with a satisfied grin on her face.

"Captain, something just happened I think you will want to know about."

"What ya got?" Mal asked, watching the grateful animals empty the container.

"I was poking around looking for any more good-sized portals when I picked up an Etheria key being charged up. Guess where it's linked to?"

"Might that be our little corner of paradise here?"

"You got it."

Mal gave a satisfied nod of her head. "Point of origin?"

"That's the strange part, it's originating from the middle of the Doldrums."

A sly smile slowly crossed the Spice Rat's face.

"Tannimore."

"Huh?"

"There's a floating city out there," Mal continued. "It's a pretty wild place. Come to think about it, it only makes sense. If you're gonna piss off an earth deity, you're safest if you surround yourself with water."

The Spice Rat saw the confused look on the Singa's face and gave an understanding smile.

"Hey," she said, "don't beat yourself up. You're from the other side of the world after all."

"You know who did this?" the lynx asked.

"No," Mal answered, "but now we've got a good idea where to find them."

This set off another round of frantic conversation among the Jissic Council. When they finished, the panda stood and walked over to the Spice Rat.

"Even though Our Lady Lardia sprouts the forest anew," the panda explained, "there must be retribution. The wrath of Elmos will not be denied. You say water surrounds whoever did this?"

"It's a city built on a dead spot in the ocean," Mal said. "They started by bolting a bunch of ships together and they just built up from there."

"Please return our brother to Zer," the panda said, pointing at the otter. "When you get back, we will have had time to rally the clans."

He then reached out and put a hand on the otter's shoulder. They met eyes. With the other he pointed to the wicker child.

"Fill the vessel with the essence of Elmos, brother," the council member commanded. "It will then be known as Lamos, child of the world tree, Lardia, and her vassal Elmos. Perhaps it will be able to travel to the places where they cannot. Once you complete this, it will awaken and know what to do."

Mal took in a deep breath then let it out slowly while her gaze traveled from her airship back to the group.

"All right," she said, "I guess it's back across the multiverse for us."

The room was oppressively hot. Twelve nervous and angry men crowded around the long table. Sweat dripped off of them while they glared menacingly at the hooded figure in front of them. They could only make out two blue eyes unnaturally shining from beneath the cowl. Two humans, whose red eyes also glowed, flanked the mysterious figure.

The mob boss, Bazo Gunda, had risen to his feet and leaned on the table's edge. His scarred, wrinkled features pulled taunt with anger and spit sprayed from his mouth.

"What kind of fucking shake-down are you trying to pull here?" he demanded.

"This isn't a shake down so much as it is a takeover," Stryder said, in a calm, booming voice.

This caused the table to erupt in angry chatter.

"You all have shown an inability to function efficiently," the hooded man continued, quieting the incensed ranting. "Instead, you seem to spend most of your time fighting each other instead of turning a profit."

He then brought his attention to the youngest man seated a distance from the others.

"I understand you were responsible for bringing certain forbidden games of chance here," Stryder stated.

"No thanks to *them*!" the young man shouted, leering at the two other mob bosses seated to his right.

"It's time for a change in management around here," his commanding voice declared.

They all could now see glowing blue lips quietly mouthing unintelligible words from under the hood. The two older gang leader's eyes went wide with surprise when their hands began slowly reaching for their daggers. Everyone looked on in shock, and a nervous murmur rippled through the group as the gang bosses tried to resist pressing the blades against their necks.

With trembling lips and bulging eyes, the crime lords sliced across their own throats. The family members, and assistants standing behind them, cried out in panic when sheets of blood erupted from the wounds, soaking the front of the boss's shirts. Shocked expressions permanently etched across their aged faces when they dropped the blades and toppled forward onto the table.

The glowing lips faded from beneath the cowl and the mysterious stranger surveyed the remaining gang members still reeling from the gruesome spectacle they had just witnessed.

"We can now get this city back on a money-making basis," his voice calmly said, before turning to the young crime boss he spoke with before. "You will now coordinate the rival factions."

Swallowing hard, the young gangster showed he understood while disgruntled murmurs floated around the table.

"Anyone unwilling or unable to serve my Lord is free to leave," he continued. "Know this, my Lord is the very essence of prosperity. He is generous to his followers and merciless to his enemies."

A scarred hand reached out from under the cloak and pointed a finger with a long dagger-like nail at those around the table.

"You must now decide where you stand," he demanded. "If you stay, you must pledge fealty to my Lord Pa-Waga and received his mark. All former hostilities between the groups are to cease and you will all work together."

Wikk Roncell, the young crime lord, stood and visibly trembled while walking over to Stryder. Standing before the dark cleric, he humbly lowered his head.

"Turn and kneel," the hooded cleric ordered.

When the young gangster complied, Stryder carved a small "X" and "I" at the base of his skull, on either side of his spine, with his fingernail. While the blood still trickled down and stained his collar, he turned and met his new lord with a smile.

All but a few of the gangsters followed suit, prostrating themselves before the Herald of Pa-Waga. The ones who refused, left the room after grumbling about not being willing to follow a dark god. One of the glamoured Na-Kab followed them out and within moments, everyone in the room could hear their screams of pain. Stryder then pulled back his hood revealing his badly scarred face and smiled.

"As I said, 'merciless to his enemies.'"

When Stryder finished etching the markings on the remaining gangsters, they stood and faced him. The Pa-Waga cleric singled out the young gang chieftain.

"What is your name?" he asked.

"Wikk Roncell, my lord."

"For official purposes you shall be deemed mayor of this city and called Wikk the First," Stryder declared. "Now tell me, is there a Kinjuto in this city?"

"Yes, my Lord, several moved here after Immor-Onn expelled them," the newly appointed mayor answered.

"Is there a Kinjuto Master among them?"

"Yes, my lord, there is Mistress Ve-Qua."

"Have her brought to me immediately."

The moon was about to set over the Free City of Tannimore, leaving only the stationary sun in the western sky for any form of light. The singular light source caused the nautically masted spires of the city to cast stark shadows stretching across the glass smooth waters of the Doldrums.

Many small and medium-sized ships bolted together on the edges of the floating city comprised what the community called the Outskirts. The distance of its occupants from the towering city center illustrated their status as newcomers.

A Bailian barge jutted conspicuously from the Outskirts, along the farthermost northern edge of the floating city. The wide flat vessel conveyed a beauty and functionality so essential to once navigating the turbulent waters around the Twilight Lands.

Nowadays, however, a constant wave of anguished cries wafted upward from the newest section of the Outskirts. Custom alterations on the four-story interior of the stationary barge reflected the needs of its newest occupant, the tenth level Kinjuto, Mistress Ve-Qua.

They had cut a large rectangle from the center of each level, creating a deep atrium in the ship's interior. A dirge of agony emanated from the second level. The masochistic wails cascaded outwards and reverberated off the empty floors below.

Mistress Ve-Qua reclined on an ornate sofa, just above in her private quarters and dungeon. She was a petite, young, naked Bailian woman with skin of such a pale blue, it appeared white. Her shoulder-length raven hair matched the thick dark circles around her eyes.

A half-inch thick metal rod pierced mid-way through her ample breasts, holding the twin orbs together and pushing them upward in a macabre, permanent cleavage. Chains led down from ominous looking bolts on each side of the breasts, hooking to the respective lips of her vagina, pulling them lewdly open.

Her eyes were closed, head tilted back in rapturous ecstasy at the echoes of misery emanating from the floor below. Her eyes leisurely opened when she felt the breeze and saw the curtains flutter. The Herald of Pa-Waga stood before her.

"I expected you a while ago," she said, calmly, closing her eyes once again.

"You were summoned," Stryder said, irritation in his voice.

"I am a mistress of Kinjuto," she said, eyes still closed. "I will not be summoned by your flunkies."

She sat up and pointed towards a bound human messenger several yards away.

"Besides," she added, "this one lacked courtesy and discipline. I hope you don't mind I took it upon myself to convey a much-needed lesson upon him."

She had stripped the unfortunate young man naked. His shredded clothing lay in a pile beside him. A large metal ring wrapped tightly around the base of his testicles bound him to a short, taut chain to the floor. It forced him to stand in a wide, bent leg position. His muted whimpers stood in stark, contrast to his engorged, quivering erection. The dark cleric gave a quick, unconcerned glance to his bound messenger.

"I come to make you an offer."

"Really?" Ve-Qua said, a touch of amusement in her voice. "I heard someone had taken over and set up a puppet mayor. This fascinates me. And pray tell, how I may play a part in this little drama of yours?"

"How would you like to fill the bottom two levels of your barge?"

The mistress briefly hesitated in contemplation before resuming her bored, elitist facade. She threw her head back and gave a mocking laugh.

"I have all the clients I need to more than maintain my energy," she said.

She sat back and closed her eyes. A look of dreamlike ecstasy descended across her face.

"You know, sometimes during the moonless," she whispered, "I'll lay here listening to their tormented pleas, masturbating. If one starts crying, it pushes me to orgasm."

"I offer you something more than just the simple and base pleasures you now enjoy," Stryder proposed, projecting an air of superiority.

The mistress of pain laughed again. "You think this is simple and base, do you? Have you any idea how difficult it is to keep that many beings on the edge of pain for extended periods and have them not go mad or die?"

"I acknowledge both your training and your status," Stryder answered calmly. "What I come to offer is a bit of a... higher calling. You could hold a serious and high position in the city."

"I have no need for a lowly municipal position," she said, contemptuously.

"I'm referring to a position on the high council."

Ve-Qua thought about the generous offer. Her eyes narrowed.

"And what do you wish from me?"

"Effective immediately," the dark cleric began, "I shall officially suspend all executions in the City of Tannimore. They will henceforth turn all prisoners over to your care. You may keep your private clients as well."

Her demeanor went from suspicious to skeptical.

"But that will produce an excessive amount of energy... wasted!" she protested.

"Not wasted," Stryder said, shaking his head. "I can contain it and use at a time of my choosing."

"Why?"

"I intend to make this city the most prosperous, shining example in the Annigan. A place where all may come to ply their trade, no matter how forbidden elsewhere. For that, I will need power, the type of power *you* can supply."

The Kinjuto mistress pondered for a moment. "They would allow me to operate without harassment?"

"So long as you do not endanger the city," Stryder assured. "In fact, you would be the sole instrument of the state's vengeance and punishment."

Stryder's last argument won over the mistress and she gave an evil smile.

"Done!" she proclaimed.

"Excellent," the dark cleric replied. "One of my associates shall be by shortly with the method of containment."

With business concluded, Stryder glanced over questioningly at his bound aide.

"Oh, very well," she conceded.

She got up and walked over to the unfortunate young man. Reaching down, she released the ring around his testicles. Immediately upon his manhood being freed, the messenger gave a guttural cry and ejaculated into a pool on the floor before him. It took a moment to compose himself.

When he attempted to straighten up, Ve-Kua gave him a savage kick to the balls, and he dropped to the floor racked in pain.

"You worthless piece of shit!" she screamed at the figure writhing in his own ejaculate. "This is the thanks I get for allowing you to release?! You learned NOTHING!"

She gave him another savage kick to his torso.

"You are not worthy to walk upright in this chamber," she scolded. "From now on, you will crawl behind your master!"

"I must admit, I admire your style," Stryder confessed. "I think I shall make him my new liaison to you."

Ve-Kua smiled cruelly watching him squirm in agony on the floor.

"He would have eventually returned to me as a client of his own volition," she said. "They always do. But thank you, I appreciate the gesture."

Racing through tunnels…
A maze of perfectly rectangular corridors

Scorched black
Above lush green woodlands

Finally arriving…
The magma pool
Where she rises

Julius' eyes slowly opened. It had been the same dream every night, but this time it was different. This time he knew. Laying there, his eyes darted back-and-forth wildly contemplating what the visions showed him.

"Are you all right, sir?" Dax's gruff voice came from outside his bedroom door. "I heard you cry out."

The Avion Prince bolted from his bed. Dax opened the door and cautiously entered the room.

"Yes… Yes, never better," he said, reaching for his robe. "I've got it!"

"Got it, sir? Got what?" the EEtah asked, perplexed.

"It was right there in front of me all the time," Julius called out, starting to pace.

"Sir?" Dax said,

"All is not as it seems. The Na-Kab… the Na-Kab are the key!"

Dak watched his master walk back-and-forth across the room. "The key to what, sir? You're talking about the fire bugs from Nocturn, aren't you?"

Julius stopped and looked up at the man-shark nodding yes, eyes wide with revelation.

239

"And their queen!"

"Their queen, sir?"

"Right in front of me the whole time," Julius muttered, getting dressed while heading for the glass doors leading to the balcony.

"Can I assist you with something, sir?" Dak asked.

Julius stepped out onto the verandah. The cool morning air flowed across the spired rooftops of Immor-Onn and through his long black hair.

"No old friend, this is something I must do myself."

"Sir, where are you going?"

"Mount Goya, home." the Avion said, unfurling his wings. "Look after things while I'm gone."

"This should be interesting," Demetrius said.

He banked the *Drakin* around the compound below, three dome shaped buildings, one large and two small, built out of branches and sticks. A swirling trail of smoke rose lazily from a hole in the top of the large building. Just west of the encampment, several humans tended a vast field of boxes housing beehives.

"So, what do you know about these Toma monks?" Demetrius asked, beginning the airship's dissent.

"Just what I've read," Okawa said, staring out the window. "It's the largest most powerful of the earth religions in the Annigan. Over at House Eldor it's the official religion of the realm. They're big into fertility and beekeepers by nature. They were also instrumental in brokering the deal that allowed humans to harvest Ukko wood from the Zerian forest. What about you?"

Demetrius shook his head, lowering the craft to the ground.

"Only by reputation," he said, shutting off the engine.

"And what might that reputation be?"

"Weird."

"That is not at all helpful," Okawa said, playfully.

He popped open the side hatch, and they exited the airship.

"Hey, what do you want?" Demetrius asked, with a shrug. "I'm just the pilot."

When they approached the buildings, several monks broke away from their activities and came to greet them. All were nude and their long, coarse hair was going through various stages of metamorphosis into delicate evergreen sprigs.

"Greetings monks of Toma," Okawa began. "We seek the one called Kesis."

The monks bowed smiling and indicated a person just exiting the beehives. Kesis was slightly taller than the rest and with a head completely covered with foliage, resembling a walking tree. Bees covered his face and upper torso—swarming off him when he moved towards the group and returning to their hives.

"I do not know your names, but I know why you are here," he said, smiling warmly.

The statement caught Okawa off guard and she gave a sheepish grin.

"You seek knowledge of Elmos and Lardia," Kesis continued.

"Good guess," Demetrius acknowledged, chuckling.

"I can help you, but, in the end, you must find the answers on your own," Kesis said, in a solemn tone.

"Yes, thank you." Okawa said, optimistically.

"Do not be so quick to thank me," the earth cleric warned, a knowing smile crossing his face. "The Vision Lodge may reveal things best left unknown."

This caused Demetrius and Okawa to exchange nervous glances.

"I came for information," Okawa resolutely said,.

"Very well," Kesis said, before leading them to one of the smaller domes by the beehives. "First, you must purify yourselves before entering the vision lodge. Remove your clothing."

Without waiting for a reply, the shaman turned and walked away into the lodge.

"Well this is awkward," Demetrius said, unbuckling his belt.

"Shush," Okawa scolded, unbuttoning her shirt. "The earth gods around this place are already pissed off enough, we don't need you insulting them."

The pilot did his best to keep his eyes averted during the disrobing but, once the process was over, they both took in each other's naked bodies.

Demetrius exhaled loudly. "I just gotta say, you are a work of art."

The seasoned agent blushed at the compliment. Stepping up to Demetrius she stroked his cheek.

"You know I've been catcalled and propositioned many times, in my life, but that was endearing."

Before Demetrius could reply the shaman returned carrying a twig with white leaves, a bowl of glowing embers and a large feather. He directed them to stand facing him in front of the lodge. He then dropped the twig onto the embers. The white leaves immediately began smoldering.

Kesis then started a low chant while moving around them, fanning the smoke over them with the feather. When he circled them three times, he set the bowl down on the ground and walked over to the nearest beehive. Lifting the lid, he reached in and broke off a fist-sized chunk of honeycomb.

Holding the honeycomb reverently out before him, he walked back and stood in front of the two naked visitors. He dipped his forefinger ceremoniously into the thick honey and dabbed a streak on both of their foreheads, between the eyes, lips, and over their hearts.

"The Vision Lodge awaits," he said, pointing to the door of the building a few feet away.

The circular room was about twenty feet in diameter. Pelts and furs of different types lined the floor. A round brazier full of glowing crystals sat in the center of the room, with a bucket and ladle next to it.

Kesis followed them in and directed them to sit facing each other to the right of the brazier. The shaman sat cross-legged beside them, dipped the ladle into the bucket, and poured liquid over the gems. The room filled immediately with aromatic steam while Kesis began a slow chant.

Demetrius felt lightheaded and instantly began sweating profusely. While the chanting continued, and the steam grew denser, he found that he couldn't take his eyes off of Okawa seated across from him.

His gaze traveled from her beautiful face, which was gaining a sheen, down to her large perfectly formed breasts. He felt a twinge of arousal watching her small brown nipples harden. When he looked back at her face, she was pursing her lips and staring down towards his crotch. Following her gaze, he then noticed his prominent erection jutting up in front of him.

Without a word, she stood and walked over to him. Kneeling down, she pulled his legs open and sat between them, wrapping her legs around the small of his back. Staring into each other's eyes, they simultaneously leaned in for a slow tender kiss, smiling when they tasted the honey.

With the ice now broken, both grabbed each other in a passionate embrace, shuddering as their wet naked bodies pressed against each other. The kiss was long and fervent.

Okawa found herself rubbing her sweat soaked abdomen against Demetrius' hardness. Her breath grew labored, and she shifted herself up onto his thighs. Reaching down, she took hold of his rigid member and guided it into her. Both gasped at her wetness and she easily slid all the way down to the base. They kissed deeply while they slowly rocked back-and-forth. With their mouths locked together, their tongues danced with each other in their coital embrace.

It was then the visions began.

Images of a lush green forest of magical wood which grew so fast no one could build there. A home for the World Tree Lardia. They saw Zer's inhabitants and their gods. A wave of understanding swept over both of them just before they lost consciousness.

They awoke a short while later still in the embrace and Demetrius buried deep within her. Finding themselves alone they discovered the Vision Lodge's door wide open and the brazier full of steaming crystals gone. Both of their eyes grew wide with surprise realizing their physical situation.

Okawa immediately slid off Demetrius leaving his erection waving conspicuously in front of him.

"Did… Did we just… you… you know what?" the pilot stammered with embarrassment.

Okawa exhaled, running her hand through her hair.

"Well, seeing how you were just balls deep in me, I'm going to say… yes."

Demetrius sighed and looked around. "I guess Toma really is a fertility god."

The Valdurian agent climbed to her feet and went out the door searching for her clothes.

"Well," she said, "at least we've got a better idea of what's going on. We gotta get back to the forum."

While she was putting on her shirt, a still nude Demetrius walked up to her. He tenderly reached out and touched the side of her head.

"You know we shared something magical back there," he whispered.

Okawa briefly met his gaze and her eyes teared before briefly looking away. When she turned back to him, the seasoned operative gave a demure smile and nodded.

Demetrius's still hard cock broke the tender moment when it accidently poked her belly. She looked down at the still engorged organ.

"But you might want to put that away before small creatures try to roost on it," she said, with an amused grin.

With the main amphitheater of the Zorian Forum under repair, it forced the Supreme council to convene in one of the smaller meeting halls. The conference was gaveled to order by the current chairman, Tate Whitmar. They were about to take a roll call, when the doors flew open and an unconscious guard toppled to the floor.

Cries of alarm rose from the seated delegates, when a humanoid ape lumbered into the room carrying a large, flat, white crystal disk. Without a sound it placed the crystal on the floor, so the flat edge faced the representatives. No sooner had he set it down, the sound of three dull thuds resonated through the hall, and the ape creature fell forward with three arrows in his back.

Archers quickly streamed into the room to see if there were any more threats. Detecting none, they lowered their weapons just in time for the crystal to crackle with blue sparks. Confused banter subsided when a projection of a black robed Stryder Aramos appeared on the floor in front of the crystal. They could see only his glowing blue eyes and lips from underneath the hood.

"Hear me Zorian Forum," he announced, "I am Stryder, Herald of Pa-Waga. I am in possession of the Ukko wood."

The statement caused the crowd to descend into perplexed banter until Pierce Calden's voice rose above the fray. "You monster! What became of the living things on that island?"

"The only thing that concerns me is the wood, and the profit derived from it," Stryder said, dispassionately.

Tate Whitmar rose to his feet and pointed the gavel angrily at the hologram.

"What makes you think we want anything to do with you and your god of destruction?"

"Destruction!?" The dark cleric laughed out loud. "My lord is one of *prosperity*, but to cultivate prosperity a seed must be planted, a token offered. This is what the investment of the Ukko wood represents if you wish to manifest the prosperity *only* Pa-Waga can provide.

"With the Golden Avatar gone, and the Pearl Avatar now in Immor-Onn, your civilization declines while the Bailian empire rises. Already the fertility in your fields and oceans, which the avatar once innately provided, is waning. Without intervention, your empires will last no more than ten grands."

"Preposterous!" someone shouted from the crowd.

Stryder ignored the remark and got right back to business.

"We shall hold an auction for the forest in two cycles in the free City of Tannimore," he announced. "Bidding will start at 100,000 secors, in the form of gold notes drawn on the Aris branch of the Imperial Bank of Zor. I invite all interested parties. There will be no further communication until the auction."

Abruptly the projection flickered, then dissolved into blue sparks and the crystal shattered onto the floor. Colonel Zekoff pulled the pipe from his mouth and leaned over to Rafel seated next to him.

"Well," he softly said, "I guess that takes the mystery out of what Lord Aramos was up to."

Okawa felt a twinge of concern while she and Demetrius watched two servants drag the body of the ape creature out of the minor amphitheater of the Zorian Forum. A cleaning woman followed behind with a pail and brush scrubbing away pools of blood.

"Not again?!" she exclaimed.

"Looks like we missed another party," Demetrius said, watching the body dragged past him leaving a crimson trail in its wake.

Okawa was already on her way into the meeting hall. It relieved her to see there was no other casualties or destruction. Across the room she could see her boss, Joc' Valdur, in an animated conversation with Pierce Calden. It ended with a handshake, and Joc' waving her over when the Calden Ambassador made his way past her.

"What in the name of the empire happened here?" Okawa asked, watching two more cleaning women get to work.

Joc' gave a frustrated sigh. "We were just paid a remote visit by Lord Stryder Aramos. He's dropped the family name and now just calls himself a Herald of Pa-Waga. He also claims to have the Ukko wood of the Zerian forest."

"How does one hide a forest and, *more importantly*, where does one put it?"

Joc' shook his head. "I don't know, but judging by his looks, I believe him. He's auctioning off the wood to the highest bidder two cycles from now. I just made a deal with House Calden. We will not be outbid."

"Between their navy and our air fleet," Okawa added, nodding, "Stryder has both of our houses over a barrel. Where's the auction being held?"

"Tannimore," he answered. "Pierce and I will be attending. You're on security detail if Demetrius can get us there. What did you find out from the Toma monks?"

"Background mostly," Okawa replied. "It makes sense now why Stryder chose Tannimore, that way Elmos can't get to him."

"Nothing like adding an angry demigod to the mix to keep things interesting," Joc' concurred.

Out in the foyer Pierce Calden stopped to scribble a quick note before handing it to his aide.

"Get this to our naval attaché in Penaber immediately."

The young man nodded nervously accepting the small piece of paper and then took off running. The message was short and simple.

Location Tannimore
Go on Operation Mimic

Even though winter was ending, cold winds swept across the northern coast of the Narrow Lands. Calden ensign Soga de Yoni stood at the end of the Memorial Dock for the City of Penaber. Pulling his jacket tighter, he stared out onto Lumina's northwestern Ocean Deep. Just beyond the horizon lay the swirling portal of the Innaca Deep. How many times had he thought about diving in and swimming for it?

Whenever he visited this final resting place of his wife and young daughter, he could still see their white burial shrouds floating off and finally sinking beneath the waters. The mind-numbing grief that constantly consumed him was exceeded only by his overwhelming feeling of guilt for being at sea when the fever took them.

How many supposed suicide missions and dangerous assignments had he volunteered for? Too many to count. It was his blatant disregard for his own life that finally landed him on a desk in this far-flung outpost of the Calden navy.

"Ensign?"

A youthful voice from behind snapped him from his maudlin trance. He turned to see a young naval courier with a folded and sealed piece of paper in his outstretched hand.

"They told me I could find you here, sir," he said, offering the paper. "Orders from the naval attaché."

Soga nodded his thanks and silently accepted the new assignment. When the courier left, he broke the seal and read the orders. When he finished, he gazed back out to sea, tore up the paper, and tossed the pieces into the ocean. They may have finally given him the mission from which there would be no return.

The lone vidette boat entered the Kusonga Ice Fields just after moonrise. Long a migration route for the Yupik, from the barren ice flows of the Frozen Sea to the slightly more hospitable tundra of the Narrow Lands, this enormous field of icebergs loosely connected the two continents. Their small craft slowly navigated the closely packed ice pillars. The pilot's eyes nervously darted around the shifting canyons of ice and his youthful face grew ashen.

Blood had stained most of the sides of the icebergs red and the still frigid air stank of rotting flesh. Partially eaten seals and Yupik carcasses hung all over. On one flat ice flow, five severed Yupik heads stared vacantly into oblivion.

A rag-tag band of armed Yupik lined the summits and ledges of the ice, peering down at the boat's careful advance through the narrow corridors. The stout, blue humanoids with oval heads betrayed no emotion towards the visitors and kept their weapons lowered.

"Don't worry about the locals," Soga said, crouching on the bow of the boat. "Just make sure we don't get crushed by shifting ice."

The pilot swallowed hard. "Yes sir."

Eventually they arrived at a flat iceberg with a narrow landing and stairs carved into the side. When the boat pulled up to the make-shift dock, Soga stood and disrobed. The naked human seemed unaffected by the cold when he stepped out of the boat.

"Wait here," Soga ordered. "No matter what you see, or think you see, don't leave the boat."

The pilot nodded and Soga ascended the staircase. The flat summit rose ten feet off of the water and was thirty feet in diameter. Soga walked to the middle and sat down cross-legged. A few moments passed before the ensign detected movement on the far rim of the ice sheet.

Two white pincers appeared over the edge, followed immediately by a bluish white Ice Scorpion a little over a foot in length. Under the watchful gaze of four Yupik clansman observing from a nearby ledge, the arachnid made an erratic, but direct path towards the telltale heat source. When the creature reached Soga, it quickly spun and stung him on the inside of his upper right thigh.

The Calden sailor winced at the initial pain, but then slumped. His eyes rolled back in his head when the neurotoxin rapidly took effect. Finally, he succumbed to the poison and toppled over.

When the scorpion turned to feed on its victim, the four Yupik leapt down beside the prone human. An older shaman, unarmed and wearing a shoulder bag slung crossway over his chest, gruffly backhanded the scorpion, sweeping it off the edge. The other three gently rolled the unconscious human onto his back while the elder reached into his bag.

The shaman retrieved four thin bone knives and place them on the ice beside Soga. Kneeling beside the sailor's head, the older Yupik gave the human a brief intense examination before reaching for the blades.

The shaman first cut across the upper forehead by the hairline. He skinned Soga with surgical precision, working delicately around the eyes nose and mouth. Once removed, he placed the intact skin of the face and neck on the ice next to him and began with the chest. He worked quickly and methodically down the front of Soga's torso and legs. As with the face and neck, he took the severed skins and laid them next to the body.

When the cutter had completely removed the human's outer layer of skin from his front side, his three assistants gently rolled him over onto his stomach and the shaman repeated the flaying on his backside.

When the older clansman nodded and the Yupik assistants rolled him onto his back once more. Soga lay there, his underlying muscles, tendons and veins exposed to the elements. Blood loss was minimal, because of the cold.

The old Yupik again knelt by Soga's head. With the same disciplined precision, the elder ice clansman began putting the skin back on the human's body, but inside out.

Down below in the vidette boat, it horrified the pilot when he watched them toss Soga's mutilated body into the frigid waters. He immediately lowered the Ukko rudder and the boat quickly closed the distance to where he saw the body fall. A tense moment passed while he leaned over the side of the boat scouring the water for any sign of life. He was both startled and elated when a forearm breached the water beside him, grasping at the air.

Reaching down, the boat driver seized the hand and pulled. When the head came out of the water, he found himself staring into his own face. Crying out in alarm, he let go of the doppelganger's hand and he fell backwards into the boat.

Yupik clansmen descended into peals of laughter on the iceberg above him. The terrorized young man stared up at the amused clansman, then back at the arm when it reached across the side of the boat and pulled itself up.

He heaved a sigh of relief when he saw Soga's normal chiseled features and bald head climbing back into the vessel. Lying on his back against the bare hull, the shapeshifting Calden sailor sputtered and caught his breath.

When Soga finally sat up, the young pilot took the rudder with an expectant look.

"I wasn't given the second destination. Where to sir?"

"Tannimore," Soga said, reaching for his clothes.

"Best possible speed, sir?"

"Just get me there."

The Kan was the only thing Che-At liked about this region of Lumina. It reminded her of home in the Land of Mists. Now, from the shadows of a nearby building, she watched the chaos at the Language Arts Center.

Her interest became piqued when she saw the human male with the long ponytail carrying the female she had seen working with the book. The female laid limp in his arms while he walked over and placed her into a parked buggy. When he jumped into the driver's seat, Che-At waited to see which direction they took. The instant he started off, the Singa bolted away on an intercept course.

One of the primary concerns of anyone driving through the Kan is speed, and this Kan was no exception. It was often said, that during the Kan, you could walk to your destination faster than a buggy could get you there.

Tysonn was having difficulty keeping the large lizard pulling the wagon under control. They bred the creature for speed and Tysonn knew one wrong turn could be disastrous. Fortunately, he didn't have far to go. Clerria House rested in the surrounding districts of the University of Marassa, just a short distance from where they were now.

The lizard hissed in protest when Tysonn pulled back on the reins. The scholar cursed under his breath when he heard a loud thump and felt something large drop into the wagon directly behind him.

Before he could react, Che-At clasped a wooden staff tightly against his throat from behind. He could feel the tickle of the Singa's whiskers against the back of his neck and his nose quivered disdainfully at her smell.

"Halt!" she gruffly ordered in Common.

Choking, Tyson nodded his head emphatically and brought the carriage to a stop. Che-At released her stranglehold then struck a pressure point on Tysonn's kneecap with the tip of her staff, doubling him over in pain. All he could do was gingerly rub his knee while the Singa easily picked up Kasha and hoisted the body over her shoulder. She pointed the tip of her staff directly at Tysonn's head.

"Give book to Tiikeri ambassador," she said, in broken Common. "Then I release woman."

With that demand, she lunged the staff forward, popping Tysonn on the temple, knocking him unconscious. The Singa then leapt over the side of the wagon with her prize and disappeared into the thick Kan fog.

From the quarterdeck of the Eldorian frigate *Reali,* Shom Eldor watched the Kan fog roll off the western Goyan coast and dissipate around them. In the distance they could see the Zorian Forum and the massive landing bays of Air Station Three jutting from the mountainside.

"We'll be docking soon," Shom said, over the fluttering of the sails.

Atina remained silent with her face cast into the wind. She carried a rare, serene smile while her hair whipped all about her.

Raising a spyglass to his face, Shom followed the buildings of the metropolis down the mountain and foothills onto the beach. He traced the horizon line to the west and settled on a massive barge riding low in the water, steering steadily southward.

"Odd," The Eldorian royal noted, keeping the spyglass to his face. "There must be something big going on in Tannimore."

The Hill Sister squinted in the direction Shom was investigating. "What makes you say that?"

"Tannimore is a wild party city," Shom said, perplexed. "The only ships you see headed out there are party boats and yachts. That's a fully loaded industrial barge."

"They could be headed somewhere else," Attina offered.

Shom shook his head. "They just caught the Tannimore Loop. That's where they're going."

"Maybe they're just catching a ride on the current."

Once again Shom shook his head. "There's nothing out there but hundreds of miles of open ocean until you eventually hit the Wild Lands."

Shom studied the massive ship hoping to see some kind of identifying mark, when he caught a flash of motion to his starboard side. Adjusting his glass, it surprised the royal to see a vidette boat rapidly approaching the barge's stern.

"Hello, what's this?" he said, now concentrating on the small, fast moving craft.

From what he could tell there were only two people on board, a driver holding the oar deep into the water for maximum speed and a person balanced precariously on the bow. The much swifter vidette easily caught up with the slow-moving ship and the person on its bow leapt onto the stern of the barge.

"Interesting," Shom said, taking the spyglass from his eye and giving a thoughtful pout.

"What?" Attina asked.

"I'm not entirely sure," Shom said, collapsing the spyglass and putting it away. "No matter, we're about to dock and we've got other things to worry about."

Soga watched the vidette boat peeling away from the barge's wake. He then spun around and took in his surroundings. The ship was easily three hundred feet long and forty feet across with a low quarterdeck and open bridge amidships. Two massive Ukko wood rudders powered the vessel.

On either side of the bridge stood two huge cargo holds covered by tarps. Somewhere on the barge, he heard crew members shouting and adjusting the rigging, but saw no one in the immediate vicinity. He felt too exposed, realizing anyone could see him on the bridge if they turned around, so he slipped into the nearest cargo hold.

The contents of the hold took Soga slightly aback. Huge rectangles of cut, polished crystals filled the entire area, instead of the usual cargo of food stores, crates and barrels. He didn't understand the importance the crystals held, but this seemed an excellent place to hide out.

"Where did they find him?" Zekoff asked, entering the double front doors of Clerria House.

"Just outside Kampo Plat in the Seven Sisters Slums," Rafel said. "Near to here, actually."

"Alone?"

"Yes sir, a patrol discovered him slumped over on the buckboard of a small empty wagon."

The old colonel nodded grimly and entered a large multi-bed infirmary. An old woman in long purple robes immediately met them.

Rafel winced slightly as he always did when he came to the Clerria House. The smell of blood, body fluids and herbal elixirs, mixed with the moans of pain, unnerved him. When it first happened, he remembered how ironic it seemed, given his line of work. He reconciled the paradox when he recognized these were the cries of the innocent, instead of the tortured wails of the guilty, and this gave him a perverse sense of pleasure.

"We're looking for the man they brought in this morning," Rafel said to the old woman.

"You will have to be a little more specific than that, Captain," she said, her face souring. "We get about half a dozen patients every morning."

"He had a long ponytail," the Zorian spymaster clarified.

The woman nodded and silently led them to one of the many beds surrounded by white curtains. Tysonn laid on his back staring at the ceiling with a large, painful looking lump in the center of his forehead.

"They took her," he said, dolefully, continuing to gaze upward with a melancholy expression.

"They? They who?" Zekoff asked, with growing unease. "What happened?"

The two senior Zorian guards traded uneasy glances while the scribe related the incidents surrounding Kasha's kidnapping last Kan.

"Lioness, you say?" Zekoff asked.

"She wore a cape with a hood and carried a staff," Tysonn explained.

"A Singa matching that description arrived with the Tiikeri delegation a few cycles ago." Rafel said, assessing the scholar's narrative. "Which is probably why she demanded you return the book to them."

"That damn book has been nothing but trouble since we started translating it," Tysonn scornfully spat.

"Where is it now?"

"Locked up back in Kasha's office," Tysonn answered. "The Bailian is guarding it."

"Let's go get that book," the old colonel said, resolutely. "Can you walk?"

Tysonn nodded, and wincing with pain, slowly got to his feet. The short trek across campus was slow going. Cha-Rod rose to his feet when the trio finally entered. After introductions, they visually searched the cluttered office and their gaze quickly settled on the blackboard filled with the binary runes.

"I'd say she was a bit obsessed," Zekoff surmised, his eyes sweeping across the blackboard. "These are the same runes Stryder Aramos was using."

"Only he wrote them in blood," Rafel added.

Tysonn unlocked the safe and returned with the book.

"The runes in *this book* are written in blood," Tysonn said, handing the tome to Zekoff. "Be careful, it can change you. Of the two scribes that copied it, one had a mental breakdown, and the other hung herself."

The colonel casually flipped through the pages.

"All from just one book?" he asked.

"Not just any book," Tysonn added, ominously, "a prayer book to a dark Tiikeri god. This was not meant for humans."

257

"Nothing from Nocturn is meant for humans," Cha-Rod concurred. "Nor *my* people for that matter."

Rafel's eyes narrowed. "I think it's time I had a little conversation with the new Tiikeri ambassador."

Zekoff nodded knowingly and a smug grin played with the corners of his mouth.

"You say the scholars here made a copy of this book?" he asked.

"The entire thing," Tysonn confirmed.

"I agree that you should pay the Tiikeri a visit," the colonel said, handing the book to his spymaster. "Just give them back the book. You know nothing about it. You're just following orders. Don't mention the Singa or anything about this affair."

"Sir?" Rafel asked, accepting the tome with a quizzical expression.

"The enemy has unwittingly revealed themselves," Zekoff said, reaching for his pipe. "Let's not show our hand. Allow them to think they've won a victory. Meanwhile, I want every member of the Tiikeri delegation under surveillance constantly."

The day went by uneventfully. Soga could hear crew members milling about on the deck, but no one seemed to be interested in the cargo.

While he sat there scratching his arm, he realized his entire body itched. He imagined this would be the new normal, a side effect of his magically reattached skin. Holding his arm up, he examined his hand. Despite the slight irritation, Soga decided he enjoyed his new ability.

He had interrogated enough Yupik to know their lore. Creatures with mimic abilities were rare and usually occurred naturally, not created like him. There was a warning given by the Yupik elders to travelers on the desolate flows of the Frozen sea. *Do not look upon the face of anyone you might pass on the ice, for they might be a mimic and will steal your face.*

Just before moonfall, Soga detected someone examining the tie downs for the tarp above him. Drawing his dagger, he silently flattened himself against the wall. A hand pulled back the corner of the covering and a face appeared through the opening. Soga reached up and grabbed the unwitting sailor, yanking him down into the cargo area.

When the young man hit the floor, the impact drove the wind from his lungs which muted his guttural groan. The sailor gasped again when he looked up and saw what appeared to be his own face looking back down at him. Taking advantage of the moment of shock, Soga gave a quick lunge, driving his dagger into the mariner's heart and killing him instantly.

Still keeping the sailor's appearance, the shapeshifter popped his head out the hatch and looked around. Several other deck hands walked his way.

"We saw you fall," one said. "Are you hurt?"

Soga nodded and waved. "Only my pride."

All three laughed and headed back towards the bow. Soga heaved a sigh of relief and climbed up onto the deck with the corpse. When the moon completely set, the weakened rays of the sun in the western sky gave enough cover for the glamoured Calden agent to slip the body over the side.

After the corpse plunged beneath the waves with an unceremonious plop, Soga could make out lights on the horizon drawing steadily closer. When the floating City of Tannimore rose before them, the steady sea breeze disappeared and the waters grew dead calm.

The reflected lights of the city and the glow of a massive purple crystal cairn twinkled together on the glass smooth water. The Ukko rudders groaned, raising almost completely out of the water and slowed the massive barge to a crawl.

This was the first time the Calden ensign had visited the infamous city of decadence and it duly impressed him. He stared upward in wonder when they passed below the entrance archway connecting the huge man-o-war ships and the seven-story structures built atop them. Just beyond, long rows of individual wharfs flanked either side of the wide aquatic corridor.

The barge came to a stop alongside three docks and a crane swung into place from up above. Immediately, deck hands began removing tarps from the four cargo holds. Soga could see more blocks of the large multi-colored crystals filling all the other containment areas.

Attempting to look busy, Soga made his way to the nearest connecting gang plank and slipped away into the city.

Demetrius was in the middle of constructing his favorite cocktail, a Zorian Whiplash, when the pounding on the front door started.

"What the…" he said, in an exasperated huff at the interruption.

This was the delicate part which called for an exact measurement. The pounding persisted while he completed the concoction.

"All right, all right!" he said, setting the glass down on the table.

The knocking seemed to pick up its pace while he shuffled across the living room of his modest apartment.

"I hear you," he proclaimed, turning the lock. "Keep your pants on!"

When he opened the door, he stood face to face with a frustrated Okawa. She wore her official green jumpsuit and pulled her hair back into a bun. He caught her with hands poised for another round of knocking.

"Perhaps I spoke too soon about the pants thing," he said, a broad grin sweeping across his face.

Without waiting for an invitation, she brushed past the pilot and briskly entered the room.

"Why Mz. Okawa, you look especially fetching," he said, watching her pace. "What brings you to my abode this Kan?"

She paused, gave him an annoyed look, then resumed her nervous stride.

"I was just mixing a cocktail," he said, closing the door and walking back to his drink. "Can I make you one?"

Ignoring the offer, she stopped in front of the fireplace.

"Demetrius, I just don't see how this can work!"

"How what can work?" the pilot asked, after taking a sip.

"This. Us! You know after what happened yesterday," she said, pointing back-and-forth at him.

Seemingly oblivious to her bluster, he smacked his lips and eyed the drink in his hand.

"This is tasty. Are you sure you don't want one?"

"Demetrius, I'm serious!"

"I can tell."

"Look it's not that I don't have feelings for you. You're different from any other guy I've met."

Demetrius's eyes twinkled taking another sip.

"Different in a good way I hope?"

"Well sure," she said, with a shake of her head just before resuming her trek across the room. "It's just in my line of work you can't become attached to people. I mean I've spent most of my life and career not trusting. Trust can get you killed."

Demetrius calmly returned to the table and began mixing a second drink.

"I'm also afraid they will use our relationship against me," she continued. "Let's face it, in my business, you're a liability."

"Uh huh," Demetrius placated, giving the beverage a final stir.

"Another thing, if we're working together, it might cause either of us to do something stupid, especially if we think the other is in danger… are you listening to me?"

"I heard every word," the pilot said, in a husky voice, offering her the second drink.

The agent paused, looked down at the glass, then back up at Demetrius.

"It'll take the edge off," he assured.

Sighing, she accepted the cocktail.

Demetrius looked her in the eye and gave an evocative smirk.

"Look," he began, "I'm not saying this won't be dangerous, but we've already been through a few scrapes together. I think you're the most different woman I've ever met. You're smart, you're beautiful and you have an incredible body. Personally, I say trying to deny these feelings is what will get in the way of us working together."

Okawa hesitated while her resolve wavered under Demetrius's disarming smile. Heaving a sigh of resignation, she raised her glass, and they toasted.

"It doesn't bother your ego that your girlfriend could snap you like a twig?" she asked, before taking a drink.

Demetrius chuckled. "No, that part's a turn on."

Rolling her eyes, she took another sip then reached back and unfastened her hair, allowing it to tumble free about her shoulders.

"Well, I'm here and we apparently have some time. What say we try a repeat of yesterday, minus the hallucinogens."

Demetrius took her free hand and led her back to the bedroom.

"Girlfriend, I like the way that sounds."

The half Bailian young man, Jer-Om, studied the papers Captain Rafel presented him and beamed with pride. While the Zorian spymaster watched the young man read, he felt a twinge of satisfaction. Another piece of the puzzle leading to Kai's undoing fell into place. He leaned back in his chair with an amused, calculating look.

"I know I speak for Colonel Zekoff," he said, "and the entire Zorian High Council in offering congratulations on your being promoted to this austere position."

"Captain, I'm honored, of course," Jer-Om answered, "but I can't help but wonder... I mean, surely there were those more qualified? After all, ambassador to the Bailian Empire is *quite* a prominent position. I would hate to think I was leaping over those..."

"Nonsense Jer-Om," Rafel interrupted. "Your mother is Bailian, so you understand the culture. You speak, read, and write fluent En'Sul. You've spent the last three grands on the Bailian desk working for me here at the forum. You've already established a network of contacts from afar. This position just puts you in closer contact with them."

"I'm honored, sir."

Rafel sat forward and lowered his voice. His demeanor turned from congratulatory to somber.

"You have your letter of introduction," he said, "and official orders, I will now give you your confidential directive."

The young man leaned forward on the desk and his large almond-shaped eyes locked on his director.

"It goes without saying you'll be keeping an eye on the palace and the queen, but I want you to keep the Bailian spymaster under heavy scrutiny."

"You mean Kai, sir?"

Rafel tensed at the mentioning of the name.

"Yes," he replied, through gritted teeth. "I want her every movement monitored, who she sees, where she goes, and no detail is too small. Make it your first duty. You will report directly to me."

"Yes sir, I'll put a team on it immediately upon arrival."

"One other thing." Rafel said, cautiously. "We must have a degree of deniability. It's best if the various members of your team are unaware of each other."

"I won't let you down, sir."

"Of that I have no doubt," Rafel said, smiling confidently. "Now, you need to pack. I want you in Immor-Onn before the next Kan."

Since awakening, Soga had taken it upon himself to get familiar with the City of Tannimore. He especially memorized the second level, in and around the theatre, where they would hold the auction this evening.

With every person he brushed up against in the congested streets his repertoire of personalities grew. Each persona added, however, caused a tingling itch to travel across his skin. He fought the constant urge to scratch himself.

On the outdoor areas, along the many rooftops and catwalks, he kept an eye on the blue skinned Gila hybrid who directed work parties placing and stacking the crystals from the cargo hold. The Calden ensign still had no clue to their purpose. They placed them in strategic spots but they appeared more ornamental than anything else.

The third level contained most of the food vendors. They wisely placed the various stalls and small shops along the outer rim of the city, known as the Outskirts, for both smoke control and proximity to the water if needed.

While Soga purchased a container of smoked fish, he spotted a group of four men eating and drinking ale at one of the many communal tables. They looked like typical rowdy men-at-arms except for their apparent leader.

The thick scar running horizontal across his forehead and weak left eye set him apart. Soga recognized the man; he had served with him in a joint operation with the Aramos Black Talons. It was a sound bet his companions belonged to the same group. The question which nagged at him was their reason to be here. He concluded it had something to do with security for the Aramos representative at the auction.

It really didn't matter. His orders were explicit and the stakes couldn't be higher.

Demetrius heard the grand turine ring five bells when they stepped onto the flight deck of Air Station Three. He did a quick glance over his shoulder at the two stone-faced men flanking Joc' Valdur and Pierce Calden. Both had the same plain, dark blue uniform and close-cropped haircut. Each man wielded a light, six-bolt magazine crossbow and a short sword.

"Who did you say they were?" he whispered, leaning over to Okawa who kept pace beside him.

"Well, they didn't introduce themselves," the Valdurian agent replied, "but if I had to guess, I'd say they're a couple of guys from the Calden Intelligencer Service who drew the short straw on this protection detail."

"I bet they're a hoot at parties," the pilot quipped.

Okawa fought back a giggle. "Something tells me those are the guys you send in to *break up* parties."

Demetrius nodded in agreement when they entered the commercial hangar.

"Well, what's all this?" the pilot said, halting in front of the *Drakin*.

Standing on top of the airship, just above the side hatch, a tiny figure stood with its arms folded curiously watching them approach. It resembled a human child constructed in great detail with twigs and branches. Its insides, filled with soil and rocks, showed through its elaborate wooden frame. It jumped to the ground in front of them and the two Calden guards reached for their swords.

"Woah there, hard chargers," Demetrius said, raising his hand. "What do you say we find out what's going on here before you start hacking away at things?"

When the two guards removed their hands from their sword hilts, the creature grinned then hugged Demetrius's legs. Then, in a single bound, it leapt back up on the top of the airship.

I am Lamos, all heard in their head. *You are going to the place in the water that is still. You will take me with you.*

Everyone was now staring around at each other in amazement.

"Did you just hear that?" Demetrius asked, to no one in particular.

"Probably because of our proximity to the Larimar crystal in the ship's new panel," Okawa surmised.

"Yeah, well, whatever it calls itself, we don't have time for discussion," Demetrius said, with a touch of annoyance. "The Kan and moonfall are only a deci away."

"Shall we remove it, sir?" one intelligencer asked Pierce Calden.

Demetrius spun to face the bodyguard. "Wow, are you guys ever wrapped tight. Look, he may be your boss, but make no mistake. This is *my* ship. I've got this."

With that admonishment, the pilot reached up to Lamos with both hands.

"Come on little guy, you gotta get down," he said. "We're in a hurry."

The creature's demeanor instantly changed to a scowl. It grew several feet in size and shook a defiant fist at Demetrius. There was the distinct sound of wood creaking when its feet morphed into long tree roots encircling the ship. The thick wooden tendrils covered both hatches and the windshield, making entry and flight impossible.

You will take me with you! it demanded.

Demetrius, along with everyone else, jumped, and the pilot raised his hands.

"Okay, okay," he relented. "I guess you're coming along."

A smile returned to the child-like face, and it changed back to its original appearance and size. Positioning itself cross legged and facing forward on the roof the *Drakin* just above the windshield, it looked down expectantly at the humans.

With a resigned shrug Demetrius opened the side hatch and the ambassador's party got onboard.

"So, who's your new little friend?" Okawa playfully queried, stepping past Demetrius and into the craft.

"Shut up…" he muttered, following her in.

High winds and rain buffeted the *Drakin,* violently rocking the airship while an early spring storm coursed across the southwestern Ocean Deep of Lumina.

An air of quiet tension permeated the cabin. Demetrius, at the controls, seemed the only one truly at ease.

"Think your little buddy's still up there?" Okawa asked, glancing upward.

"Probably, you saw the way he latched onto the ship." Demetrius said, squinting out the windshield.

The weather's instant clearing visibly startled the Valdurian agent. They could now see streamers of sunlight poking through the storm clouds in the east. To the west, the setting moon cast dim illumination. A wide-eyed Okawa spun in her seat taking in the tempest all around them, held at bay by an invisible circular barrier.

"First time in the Doldrums?" Demetrius asked, gently banking the craft to the southwest.

She nodded, staring about in wonder.

"I'd only heard about it."

When the airship altered course, the free City of Tannimore came fully into view, sitting placidly on a calm sea.

"It's even bigger than when I was here last," Demetrius noted.

"I almost pulled an assignment here several grands ago," Okawa said, examining the approaching city.

"Really?" Demetrius asked, amused. "What was that all about?"

The immediate silence caused the pilot to look over at his girlfriend who was giving him the 'stupid question' look.

"Sorry," he weakly said, returning his gaze outward.

When the *Drakin* drew close enough for a landing Demetrius circled the city studying the rooftops below.

"Hey, it looks like they've added landing pads," the pilot said, optimistically.

His brow furrowed the moment he saw the multi-layered crystal cairns strategically placed around the city.

"These look familiar," he added, "and not in a good way."

Okawa closed her eyes and let out a loud frustrated sigh.

"Those cairns mean Stryder controls this city," she pointed out. "Are we just going to deliver ourselves to him?"

By now, both ambassadors had joined them at the command chairs and peered down at their destination.

"We really don't have a choice," Joc' said, bleakly.

From Tannimore's upper docks, they watched the airship slowly circle and begin its descent.

"Here come some more rich fucks for the auction," Marko said, his voice dripping with disdain.

"Wouldn't mind getting my hands on some of that money," Danzig said, scratching the stubble on his neck. "They say whatever it is they're bidding on, starts at a million gold pieces,"

The two others whistled in appreciation.

"Heh, I didn't think you could count that high," Marko said, sweeping back a strand of sweat drenched black hair.

Danzig gave an evil chuckle. "I don't need it all, I ain't greedy."

A third man, substantially younger than the other two, with short blonde hair and a baby face, shook his head condescendingly.

"There's plenty of prosperity here to go around if you would just embrace it."

Marko sneered at the thin young man. "Look at Oreus over here, all high and mighty since he got those marks on the back of his neck."

Oreus remained unfazed by the insult. "You had your chance. You refused the invitation. I embraced the lord, now look, they have placed me in charge of you two. I will continue to advance and prosper while you toil on the docks for the rest of your lives."

Marko became indignant. "Yeah, well I got the Whitmar brand on my back. I made a promise to myself on my last day in punishment slavery; no man would mark me again. You can keep your damn god and your prosperity."

The young man gave a shrug of indifference. "Suit yourself. The lord only wishes those who come to him of their own free will..."

"Hey, look at that!" Danzig interrupted, pointing towards an object falling from the airship.

"The damn thing's falling apart," Marko said, mockingly.

All watched while it plummeted. They heard it crash onto a nearby dock.

"What was that?" Marko asked.

"Don't know," Danzig replied, staring the direction it landed. "Too small to tell,"

"Come on, it could be something important," Oreus said, starting off. "Let's go check it out."

"I don't give a shit what it is," Marko said, defiantly.

The young man's demeanor turned commanding. "And I don't give a shit that you don't give a shit, come on."

With the order given, he headed in the direction the object fell with the two dock workers reluctantly in tow. The search ended in a warehouse by the lower docks. They cautiously approached a set of double doors pulled off their hinges.

"I don't like the looks of this," Danzig said, nervously.

Oreus scowled and drew his dagger. With a motion of his head, he led the two into the storage area. The room smelled musty and their nostrils flared. Oreus tapped a crystal on the wall bathing the room in warm orange light.

Amongst the various crates and barrels, they saw a small wooden figure in the far corner standing with its arms folded.

"You think that's what fell from the airship?" Marko asked, moving warily into the warehouse.

"I seriously doubt it was here before," Oreus replied, moving towards the mysterious figure.

"What is it?" Danzig asked. "It looks like an idol."

"And how the fuck did it get in here?" Marko wondered aloud. "Somebody broke that door open."

All three now stood in a semi-circle a few feet from the figure, staring intently.

"We should report this to someone," Oreus suggested.

"And say what?!" Marko challenged. "People from the sky are throwing dolls at us?"

All three jumped back in surprise when the figure uncrossed its arms and raised them.

"The fucking things alive!" were Marko's last words.

With the sound of creaking wood Lamos' body seemed to explode and expand, transforming into dozens of branches and briars filling the room. A half a dozen inch-thick sharpened limbs impaled both Markos and Danzig, while a thorny vine tightly entangled Oreus.

Held immobile, the young acolyte could do nothing but watch in horror while multiple small thorns pierced his clothing and a long barb wavered inches from his throat. The sound of groaning wood preceded the branches shifting and moving in rapid gyrations and shredding the two human corpses. Oreus shrieked while their various body parts flew about and showered the room in blood.

From off to his left, another thick, barbed vine, with the head of Lamos on its end, undulated to within inches of the terrified human's face. Its eyes blazed with hatred and the mouth twisted into a scowl.

You will take me to the plunderer! the voice thundered in Oreus's head. *The one called Stryder!*

Appearing as a guard, Soga moved unnoticed through the streets of Tannimore and into the theatre. The Calden ensign was getting used to his new ability and enjoyed the sensation of changing at will.

The large chamber was empty, but he knew soon it would teem with representatives of various houses and factions, all vying for the precious Ukko wood of the Zerian forest. He would have to act quickly, and he would only have one chance.

Making his way backstage, he hid behind a curtain in the preparation room. His wait was brief, and he drew his dagger when he heard the back door open. The general feeling of unease permeating the area and the substantial rise in temperature made him certain it was Stryder.

"Make sure this back door is secure," Stryder's deep voice commanded.

"Yes sir."

"You two position yourself on the stage," he ordered. "Our guests will arrive soon."

There was no response, but he heard them leave and the temperature returned to normal. Soga peeked out and saw his target for the first time. The bald, black robed man stood with his back to him, rune scars covered his head and neck. A nervous looking young man stationed by the rear door served as his only guard.

Soga felt certain he could get to the dark cleric before his security would have time to intervene. The time was now. Slipping quickly between the curtains, the Calden assassin covered the distance to his target in a single bound.

The startled look on the lone guard's face caused Stryder to spin. The thrust of Soga's dagger stabbed through a corner of the dark cleric's robe and became entangled as he turned. This gave Stryder time to reach down and grab the assassin's arm.

The cleric's solid black eyes locked onto the assassin and glowed blue while a maniacal smile crept across his face. Soga wrenched in pain when the runes on the back of the dark cleric's hand also began to glow.

"Is this any way to treat someone bringing you an offer of salvation?" Stryder gloated.

Soga suddenly began violently convulsing. His eyes rolled back in his head and his face changed back to his own, then promptly switched to another. Then, one after the other, in rapid succession, the Calden ensign's face transformed into a seemingly unending cavalcade of various personas.

He dropped to the floor at Stryder's feet, still convulsing and cascading through an endless stream of personalities. Through the spasms, Soga watched Stryder's eyes narrow with rage, peering at the young guard. The Herald of Pa-Waga slowly levitated toward him.

"Tell me," he said, in a calm, but threatening tone. "What do you call a bodyguard who does not guard?"

The young sentry trembled uncontrollably, his eyes wide in terror. He shook his head and tried to speak only to find no words would come out. Soga could do nothing but shudder and randomly shape shift on the floor while he watched Stryder halt a few feet away from the horrified youth and the dark cleric softly answered his own question.

"Worthless."

The runes on his lips glowed blue while he softly mouthed a string of unintelligible words. The disgraced guard looked down and saw his hand remove the dagger from its sheath.

"Redeem yourself in the eyes of the lord," Stryder ordered in a low voice.

The guard's wide, panic-filled eyes watched his muscles protest in vain as he brought the blade up to his own throat.

"Slowly," Stryder said, in a sensuous whisper, "savor the moment."

Unhurriedly and reluctantly the young guard obeyed, pulling the blade across his throat. He gurgled while a sheet of blood flooded the front of his shirt and he toppled to the floor next to Soga.

As the young man's lifeblood flowed out onto the floor, it pooled around Soga's head. When the blood touched the dying Calden assassin, he polymorphed one last time into the dead guard lying beside him.

Stryder stared down at the two identical looking men lying beside each other and gave a condescending sneer.

"Some are not meant to witness the majesty of the lord," he said, watching Soga do a final shape shift as he died.

When the Calden assassin finally perished, he reverted back to his mutilated body, with his bloody skin flayed and inside out, just as the Yupik shamans had left him.

"Looks like we've got a welcoming committee," Okawa said, while the *Drakin* settled onto the landing pad.

She then spun around to Joc' Valdur seated behind her.

"Boss, from a security standpoint, this is a bad idea."

"As I mentioned before, we don't have a choice," the Valdurian ambassador replied.

She stared at the passenger's resigned faces and then stood up.

"Well," she said, "all right then, let's do this."

While everyone else was getting to their feet, her gaze settled on the pilot.

"Once we're away, you take off and hover just out of ballista range and..."

"I know, I know, wait for your signal," Demetrius finished her thought.

Smiling she reached down and gently caressed his cheek while nodding yes.

"You just be careful," he said, gazing lovingly into her eyes.

When Okawa looked back up everyone in the cabin was staring at them, and Joc' had broken out into a grin of recognition. With an embarrassed smirk she checked the pistol crossbow on her hip.

"Let's go," she said.

When they stepped out onto the roof, the *Drakin* silently lifted off. Joc' leaned over to her.

"You two?" he asked, with the same grin.

The Valdurian agent averted her eyes and blushed.

"You look good together," Joc' said, nodding in approval.

The two men who waited for them to land approached. One was much older with short grey hair, the other in his twenties with freckles and an unkept red mane. Both wore identical black tunics.

"Welcome to Tannimore," the older man said, with a somber look on his wrinkled face.

Pierce Calden's eyes bore into him. "You're extorting us, sir. I think we can drop the facade of civility."

The two shared a long, tense moment staring each other down. The old man sucked on a tooth while he assessed the Calden ambassador. Finally, he stepped aside and motioned to the younger redhead.

"Very well then," he said, tensely. "Piros will show you to your seats. The auction will start soon."

The young man led them down through the second level of the city and to a large partially filled theatre and escorted them to a private balcony.

Along the way, Okawa noted four men-at-arms lining the aisles on the floor of the theatre near the stage. They hardly looked like they could afford to be at the auction. One of their numbers, presumably the leader who had a large scar on his forehead and a lazy eye, quietly issued orders.

When Okawa and the group walked past, the leader stopped talking and the four stared at the group as they traversed the stairs to their private box seats along the theatre's back wall.

The room was small, with only a single curtain for a door. There were two chairs facing out into the theatre. On one chair was a yellow paddle with the number twenty-three printed on it.

The ambassadors took their seats with Okawa standing next to Joc'. The two Calden intelligencers positioned themselves on either side of the curtain. While the Valdurian agent watched more potential bidders get seated, her attention kept returning to the man with the scar and his three companions. She couldn't shake the feeling that he looked familiar.

Stryder's booming voice snapped her attention to the stage. He was there, levitating a few inches above the floor. He pulled his hood back and a collective gasp ran through the crowd when all could see his marked bald head and face. Standing on either side of him were two humanoids with glowing red eyes.

"All of you here this evening are witness to, and a part of, a new age of prosperity. I know it is difficult to see it now, but the seeds planted today, will ensure the blessings of the lord and shall bear abundant fruit."

The allegedly prophetic soliloquy caused an indignant grumble to rise from the audience. Ignoring the unrest, Stryder extended his right hand with the palm up. The runes carved there glowed blue and a shard of purple Etheria crystal levitated just above his outstretched palm.

"Behold," the dark cleric continued, "you will bid on this key. With it, the winner will take possession of their Ukko wood. I trust all bidders to have the necessary funds deposited in the Aris branch of the Imperial Bank. Payment will be immediately transferred from your account. The bidding will begin at one hundred thousand secors."

From the balcony of his booth Stryder saw Pierce Calden immediately raise his paddle with a contemptuous sneer. The bidding proceeded in increments of ten thousand secors and during that time the Calden ambassador never lowered his paddle. While the bidding climbed, more factions continued to drop out until only the agent from House Whitmar remained. When the price reached two hundred thousand, he shook his head.

Stryder looked around the room. "Last call for bids."

The room became a sea of murmurs, but they raised no other paddles.

"Sold to the Calden Valdur alliance for two hundred thousand secors," Stryder announced.

He reached over to a large round flat crystal on a small table. When he placed his hand on the milky white facade, the face of Harper Aramos appeared in the cloudy surface.

"Transfer one hundred thousand secors from the accounts of both House Valdur and Calden," he ordered.

The Aramos cousin nodded and his image faded.

Payment details completed, Stryder returned his attention to the victorious pair. Extending his arm, the purple shard floated from his open palm across the room towards its new owners.

When the crystal floated over the heads of the four suspicious men at arms, Okawa couldn't help but notice the envious looks on their faces following its path. She had been monitoring them the entire time and the fact they had not bid once, only heightened her uneasiness.

While the gem levitated across the theatre, tremors shook the room. The sound of wood creaking and groaning preceded a loud cracking, when a massive fissure opened in the floor just before the stage. The audience panicked when an enraged Lamos, now a full twenty feet tall, burst through from the level below.

With Stryder startled, his concentration broke, and the shard toppled to the floor amongst the out-of-control crowd.

When the men-at-arms saw the gem drop, they drew their weapons and began hacking their way through the throng toward where they saw it fall.

Lamos' height had grown almost as tall as the ceiling and he directed his fury toward the man on the stage.

"PLUNDERER!" its voice thundered, reaching for Stryder. "PREPARE TO PAY FOR YOUR SIN!"

Both ambassadors were now on their feet viewing the violent spectacle below with dread.

"The key!" Joc' cried out, pointing to the men-at-arms pushing through the chaos below.

"I knew those bastards were up to no good!" Okawa shouted, pulling her pistol crossbow. "Get the ambassadors to the roof!"

The agent cocked the weapon, and a bolt dropped in from the magazine. Not waiting for a reply or argument from the Calden bodyguards, she bound over the railing of the balcony and landed in a crouch next to several mangled and bleeding bodies. Her position was directly in the path between the swordsmen and the assumed position of the key.

Through the maze of rushing people, she saw the four headed her way. When the leader ran his blade through an unarmed attendee, she fired from her crouch. A bolt struck the leader in the temple while he attempted to free his sword. Its force catapulted his body into the comrade beside him, knocking him to the ground, and under the feet of the stampeding attendees.

The other two streamed forward, swords raised to strike. With little room to navigate, Okawa rolled forward just under the swords swing. While she tumbled, the Valdurian agent cocked the crossbow again. Landing on her back, she fired upward at point blank range, striking one attacker directly in the crotch. He screamed in pain and dropped his sword before following it to the ground.

The second assailant spun around for another strike. There was no time to load her weapon, so Okawa grabbed the sword off the ground from the man she had just shot in the groin. She got it up in front of her just in time to intercept the blow, but the force of the strike sent the sword flying from her hands.

The attacker raised up for another swing when a still growing Lamos smashed through the roof, raining debris down on the theatre's interior. He looked up in time to see a broken wooden beam falling straight for him. Okawa took advantage of the distraction and lashed out with a vicious kick to the knee then rolled to the side. The attacker screamed and fell beneath the beam which crashed down crushing him.

Demetrius was growing concerned. He could tell there was some altercation taking place in the theatre but couldn't determine anything specific. He bolted upright in his seat when the roof of the structure exploded and the upper torso of a giant Lamos protruded through.

The once tiny wooden figure now held Stryder in its outstretched hand, which now resembled a crude wooden cage. Runes strobed furiously all across Stryder's body. Their flickering blue lights induced a slight paralyzing effect on the wooden colossus, slowing its motions to a crawl.

Demetrius banked the craft around the besieged theatre complex, frantically searching the surface for his passengers, when he heard a loud creaking and popping of wood breaking. The wooden attachments of Lamos' chest cavity were breaking open under Stryder's magical assault, causing the dirt and rocks inside to spill out. The gigantic figure, now wounded, screamed in rage at his captive. In a single constricting motion, the forest guardian collapsed his cage hand around the dark cleric.

The force quickly crushed the former quartermaster's body, pulping it into a visceral paste which squeezed through the bars of the cage. The blue runes continued flickering wildly across the surface of the gelatinous form. Once it pressed outside the confines of the cage, its various visceral parts rejoined into a large amorphous blob that dropped out of sight into the ruins of the theatre.

The pilot sat speechless, watching the ferocious spectacle, until he saw a door opening onto a nearby roof. Four people bolted out onto the flat surface. He could make out the long-haired features of Joc' Valdur.

"Nothing like playing it close," he said aloud, banking the ship downward.

The *Drakin* was almost on top of the fleeing ambassadors, when the two Na-Kab shot columns of fire out through the open roof from somewhere within the theatre's interior. The blast set Lamos ablaze and forced Demetrius to swerve the airship to avoid being hit. Burning chunks of the immense wooden creature fell, setting structures in the area alight.

"Where's Okawa?!" Demetrius demanded, when the ambassadors climbed in through the side hatch.

"She went after the key," Joc' panted. "We lost track of her."

"I'M NOT LEAVING WITHOUT HER!" the pilot screamed, defiantly.

From off to their immediate port side, a section of burning roof collapsed with a rumble and shower of sparks. Joc' watched more burning debris falling all around them.

"If you don't get us off this roof," he said, "none of us will make it!"

The pilot scowled and reluctantly took the ship airborne just before one of Lamos' burning limbs came crashing down where the craft had been sitting. Demetrius pulled the *Drakin* upward and performed a tight circle around the burning area all the while keeping a close eye for Okawa amongst the fleeing citizens.

"There!" Joc' said, pointing.

A figure sprinted through the Outskirts to the city's edge. Between her size and the trailing ponytail, Demetrius knew it was her. He did a quick bank off to port and came in low just behind the racing woman. The airship was almost upon her, when she leapt over the side into the calm waters of the Doldrums.

The craft was hovering inches above the water when she surfaced. Once they pulled her aboard, the exhausted agent sat bent over, forearms resting on her thighs while she caught her breath.

"What about the key?" Pierce asked.

She shook her head without looking up.

"Too much fire and confusion," she said, in a defeated, weary voice.

The disappointment was obvious on the ambassador's faces. Pierce exhaled hard running a hand through his hair.

"That was a *lot* of money," he said.

Joc' watched the fire control water towers douse the area around the flames, but like before, the water had no effect on the Na-Kab fire. What remained of Lamos plunged into the sea when the floor beneath it burned away. The figure continued to burn, lighting up the depths while it plummeted into the blackness of the ocean.

"Maybe we can get in there once they've got the fire out," Joc' offered.

"It's worth a try," Pierce said, in desperation.

What they witnessed, when the *Drakin* circled over the destroyed theatre, dashed any glimmer of hope. Fire had burned through the level exposing the still water below.

"The damn thing is on the bottom of the ocean by now." Pierce grumbled in frustration.

"What now?" Demetrius asked, over his shoulder.

Joc' sighed in defeat, slumping back in his chair. "May as well head back to Zor."

"The Kan will be lifting soon," Bodil said, jiggling the lock on a butcher shop front door. "I hope that lazy bastard Howland and his team are ready to relieve us at shift change."

Churro adjusted his sword belt and nodded in agreement.

"You should report him to Captain Gasata," he said. "I mean, it ain't fair. We was on our feet all Kan."

"Yeah, and it's those fuckers keeping me from that first pint," Bodil said, moving to the next door.

"Yeah," Churro chortled, "that's the *real* reason you're pissed."

"You don't get between me and my ale," Bodil laughingly confirmed, checking the handle.

"Hey," Churro said, motioning down the street.

A lone figure slowly staggering out of the Kan fog staggeringly approached them.

"Someone coming from the Seven Sisters," Bodil noted, starting for the teetering figure. "Looks hurt."

By the time the Zorian guards reached the human, she had stopped walking and leaned against a wall. She was naked from the waist down, holding shreds of her nightgown feebly covering her naked breasts. Scratches and bites left her thighs and genital area swollen and bloodstained. Blood matted in her face and hair from the scratches across her head and face.

"I got you, lady," Churro said, catching her as she pitched forward.

The guard reeled when he caught a whiff of her.

"Damn, she reeks of cat piss!"

"She's in bad shape too," Bodil assessed. "Ma'am, can you speak? What happened?"

"Cat people," she said, in a horse whisper.

The two patrol guards traded perplexed glances.

"Do you know what she's talking about?" Churro asked.

Bodil shook his head and then leaned in closer to the woman's face. "Ma'am, what's your name?"

The woman stared vacantly down the street.

"Can you tell me your name?" Bodil inquired again.

She gazed at him with a pained expression.

"Kasha," she whispered, weakly.

"Well Mz. Kasha, we're gonna take you over to Clerria House to get you taken care of."

While the *Drakin* did a slow circle of Zor heading for the air station, all in the cabin noticed the flock of gulls circling the commodities exchange. A frenzied crowd flowed in and out of the large round building.

"I'm not sure I like the looks of this," Pierce Calden said, his brow furrowing.

"I'm afraid I have to agree," Joc' said, surveying the hectic scene below. "There's a small plaza, put us down there. Then you can take the *Drakin* in."

"You got it," Demetrius chirped, guiding the craft gently down.

After pushing their way through the throng outside, the two ambassadors discovered an even more chaotic spectacle on the trading floor. King Shom stood just inside the doors with his hands on his hips staring up at the trading board. A frenzied crowd of traders rushed about all around him shouting and waving pieces of paper. Now and then, a flustered trader would brush too close to the Eldorian sovereign and Attina would violently shove them away.

"I just got here," Shom said, when the two ambassadors joined him, "but someone just cornered the Etheria market with one enormous buy."

"Any idea who?" Pierce asked, watching the price of Etheria notes continuing to climb.

Shom shook his head. "No, but you have to ask yourself; who just came into a windfall of money?"

"Sure, would like to know how they pulled this off," Zau said.

She stared in wonder as a herd of deer emerged from the massive trunk of the world tree and bounded off into the new growth forest of Zer. A large flock of birds immediately followed, appearing in a shower of blue sparks from the leafy canopy and taking to the cloud filled skies.

"Like I said before, the Jissic run this island," the Spice Rat said, watching the birds until they disappeared and then turning to the panda. "Well, this could take a while. We should be going. Remember to keep them coming, we don't know how long that portal will stay stable. It's a… what do you call it?"

"A mirror portal," Zau said, in response. "The actual portal is right over there in the form of Lardia the World Tree. When they snatched the forest a mirror of her was…"

"Yeah, yeah, we don't need a lecture on it," Mal interrupted.

"You asked!" the Singa replied incredulously.

"I asked for a name, not a fucking speech."

"Fine!" Zau snapped.

"We owe you our very lives," the panda said, ignoring the bickering. "You are forever welcome on the Island of Zer and have found great favor in the eyes of Lardia."

Reaching inside his tunic he pulled out an Ukko wood amulet of a tree in a circle.

"With this they shall know you as a friend of the Jissic," he said, placing it around Mal's neck. "It will afford you safe passage throughout Zer and cooperation of the ranger clans."

"Thank you," Mal said, her voice beaming with pride.

"Is there anything else you desire?" the panda asked. "Name it, if it is within our power to give, it shall be yours."

A calculating smile crossed Mal's face. "I couldn't help but notice a shitload of Impia mushrooms growing a little way from here."

ACT THREE

The Corporeal Reach

T he weak rays of the sun in the far western sky cast long shadows down the windswept streets of Immor-Onn. High above the virtually empty avenues, the wind chimes kept a melodic cadence while the city slept.

A compact, open-top carriage pulled by a large, agile lizard stopped in front of the Whispering Zephyr. The lone driver checked up and down the street before directing the carriage into an alley beside the inn and orphanage. With a hiss of protest from the lizard, the wagon came to a stop in front of a row of windows.

Pulling a bandana up over his nose and mouth, the Bailian reached down on the floor of his buckboard and retrieved a round object about the size of a melon. With his free hand, he unsheathed a dagger and carefully punctured the object. Immediately a stream of green gas began hissing outward. Not bothering to sheath the dagger, he heaved the leaking orb through the nearest window.

The sound of glass shattering echoed off the alley walls. He snapped the reigns, and the lizard took off at a gallop. When he rounded the corner onto the main street, he pulled down his bandana and sped off into the city.

Within moments, the interior of the Whispering Zephyr turned into pandemonium and cries of "WAKE UP!" and "GET OUT!" resonated into the moonless. The shouting led to doors bursting open and a dozen children rushing out into the street.

By now lights were coming on in the nearby buildings and a marine patrol whistle chirped in the distance. Kai had just finished taking a head count when the Valdurian marines trotted around the corner with the crossbows on their backs clattering loudly.

"I've got three missing," she said to the patrol sergeant.

The outer clan EEtah sniffed the air. "We have to air the place out before anyone can go in."

"There are three children still left in there!" Kai protested.

The EEtah jerked a thumb in the building's direction.

"Smell that?" he asked. "That's Meleno gas. It can kill you pretty quick in a closed space and its not pretty. You all are lucky to have made it out."

Once the windows and doors were open, the sickening sweet almond smell dissipated and the odor of human feces replaced it. They cautiously entered and Kai sorrowfully lowered her head. The three beds by the broken window each contained a corpse. Two boys and one girl lay contorted into twisted positions. Foam covered their mouths, and they had shat their beds.

One of the Bailian marines picked up the now empty bomb and handed it to the EEtah.

"This stuff is complicated to make," the sergeant said, holding up the orb. "You don't just mix a few items together. You need a fairly sophisticated operation."

"This was meant for me," Kai said, her voice turning cold and hard. "Leave that with me. I've got some questions for a few select individuals."

"Sovereign or not, these people will not wait for us, sire!" Attina admonished, wrestling a bag of Shom's belongings across the flight deck of Air Station Three.

"Nonsense," Shom said, casually watching the *Haraka* settle into a nearby slip. "I'm counting on you making a suitable justification."

The seneschal spun and faced her king, protectorate, and lover with an exasperated look.

"Shom!"

The royal was unphased and glanced down at her naked breasts with a smirk.

"Has anyone ever told you that your nipples get incredibly hard when you get frustrated?" he asked.

"Shom!"

"It's really quite becoming."

The Hill Sister gave a resigned sigh and rolled her eyes. The royal stepped up and put his hands on her shoulders.

"Look, your breasts notwithstanding, get our belongings on board," he said. "Remind the captain that if he wants to retain docking privileges in Rophan, or any Eldorian port for that matter, he can wait for a few extra centi."

He then nodded to the *Haraka*, whose side hatch was dropping.

"I've got some folks to say hello to."

Mal came down the ramp first. Her face lit up when she saw Shom.

"Hey, you clean up pretty good," she said, when they embraced.

"Yes, I must say I'm rather getting used to the royal life."

"It's the funny little man!" Zaad thundered, approaching the two of them. "I mean… your majesty."

"My name is Shom," he said, with a grin when they clasped forearms.

The EEtah chuckled. "I know."

"Wow, you really *do* keep turning up like a bad copper," Zau said, keeping her distance.

"And I see you're just as charming as ever," the Eldorian sarcastically noted. "What did you say your name was again?"

The Singa scoffed. Shom's gaze fell on Wostera.

"I remember you from that dust up back in the fields of Amarenia," he said.

The bowmistress smiled and nodded but remained silent.

"Where's Alto?" the royal asked, looking around.

Mal's face briefly fell into a sad smile. "Teaching school in Makatooa."

Shom gave an understanding nod. "Well, that was his dream."

The sovereign then brightened up and changed the subject. "So, what brings you back to civilization?

"We've got a bunch of mushrooms to sell. What are you doing here?"

"There was a bit of a financial mess and now I'm off to Aris following the money trail."

Mal's face scrunched in uncertainty. "Now that you're king, I would think you have people to handle that."

"Yes, well, a certain amount of authority is called for when you're dealing with House Aramos and the Imperial Bank."

Mal placed her hands on his shoulders and chuckled. "Look at you, being all responsible and shit."

Shom returned the smile. "I must admit, I surprise even myself."

He noticed Attina standing impatiently in the doorway to the airship. "Speaking of which, I really should be off duty calls."

The room was stuffy and smelled like Sulphur. Light streaming in from several large windows cut the dust filled air in wide beams. A floor to ceiling bookcase lined one wall flanking the window. An old Bailian alchemist, with long, stringy grey hair, bent over and intently studied a beaker containing a bubbling clear liquid on a worktable along the opposite wall.

A sudden gust of wind flung the door open, and then slammed it shut, causing him to jump and look around. His attention returned to the boiling liquid when he saw no one.

The shell of the empty gas bomb clattered on the table beside the beaker, and the noise startled him again. He stared wide-eyed while it rocked to a standstill, recognizing his own handiwork.

"Wouldn't happen to know anything about that, would you?" a female voice asked from behind him.

Spinning around, his long hair fanned out behind him. Kai stood in the shadows of the bookcase.

"What's the meaning of this?!" he incredulously bellowed. "How did you get in here? This area is off limits!"

"Those questions really aren't that important," Kai said. "What *is* important is that gas bomb."

He shook his head in agitation and dismissively waved his hands in front of his chest.

"Go away, you annoying little woman. I'm terribly busy!"

She held his gaze, reached out and pointed a finger at the beaker. A small blue phantasmal dagger shot out. It struck the glass container with a loud crash and spilled its contents on the tabletop. The alchemist looked on in shock while the steaming liquid dripped onto the floor.

"Not anymore," the one-armed woman said, ominously. "Now, let's talk about that bomb."

Mal heard the window open several stories above her. The audible clue afforded her just enough time to flatten herself against the alley wall. A stream of foul-smelling liquid crashed in the middle of the narrow thoroughfare. It landed in front of Zaad, who stood right behind the captain carrying the large sack of mushrooms.

She winced from the stench. He glanced down at the splattering's and unidentified chunks on his pants then back up at the window.

"Hey!" he growled. "Watch where you're slinging that crap!"

The woman, her bucket now empty, had already retreated inside and missed the EEtah's rebuke.

"You would think a merchant who can afford to purchase our cargo could live in a better location," Wostera said, checking her robe for spray.

"I wouldn't exactly call Zabor a merchant," the Spice Rat replied, starting off. "He's more of a broker for sensitive items. He's set up between the docks and the Seven Sisters because that's where a lot of his clients hang out."

They only proceeded a few steps when the double doors at the end of the alley swung suddenly open and three men stepped out. Two wielded light crossbows loaded and pointed at Mal. They flanked a meticulously groomed, unarmed man in his thirties. His short brown hair and trimmed beard framed thin, cruel facial features. His blue silk robe spoke of wealth.

"Maluria," he greeted her, voice dripping with condescension. "I knew it was just a matter of time before you darkened my door again."

"Hello Zabor," Mal said, ignoring the attempted intimidation.

"You gotta lot of nerve showing up here," he said, with a sneer. "But I guess it saves me hunting you down."

"What's with all the hostility?"

This caused the broker to break into a frustrated chortle.

"Are you kidding me?" he asked. "Have you conveniently forgot about the Creos run a while back?"

The Spice Rat appeared perplexed. "You weren't the one that hired me."

The disbelieving smile transformed into an angry scowl. "You cost me a lot of money on that one."

"Me?!" Mal screamed. "Is it my fault you hired a bunch of fuckers who couldn't find their dicks when they're holding them?"

"Tell ya what," Zabor said, a sly smile returning to his face. "I'm in a fairly good mood. So here's the new deal, you have the big fish hand over the bag and I'll let you all live."

"BIG FISH!" Zaad incredulously roared.

Mal watched the two henchmen nervously fidget with their crossbows.

"You do realize those are just going to piss him off?" she asked.

"Oh those two are for you," Zabor countered. "I've got something special for your toothy friend."

He gave a high whistle and there was a commotion at the alley entrance. They turned to see a man quickly set up a small ballista on a monopod.

"So, what will it be?" Zabor asked, smugly.

"Go fuck yourself," Mal sneered.

"I could just kill you and take it," he said, in an overly friendly tone.

"Go fuck your..."

A loud thump from behind them cut short Mal's condemnation. Zabor's eyes went wide in shock when his ballista operator toppled to the ground, the tip of a crossbow bolt protruding from his forehead. Okawa stood behind him, pulling back the side lever of her pistol crossbow, cocking the weapon and dropping another bolt into place.

Zaad immediately charged the trio with a thunderous bellow. Both crossbowmen fired their weapons, but Zaad threw himself between them and Mal. The bolts struck and lodged ineffectually in the EEtah's chest.

The alley was too narrow for the man-shark to draw Bowbreaker, so Zaad backhanded the first crossbowman he encountered sending him smashing into the wall. He then grabbed Zabor and lifted him off his feet in front of his face.

"What was that about a big fish?!" he growled, before biting out his throat.

The last crossbowman frantically tried to reload. Wostera readied her bow, nocked an arrow and fired in a quick fluid motion. Her target was so absorbed with reloading that he never saw the projectile coming. When the blunt tipped arrow struck mid-chest, it blew a massive hole in his torso, showering the wall behind him with the man's innards.

The arrow disappeared in a shower of blue sparks when it exited the thug's back, then reappeared in the bowmistress' outstretched hand. Okawa put the pistol crossbow back on her belt when she entered the alley. She walked up to Mal, surveyed the carnage, nodding appreciatively.

"You all make an effective team," she noted.

"Thanks for the hand," the Spice Rat said, eyeing the weapon on her hip. "That's a pretty nice toy you've got there."

"It comes in handy," the Valdurian agent said, patting it. "I remember you from over in Nocturn."

"Yeah," Mal confirmed, "it seems like I keep hopping from one prickly situation to another."

"I know what you mean," Okawa said, with a chuckle.

"So, what are you doing here?" Mal asked. "Don't get me wrong, I'm glad to see you and all."

Okawa glanced over at Zabor's still oozing corpse. "Well, I *was* keeping an eye on him. Joc' figured he was the only one able to broker that much Ukko wood."

Mal shook her head. "Nah, he's not involved."

"How can you be so sure?"

"Because I know where the wood is," the Spice Rat said, with an impish grin.

Rafel's choice for spy chief in the Bailian empire pleased him. Jer-Om went straight to work galvanizing his network of informants and, just as ordered, he sent frequent detailed reports. The newest one, now sitting before him on his desk, was the most interesting to date.

According to the dispatch, Kai repeatedly arranged clandestine rendezvous with an attractive female Ash-Ta of the Desmodus clan. The relationship was definitely not professional and obviously more than just friendship.

He sat back staring off into space and played with a strand of hair, contemplating a change in strategy. His stomach knotted and throat tightened every time he thought of Kai. He angrily tugged at the lock of hair. Killing Kai would briefly be very satisfying, but why not prolong her agony? She should have to live with the constant ache only attainable by profound loss.

Yes, a new tactic and a new target, he thought, anger transforming into sinister anticipation. For the first time since Hoyt's murder, Rafel smiled.

"Well, she sure is big enough," Demetrius said, his eyes sweeping over the transport airship.

"What's she called?" Mal lovingly queried.

"The *Prevoz*," Demetrius replied, his gaze transfixed on the craft.

"Can you fly it?" Mal asked.

"Sure," Demetrius replied, nodding. "I'm just not going to try anything tricky with it."

"So, I guess we won't be going *upstairs* in it?" Okawa asked, making her way to the side hatch.

"Not in this thing," the pilot confirmed. "Believe me, you wouldn't want those Etheria cairns bouncing around the cargo area. Besides, Zer is just across the pass."

"Yeah, but the dicey part is the portal," Zaad said, climbing the ramp.

"You let me worry about the portal," Zau said, trailing behind the man-shark.

"You just be ready in case we encounter complications."

"Complications?" Wostera pressed, bringing up the rear.

The Singa shrugged. "Hey, it's the Middle Realms, things can get complicated real quick."

"That's why we get the big money," the Spice Rat said. "It's not just anyone who can move a forest across the fucking multiverse."

"You sure this will work, Captain?" Zaad asked.

"Anyone has a better idea and I'm all ears," Mal replied. "Besides, they already paid us."

The interior of the ship was designed for cargo. The bow contained the usual two command chairs, for navigator and pilot, with a row of six seats mounted directly behind them, and the rest of the spacious craft was empty.

"How fast can you get us there?" Mal asked, while everyone settled into their seats.

"Well, like I said, Zer is just across the pass," Demetrius reiterated in a distracted voice while nonchalantly familiarizing himself with the controls. "I can get you just about anywhere in the Annigan fast. The real question is, how well you can hold down your last meal."

"Well, seeing how it's just across the pass," Mal rationalized apprehensively.

"Right," the pilot responded, turning on the twin Etheria power cores.

The trip from Air Station Three, in the High Holy City of Zor, to the Island of Zer was brief as promised. All could see the busy ship traffic below in the wide pass between the two island continents. As the *Prevoz* descended, the rate of the forest's regrowth amazed them. Lardia's massive crown towered above the lush treetop canopy.

"Okay, lucky for us these cairns are all on the beaches." Demetrius said, concentrating on the coastline.

"They stacked the cairns in sections," Okawa said, checking her pistol crossbow. "I've seen what these things can do firsthand. We must carefully separate the disks, quickly and in order, starting from the top. Then, when we rebuild the cairns, reassemble them in the same order we found them. No mixing them up. Got it?"

All nodded their confirmation.

"Speaking of which," Demetrius announced, "we've arrived at our first destination."

The craft settled with the crunching of crushed shells onto the pebbly, thirty-foot-wide beach next to a circular Etheria disk cairn composed of five separate tapering layers.

All stood when the ship settled. Mal slipped on her sword and put the Jissic's pendant around her neck. Okawa gave a puzzled glance at the ostentatious bauble.

"An odd time for jewelry, don't you think."

"Any other time I would agree with you," Mal said, making her way to the lowering hatch. "but this might placate any locals we may come across.

"Sure hope it works."

"Me too."

Something was amiss, but Shom couldn't quite put his finger on it. He felt it the moment they disembarked from the airship onto the docks of Aris. The royal mentioned nothing because this was only his second visit to the Aramos ancestral home, and points of reference were cloudy at best.

The nagging feeling persisted while they stepped out to the street and Attina hailed a carriage. It only got worse when a young man with long dark hair pulled a small wagon up to the curb to pick them up.

"It is truly a beautiful day the lord has made," he said, with a placid smile. "Where may I take you?"

"The Imperial Bank," Shom said, climbing in.

"Ah, the temple," the driver said, starting off down the busy street. "Are you here for the festival?"

Shom and Attina glanced at each other questioningly.

"No," Attina answered. "What festival might that be?"

"We will gather in the temple when the Kan fog rises and pay homage to the Ascension of the Proffitt."

"I'm sorry, what Proffitt are we referring to?" Shom asked, curiosity getting the better of him.

The young man sat up proudly in his seat.

"Saint Stryder recently joined our blessed lord in the heavens ensuring prosperity for the faithful," he said.

"And I suppose you consider yourself one of the faithful?" Shom asked, warily.

"Oh yes," the driver enthusiastically confirmed. "I wept when I heard of the blessed Proffitt sacrificing himself for us. I immediately donated my life savings as seed money, then received his mark. *And it worked.* Soon after, he blessed me with this carriage so I may seek my blessed fortune."

"Well, I wish you blessed luck in your blessed endeavors," Shom said, fighting to keep a straight face.

"I do not need luck," the young man proclaimed confidently. "I now walk in the light of the lord."

No greater fanatic than the recently converted, Shom mused to himself. He was beginning to understand the nature of his trepidation.

They had only travelled a short distance through the crowded streets when a commotion erupted on the right side of the road. Several men dressed in red shirts and black capes thrashed a shabby looking man with thin wooden rods. The unfortunate recipient of the beating cowered against the wall, covering his face and pleading.

"Here now, what's this all about?" Shom asked, grimacing with each cracking blow.

"The Piety Watch must have caught him begging," the driver said, nonchalantly.

Shom's face crumpled in disbelief. "Begging is illegal?"

"By recent decree," he confirmed. "The Proffitt says, 'Productivity is the only path to prosperity.'"

The rest of the ride thankfully went in silence. Shom now took in a greater assessment of his surroundings. All the residents they passed appeared busy with some project. No one sat idle. From repairing buildings to sweeping the streets, all citizenry performed mandatory occupations.

When they approached the wide porch of the bank, the Eldorian sovereign noticed they had replaced the traditional EEtah detail guarding the double wooden doors of the entrance with human sentries in Piety Watch uniforms. The wide collars of their black capes rose above the back of their heads, resembling cat ears. They held spears at their sides, pointed outward at forty-five-degree angles blocking the entrance.

Odd symbols for a bank, Shom thought, gazing up at a bronze placard composed of the runes "X" and "I," just over the doors.

The duo got out of the carriage and Shom generously paid the driver a single struck gold coin. The young man's face lit up at the amount.

"Bless you sir," he chimed, "have a profitable day!"

He then sped off, leaving Shom and Attina staring up the wide stairway leading to the porch.

"Not very inviting for a bank," Attina noted, starting up the stairs.

"Nor a temple," Shom added.

When they reached the porch, the guards shifted their spears, so they faced forward and adopted a more aggressive stance.

"Ah yes, matching lackeys," Shom quietly remarked to Attina.

"Halt," the guard on the right ordered. "State your name and your business with the Imperial Bank."

The Hill Sister took a confident step forward.

"You are addressing Shom Eldor, patriarch of House Eldor."

This took the two sentries by surprise and they hesitated.

"I am here to see Harper Aramos," Shom said. "Would you kindly announce me?"

"Do you have an appointment?"

"I'm afraid not," Shom confessed.

The guard's face went grim. "The High Priest is very busy. He sees no one without an appointment."

"The royal sovereign of Eldor needs no appointment!" Attina said, adamantly.

The watchman's eyes swept over Shom's well appointed, yet relatively modest attire.

"You don't look like a king."

"An observation based on your extensive dealings with royalty, no doubt," Shom said, sarcastically. "Now why don't you be a good lad and tell Harper I'm here."

The two guards exchanged uncertain looks before one disappeared inside. He returned moments later and silently escorted them through the ornately carved doors.

The starkness of the main lobby struck Shom when they entered it. Other than Shom and Attina, the room appeared empty. A large receiving desk sat on one side and an ornate but uncomfortable looking couch on the other.

Rich, dark wood panels covered all the walls except for where a huge painting of Stryder displayed above the entrance door. A sign hung below the portrait, comprises several lines of the binary runes.

"If you don't mind," Shom said, indicating the sign. "What does that say?"

"It is the first edict of the Proffitt," the guard answered, reverently. "'Productivity is the only path to prosperity.'"

Shom's eyes narrowed suspiciously at the translation while the sentry knocked on a door beneath the portrait.

"Wait out here," Shom softly ordered Attina. "We're not to be disturbed."

She nodded and then positioned herself by the door handle. Shom stepped through the threshold and closed the door behind him.

Once inside, the sentry began a formal introduction, "I present Shom Eldor, Sovereign of House Eld..."

"Yes, yes, we know all that," Shom interrupted, brushing past the guard.

Embarrassed, the watchman lowered his head, then quickly left.

"Shom Eldor!" Harper Aramos rang out in a friendly voice. "It's been ages!"

Harper appeared almost exactly as Shom remembered him. Neatly trimmed hair and beard framed a slightly handsome face, offset by a dark brown receding hairline. He wore ornate black and red robes draped across his thin frame.

"What brings you to this holy place?" he asked, offering his hand.

"I had no idea banks were holy." Shom replied with a firm grip.

"To our lord they are," Harper said, offering a seat.

"You are a man of wealth and taste," the Aramos' high priest said, once Shom took his seat. "You would do well in the service of our lord."

"No, thank you," the Eldorian royal said, chuckling. "I prefer to get my money the old-fashioned way, by family name."

"And a little conquest," Harper countered. "I mean, it was *your* father who started the Unification War. He transferred lots of fertile farmlands from House Valdur to Eldor."

"My father is dead," Shom countered. "I'm working tirelessly to mend fences with the Valdurians."

Harper smiled smugly. "I couldn't help but notice you have returned none of the annexed lands."

"Well, let's not get crazy here," Shom defended, shifting nervously in his seat.

Harper maintained his self-assured grin. "Face it, you like having the food market cornered for the Goyan Islands."

"It comes in handy when I want a loaf of bread," Shom jested.

"So how goes the fence mending?"

"Well," Shom began, "they let me ride in their air ships now."

A brief mutual laugh brought them to an uneasy silence.

"So, what do I owe the pleasure of this visit?" Harper asked, sitting back in his chair.

Shom cleared his throat and leaned forward. "Two cycles ago, someone transferred two hundred thousand secors worth of gold notes to this bank and immediately used them to purchase the bulk of the Etheria notes in a crashed market. Care to tell me what happened?"

The smile disappeared from Harper's face and his demeanor changed to serious and guarded.

"What of it?" he asked, defensively. "We had a large deposit, and I chose to take advantage of a depressed market. Some might call that an astute business move."

"Some might," Shom agreed. "Unless they knew you got the investment capital through extortion."

"I have no idea what you're referring to," Harper lied. "I can not question the nature of every deposit."

"Even when it comes from your cousin?" Shom asked, jerking a thumb over his shoulder indicating the portrait hanging in the next room. "You know, the Proffitt?"

Harper's face flashed with anger. "I cannot sit here while you blaspheme!"

"I meant no disrespect," Shom said calmly, "but I was in the Calden Commodity's Market when it crashed across the board. You then used the money from the auction of the Ukko wood to corner the Etheria market."

The Eldorian sovereign paused for effect. "Any of this sound familiar? If not, perhaps I should take it to the Zorian Monetary Council?"

Harper's face was a mixture of fear and controlled rage.

"I'm afraid I will have to ask you to leave."

"Oh, you don't have to be afraid, Harper," Shom said, in a superior tone. "I was leaving anyway."

Shom stood, he looked down at the still seated High Priest of Pa-Waga and smirked.

"So, I've cornered the market on food and you have all the Etheria crystals," he said. "We'll see which one is more useful when you're hungry."

Admonishment completed, the royal brusquely left. When the door clicked closed, Harper looked down at his badly trembling hands. He would have to do something about this before the Zorian Monetary Council became involved.

"Did you hear all that?" Harper asked out loud, glancing over to a far corner of the room.

From the cracks in the floor, a thick black ooze slowly rose. It pooled and built until it formed a large clump of quivering gelatinous material. From across its surface runes flickered blue, and the blob rose and took on a humanoid shape. When it finished, the runes faded and left the crude outline of Stryder staring at his cousin.

The Vicar of Pa-Waga had changed again. His body was all but featureless except for the various fields of "X" and "I" which now completely covered his black skin. The shape of his head took on a distinctly feline quality, displaying pointy ears and a short snout.

"Yes, I heard," Stryder said, in a deep ominous gurgling voice, although Harper could make out no discernible mouth on his almost featureless face. "It is of no consequence."

"He must be stopped!" Harper cried out close to panic.

"Where is your faith?" Stryder asked. "The Council will be powerless to stop us."

"They can pull our charter!"

"Let them, we do not need them anymore," Stryder said, with a sinister laugh. "We have achieved a glorious victory and now control the world's Etheria. Your thinking is far too small. Remember, you serve a mighty god."

Harper nervously shook his head. "It will just cause unnecessary trouble if the council becomes involved."

"It matters not to me," he said. "Deal with the Eldorian as you see fit."

Stryder nonchalantly waved a loosely structured hand, and the runes once more lit up on his amorphous body. His humanoid shape melted while reverting to the jellylike form and seeped back through the cracks.

Kasha slowly opened her eyes and looked around. She laid beneath the sheets in an infirmary bed at Clerria House. They had bandaged her head and body and she ached all over, but especially between her legs.

Tysonn and Cha-Rod sat beside the bed, just inside the privacy curtain. She groaned in discomfort and stirred. Tysonn got up and leaned over her.

"Hey beautiful," he said, greeting her with a smile. "Good to have you back."

He reached down and tenderly touched her arm.

"You gave us all quite a scare."

The wounded linguist rocked her head back-and-forth, mumbling something unintelligible. Tysonn leaned in closer. He could only discern one word.

"What?" she was asking, in a raspy whisper.

"The city guards found you wandering the streets yesterday morning," Tysonn answered, softly. "You passed out the moment they brought you here."

Kasha sobbed and jerked her arm away from his touch. Tysonn glanced over at Cha-Rod with a painfully confused expression. The old Bailian motioned for him to step out of the enclosure, his face painted with sorrow.

"She's been through quite the ordeal," Cha-Rod whispered, once they were beyond the curtain. "You're one of the few people she can talk to, so be there for her when she's ready."

Tysonn nodded sadly and was about to return to Kasha's bedside when a purple robed Clerria appeared. She held a goblet in her hand filled with a thick milky white liquid. Stopping, she gave both men a serious stare.

"I'm afraid I will have to ask both of you to leave and give the young lady some privacy," she said, firmly.

She softened when she saw Tysonn's puzzled look.

"During her imprisonment it appears Kasha was sexually ravaged," she explained.

Tysonn's mouth dropped open in horrified shock.

"By the gods," he stammered. "Surely you don't think she's..."

The young Clerria stayed composed with compassionate professionalism.

"It's too soon to tell if she is with child," she answered, "but given the nature of her captor's we can't take a chance."

"This will purge her womb," she said, glancing down at the goblet.

"Will it harm her?" Tysonn asked apprehensively, peering into the viscous liquid.

"It shouldn't," she replied. "However, it won't be pleasant and can be bloody. The process will take a few cycles and it's no place for a man. Don't worry, there will be several Clerria in attendance when the purge finally happens. She will be well cared for."

Tysonn weakly nodded, and the Clerria gave a conciliatory smile. "Now, I'm sure you gentlemen have business elsewhere."

By the time the healer disappeared behind the curtain, Tysonn's mouth had tightened into an angry sneer.

"I will end this!" Tyson said, in a low growl.

The mild-mannered scholar's aggressive fervor left Cha-Rod slightly taken aback.

"What exactly do you propose we do?" the Bailian asked, somberly.

"I'm not sure yet," Tysonn said, turning to leave with a look of grim determination. "I've got to find out more about what we're dealing with here. That's okay though, I've got the greatest university in the world at my disposal."

Catching an updraft in the Salar Winds, Julius did a slow circle of Mount Goya and pondered at how things seemed strangely different. True, it had been awhile since he had returned home, but now he felt peculiarly disconnected to the place he had grown up.

He watched the steady crawl of magma from the breech in its southern face making its way into the Shallow Sea. The lava carried with it the haunting call from inside the mountain. He shook his head to clear the voices. Julius repeated the mantra taught him by the shamans which allowed him to function in this world and deal with the voices when they plagued him.

In the moment.

In the moment.

In the moment.

He well knew that acknowledging the calls and engaging in their conversation, would lead him back down into the pit of madness from which he had struggled to escape.

In the moment, he repeated to himself once again.

To the east he saw the Azorith Monastery and the Valley of Chains. He gasped when he caught sight of the purple Etheria pillar jutting from the ground.

What's this? he wondered; his mind awash with visions of Na-Kab flooding from it.

Running along the steep slopes of the northern and western face was the Avion City of Darmont, home to House Pyre. Julius hovered before the main entranceway cut into the cliff face and took in the tall, graceful, stone arches carved out of the mountainside.

He closed his eyes momentarily to compose his thoughts. He had to hold it together for father and the Nine Golden Masters.

In the moment, he repeated one last time before coming to rest on the wide landing and folding back his wings.

The main portico led directly into the great hall. Just beyond, a massive arched balcony overlooked the bubbling cauldron of molten rock they worshiped.

"Julius!" his father's greeting boomed. "What a surprise."

The Avion watched his father, Yekem, First of the Nine, stride across the polished granite floors towards him. The two could have been twins, with their lean chiseled features and long, jet black hair.

"Father!" the Avion prince cried out, opening his arms.

Their embrace was warm and genuine. Afterwards they held on to each other at arm's length.

"What brings you home son? Don't tell me you're tired of dealing with the blue people already."

"No father," Julius answered, laughing, "the Bailians are a wonderful people and Immor-Onn is a beautiful city. They have welcomed me with open arms."

The Avion king tilted his head and gave a puzzled look.

"I'm glad to see you, Julius, as your mother will be, but..."

"No!" Julius yelled, suddenly.

He stared behind his father in horrific shock. A swarm of Na-Kab climbed out of the lava and spilled over the balcony railing. Their barbed tail telson phalluses raised and weeping, on the verge of attacking.

Julius shrieked in panic and gripped the side of his head. He rocked back-and-forth with his eyes closed. A shocked Yekem reached out to steady his son.

"We need some help over here!" his father yelled.

When Julius opened his eyes, the Na-Kab vision vanished and with labored breath, he focused on his father's worried face.

"No, I'm all right," he gasped.

"Are you sure?" Yekem asked, still uncertain.

Julius nodded, his breathing returning to normal. With an immediate personality shift, the Avion prince's face grew elated. Julius reached out gripping his father's arms excitedly while he gazed into his eyes.

"Father," he cried, "I have been summoned!"

"Summoned, by whom, for what reason?"

Julius stared over at the balcony overlooking the magma chamber. "I need to speak with the Nine Golden Masters."

Yekem gave his son a sympathetic smile. Since his son's brush with insanity, he had entertained many a strange requests and notions.

"Son?"

"Father, I'm serious!"

"Serious," he said, understandingly. "Like the time you had me call a council meeting, and all you wanted to talk about was footwear?"

"Father!"

"Or the time you proposed an anthem for our house? Then you sang it for the council."

"I thought it was a rather stirring hymn," Julius meekly defended, before resuming a more anxious tone. "Father, this is different!"

"How so?"

"The visions."

The council chamber for the Nine Golden Masters of Avion House Pyre is, mostly, a large empty room. A number of stoic painted murals, depicting various scenes of historical significance, cover the walls. An enormous closed front desk, in the shape of a horseshoe, filled the center of the room. The midpoint of the imposing bench rose to an impressive twelve feet tall and gently sloped to eight feet at the ends.

Julius now stood before that horseshoe looking up at the nine faces staring impatiently at him.

"Golden Ones," he began. "I thank you for this audience on such short notice."

"Perhaps you would like to sing us another song Lord Julius?" asked a scowling councilman to his left.

Julius brightened at the suggestion. "No, but funny you mention. I've heard quite a few Bailian ballads I could perform if you wish?"

"We most certainly would not!" the councilman growled, halting Julius as he took a deep breath to sing.

"Personally, I would like to know what is important enough to have one of my ambassadors leave his post," asked a pale female councilwoman with straight blonde hair.

Julius bowed. "I apologize Seventh of the Nine, but I come with important news." He then turned to his father at the head of the table. "And a request."

"You have our attention," Yekem, First of the Nine said, watching his son vibrate with excitement.

"Golden Ones," Julius said, giddily. "Holy Mother Mountain has shown me things. It spoke to me in my dreams a half a world away."

A collective groan travelled around the table which had a sobering effect on the Avion prince.

"Go on," said the female seated to his father's left.

"We all are aware of the war in the darkness which took place a short time ago," Julius continued. "House Awa's oyster beds are all but decimated and it will take a thousand grands to recover. The Golden Avatar sacrificed itself to defeat the forces from Nocturn."

"These are Otick matters," an elderly male to his right interrupted, "What has it to do with us?"

Julius continued, undeterred, "The avatars stimulate fertility throughout the Goyan Islands. Something must replace the avatar or all of our lands will decay."

"How can this happen," the same male argued. "We are children of the Holy Mother Mountain. She will provide for our needs."

"I agree Ninth of the Nine," Julius concurred, "but she needs a catalyst, something to make her holy fire more palatable to everyone else."

"Why in the name of the gods should we care about everyone else?" asked a handsome male with short blonde hair. "As far as I'm concerned you can start with the humans, purge them from the Annigan with the Mother's holy fire."

"I used to feel as you do Fifth of the Nine," Julius said. "I too believed the Idonian philosophy was correct. However, after much reflection, I now realize that thinking is flawed."

Julius paused for effect. Several councilmen grumbled their disapproval.

"Whether or not we like it," he added, "the human now plays an integral part in the balance of our world. Think of them as bottom-feeding fish; repulsive and lowly, but necessary. But I digress…"

"Julius, what is the point to all of this?" First of the Nine asked, in a calm, metered tone.

"Holy Mother Mountain has shown me the catalyst, and it is right below our feet!"

This caused another murmur to pass around the table.

"They are a race new to our lands, but they embrace the Mother's fire and all will soon enjoy their aftereffects."

"I have a feeling there's more son," Yekem said, suspiciously tilting his head.

Julius averted his eyes. "They need our help."

Shom lay on his back, savoring the sensuous feeling of a thick down mattress and expensive sheets. His hips bucked and twitched furiously while Attina rode him to the rhythm of the loudly creaking bed.

The royal looked up at his seneschal and lover and lustfully contemplated he had the best of both worlds. He couldn't decide which of her hermaphroditic features drove him maddest with desire. Was it her sweaty, undulating breasts which buoyantly swayed and glistened, or her rigid member which slapped against his stomach with each downward stroke? Or perhaps it was her uncanny ability at deftly impaling his own erect organ, alternating between both orifices without missing a stroke?

Whatever it was, Shom could feel release quickly building. His loud moaning covered the soft click of the latch turning on the door. Before he could announce he was about to cum, Attina quickly slid off and dove to the floor. A shock of cool air replaced the wet warmth around his cock and Shom bolted up in surprise.

The Hill Sister retrieved her short sword just as the door burst open and three men armed with swords stormed in. With an enraged cry, she threw the blade, burying it deep in the chest of the first man. He gasped in disbelief, staring down at the short sword protruding from his torso.

Attina was on her feet. She grabbed the hilt of her sword and pulled, while giving the dying man a savage kick to the belly. The blade dislodged, and she drove the man back into his two companions.

As the remaining two struggled to untangle themselves from their dead companion, Attina reached over and stabbed one in the throat. He gurgled and tried to cover the wound with his hand to no avail. Blood erupted through his fingers.

He fell backwards and his rapidly beating heart sent a shower of arterial spray throughout the room.

The last thug swallowed hard, frozen in wide-eyed disbelief at the sight before him. The woman stood a full six feet tall, naked and covered in blood. Her large breasts heaved with ragged breaths and the jutting erection towering in front of her, seemed to throb with a life of its own. Her attractive face was contorted into a murderous sneer.

The brief distraction was all she needed. With another ferocious cry, she brought her sword down on the top of the would-be assassin's head. The heavy blade cleaved into the skull with a sickening crunch. The momentum carried the short sword all the way through, lodging in the base of his neck, and drenched the area in another torrent of gore.

A naked and completely stunned Shom managed to bumble out of bed and draw his sword. He reviewed his lover's grim handiwork with labored breath.

"Well, there goes another ruined orgasm!" Shom said, exasperated.

Slowly, Attina looked up and eyed the royal with a hungry gaze. Dropping her weapon on the floor she maintained eye contact walking past the bodies towards him. She hesitated in front of Shom briefly, before grabbing him and giving a heated kiss. Shom's thin bladed sword dropped while he returned the kiss. He felt the slickness of the blood on her skin smearing across his upper body and face.

The kiss became more and more passionate until she broke with a start. Shom saw the wild look in her eyes and knew what was coming. With a licentious grunt she grabbed the prodigal king and threw him face down on the bed.

"You lost your turn, it's my turn now," she said, in a husky voice while parting his buttocks.

When he felt her shaft glide between his ass cheeks, he knew this would be neither romantic nor gentle. The battle awakened ancient, primitive passions, and there would be no stopping until she got it out of her system. Arching his back to make it easier for her, he only hoped she finished before the city guards arrived.

The tunnels below Mount Goya got progressively smaller the farther down they traveled.

"Any place where I can't extend my wings makes me nervous," Julius said, staring at the encroaching walls descending into the darkness.

The female Avion walking beside him smiled and looked away. Her brown, shoulder length curls swept past the tops of her folded black wings.

"My discomfort amuses you, Second of the Nine?" Julius asked.

"Please, the council is not in session. No need to be so formal. Call me Bigarren."

Raising the glowing orange crystal, he peered down at the petite Avion. Her face was pleasing and the low-cut, floor-length dress suited her.

"Well Bigarren, you didn't answer my question."

"It's not that it amuses me, I was just thinking about our differences. I am most at home when I am close to the Mother's bosom."

"Here I was thinking I was the only one crazy enough to come down here. Well, you are the High Priestess of Goya," Julius conceded. "I should expect nothing less. It's also not surprising that you sit at my father's right hand."

The Avion prince suddenly turned serious. "Yesterday, in the council meeting, you and my father were the only ones that didn't scoff. Why?"

"Well, I'm fairly sure your father didn't scoff because he loves you. As for myself, I too have felt the presence of something down here, I just couldn't quite place it."

"They're called Na-Kab," Julius said, straining to see ahead of them. "They used to inhabit the volcanic tunnels running under Mount Natal in Nocturn. How they got here, I do not know."

"You said they needed our help."

"Yes," he replied. "I don't know the exact nature, but for them it's dire."

"If they're from Nocturn, how will you communicate with them?"

Julius pointed to a small white disk with blue striations embedded in the oval buckle keeping his two crossed belts closed across his muscular chest.

"The Bailians call these Diplomat Disks," he explained. "This was a gift from the queen upon my deployment to Immor-Onn. It gives the power of tongues."

"Is it some kind of magical amulet?"

"It's made from Etheria crystals. There are all kinds of these crystals in the Twilight Lands and Nocturn. Many, *many* kinds, both above and below those lands. Black crystals, white crystals, red crystals, blue crystals, green crystals, gold crystals, orange crystals, chartreuse crystals, purple crystals, garnet crystals, lavender crystals, aquamarine cry…"

"Julius…" Bigarren interrupted. "Many colors, I get it."

"Yes, yes, yes," the Avion prince stammered, tapping his temples punitively. "Sorry."

In the moment, Julius thought, *in the moment…*

"Now… Where was I?" he began again. "Yes! As I understand it, each crystal color represents a different crystal type, and each crystal type carries different magical endowments. Because of this, Etheria crystals provide the catalyst for most magic throughout the Twilight Lands and Nocturn."

"So the crystals in your Diplomat Disk allow you to speak other languages?"

"Not as such," Julius clarified. "You speak your own language, but anyone within earshot will hear their own tongue in their head. The reverse is also true."

"That's amazing," the high priestess marveled.

They felt the temperature rise when they approached a large opening in the wall to their right. They could detect a reddish glow and the distinct smell of sulfur coming from just beyond the outlet.

Peeking in they could see a cavern, two hundred feet across and fifty feet high. A steaming and bubbling lake of glowing magma dominated the center of the room. Two rivers of flowing molten rock extended outwards on either side of the lake and down their own tunnels.

Both Avions cautiously entered and looked around.

"This is it," Julius said, inspecting the ceiling. "This is the place in my visions."

"Lord Julius?" Brigarren's voice was unsettled. "Something just moved in that lake!"

Julius turned in time to see an area by the shore rippling and bubbling. A figure rose from the magma. It had a mantis head with no eyes and a humanoid torso with no arms. When it faced Julius and Brigarren it let out a sustained, high pierced shriek and its long black tongue snaked out of its conical mouth.

From down the various corridors, cries of response filled the air. Within moments, a dozen Na-Kab scampered into the cavern and froze in shock when they saw the Avions.

"Fleshy ones in the queen's chamber!" one shrieked.

Julius watched several open their mandibles, their mouths displaying a fiery interior.

"They're preparing to attack!" he warned.

Brigarren extended her arms out in front of her and clapped her hands together, sending a shower of sparks cascading to the floor. She then trailed her arms over her head and lowered them back down. A wavering curtain of super-heated air descended around them.

Three Na-Kab attacked, simultaneously sending bursts of fire at the invading couple. The fire disbursed like water on glass when it struck the barrier. When two more fire bugs joined the assault, she turned to Julius.

"I don't know how much longer I can keep this up," she said, straining from the effort, "especially if any more join in on the attack."

"Na-Kab, cease this senseless violence!" Julius yelled. "We are here to help you. Where is your king?"

Upon hearing their own language spoken with Julius' noble confidence, the creatures stopped and stared at the strangers in stunned silence. Several circled them warily, looking them up and down, sniffing furiously, their tails undulating menacingly while the penis-shaped telson stingers wept.

"I am King Krol," the largest of the Na-Kab said, stepping forward. "Why would fleshy ones help us? Fleshy ones are all liars! Fleshy ones deceive Na-Kab!"

"If you have been dealing with humans, I understand your feelings," Julius agreed with a sympathetic nod, "but we are *not* humans. We are Avion."

"*All* fleshy ones lie!"

"No!" Julius renounced adamantly. "*Humans* are the scourge. Give me a chance to prove our intentions."

Krol assessed the young Avion. "How?"

"Is that your queen?" Julius asked, pointing to the blind, limbless creature in the lake.

"Yes, behold the deceit of another fleshy one," King Krol growled. "It promised us a queen but mocks the end of us."

"What if I told you I think I can make her whole, save her and your kind?"

"More empty promises from the fleshy ones!"

"Put me to the test," the Avion prince said, confidently.

The Na-Kab hesitated once again, assessing the brash stranger's claim. Sensing he was getting somewhere, Julius hammered home his argument.

"What have you to lose?" he asked. "If you do nothing, your race will slowly fade away. Killing us destroys perhaps your last chance at survival and a life here in your new home. A land of your own where you can live and tunnel in peace without the worry of warring Do-Tarr."

Julius' last statement seemed to work and King Krol visibly relaxed. It lowered its tail and the other Na-Kab followed suit.

"Very well, winged fleshy one, save our queen and we will live in peace with the beings of this new land," it said, and then held up two fingers. "You have two fog cycles. If we are to die, we will not die alone. The countryside above and all that live there will burn!"

"Fair enough, two cycles," Julius confirmed.

Julius was unusually quiet while the Avion pair made their way back to the surface.

"So, what are you going to do?" Bigarren asked, stepping out into the sunlight. "Two cycles isn't a lot of time."

"I have a Bailian friend of mine, an Etheriat back in Immor-Onn. If anyone knows, it will be him. I just hope I can make it halfway around the world and back in time."

"May Goya guide you," she said, when he launched himself into the sky.

The moon was setting over Immor-Onn. Drucilla perched atop one of the few remaining buildings on the edge of the now almost completely occupied Available Regions of the city. She had little inclination to ponder the fate of her hunting grounds because once again, hunger raked across her stomach like claws. It dominated her thoughts and clouded her mind.

The streets were steadily emptying for the moonless with most citizens going home. Soft melodic ringing of the city wind chimes joined the bells of the new turine. She was counting on the wind picking up, as always, at moonfall. The increased chiming should cover any sounds of alarm her prey might make.

When she saw the woman turn off the main thoroughfare and head her way she started salivating. It was a human prostitute. This was almost too good to be true. Humans were her favorite food. She had learned her lesson about keeping a low profile when she killed the Calden sailor a little while ago and now she kept her diet to the lower denizens of the city, the ones that few would miss.

When the woman drew closer, Drucilla took off and circled her prey. She was about to strike when she saw two more humans, a man and a woman, approaching the prostitute from the alleyway. Deciding there were too many to attack, and remembering her rule against rash killing, she perched on a nearby roof top and observed.

The woman handed something glittering to the man. Whatever she gave him definitely displeased him. Drucilla could only hear parts of the dispute but she heard the term 'holding out on me.' This preceded a savage punch to the stomach which doubled the woman over.

All pimps are the same, she angrily thought, watching the man remove his belt to whip the woman.

His long greasy hair swayed while he flailed away at her back and she remained bent over. The other prostitute cowered a few feet away. Drucilla could now hear his angry shouting while he continued the assault.

"I didn't bring you whores halfway around the world for you to hold out on me! I got expenses, I got overhead!"

It ended as quickly as the beating started, with the muscular man huffing in exhaustion. He then pointed a finger at both prostitutes and his voice lowered. Once again Drucilla couldn't make out what he was saying but the threat was clear.

The two women left the alley with one assisting the other.

The man walked back down the alley assessing the number of gems in his hand. Drucilla sneered in contempt when she took to the skies. He was meatier and cruel. He would not be missed.

Coming up behind him, Drucilla silently swooped down. Her blow to his back propelled him forward, deeper into the alley, knocking the wind out of him. He gasped trying to regain his breath. The Ash-Ta's momentum carried her forward, right behind the surprised human. Drucilla grabbed him with her talons by the shoulders. She easily dragged the winded and disoriented pimp still deeper into the alley and away from prying eyes.

The turine ringing outside the harbors reminded Julius of the hour. He studied the three-foot-long, deep pink Etheria crystal rod in his hands, then peered back up at the older Bailian man standing behind the counter.

"Thank you for staying open for me," Julius said. "This is magnificent. You are truly the finest Etheriat in all of Immor-Onn.

"Thank you, Lord Julius," the Bailian beamed. "I am happy to be of service to the Crown and to House Pyre. That is some of the finest Cobalcite I have ever come across. It just arrived a few lunas ago from the Dark Waste."

Cobalcite for healing, Julius thoughtfully considered running his hands lovingly across its smooth surface. *It should be enough.*

"I'll take it," the Avion said, wearily. "Please put it on my account."

"Of course," the Etheriat confirmed. "If you don't mind me saying so, you look tired Lord Julius."

"If you just flew a thousand miles non-stop, you'd be weary too. At moonrise I have to fly back."

The startled pimp landed face first on the ground with Drucilla's claws firmly gripping his shoulders. Before he could cry out, the Ash-Ta landed on top of him and bit through the back of his neck. She tore into his flesh. His bones snapped and crunched loudly when Drucilla ripped most of the spinal column out of his body. By the time the turine's ringing stopped, Drucilla perched on the body catching her breath, her claws and mouth bloodied.

She shredded the man's clothing in a single rake of a claw and eyed his meaty arms and thighs. Leaning down, she took another large bite and savored the sweetness of a fresh kill.

Drucilla swallowed and prepared to take another mouthful, when a heavy crossbow bolt struck her violently from behind. It plunged into the middle of her back catapulting her forward. The wounded Ash-Ta landed beside her victim and writhed in agony with the crossbow bolt's broadhead jutting from her chest. She could taste blood filling her mouth, when she heard the crossbow cock again.

Gazing up through the fog of pain she watched a small Bailian man, she didn't recognize, step out of the shadows.

The assassin calmly walked over and aimed the crossbow at her head.

"So predictable," the figure said, calmly pulling the trigger.

Julius's eyes went wide in shock. He lurched forward uncontrollably and dropped the Etheria rod on the counter. Searing pain shot through his back. Clumsily reaching for the affected area he could find no offending projectiles. Groaning he looked down at his chest, confirming nothing protruded there.

"Lord Julius what's the matter?" the Etheriat asked in a panic.

"Shot," was all the Avion could utter.

Another spasm followed. Julius grabbed his neck, gurgled several times, and fell unconscious to the floor.

Stryder was gone. Where and for how long was anyone's guess. Harper rose from his desk brooding, distraught that the Vicar of Pa-Waga had refused to see the looming threat.

He knew he would have to do something drastic, something he had never attempted before. Now, *he* would have to be the one to call directly on Pa-Waga. It would be up to him to serve the lord as high priest and lead the way into this new era of prosperity.

The hairless cat lay unconscious on the nearby table. He walked over and stared down reluctantly at the stray animal before him. These cats roamed everywhere in the city and most generally considered them a nuisance. Harper had never performed a sacrificial ceremony before, he had always left that to Stryder.

Although uncertain of his own abilities, he *was* certain of one thing; he could not allow Shom Eldor to go to the Zorian Monetary Council. He had been left no other choice. The assassin's attempt failed the night before when Shom's bodyguard proved too formidable. It would take something far more esoteric to deal with the Eldorian sovereign.

He lifted the animals head, placed a shallow bowl underneath, and picked up his dagger. He made a mental note, if he would perform these rituals in the future, he would need a dedicated area and better tools.

Harper sighed, cleared his mind, then dragged the blade across the cat's neck. The bowl filled quickly with the animal's blood and when the bleeding subsided, he placed the vessel next to the now dead animal.

Harper laid the lifeless cat on its side and dipped his forefinger in the bowl. He then inscribed two lines of "X" and "I" with the bloodied fingertip, running the length of the body. Then he double checked the second line, making sure it read *Shom Eldor*, and picked up the knife again.

Keeping the image of Shom in his mind, he made a deep incision between the lines of runes and winced squeamishly when the bones of the cat's ribcage cracked under the heavy blade. Harper considered stopping, but it was too late. He didn't even know what would happen if he ended the incantation early. Pa-Waga was an unforgiving god.

When the cat's body cavity opened completely, the animal's corpse vibrated and Harper stepped back. He could see wisps of smoke rise from the incision. The volume of smoke steadily increased, hovering over the body like a living mist. When the cloud grew as large as the table, it began undulating.

Harper watched in uneasy amazement while the smoke slowly took on the form of a ghost-like panther. It crouched on the table over the dead street cat. Looking around, it growled once, and then leapt for the nearby window.

Just before it reached the pane of glass, it returned to a formless shape and flowed through the surrounding cracks. Once outside, it resumed its feline spectral form and bound off, blending in perfectly with the thick Kan fog.

"Enjoy," Cha-Rod said, handing the skewer to Tysonn and sitting down next to him.

"Thanks," the scholar replied, examining the impaled chunks of beef. "Meat on a stick, common in one form or another to just about every society."

"Well, it's not eel," Cha-Rod said, before taking a bite, "but the only street vendors open during the Kan are next to taverns. Selection is limited."

"Quite all right," Tysonn replied. "I appreciate you venturing out in the fog."

"Have you discovered anything?" Cha-Rod asked, gesturing towards the several piles of books and the stack of Kasha's notes littering the desk in front of Tysonn.

"There's virtually nothing on the Tiikeri race, much less on their pantheon of deities," Tysonn replied, before taking a bite. "There are some writings on dealing with deities in general, however. The bad news is you can't kill them. The only way gods die is if people stop believing in them. All we can hope to do is drive its presence from here in the Corporeal Reach back to where it came from."

"That sounds frightening," Cha-Rod noted, worriedly.

Tysonn nodded in agreement and continued, "Then, of course, we've got the copy we made of the Cisla a Moc. Thank the gods Kasha kept detailed notes."

"At least the copy isn't written in blood," the Bailian added.

"That's some comfort," Tysonn conceded.

"Does that tell you what to say?" Cha-Rod asked, looking at the pages marked with artistically designed rows of "X" and "I."

Tysonn shook his head. "This is not a spoken language. There are only two binary type runes. If combined in specific groupings, they can represent and effect the physical world."

"This world?" the Bailian asked, puzzled.

"Any world in the Corporeal Reach," Tysonn explained, "or the entire multiverse for that matter. These runes represent the very building blocks of reality."

There was a moment of reverential silence.

"Pardon an old man's misgivings, but that sounds dangerous," Cha-Rod finally uttered.

"That's because it is," Tysonn said, pointing to the script. "Fortunately, it's very complex. To the average sentient, it would be meaningless and harmless."

"Unless it's written in blood," Cha-Rod qualified.

"Unless it's written in blood." Tysonn agreed, nodding. "Then it acts as a conduit to the deity because it's a prayer book."

"So, what does all this mean?" Cha-Rod asked, noting all the reference material.

"This is a Tiikeri god. They call it Pa-Waga. But that is only their name for it. These runes are vastly more primal. They reveal its true name, the unspeakable one. And here's the best part, if one knows an entity's true name, one can control it!"

"Or in this case, banish it," Cha-Rod added.

"There's just one thing," Tysonn said, his expression dire. "First, we have to summon it."

Attina's eyes narrowed suspiciously at the sounds coming from behind them. All of her senses tingled. She inherently knew she was being stalked. She kept a hand on the hilt of her short sword and peered over at a very drunk Shom, staggering next to her.

"I probably shouldn't have had that last drink," the royal slurred.

"You probably shouldn't have had the last *three* drinks," the Hill Sister said.

"Nonsense!" Shom blustered. "If there's one thing I can do, it's hold my liquor."

The seneschal was about to make a snide comment when Shom tripped over a cobblestone and toppled to the ground.

"I'm okay," he immediately proclaimed. "Thankfully, the road broke my fall."

She was about to reach down to help the sovereign up when she caught movement in the fog. The Amarenian only had time to pull her sword halfway out of its scabbard, when the ghost cat roared and sprung. Two enormous spectral paws connected with Attina's chest sending her reeling backwards onto the street.

The beast roared again at her but didn't attack. Instead, it turned its attention to a terrified Shom, who attempted to crawl away while drunkenly fumbling for his blade.

Crouching, it snarled, and lunged, landing directly in front of Shom. The Eldorian cried out and raised his blade in front of his torso when the cat swatted him. The claws entangled with the blade, but the force sent Shom crashing into a nearby wall.

Attina was back on her feet, swinging at the phantasmal panther and struck it in mid frame. It roared but the Amarenian's blade passed through the beast with no obvious effect. Crouching again, the ghost cat prepared another attack on the now unarmed royal.

The Hill Sister swung once again, this time with the flat of the blade. The monster bellowed in defiance as the sword swept away a large swath of its body. It briefly paused its assault as the smoky wound filled back up.

Tysonn glanced nervously over at the book open a third of the way through and laying on the desk. He reached into a drawer and retrieved a small knife, candle, and a sheet of fine linen paper.

"Once we get started, we will have to work fast," Tysonn said, assessing the items before him. "We don't want to give that thing a chance to latch onto one of us."

"What do you want me to do?" Cha-Rod asked, hefting his cane.

"Well, that won't have any effect on it," Tysonn said, eyeing the ornate cudgel. "I need you over by the door. I can't be disturbed once I get started."

The Bailian positioned himself where requested while Tysonn lit the candle and picked up the knife.

"You sure you want to do this?" Cha-Rod asked, when Tysonn brought the tip of the blade up to his extended forefinger. "I mean, you just went through a whole ordeal because of that book and blood."

Tysonn gave him an apprehensive glance. "No, I really don't, but it's the only way."

The linguist winced as he lanced the end of his finger. When the blood flowed, he put his fingertip to the paper and wrote six lines of runes.

IIXXXXXX
IXXXXXXI
IXIXIIII
IXXXXXXI
IXXXIIII
IXXXXXXI

When he inscribed the last glyph, the temperature plummeted and the dank smell of ammonia permeated the room.

"It's here," Tysonn announced, he could see his breath.

Ignoring the paranormal signs he held a corner of the paper over the candle's flame. It ignited immediately. The windows and doors rattled. Hissing and roaring filled the air. When the flames consumed more of the paper, the room shook violently, and the howling grew more fever pitched.

Cha-Rod glanced around the room nervously when loud scraping sounds accompanied giant claw marks gouging the walls. Tysonn stood silently through it all, holding the burning paper in his outstretched hand. When the sheet was half engulfed, the floor cracked and a deep fissure opened running the length of the room.

The first floor, which should have been below them, was not visible, instead only an inky, bottomless darkness. They heard growls and otherworldly shrieks emanating from the blackness of the abyss before them.

Tysonn concentrated on the burning paper in his hand and didn't notice the large patch of black ooze crawling rapidly out of the fissure. Fields of "X" and "I" runes fired up across the creature's malleable surface. The blob slithered on the ledge stalking an oblivious Tysonn. It undulated wildly and rose into the abominable, new transmutation of Stryder, the Vicar of Pa-Waga.

"Look out!" Cha-Rod cried out.

The warning came too late. As Tysonn spun around, Stryder knocked him backwards with a whipping back hand. The scholar let go of the paper just as the flames had nearly consumed it. The Bailian watched the burning page hover over the abyss which was too wide for him to jump.

Stryder lashed out with an inhuman growl and grabbed Tysonn by the neck. The creature lifted him up violently and stared into his panicked face, who kicked and flailed wildly.

"YOU LITTLE FUCKER!" it roared with a force shattering the windows. "YOU REALLY THINK YOU CAN HARM ME?!"

Cha-Rod helplessly watched his companion being strangled, when an idea suddenly occurred to him. Rearing back, he tossed his cane at the cat-headed assailant. When it made contact in the center of Stryder's back, the bronze colored Ukkonite Etheria crystal flashed. The impact knocked Stryder off balance and forced Tysonn's release, who fell to the floor.

Stryder turned angrily, but before he could do anything, the flames completely overtook the paper. Instead of falling immediately, the burning note hovered above the gaping cavern for a moment, before dropping into the abyss.

An invisible force grabbed Stryder, pulling him into the fissure along with the falling ashes. The Vicar of Pa-Waga roared in frustration and abandoned his humanoid shape, as the force dragged him towards oblivion. Before going over the edge the gelatinous monstrosity extended a slime tendril that enveloped Tysonn's legs.

The prone scholar strained and tugged unsuccessfully, trying to break the thing's grip. Cha-Rod watched helplessly as the amorphous Stryder dragged Tysonn screaming over the edge, disappearing into the darkness of the cavern. The room shuddered one last time, before the fissure closed back up behind them, and silence descended on the chamber.

When he finally collected himself, the Bojo-Vat master found he was alone. They had reduced the room to shambles, with books and papers strewn everywhere. The ceiling looked as if it could collapse because of the damage dealt to the walls, doors, and windows. He could hear rapidly approaching footsteps from down the hall.

Walking over to his cane lying on the floor, he picked it up and inspected it. He sighed in relief that his staff was unharmed then braced himself for the inevitable flurry of questions and considered what he would say.

The Ghost Cat pinned Shom to the ground and poised to take a bite out of his throat, when Attina fanned the sword through its head. It disappeared in a trail behind the blade, swiftly replaced by a new one behind her. Attina spun to strike again, when the southern sky erupted in a blue flash and the spectral creature dissipated into the Kan fog.

"What in the name of the gods just happened," Shom asked, when he caught his breath.

Attina sheathed her sword and helped her sovereign lover to his feet.

"It's only a guess," she said, "but I'd say whatever powered that thing, just left."

"Well, I'm not drunk anymore," Shom said, with resignation. "Nothing like a serious jolt of adrenalin to kill a good sousing."

The Eldorian put his arm around his seneschal and began directing them both back to the pub. "Please allow me to buy you a drink as a thank you for saving my life."

"Are you kidding," the Hill Sister scoffed, "after that you will need to buy me a lot of drinks."

Kai felt her stomach knot up and throat tighten the moment she stepped into the alley. The two bodies were lying midway down the narrow back street, one on top of the other.

The one on the bottom was a male, probably a pimp. She found him lying face down, with the back of his clothes ripped open. The top of his spine, pulled from his body, jutted upward like a macabre cobra. A bite mark in his upper right thigh left a sizable chunk of flesh missing and blood everywhere.

The body of Drucilla lay on top of the pimp's lower back, slumped over on its side. Crossbow bolts impaled both her upper body and neck.

The Priestess of Orad, though numb from witnessing countless scenes of death, fought back tears. She struggled to keep a professional demeanor. No one could know of their relationship. Public grief would be an emotion denied the spymaster.

She stood staring at the bodies through a foggy tunnel vision until the EEtah sergeant stepped up beside her.

"Your people?" she asked.

"Nah," the EEtah grumbled. "Our patrols use medium crossbows. These two bolts came from a heavy crossbow. They could have penetrated armor."

Kai numbly nodded.

"Looks like we caught the creature red handed," the Valdurian sergeant continued. "It's a safe bet that's what's been killing and eating folks around here lately. Whoever did this saved us a lot of trouble."

An immense wave crashed over the bow of the Calden Frigate *Valborg,* drenching a wide-eyed Joc' Valdur while he tightly gripped the railing. The Valdurian ambassador looked around nervously at the seven-foot swells.

"Don't get out on the water much do you?" Pierce Calden asked, with a knowing grin.

Joc' shook his head and looked suddenly away from the surrounding white caps. "I fly over it. Does that count?"

"Not really," the Calden ambassador said, grinning.

Pierce watched the flotilla of ships bobbing about in the swells of Lumina's northwestern Ocean Deep. He gazed up at the bright blue sky streaked with wispy clouds.

"Be glad the weather's good," he said, "it can really get dicey out here in a storm."

"You would think they would have chosen a calmer spot." Joc' yelled over the roar of the waves.

Pierce pointed out over the bow.

"The Innaca Deep is about ten miles in that direction," he said. "It's the only portal big enough to handle a transfer of this size. Just think, you're in a part of the world very few people have ever seen. We might have to make you an honorary Brightstar."

"There!" Joc' cried out.

He pointed to the horizon as the transport ship *Prevoz* shot out of a giant whirlpool portal into the skies above. An eruption of dead trees followed the airship, propelled high into the air filling the immediate sky. The massive arboreal fountain continued spewing, sending the bald, hundred-foot logs splashing down amidst the deep rolling waves.

The *Prevoz* leveled off and circled around, making sure it stayed clear of the flight path of the incredible volume of Ukko wood being spit out of the Middle Realms into the Corporeal Reach.

"Did someone order a forest?" Joc' said, visibly relieved.

"They pulled it off," Pierce said, astonished.

"Mal and company rarely disappoints," Joc' replied, with a satisfied nod.

The *Prevoz* pulled alongside the pitching and rolling Calden naval frigate. Mal stood in the open side hatch giving both thumbs up before the airship rose and banked eastward toward Zor.

"All right then," Joc' said, watching the last of the Zerian forest plunge into the ocean, "this is where your Brightstar people earn their keep."

Pierce slapped his friend on the back while on his way to the bridge.

"Let's go get our wood."

"What took you so long?" Bigarren asked, her voice in a near panic. "The Na-Kab are preparing to attack the surface."

Julius's face was a mask of pain and sadness walking past her carrying the pink Cobalcite rod. The Avion high priestess fell in behind him while they descended once again into the sprawling tunnels beneath Mount Goya.

"My sister is truly gone this time," the Avion prince said, morosely. "Perhaps it is for the best. She was miserable in that Ash-Ta body. At least she and Kai had the chance to make up before the end."

"Will you avenge her?" Bigarren asked.

Julius sadly shook his head. "I've had enough killing."

From up ahead in the first enormous cavern they heard a commotion while a large group of fire bugs made their way to the surface.

"You will be the first to die, winged fleshy ones," King Krol spat. "Your time is up!"

"The second fog has not yet risen," Julius proclaimed defiantly. "I was under the impression the Na-Kab kept their word!"

"It is about to rise," the lead bug argued, "and yet we still have no queen!"

"Take me to her chamber," Julius said, confidently, raising the pink Etheria rod. "If we fail, then we have not kept our end of the bargain and you can do as you will."

The mantis creatures hesitated while they chattered across their hive mind.

"Come," the Na-Kab king said, reluctantly.

He led them back down the tunnel. The two Avions strode directly over to the magma lake when they arrived in the queen's cavern. The Na-Kab horde crowded around them, spilling out into the passageway.

There was no time to lose. They already detected wisps of fog as the Kan began setting in. The Na-Kab, much like their cousins the Do-Tarr, were unbending with their word. Late and almost were not a part of their lexicon. If they didn't have a queen by the time the passages filled with fog, they would consider the promise broken, with all its dreadful consequences.

Julius stood beside the magma pool holding the Etheria rod out at arm's length, when Bigarren came up beside him. She reached out and touched the rod. While Julius slowly lowered the crystal into the pool, she began a prayer to Goya under her breath.

The rod melted when it entered the liquified rock, turning into a swirling pink puddle before dissipating. After a long, tense moment of silence, the pool suddenly bubbled. When the magma's agitation increased, Bigarren took Julius by the arm and backed him away from the shore.

The boiling lava began to pop and build, slowly coalescing into a single, mammoth sized glowing red bubble. When it reached twelve feet tall, it ceased expanding and started to quiver.

Bigarren's eyes widened with the realization of what was about to happen. She quickly slapped her hands together resulting in another shower of sparks. Arching her hands over their heads she initiated the protective shield of super-heated air just when the bubble exploded, filling the cavern with a shower of volcanic spray. Like the Na-Kab fire, the molten spittle ran harmlessly off the barrier and collected on the floor.

Silence once again enveloped the cavern, and the pool resumed its normal ebb and flow. All stared intently at the surface. The Na-Kab noticed it first, and they began chattering deliriously. There was definitely movement in the molten lake which grew considerably larger than before.

When the queen's fully formed mantis head broke the surface, the Na-Kab began jumping about excitedly and the Avions heaved a sigh of relief. Its humanoid torso rose next, complete with the six teats full of her fiery nectar, followed by an insectoid thorax, fully formed with plates covering her molten bowels.

She stood a full ten-feet tall on her eight legs and gazed down upon her subjects with magma red eyes. The hive of ecstatic mantis creatures swarmed their queen, all hoping to be the first one to touch her. She looked down at the two Avions staring up at her in admiration.

"You saved my people, our civilization," she said, in a tone as thankful as their race could muster. "We embrace your god Goya as our own. This is truly a sacred union."

"And you just saved ours," Julius said, with a grateful smile. "Blessed be the Holy Mother Mountain."

"Are you going to return to your post in Immor-Onn or come back home?" Bigarren asked, when they exited the reborn Na-Kab fire hive.

"I go to see my father," Julius said, distantly, lost in thought. "I must renounce my crown."

This visibly stunned the Avion priestess of Goya. "What! Why?"

"The visions I've been having and the recent events have shown me the delicate balance of the Annigan," Julius said, keeping his serene pace. "I seek seclusion to meditate on these things. I feel I'm on the verge of a higher calling beyond the novelty of being a mad prince."

Moonrise found the palace in Immor-Onn busy as usual. Bailians bustled in and out of hallways and offices conducting the business of the state. When Kai saw the Finance Minister leave the queen's chamber, she swept through the wide double doors, nodding to the guard as she passed.

Queen Shula sat on her throne stroking her pet Cheepa, Manar, cooing on her lap. The trilling creature evoked the usual calming effect when the queen gently stroked its furry belly. Glancing up she waved her spymaster over.

"My queen," Kai said, bowing. "My people have just confirmed earlier reports that the Tiikeri have built a settlement on Gar-Yesh Point."

"Is this something which should concern us?" Shula asked, keeping her serene disposition. "I mean, it is on the other end of the continent."

"I don't trust the Tiikeri," Kai said, disdainfully.

"You're the royal spymaster," the queen said, chuckling, "I didn't think you trusted anyone."

Kai gave an embarrassed grin. "Especially not the Tiikeri. They're just a little too aggressive about empire expansion, among other things."

"I'll speak with ambassador Jo-Rakk, just to let them know that we know. Was there anything else?"

"Yes, my queen, I would like to request a temporary leave of absence. No more than four lunas."

"Of course, my little savior." Shula tilted her head and gave her a curious look. "Personal business?"

"Mending bridges and tying up some loose ends."

The queen nodded her consent and the one-armed woman bowed before making a hasty exit. When the queen settled back in her seat, she detected movement on the other side of the room.

"Greetings queen Shula," came a monotone voice.

A lone albino Bailian stepped from behind some curtains. "We are Orich-Ta."

Queen Shula watched the blue robed figure approach.

"You said 'we,'" she said, "but I only see you."

Ignoring the question, he stopped at the stairs leading up to the throne.

"We are a Harbinger of Balance," he said, calmly, "and we bring joyous news."

The queen shook her head in confusion. "You're a what? How did you get in here?"

"A major event on the far side of the world in Lumina has restored balance to the Annigan. The Black Mural is no longer poised to fall."

"What event?" she asked. "The Black what?"

"This is my message," he said, with a bow.

With that, Queen Shula watched him wordlessly back away and disappear behind the curtains. She stroked Manar a few times, deep in thought, before alerting the guards.

Joc' Valdur stood and came out from behind his desk when the Avion entered.

"Lord Julius," he greeted warmly. "What can I do for House Pyre?"

The Avion prince surprisingly offered his hand. Joc' seemed to recall Avions abhorred physical contact with humans.

"It is what I can do for you," Julius said, while the two shook hands. "And I have renounced my position and title, so you no longer need to refer to me as lord."

This surprised the Valdurian ambassador.

"As you wish," he said, offering a seat.

"Thank you, no," Julius replied. "I shouldn't be here that long."

"You said you could do something for us. I apologize for my misunderstanding, but in the past you have always held my race in contempt."

The Avion gave an introspective smile. "Recent events have caused me to reconsider my prior prejudices. I have a gift for you."

Reaching inside his tunic he pulled out a four-inch-long metal pellet and placed it on his desk.

"You have new neighbors," he said, "courtesy of the late Stryder Aramos."

"Oh?" Joc' replied, picking up the pellet to examine it.

"Yes, they are called the Na-Kab, and he brought them here from Nocturn."

Joc' gave Julius a silent, concerned stare.

"They are fire mantis creatures from Mount Natal in the land of Mists," the Avion continued. "Queen-less, their race was dying, and they were desperate. This caused them to become aggressive and ruthless."

Joc's concerned stare quickly transformed into worrisome.

"Be at peace," Julius said, when he saw the troubled expression. "We have restored their queen and they are now under Mount Goya, doing what they do best, tunneling."

"What is this?" Joc' asked, holding up the pellet.

"Na-Kab Carbon," Julius answered. "They consume molten rock and this is a byproduct of their waste. It is strong, lightweight, and infinitely forgeable."

"Na-Kab Carbon," Joc' said, eyeing the metal with fresh interest.

"I think you will find the Na-Kab more than willing to trade," the Avion proclaimed. "It could be a significant advantage to your house."

Joc' nodded in agreement, his mind racing.

"There's more," Julius continued. "The byproduct of their tunneling and processing volcanic minerals from Holy Mother Mountain will restore the sacred fertility lost with the passing of the Golden Avatar."

"That means Stryder was wrong when he predicted our civilization would be in decline."

Julius shook his head. "No, he was initially correct but the Na-Kab changed all that."

"The intervention!" Joc' blurted out.

"I beg your pardon?"

"When Stryder initially contacted us about the auction, he claimed without an intervention our civilization had only ten grands. This is the intervention!"

"I don't know if it was intentional or not, but it is no matter. We *have* restored the balance. The Black Mural is still."

"So, what about you?" Joc' asked. "What will you do now that you've renounced House Pyre?"

"I have been shown many things recently. The true fate of the Annigan rests with the symmetrical harmony of its inhabitants' actions. I will remain in Goya as a Harbinger of Balance, a herald if you will."

"Well I'm not sure what any of that means, but House Valdur thanks you for your gift and your insight. I hope it means greater cooperation and perhaps even friendship between Avion and human."

"One can only hope," Julius said, extending his hand once more.

The taste of revenge is not so sweet, Rafel pondered, taking another drink.

The liquor burned going down and the Zorian spymaster stared despondently into the fire. He had killed the Ash-Ta and he could feel Kai's pain, but it offered no solace to him. He had imagined himself reveling in her grief, savoring her loss. All it did was magnify his own sense of sorrow.

Rafel cursed when a sudden gust of wind blew the window open. He rose from the floor in front of the warmth of the fireplace and shivered as the Kan fog outside chilled his naked body. Once he closed the window, he made sure to latch it this time.

"So, what do we do now?" asked a female voice from behind him.

Rafel spun in a panic. Kai stood by the door; her face bathed in melancholy. The spymaster froze in place, his eyes wide with fear.

"Where do we go from here?" Kai asked, in a low voice. "Do we continue this dance of retaliation or do we end it?"

"What do you mean?" Rafel choked out, when he finally found his voice.

"We've both experienced the loss of someone dear to us by each other's doing. Mine by contract. Yours for revenge. We are even in our anguish. So, I ask again, do we continue this insanity, or does it stop here and now?"

"What makes you think it *can* stop?" he asked.

"Our sense of duty."

Rafel silently contemplated her point.

"It serves no purpose to have the spymasters of two great powers at odds with each other," Kai reasoned. "Especially with what we will soon be up against."

"I'm not sure I take your meaning?"

"The Tiikeri empire is on the rise," Kai said, with conviction. "Contrary to what our leaders would like to believe, the Tiikeri's are *not* our friends. They are cunning, aggressive, and more than a little ruthless. You and I don't have to like each other, but unless we want our peoples annexed and enslaved, we will need to work together."

Rafel silently walked over to where the liquor bottle rested on the floor, his mind was awash with potential plots and scenarios. Sitting on the floor, he hefted the bottle in her direction.

"May I offer you a drink?"

Kai considered the offer and a melancholy smile descended on her face.

"Sure."

She sat down facing the naked Rafel and accepted the bottle. Rafel watched Kai take a sip.

"You know," he began, "I thought exacting revenge would bring me some kind of peace, a sense of closure. All it did was make the hole in my heart bigger. Now there are two people in pain, not just one."

"I know you must miss him terribly," Kai said, handing the bottle back.

Rafel slowly nodded before taking a drink.

"I miss the discipline he brought to my life," he said, with a sad chuckle, peering down at his lap. "Our first time together he made me bleed."

Kai embraced his nostalgia with a sorrowful smile.

"I'll do you one better," she said, raising the stump of her missing arm.

"That must have been some lovers quarrel," he replied, lifting the bottle to his lips.

"She was an Avion," Kai explained. "We weren't supposed to be together. When she died and I arranged to bring her back from the Middle Realms, an Ash-Ta was the only available body. She was angry, and she took it out on my arm."

"Anger between lovers cuts the deepest," Rafel replied, passing the bottle back to her. "I'm glad you had an opportunity to make up."

"It took awhile," Kai acknowledged. "She *really* hated that body."

"I guess it's fortunate that love doesn't care what you look like.

Kai nodded solemnly in agreement while she stared down silently. They sat quietly for the next few moments occasionally handing the bottle back-and-forth. Kai finally looked back up when she heard Rafel sob.

"I really loved him," Rafel bemoaned, tears streaming down his cheeks.

"If the gods are merciful, we will be together again." Kai said, feeling her tears well up. "Until then, I guess we just have to get used to their absence."

With a sniffle, Rafel stopped crying and stared at Kai with a softened demeanor.

"To absent loves and new friends," he said, taking a drink and raising the bottle.

Kai took the bottle when he offered it and also raised it in front of her.

"To absent loves and new friends."

By the time the turine in the harbor rang thirteen bells, thick Kan fog enveloped the Makatooa docks. The nude human female peeked out from behind the stack of shipping crates and cautiously scanned the area. Confident there was no one around, she scampered towards a nearby covered quarantine zone.

The thirty-foot square area contained three rows of unstacked large barrels. She had seen the fishing boats return from the Ocean Deep and unload their catch. They transferred their harvest of Derin Krill with shovels into the barrels and then salted them down. They would quickly sell the rare delicacy for a large profit when the market opened at the lifting of the Kan.

Her stomach growled, and she salivated at the thought of the miniscule creatures which inhabited waters much too deep for her to dive. Wasting no time, she tore the lid off one and reached in. Pulling up a handful of the tiny crustaceans she jammed them into her mouth raw. Her eyes rolled back ecstatically in her head, accompanied by the crunching sound of shells being crushed and devoured.

She was about to reach her hand in again when she heard a creaking sound above her. She glanced up in time to see a large bucket of water being pulled off a ceiling beam by a long rope. Cold water doused her petite frame, plastering down her long blonde, highlighted hair.

She cried out in shock when her legs fused together and develop scales. The lower half of her body transformed into a v-shaped fishtail and she toppled helplessly to the deck.

"There you are!" came a loud nasally lisp over the sound of her flopping around on the damp planks.

She watched as seven men appeared from out of the fog. Six of them appeared to be common street thugs, but it was the leader who was truly unsettling.

He stood tall and thin with a bone white pallor. Dressed in a formal, thigh length dinner jacket with no shirt, she could see his ribs straining against the taunt skin. Shoulder length white stringy hair cascaded out of a black top hat. Sunken bloodshot eyes leered from a long and angular face, giving him a ghoulish bearing.

It was his mouth however that was the most disturbing. He had no lips, which gave his yellow teeth the appearance of being freakishly long.

"I have been chasing you all over the Spice Islands. That was until I said to myself, 'Self, you're going about this all wrong. You've got to bring her to you. What would be her favorite food?'"

He did a quick lick of his teeth and shrugged.

"And here we are."

Two of the men grabbed her by the arms and drug her out onto the main dock. He knelt down beside her and brought his face close to hers. She winced at the sour smell of cucumbers, dill, and garlic.

"So," he said, the corners of his mouth turning upward in a maniacal smile, "if I've been all over the western Goyan Islands looking for you, can you guess why?"

"The totem," she weakly said.

He suddenly leapt to his feet and waved his arms enthusiastically.

"That's right!"

His face then took on a mockingly sad presence.

"So you can see what I have to do." He paused and smiled again. "But not to worry, it will be quick and your essence will live on in my wardrobe. I'm sure those green scales and perky tits will make an excellent shirt."

"I do not think the sentient is enjoying your company," a calm voice came from behind.

All spun to see a man of average height and build with long brown hair and a goatee. The wide sash that held his long black robes closed, cradled three blades of varying lengths. The leader placed his hands on his hips and assessed the brash young man.

"Boys," he said, addressing his companions. "What we have here is a hero. I hate heroes. Ya know why?"

He halted and faced Alto.

"Rules," he said, without waiting for anyone to answer. "Heroes always have rules, a code."

A long bony finger pointed at the swordmaster.

"You, for example," he said, "I'll bet you have a code, don't you?"

"I was passing by and heard the cry," Alto said, with an amused grin. "She *is* unarmed."

The leader instantly became animated again, addressing his men.

"See, see, I told you, always with the fucking rules!" he exclaimed, before a resolved look swept over his face. "Kill him."

The two closest to the swordmaster drew their daggers and stepped forward. Alto's blade, Defari, let out a loud baying howl, which echoed down the wharf, when Alto unsheathed her. The blade travelled upward, diagonally slicing through the first attacker.

It made snarling and biting sounds while it travelled horizontally through the second, sending a curtain of blood spraying across the group.

Both severed bodies toppled to the dock while they silently bled out. The leader's face displayed both shock and amusement. He grabbed the brim of his hat and did an excited hop.

"Whoo Hoo!" he yelled. "That was impressive!"

The rest of the mobsters froze in disbelief staring at the growling sword. Seemingly unfazed, the leader stepped over to Alto with a look of awe.

"You know," he said, "it is so refreshing working with a professional. Most of the time I'm stuck with, you know..."

His eyes flitted playfully around indicating his henchmen.

"...the local talent."

He licked his teeth again and took on a conciliatory demeanor.

"But fun and games aside," he said, "I'm going to have to ask you to drop your sword."

When Alto returned a playful smirk, the leader stepped aside and revealed one of his thugs holding a dagger to the mermaid's throat.

"Put your weapons down and back away," Alto demanded, softly. "And I'll let you live."

The leader excitedly addressed his men again, "There it is! Another reason I love dealing with professionals. Confidence! I like a man who's confident in his abilities."

In an instant, his continence changed again.

"In all seriousness, drop the sword or we will carve fillets out of the fish lady.

The mermaid gasped in terror when the blade pressed tighter against her neck drawing blood. Alto paused, then lowered Defari. Reaching beside him, he let go of the sword. It hovered in midair giving off a low menacing growl.

"Stay," the swordmaster ordered.

The leader's jovial mood instantly returned.

"Once again, impressive," he said, assessing the hovering Etheria sword.

His attention then returned to everyone.

"There, you see, we can all be reasonable." He gave a weary sigh. "All right, *now* you can kill them both."

Before anyone could move Alto whistled and pointed at the one with the knife to the mermaid's throat. Defari streaked with a loud growl across the dock and embedded itself in the hooligan's forehead, catapulting him onto his back. The mermaid screamed when an arc of blood showered her and the entire area.

The leader laughed manically and pointed at his impaled henchman. Alto drew his short sword and slashed upward along the chest of the nearest man charging him.

The two remaining ruffians all but froze in fear. Seizing the opportunity, Alto bound over to his long sword and pulled it out of the dead man's forehead, just as the mermaid slipped over the side of the docks into the water.

The determined swordmaster now stood with a blade in each hand. When the leader broke and ran, the last two hoodlums followed suit. Alto sheathed his blades surveying the carnage while the leader's demented laughter faded off into the Kan fog.

Wostera examined the stack of eight, one thousand gold piece commodity notes in her hands and gave a perplexed grin.

"Thank you, Captain," she said, handing them back to Mal, "but I don't know what this is for."

"It's your share," the Spice Rat replied. "You know, for kicking ass across the multiverse with us. Two percent of two million, which was the winning bid for the forest divided by five, is eight thousand."

"Valorous I appreciate your fairness," she said, "but when I petitioned you to come along, I said that during my So'Gen I would not require compensation."

"More for the rest of us!" Zau said, with a touch of greed.

"I don't need it either," Kumo said, handing her notes back to Mal.

"Now were talking!" Zau blurted out, enthusiastically.

The Singa fell silent when the captain shot her an annoyed glance.

"Fair enough," Mal conceded, "but we're using the extra gold to pay for some upgrades to the *Haraka*."

Zau crossed her arms in front of her and scoffed loudly. "Fine!"

Mal shook her head in frustration. "You know, you don't have to act like you've got a spike up your ass all the time!"

"Me?!" the Singa bellowed.

"Yes you," the Spice Rat replied. "Sometimes it's like you're my, my... You're not my mother!"

The lioness recoiled at the statement.

"I'm not your mother!" she yelled. "Your mother's dead! Do I look dead to you?!"

Both females turned away from each other in frustration.

"Joc' said there was a secret base in the mountains of Atar Island called Landagar." Mal said, addressing the rest of the group. "It's where they develop their specialty equipment. We've been invited."

She then pointed to the bag of mushrooms in the cargo area.

"But first we've got to convert those into something a little more useful."

"Yeah, like gold," Zau commented, sarcastically.

"Like gold," the captain agreed, "and there's only one person who can handle a shipment of that size, my friend, Asad."

"Asad, huh," Zaad chuckled. "You mean a trip to Makatooa?"

"You sure there isn't another reason to visit Makatooa?" Zau poked.

"Maybe one more," the Spice Rat said, blushing slightly.

Agents of the Void

GLOSSARY

Spoiler warning: The following is a master glossary for all the books in this series. Reading beyond a specific word or phrase searches could result in spoilers.

Adad Sunal – EEtah war collage belonging to House Bran, specializing in conducting internal security for House Bran.

Agress – A green Etheria Crystal with red striations which opens and closes doors, windows and hatches, negating any locks but not traps or wards.

Aiken – Semi-sentient clouds sent out across the Annigan from Mount Ghas-Tor, recording everything they witness on the ground and in the air. They are indistinguishable from other clouds against the backdrop of a blue sky. Aiken constantly send visuals back to the mountain, but recent images remain in their limited memory. Those possessing psychic abilities can access their recent memories by flying through and communing with them.

Akina – Humanoid fox creatures native to the Barrens in the Twilight Lands. Often sly and excellent thieves.

Amarenian – Female human race formerly noted for their hatred and slavery of men and piracy.

Angona – Roasted eel on a stick. Sold from vendors' carts all over the City of Immor-Onn.

Annigan – The name of the world which is the setting for the various stories in the Tales of the Annigan Cycle. It includes the two hemispheres of Lumina and Nocturn separated by the Twilight Lands.

Anointed Sister – The title for the Amarenian Queen.

Aquamarine – Pale blue Etheria Crystal which reveals something's true nature.

Ara-Fel Party – Political party of Amarenian farmers.

Arapa Fish – A large fish native to the back waters and tributaries of the Otoman River. Their tough scaly skin is coveted among the Dreeat as armor. The scales by themselves are so abrasive they are also sold as nails.

Ash-Ta – Avion term (winged monster) for the widespread colonies of humanoid bats inhabiting the rocky crags stretching across of the Spine of the World. Avion scholars record six tribes: the Molossi, Acero, Chiro, Ptero, Diaemus and Desmodus. The Ash-Ta allied with the Tiikeri due to their shared enemy, the Do-Tarr.

Astute Sister – Amarenian title for high level politician.

Aur-Quaz – Iridescent Etheria Crystal stimulating energy.

Available Regions – Uninhabited areas of Immor-Onn waiting for the residents displaced by the recent Black Pearl Revolution to return and inhabit.

Avion –Proud sentient rulers of Lumina's sky. Incredibly beautiful and graceful to behold and unabashedly elitist, especially towards their distant cousins, the Humans. Avions refuse to wear any armor and yet have led the way in almost every major war fought. Their scholars contributed a great deal to the knowledge of Lumina. Their four Great Houses occupy the airspace and mountain tops of the Goyan Islands.

Avion Great Houses:

House Azar - Avion House inhabiting the City of Mitar, on the Island of Dal, in the Tellasian chain, ruled by Queen Averin. Their territories include the skies over the Tellasian Chain, Otomoria, Zer-Tal Twins, and the Zerk

Atoll. They are known for their healing Clerics of Neami and their beautiful music.

House Eacher - Avion House inhabiting the Island of Wou, City of Picon & surrounding airspace. Ruled by King Sindil.

House Solas – Smallest of all the Avion houses. They inhabit the city of Adean on the Island of Temil in the Outer Zerians and control the surrounding airspace.

House Pyre - Eldest, largest, and most powerful of all the Avion Houses. They inhabit the skies above the Island of Goya. Their city stronghold, Darmont Keep, sits on the north face of volcanic Mount Goya. Unlike the other Avion Houses who utilize Air Magic, they mastered Fire Magic drawing their power from the volcano.

Awal – First of the ten Quinte Grand Cycle, Spring.

Azurite – Purple Etheria Crystal which connects to the Middle realms.

Bailian – Predominate race of the western Twilight Lands. Descended from the Piceans, they are a beautiful humanoid race with pale blue skin and large eyes.

Banja – The seventy-seven Amarenian noble families, eleven for each of the various seven provinces called Dors.

Banok Atoll – Island ring in the Southeastern Ocean of Lumina housing one of the largest permanent Flavian portals. Its psionic ripples extend out hundreds of miles and affect the entire southeastern Deep Ocean of Lumina.

Banok Run – The final test for admittance to the elite Brightstar Sailors where they must navigate a tight circle around the turbulent seas surrounding the Banok Atoll without being pulled into its giant Flavian portal.

Bespoke Lords – Members of prominent families who have Bespoke Names and serve as advisors to the sovereign in a respective noble human house in the Goyan Islands.

Bespoke Names – Honorary family names only bestowed by a Goyan Island governor or higher as reward for exemplary service to the crown.

Black Mural – A magical record of the Annigan located deep in the Rod-Ema Trench in the Ocean Deep of Nocturn. It slowly grows in size as it records every act of imbalance on the planet. If it grows too large, it will penetrate into the planet's core, killing all life and allowing it to start anew.

Black Talon – Special forces of the Aramos Army, the Fosvara Guard.

Boustian Mage – Bards who perform magic by singing, playing music and storytelling, found predominantly in the larger cities of the Goyodian Chain of islands.

Brightstar – Elite sailors of House Calden qualified to sail the Deep Oceans and the storm-tossed seas of the Twilight Lands. Captains in the Calden Navy must be Brightstar qualified. Brightstar only allows acceptance to their ranks upon completion of the treacherous Innaca or Banok Runs.

Brom – Horse size dragonflies inhabiting the steep southern foothills of the Amaren Mountains.

Calcite – Clear Etheria Crystal which aids in navigation.

Caldani – Privateers hired by Human House Calden to patrol their waters.

Calden Intelligencer Service – House Calden's elite spy agency and secret police. They draw recruits mostly from the Calden Maritime Legion.

Calden Maritime Legion – Marines for House Calden

Calisma – Main library in the University of Marassa.

Cali – Branch libraries and scriptoriums in the five Human capital cities in the Goyodian Island Chain.

Carbana – Chewing tobacco rolled into a tight tube.

Cavernite – A pale green Etheria Crystal with pink striations that can increase the physical dimensions of the interior of any structure it is placed within. The size increase depends on the amount of Cavernite used and the level of PSI used to power it. Without a constant supply of PSI power, the dimensions revert back to their original size. Often used with an Obsidian PSI battery backup.

Centi Elipse – Called a Centi for short. Unit of time in the Goyan Islands equaling a minute.

Celot – Amarenian term for a priestess.

Cevot – Large sentient spider creatures known for their silk, inhabiting the Os-Oni Mountains of the Twilight Lands.

Ched – Seventh of the ten Quinte Grand Cycle, Autumn.

Chanakans – An ancient race of sentient octopoids dwelling in vast underwater cities in the Ocean Deep of Nocturn. They worship the ancient ones of the abyss and practice a powerful water magic.

Cluster – The name for ten cycles, the Annigan's version of a week. There are five clusters to a Quinte (month).

Cobalcite – Deep pink Etheria Crystal used for healing.

Code of Tisina – Mobster code of silence in the City of Zor. Because of Zor's zero tolerance for organized crime, the various independent criminals adopted a "no cooperation" rule with city officials. The slightest violation of this code is punishable by death.

Common – The Common Tongue, a spoken only language used mostly by humans and those in business with them.

Cocoonessa – Cocoon city of the Tinian Moth people on Mount Natal in the Land of Mists. Also called the Silk City.

Corporal Reach, The –The prime material plain of the middle realms where the Annigan resides.

Coxeter – Both the language and magic system of the Tinian race based on a complex form of three-dimensional geometry. The written language is made up of cryptic mathematical notations using lines and dots. Tinian minds perceive all math as the three-dimensional mapping, best displayed in their silk weavings of intricate geometric patterns. When combined with Etheria Crystals, these patterns can be used to perform spells.

Croquis – Magitech mapping devise projecting a scalable three-dimensional holographic image of a desired location, including the other planes of the multiverse.

Cub Prince – A rare black tiger heir to the throne of the Tiikeri Empire. Once every generation, the Tiikeri king must breed an heir. All prominent Tiikeri families offer their most eligible daughters for breeding, but only one will conceive of a black tiger. All other cubs produced from this royal union are killed at birth. They move the complete family of the female who gives birth to the Cub Prince into the palace and considered them nobility. They immediately begin grooming the Cub Prince for the throne, and, when he comes of age, he must kill his father to take it.

Cul-Ta – Humanoid rat creatures found in almost every City in Lumina.

Cycle – Time period equivalent to a day.

Dag – Amarenian term for a common slave. A derogatory slang word for a male.

Darek Witch – Amarenian earth shamans acting as midwives and performing other shamanistic duties.

Darian Silk – High quality silk spun by the Cevot Spiders traded to the On'Dara.

Darwan – A cross between the Balians and the Fudomi, this race is the most prolific humanoid native to the Barrens. They situate their villages around Ghorn temples and must pay tribute to the Onay hordes of the region. Villages close to the borders of the hordes remain under constant threat. Darwans raise a herd animal called the Ng'Ombe which provides the major staple food in the Barrens.

Dasam – Tenth of the ten Quinte Grand Cycle, Winter.

Deci – Time unit equivalent to one hour.

Derde – Third of the ten Quinte Grand Cycle, Spring.

Diamond – Clear Etheria Crystal which transfers power.

Doggin – Derogatory term used for slave dock workers in the city of Aris.

Dolin – Etheria gem hunters, mostly of the Gila race, traveling the Barrens in small caravans and harvesting raw Etheria Crystals to sell to the Zadim lapidaries of the Oasis in the Dark Waste Desert.

Dor – Title of the seven various provinces in Amarenia. Taia-Dor, Denat-Dor, Mivira-Dor, Amoso-Dor, Kinning-Dor, Rackam-Dor, Durik-Dor.

Do-Tarr – Sentient, hive-minded mantid creatures from the Land of Mists in Nocturn. They comprise two large hives in the north and south with precise subterranean tunnels connecting them. They are expert builders and remain neutral in all forms of politics.

Dreamer in the Lake – Demi-God of the Os'Tor Forest and a Harbinger of Balance. She rests at the bottom of a large lake encased in mud and manifests herself on the lake's surface as a multicolored lotus. Her accolades, sentients from every race, sleep around the lake's shore, sending their ethereal bodies out into people's dreams and guiding them.

Dreeat – Humanoid crocodilians inhabiting the end of the western fork of the Otoman River in Otomoria. They grow sugar cane and make magical healing candies from it. They harvest river fish as a major part of their diet. For thousands of grands, ever since the arrival Human race, the Human families have tried to eradicate them.

Dronning Mare – Female horse chosen to breed with the On'Dara chief.

EEtah – Large, powerful and aggressive sentient humanoid shark creatures trained in martial schools known as Sunals to become the professional warriors of Lumina. After their egg birth in the hatcheries and their first year in the nursery, they are sorted into one of the various Sunals of their House. Females enter House Nur and the males go through a highly competitive Sunal scouting and recruiting process with the nursery's called the Garess. Sunals hire out bodyguards, sentries, mercenaries and virtually anything martial. This, along with weapon manufacturing and sales, provides the main revenue stream for the great houses.

EEtah Great Houses:

> **House Nur** – This Noble house is female only. Co-ruled by a secular Queen Mother and spiritual High Priestess.
>> Temple of Drulain headquartered in the High Holy City of Zor.
>> Specialty: Scribes, Clerics, Healers, Politics, Domestics.
>
> **House Crom** – Three Sunals in the Tellasian Chain.

Sedar Sunal on Roe Island. Specialty: Bodyguard.
Boril Sunal on Uma Island. Specialty: Crom Internal Security.
Zorod Sunal on Tel Island. Specialty: Castle and Town Defense.

House Bran – Four Sunals in the Goyodian Chain.
Garf Sunal on Quell Island. Specialty: Long term inland duty.
Tukk Sunal on Mobis Island. Specialty: Shipboard Security.
Adad Sunal on Creos Island. Specialty: Bran Internal Security.
Farak Sunal on Roust Island. Specialty: Bounty Hunter, Vengeance.

House Zed – Three Sunals in the Wouvian Islands.
Dakor Sunal on Owling Island. Specialty: Shock Troops.
Jut Sunal on Tor Island. Specialty: Zed Internal Security.
Morrak Sunal on Billow Island. Specialty: Police, Executioners.

Elipse – A unit of time equaling a second.

Ellie – Slang and abbreviation for an Ellipse.

Esteemed Sister – Amarenian title for Ambassador.

Etheria Crystal – Crystals containing magical properties mostly found in crystal trees in the Barrens of the Twilight Lands. Residents of the Dark Waste Desert harvest and process the oases' crystals. These crystals provide the primary form of magic in Nocturn.

Flavian Portals – Portals through space making different points in the Annigan instantaneously accessible by passing through the inter-dimensional Middle Realms. Each portal is different. There are several large, fixed portals on both Lumina and Nocturn and hundreds of smaller dedicated Flavians. Certain animals, intoxicants and magical items can open smaller portals.

Frozen Sea – The vast expanse of ice flows covering the majority of Nocturn and the largest centrally occupied area in all of Annigan. The ice ranges from a slushy mixture with icebergs near the land masses to several hundred feet thick in the eastern areas.

Forsvara Guards – A rank-and-file foot soldier army of House Aramos.

Fudomi – Sentient humanoid ram creatures inhabiting the western Os-Oni Mountains of the Twilight Lands. They steal and sell the Cevot Spider broods' silk and eggs, which they consider a delicacy.

Galeb – Sea Gulls with a psychic connection to a handler. They are used to transport messages across Lumina.

Garf Sunal – EEtah War college belonging to House Bran. Their specialty is long term inland duty.

Gar-Kal – Fish head humanoids living on the ocean floor of Nocturn. They are of low intelligence and aggressive.

Geta – Amarenian title for a master at a skill or craft, especially if they teach it.

Ghas-Tor – This is the tallest peak on the Annigan. It reaches upward 32,000 feet in the Os'Ani Mountain range of the Twilight Lands. More than a mountain, it is a sentient being and the epicenter of Air Magic in the world.

Ghorn – Necromancers of the Barrens in Twilight Lands.

Ghost Suit – A gray, skintight jump suit used mostly by Valdurian forces to blend into the Kan fog.

Ghosts of the Kan – Mariner's term for Rayth raiders. Due to their ghost white chalk covering their bodies and acting as camouflage when they attack during the Kan fog.

Gila – The main sentient race populating the Dark Waste. Hybrids comprising Bailian pilgrims and a now long-gone sentient lizard native to the region. They are an advanced race occupying the three large oases of the desert.

Golden One, The – Otick term for the Golden Avatar.

Goy-Ardia – Goyan fire mages trained at the University of Marassa.

Goyan Calendar – Method of time keeping found only in the Goyan Islands. It consists of a Grand Cycle (year) which is comprised of ten Quinte (months) named; Awal, Teine, Derde, Kvara, Peto, Sesto, Ched, Merve, Tisa and Dasam. Each Quinte is divided into fifty Cycles (days) with each cycle being divided into fifty Deci (hours) twenty-five in sunlight and twenty-five in Kan. Ten cycles equal a Cluster (week) with five Clusters per Quinte.

Goyan Rise – A 300-mile-wide sea mount in central Lumina acting as the floor of the Shallow Sea. Its volcanic vents fuel the volcano of Mount Goya.

Grand – Short for Grand Cycle. Unit of time equivalent to a year.

Grass Eater – Singa insult

Gustare' – Amarenian bath house and tavern.

Hackney – Etheria driven floating carriages found throughout the major cities of Lumina.

Hand of the Wind – The Assassin's Guild of Annigan. All members worship Orad, goddess of death. The upper levels are clerics of Orad.

Hakim – A judge in the High Holy City of Zor.

Harbingers of Balance – Sentient creatures of all types called to a secret society monitoring the balance of the Annigan and warning when something upsets it.

Hasteen – City of the Dreeat crocodile people.

Hill Sister – Hermaphroditic warriors inhabiting the northern foothills of the Amaren Mountains in Amarenia. Though they possess both male and female sex organs, they cannot procreate. Popular with Amarenian nobility as seneschal/bodyguards partly because they can have sex with them and not violate their "no man" pledge.

Hoon – Word used in Zor to denote a pimp or the manager of a brothel.

Howlite – Gray Etheria Crystal used for glamour, disguise and polymorphing.

Humans – The Human race descended from the Avion race. In 5070 PA, the rebellious Avions which joined Xandar the Mad's doomed Great Kraken Incursion had their wings severed as punishment before being banished and scattered to the Goyodian Chain. 171 years later the Seventh Avatar sang the "Song of Rebirth" evolving them into a separate race. They formed their Great Houses, spreading out across the Goyan Island Chain and beyond the Shallow Sea.

Human Great Houses:

House Aramos –The largest and wealthiest of the great human families directly descended from the First Men. The capital city of Aris is located on the Island of Vakai in the Goyodian Chain of Islands in the Northern Shallow Sea. They control banking and finance in Lumina and constantly hatch Machiavellian plots to expand their power over the other houses.

361

House Calden – This great house controls the seas with the largest military and commercial fleets. Their Capital City of Nader is on the Island of Tarla in the Goyodian Chain, but they command the island chain of the Zerk Atoll where their sailors are trained.

House Eldor – This great house controls virtually all the agricultural islands of the eastern Goyan Islands. Their Capital City of Rophan is on the Island of Tolle in the Goyodian Chain of Islands in the Northern Shallow Sea.

House Valdur – This house is known for their incestuous practices to keep the family bloodline pure. Their capital city of Dryden is on the Island of Atar in The Goyodian Chain of Islands in the Northern Shallow Sea. All but destroyed in a surprise invasion by House Eldor called the Unification War, only the discovery of lighter than air travel and a fleet of war balloons saved their home island. They lost the rest of their agricultural lands to Eldor. Their entire culture revolves around their powerful air guild, the Valdurian Air Service.

House Whitmar – This family runs the organized and sanctioned slave trade on Lumina from the City of Nier on the northern Goya coast. Their Capital City of Brinstan is located on the Island of Umin in the Goyodian Chain in the Northern Shallow Sea.

Immor-Onn – Large city known as "the Shining Jewel of the East" located on the western coast of the Twilight Lands. Home of the Bailian Empire.

Idonian Philosophy – The Avion prejudice that Humans are a scourge which should be wiped out. The driving belief of the Idonian Cabal of Avion House Pyre and Solas.

Innaca Deep – Giant whirlpool in the Northwestern Ocean of Lumina housing one of the largest Flavian portals. Its psionic ripples extend out hundreds of miles.

Innaca Run – The final test for admittance to the elite Brightstar Sailors where they must navigate a tight circle around the turbulent seas surrounding the Innaca Atoll without being pulled into its giant Flavian portal.

Ironmark – Brutal enforcers of the Quartermasters in the Goyan Islands of Lumina. Each island chain has their own Ironmark specializing in their own unique form of torture.

Itori – Insect Shamans found throughout the agricultural western Goyan Islands. Although they control mostly locusts, they can command any insect and are immune to all insect venoms and stings.

Jangwa – Elite desert commandos defending the outer parameter of the two civilized oases in the Dark Waste Desert. Capable of traveling under the sand and rapidly over the surface of the desert, they make frequent scouting missions to the untamed Qua-Raman Oasis and the Buried City of Nof-Saloom.

Kaefom – Traditional Amarenian breeding ritual overseen by the Darek Witches.

Kan – Period of the day in the Goyan Islands when the thick sea fog rises blotting out the sun, used mostly for sleep. It is an effect caused by geothermal activities only found in the Goyan Islands and Shallow Sea.

Kel – Flying lizards bred and tended by Avions for food and as beasts of burden.

Kharry Institute – Tiikeri medical facility located outside the Tiikeri capital city of Hai-Darr and run by the brilliant and ruthless Dr. Met-Ge, specializing in crossbreeding Mawl races to produce Mongrels for specific duties. The Institute created Cheepas and the Ves-Lari.

Kinjuto Dominator – Sex mage using BDSM techniques.

Konaleeta – Called the Island of the Lost. The entire island is caught in a permanent Flavian Loop. It bounces around from location to location across any of the planes of the Middle Realms, never staying in anyone place for very long.

Kusars – Mawl bandits from the Dasos region in the Land of Mists.

Kvara – Fourth of the ten Quinte Grand Cycle, Summer.

Ky-Awat – Sentient rat creatures of the Dark Waste Desert. They have bred them up from the Cul-Ta and are larger and more aggressive, but no smarter. Various factions use them as cannon fodder. They breed quickly and are plentiful, especially around the three main oases.

Land of Mists – The largest land mass in Nocturn. So named because the mixture of cold temperatures in the air combined with the warmth of the ground results in a uniform constant low hanging fog over the entire continent. Three distinct landscapes cover the surface of the land, separated by the Kel-Raku Mountain range and dimly illuminated by bioluminescence, outcroppings of Etheria Crystals and the moon and stars. The thick rainforest of Arboro lies to the north, and the vast savannah of Rovina runs to the south. They're connected by the Bor-Kaa Pass. The dense jungles and swamps of Dasos lie to the east.

Landagar Group – Research and Development Division of the Valdurian Air Service located in the balloon city of Landagar high in the mountain peaks of the Valdurian home island of Atar.

Larimar – The "Talking Stone," a milky white Etheria Crystal with blue striations, used for psychic communication between parties within proximity of the gem.

Learned Sister – The title given to Amarenian teachers, scribes & academics.

Legates – Suicide messengers hired through House Whitmar. Candidates are usually elderly or terminally ill. Upon their death, House Whitmar agrees to care for their surviving family for their remaining lifetimes.

Lor-Danta Oasis – The eastern most major oasis in the Dark Waste Desert. The large Obsidian field stretching from its shore contains six Tanum Charts of the skies used by the Arron-Nin Astrologers dwelling there.

Lumina – The hemisphere of the world in constant sunlight.

Luna – Term for the lunar cycle used by every culture in the Annigan except the humans in the Goyan Islands, who cannot see the moon.

Luroh – Bolo/sash weapon used by the Mahilia. The sash contains the person's rank and record. The two metal balls at either end become an effective weapon when twirled.

Magitech – The fusion of magic and technology. Mostly referring to the use of Etheria Crystals and specific mechanical items. i.e., Airship engines.

Mahilia – City guards in Mostar, the capital of Amarenia.

Makari – Inter-dimensional race of sentient spiders from the Pasture Plain of the Middle Realms. They seeded the Cevot race in the Os'Tor Mountains in the Land of Mists. The males resemble hairy wolf spiders, the females resemble black widows. The females have been known to allure any male of any race. They compulsively kill after sex.

Malachite – Light green Etheria Crystal, absorbs energy.

Marassa – A professor at the University of Marassa.

Masha – Amarenian for master.

Maudo Grass – Tall grass with a bright blue flowering tuft growing in the Land of Mists. The flowers are a favorite intoxicant for Mawls and especially coveted by the Tiikeri.

Mawl – Overall name for the humanoid cat races of the Land of Mists. It is also the term used for the common language they share.

Medikua – Medical officer aboard Calden naval vessels.

Merve – Eighth of the ten Quinte Grand Cycle, Autumn.

Middle Realms – Constantly shifting inter-dimensional plane between worlds. Sometimes referred to as the Fairy or Dream Realms.

Mongrel – The product of cross breeding between the Mawl races found all over the Land of Mists. Pure breeds mostly shun them and the Tiikeri use them for slave labor.

Moonfall – Period of the cycle when Nocturn's main illuminating body, the moon, dips below the horizon issuing in the Moonless

Moonless – The "night" period of the cycle when Nocturn's main illuminating body, the moon, orbits around to the Lumina side of the Annigan.

Mora – Term used for teacher or master in the Whovian Sword Schools of Rohina Takki.

Morasian Puff Boy – Male prostitute from the Port City of Moras on Goya's west coast. Known for their distinctly feminine demeanor.

Mostas – Capital City of the Amarenian Empire on the western shore of Amarenia.

Najuka – Amarenian emasculation ritual performed on all males except those used for breeding purposes in the Kaefom Ritual.

Na-Kab – One of the three insectoid groups originating from below the Land of Mists. They occupied the easternmost hive closest to Mount Natal. Their exoskeleton is made up of fire magic. Their tail has a penis shaped stinger capable of impregnating any living thing they sting.

Namesake – Term used for spouse when they share a bespoke last name.

Narrows, The – Remnants of an old iron mine forming the slums of the Hidden City of Toriss in Otomoria.

Nocturn – The hemisphere of the world in constant night

Nolton Boat – Ships made of Ukko wood in a secret shipyard on the Island of Zer, mostly used by Brightstar sailors. Hovering less than an inch above the water, their Ukko rudder guides and propels. The specific construction of the hull makes the boat unsinkable.

Noma – Poison from the Noma Viper.

Nurian Edicts – EEtah rules of conduct set down by House Nur forming the basis for all Sunal laws. The various Sunals add their own individual laws to this baseline.

Nyanja – Large seahorses ridden as sea cavalry by the Calden Navy.

Obsidian – Black Etheria Crystal storing psychic energy.

Ocean Deep – Name referring to any of the deep oceans of Lumina or Nocturn.

Ol'daEE – Person able to cast spells while having sex under the influence of Oldust.

Oldust – Hallucinogenic powder derived from the spores of the rare Impia Mushroom, increasing magical abilities and is essential for individual travel to the Middle Realms.

Onay – Humanoid wolf men of the Barrens, banding their various packs together in three distinct hordes.

On'Dara – Sentient horse creatures living on the Plains of Taka-Vir in the southeastern Twilight Lands. They raise and train horses, trading them for silk with the Cevot Spiders and selling them to the rest of the Annigan.

ooD – Shell worn on the back of the male Otick warriors as armor. They mark the warrior's rank and house on the outside of the shell and inscribe a record of their deeds on the inside. They place the ooD over the entrance to their homes in the sand.

Oracle of the River – Demi-God who dwells in the cypress swamp at the end of the western fork of the Otoman River for thousands of grands. It appears as a partially submerged giant catfish with its many whiskers sunken into the water. These whiskers perceive anything happening in, on, or around the waterway.

Orad – Air goddess of death and predominate deity of the assassin's guild, the Hand of the Wind. Her creed: *She comes as the wind. And takes whom she wishes. Her name is Orad. And she is death.*

Orad Dex – Initiates to the Orad priesthood. Street/entry level assassins.

Orad Con – (Taker of the Divine Wind) These are full priests of Orad. Their special skills are the Kiss of Death, the Poison Breath and the Phantom Dagger.

Orad Sto – (Giver of the Divine Wind) High priests of Orad who can also restore life.

Otick – Humanoid crab people inhabiting the Shallow Sea. Among the first sentient creatures to rise from the ocean floor they evolved into a proud, deeply spiritual and noble race. Goya's volcanic warmed waters provide home to the

Otick's prolific oyster beds littering the floor of the Shallow Sea. From these beds arose the five great Pearl Avatars, creation gods whose songs brought life and sentience to Lumina. Otick society is divided into a highly structured caste system: Worker Class, Warrior Class and Mother Class, and organized into two main categories: domestic and military. The Shelled Triad, the three Otick Great Houses, tend their own oyster beds and compete for the birthplace of the next Avatar.

Otick Great Houses:

House Awa – Home of the last two avatars. Located in the Tellasian Chain, in the capital city of Hidet on the Island of Zod. Mother Class specialization.

House Pewa – Located in the Goyodian Chain, in the capital city of Oniack, on the Island of Zak. Worker Class specialization.

House Sensu – Located in the Otoman Group, in the capital city of Sunico, on the Island of Lakia. Warrior Class specialization.

Otomoria – Large Island continent in the western Goyan Islands. The main grain producing agricultural island.

Outer Clan EEtah – Humanoid shark creatures smaller in stature than regular EEtahs and cast out from the three great EEtah Houses hatcheries. The survivors band together into loose clans, contracting themselves out as deck hands or recently volunteering in the Valdurian Marines.

Padi – Regional demi-god of water worshiped in and around the High Holy City of Zor, associated with the peace and calming effect of water and represented by a calm pond.

Palu EEtah – Rare hammerhead EEtahs. They are as big as the Outer Clan EEtah but extremely intelligent. They tend to be reclusive loners.

Pappia – Members of the child street gangs of the Hidden City of Toriss in the slum section of The Narrows.

Pa-Waga – Lawful evil god of greed worshiped mostly by the Tiikeri. Its clerics practice binary blood rune magic comprised of the letters "X" and "I."

Peace Babies – Children born of a union between any of the five major Human noble houses.

Peto – Fifth of the ten Quinte Grand Cycle, Summer.

Piceans – Humanoid fish people of Lumina. Capable of breathing above and below the water and impervious to the ocean's depths. They have gill flaps large enough to fold over their ears and when the vocal sound waves pass through the membrane, it translates it. This makes them valuable translators in the seaports of the Goyan Islands.

Piety Watch – Militant, religious police faction of the Pa-Waga church. They arrest anyone caught begging, idle, or not being productive. Minor offences are punished by a beating with thin cane rods. They wear red shirts under black capes with high pointed collars resembling cat ears.

Pisar – Bailian title for a scholar.

Pomaku – Humanoid leopard people (Mawl) native to the Arboro region in the Land of Mists, Nocturn.

Protocol 13 – EEtah House Nur code phrase requesting a meeting between an intelligence asset and their handler.

Qua-Raman Oasis – An oasis in the central Dark Waste Desert. Due to its location just south of the Tur-Qua Pass, it serves as a major trading post for gems harvested in The Barrens to the north.

Quartermaster – Collector of taxes and tariffs in the Goyan Islands who use the Ironmark to enforce their rule.

Queen's Envoy Service, The – The Amarenian Empire's spy service and member of the Society of Whispers.

Quinte – Time period equivalent to a month.

Ramu – A gambling dismemberment game banned everywhere in Lumina, except the Free City of Tannimore.

Rayth – Pirate faction of the Amarenian people in open revolt and attempting to form their own nation.

Rod-Ema Trench – Massive abysmal fissure running along the equator in the western ocean floor in Nocturn. At its head is the Agar Goyot and the Black Mural is found on its north wall dipping into the ocean depths.

Rohina Takii – Sword school originating on the Island of Wou. Known for its strike while drawing technique.

Sardor – Amarenian title for a female warlord.

Salar Winds – Turbulent winds surrounding the peak of Mount Goya which must be navigated to enter the Avion City of Darmont on the mountain's northwestern face. Avion term of exasperation, "By the mighty Winds of Salar!"

Secor – Street name for the Imperial Gold Ingot equivalent to ten struck gold coins.

Sesto – Sixth of the ten Quinte Grand Cycle, Autumn.

Shallow Sea – The body of water surrounding the greater Goyan Islands covering the Goyan Rise. The depth is no more than thirty feet deep at its lowest point.

Si – The term for "mister" in the Common Tongue spoken in the Goyan Islands.

Sikari – Female Singa hunter/killer squads, traveling in groups of two or more. They arm themselves with crossed bandoleros covering their chests and filled with sickle shaped throwing blades.

Silent Partner – Seven cabals of organized crime families in the Goyan Islands.

Simikort – Round engraved coin acting as an Amarenian noble's calling card.

Singa – Humanoid lion people (Mawl) inhabiting the southern Rovina area of the land of Mists.

Skirting the Upwinds – Dangerous maneuver practiced by few airship pilots. It involves taking the airship up to the edge of the atmosphere and then plummeting down to your destination. Allowing long-distance travel in a short period.

Society of Whispers – The general intelligence cooperative of the five Human noble houses, the Zorian Spymaster, the Calden Intelligencer Service, Suusho, and the Queen's Envoy Service.

Spice Rat – Smugglers operating in the Spice Islands chains (Zerian Reef Chain and Outer Zerians) and occasionally in the entire western side of the Goyan Islands.

Spooks – Street term for spies and operatives in the Society of Whispers.

Strasta – Ancient prophet in the folklore of the Cevot spider people of the Os-Ani Mountains.

Sunal – EEtah war college specializing in martial skills.

Suusho – The Bailian Empire's spy service and member of the Society of Whispers.

Szoldos Mercenaries – One of several small private armies for hire on the Goyan continent.

Taking it Upstairs – Airship slang for skirting upwinds

Tanum Charts – Six maps of Nocturn's night sky. The Arron-Nin Astrologers use them for divination and sometimes the opening of Flavian portals.

Teine – Second of the ten Quinte Grand Cycle, Spring.

Ten/Fifty— Cliché phrase in the Goyan Islands referring to the ten cycles (days) in the cluster (week) and fifty decis (hours) of the cycle (day). The equivalent of 24/7.

Tenable Sister—Title given to Amarenian lawyers.

Tiikeri – Sentient humanoid Tiger creatures of the Dasos region in the eastern Land of Mists.

Tisa – Ninth of the ten Quinte Grand Cycle, Winter.

Trinilic – Orange Etheria Crystal, fire magic connection.

Turine – Tidal clocks used in the Goyan Islands.

Twilight Lands – Area between Lumina and Nocturn in constant state of Twilight. Due to converging hot and cold air masses its weather remains perpetually stormy.

Ukkonite – Bronze Etheria Crystal with natural repellant properties. It is the crystal equivalent to Ukko wood found only in Nocturn.

Ukko Wood – Magical wood from the World Tree, harvested only on the Island of Zer in the eastern Goyan Islands. Its natural repellant properties are used in shields, weapons, Brightstar Nolton Boats and used as currency.

Ulana – Chaotic evil sea goddess worshiped by a small sect of Amarenian Rayth in the province of Durik-Dor

Unification War – Conflict started by House Eldor in 2 P.A. against the eastern agricultural islands of House Valdur. It ended as quickly as it began when House Aramos forced them to the negotiating table by threatening to freeze both houses' accounts in the Imperial Bank.

Valorous Sister – Amarenian title for heroic acts which affected the realm.

Vedette – Small fast Nolton Boats crewed by a single ex-Brightstar sailor and used for fast, anonymous travel around the oceans of Lumina.

Velocomite – Pale blue Etheria Crystal with red bands, increases or decreases an object's speed travelling.

Veros Pearls – Highest quality pearl cultivated in the Otick oyster beds. They are capable of holding a magical charge.

Ves-Lari – Mawl mongrels bred by the Tiikeri for rowing and poling. They are a combination of Pomaku (leopard) and Duma (Cheetah). Crews can pole or row for hundreds of miles at a time without stopping.

Vurr Carts – Carts used by the Vurr Clerics to collect the City of Zor's dead and garbage. There are two types: stationary carts situated on every major street where citizens can deposit their waste and roving carts mostly dealing with collecting the bodies of the dead.

Vurr Clerics – Accolades of the Free God Vurr serving as waste disposal in the City of Zor. Once maintaining constantly pyres burning everything from corpses to ordinary refuse. The city upgraded the pyres to full crematoriums. Vurr clerics smell of smoke and generally work nude, wearing only a simple cloak.

Wraith – Deep cover agents for House Aramos drawn from the elite Black Talons unit.

Yagur – Humanoid jaguars (Mawl) from the Arboro region of the Land of Mists. They are seers, healers and shamans, serving all the various Mawl races.

Yudon – Harpoon with a rifled the shaft for throwing accuracy. The standard weapon of every Sunal EEtah.

Yupik – a.k.a. the Ice Clans, one hundred and sixty-five clans divided into three major groups. The nomadic wanderers of the Western Flows compete for resources while the Ash-Ta constantly hunt them as prey. The largest group inhabits the vast Eastern Flows with semi-permanent settlements surrounding the Ice City of Mos-Agar'.

Zadim – Lapidaries operating in the Dark Waste Desert.

Zerian Rangers – Woodsmen fighters belonging to any of nine different clans occupying the forests of the Island continent of Zer in the Goyan Islands.

Zoldak Group – A private mercenary army comprised of former Black Talons of House Aramos.

Zorian Monetary Council – A ruling body founded in 3850 P.A. controlling all banking in the High Holy City of Zor. The council coordinates with the Calden Commodities exchange to regulate the exchange of money, goods and services, and uses the Quartermasters Guild for the collection of taxes and tariffs.

MAPS

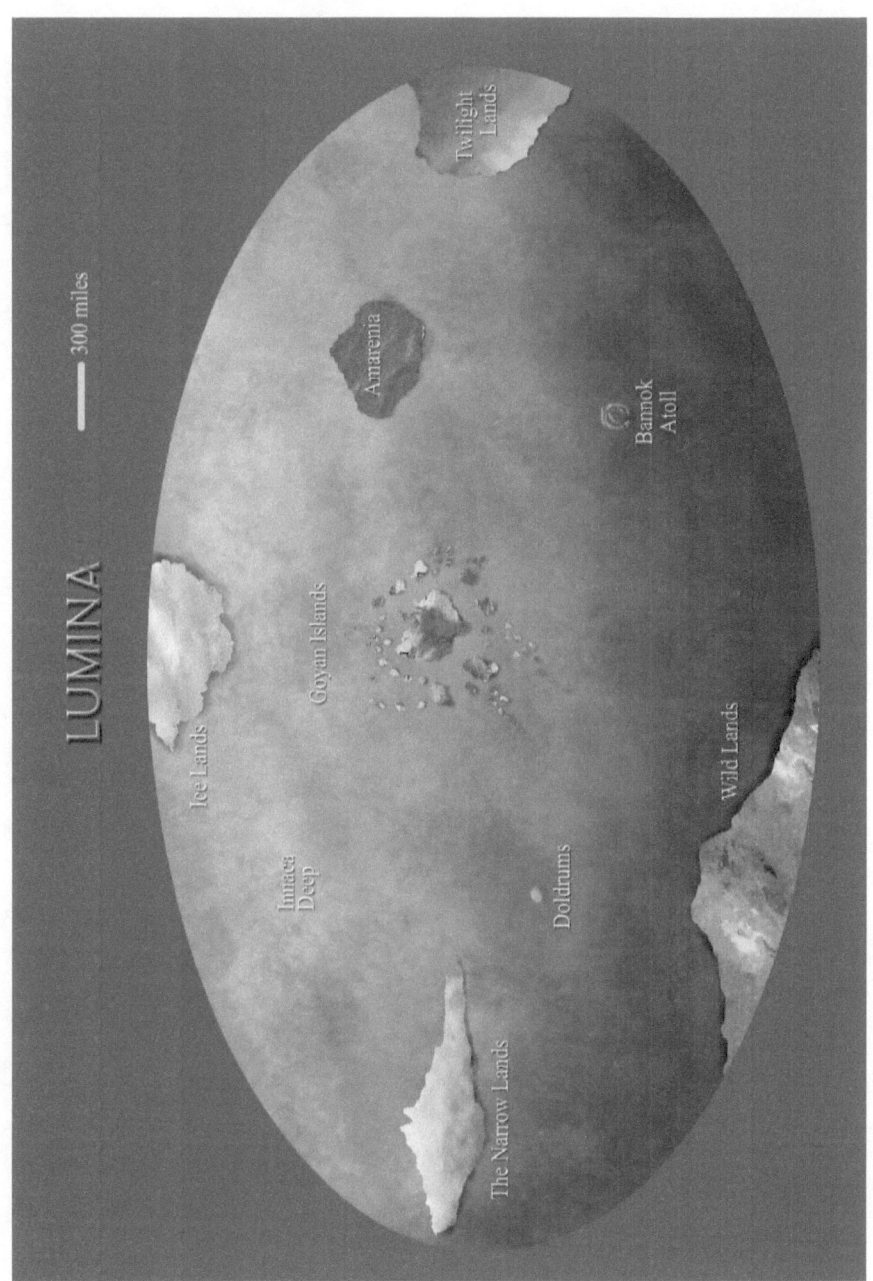

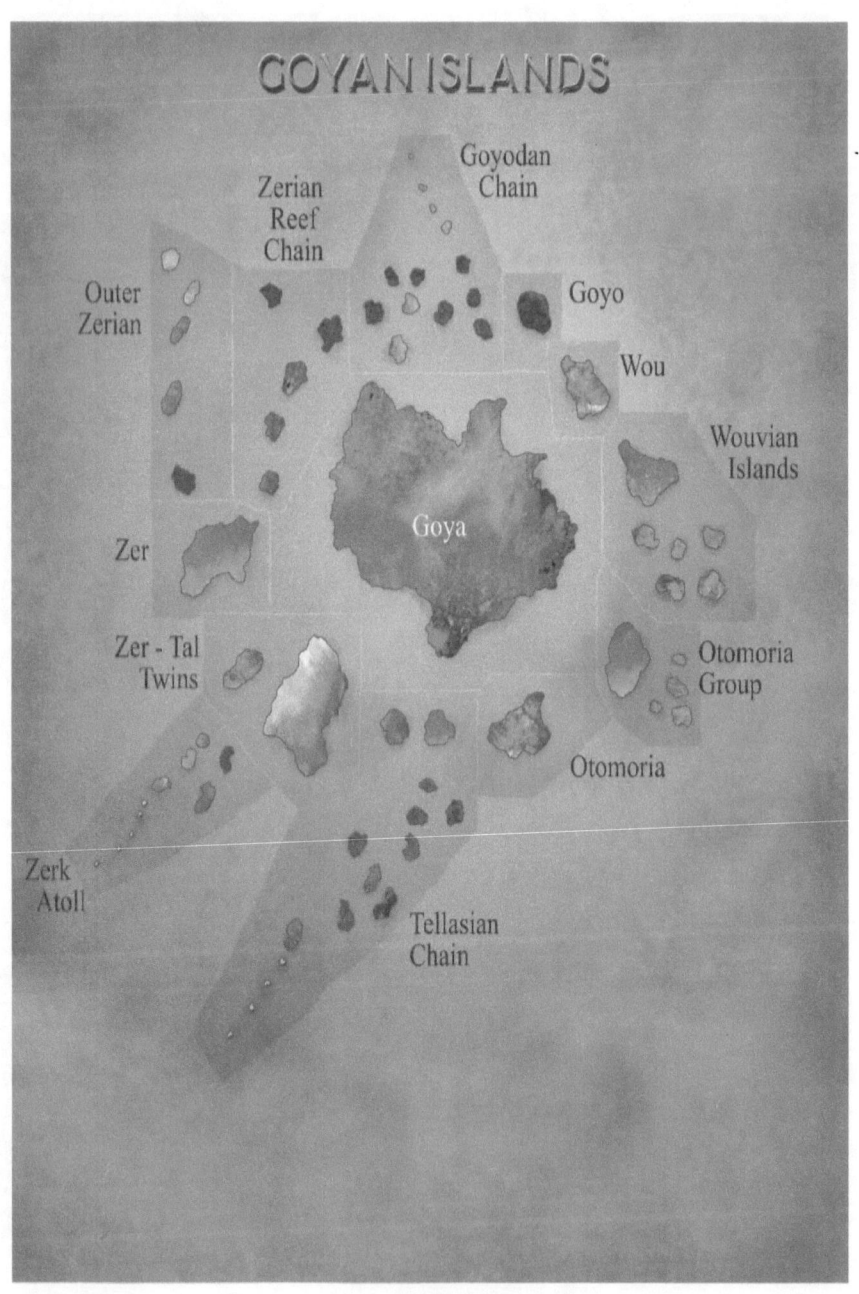

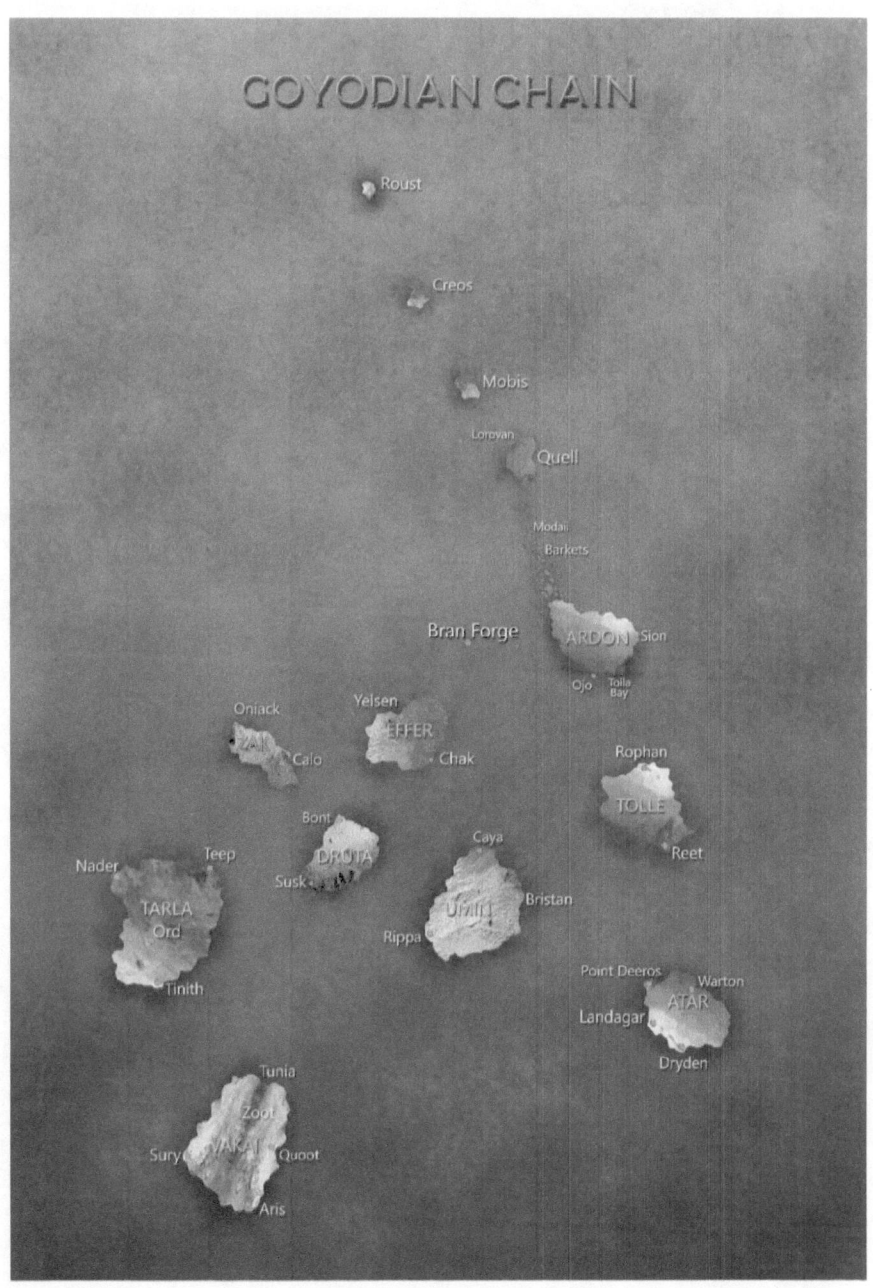

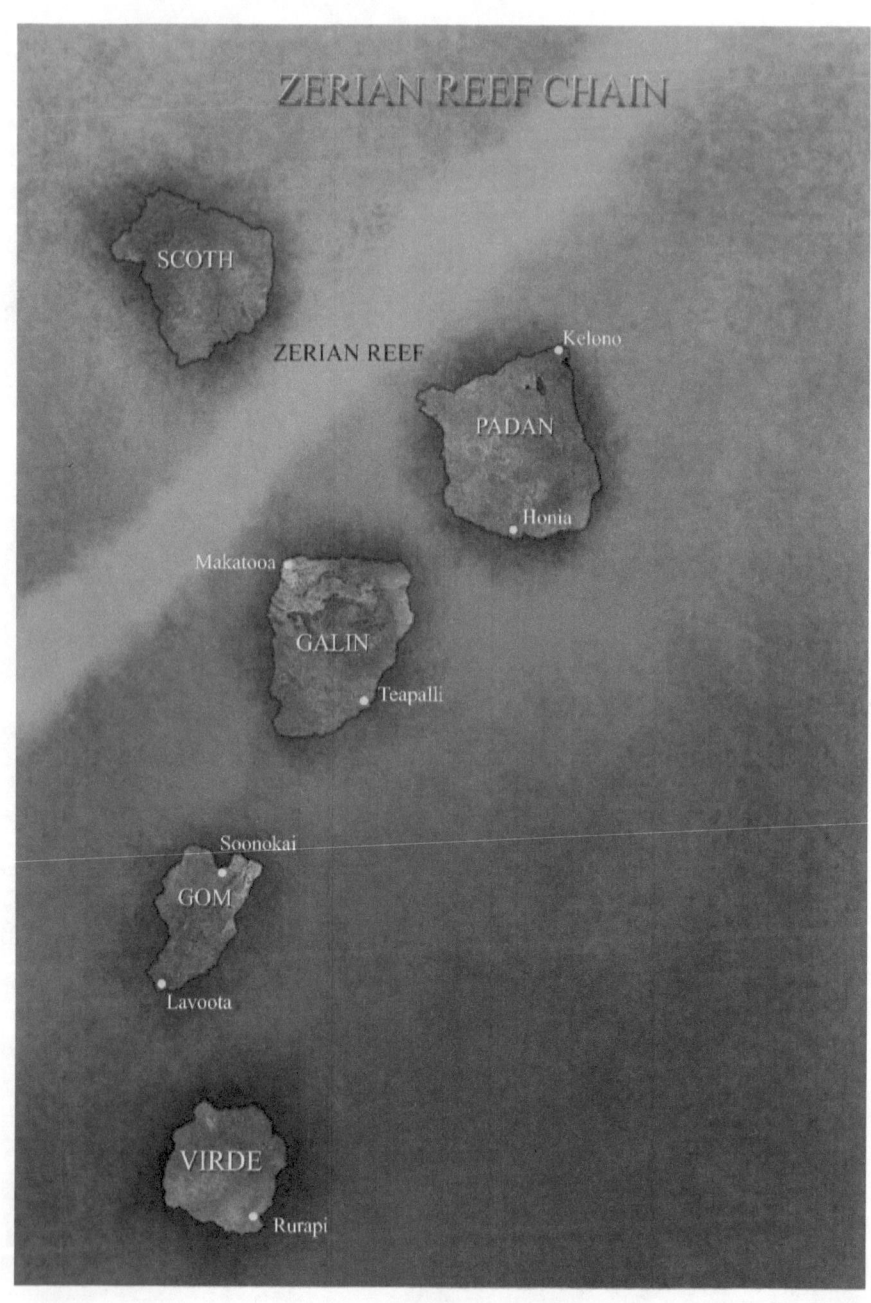

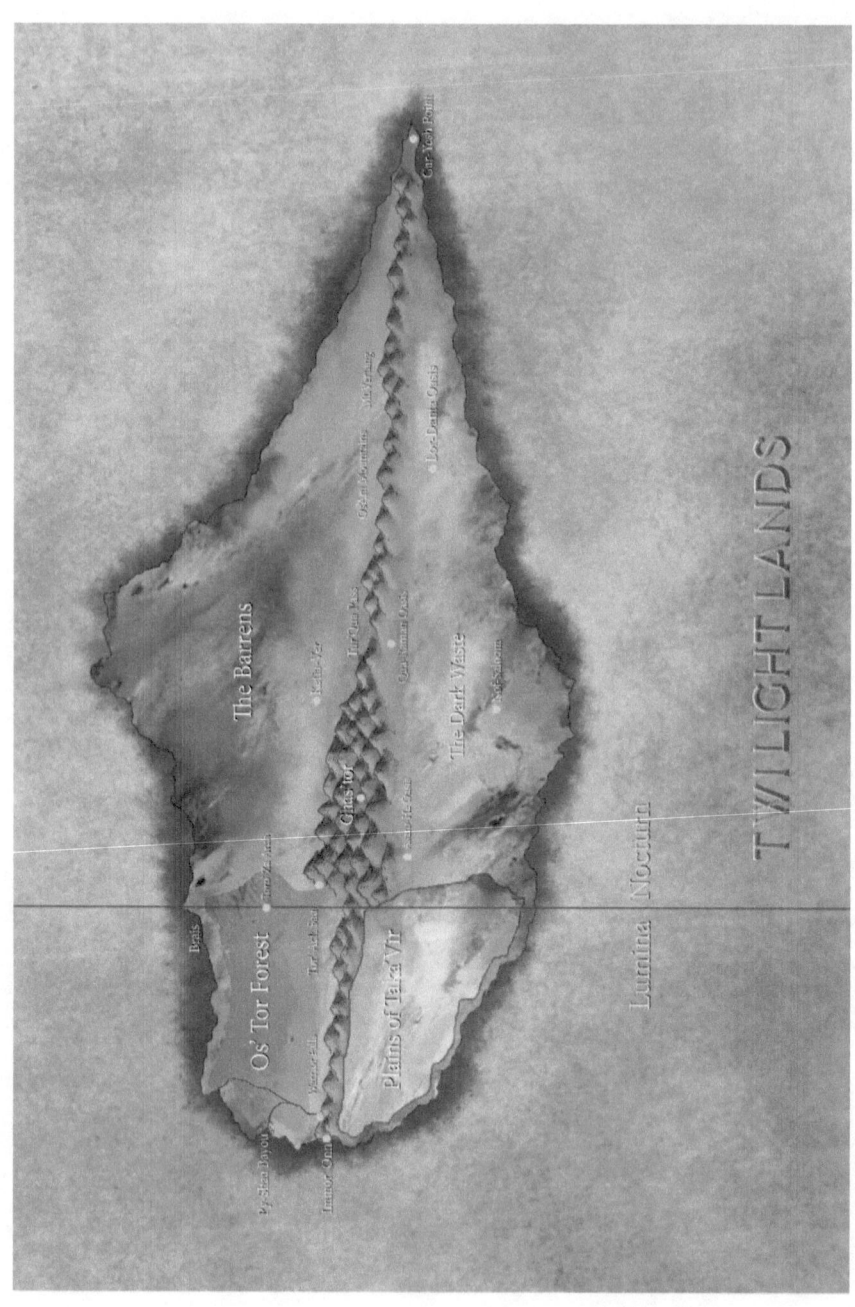

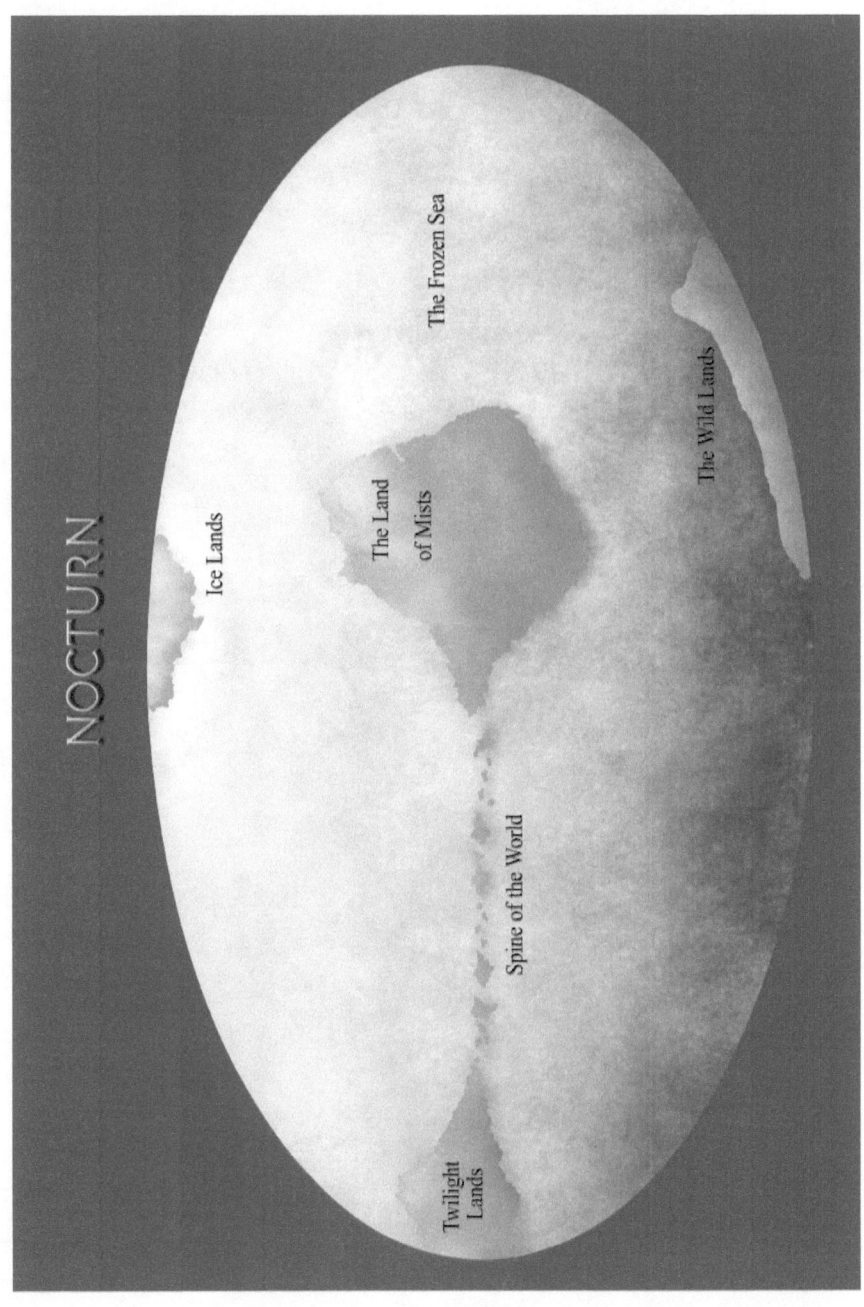

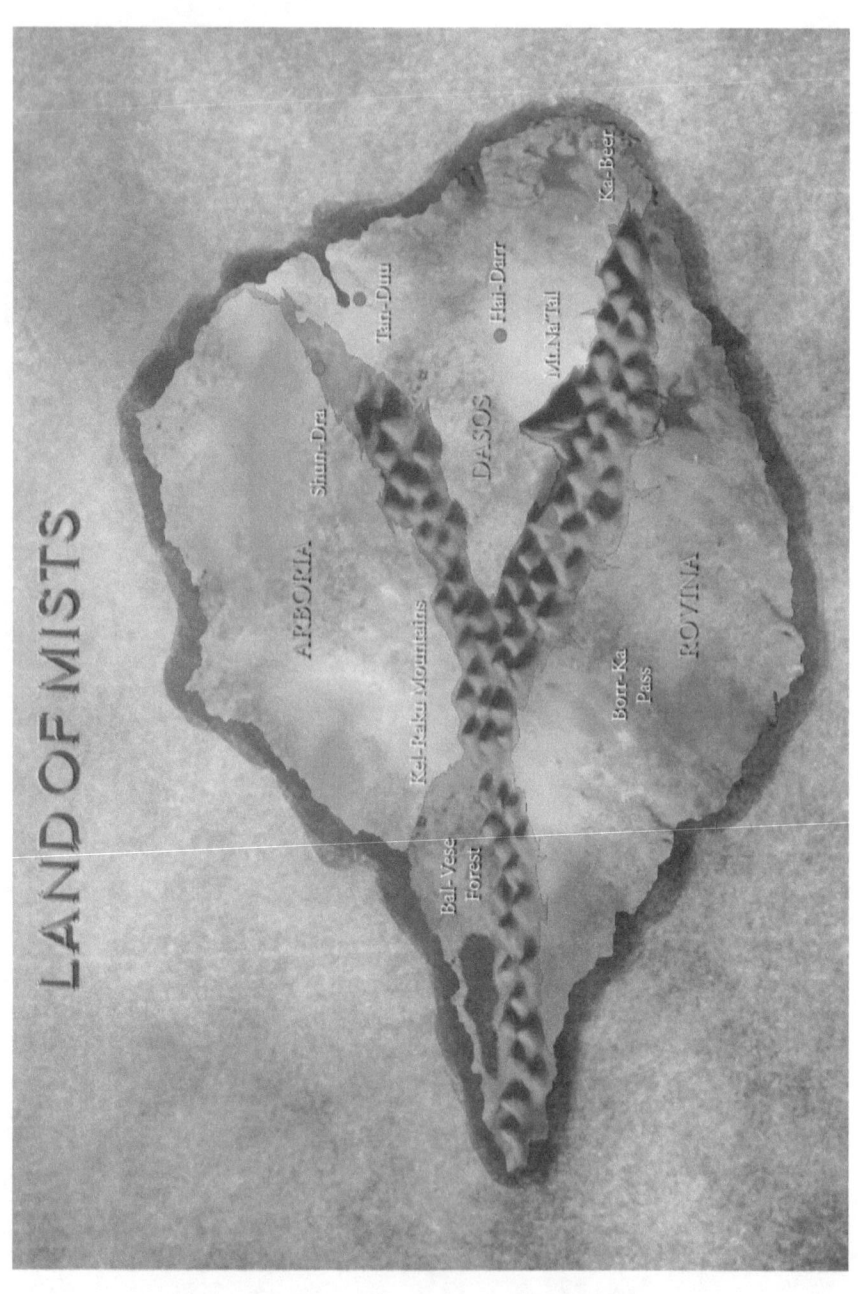

ABOUT THE AUTHOR

R.W. Marcus spent most of his life selling books. Along the way he managed to become a Falconer, 2nd Dan Black Belt in Yoshukai Karate, Freemason, Freelance Photographer, Ad Copywriter and WMNF Radio Disc Jockey. Marcus' radio commercials and freelance photography won numerous awards, including Best of Shows and Best of the Bay Addy Awards for work with Creative Keys and Laughing Bird Productions. R.W. Marcus was also Founder and Creative Director of United Game Masters, where he cowrote the UGM Universal Gaming System which he used to create and playtest a role-playing game based in the world of the Annigan Cycle. He formally held the title of Director of

Incunabula at Griffon's Medieval Manuscripts, where he penned his first nonfiction title, *The Ship of Fools to 1500*, which Amazon called "an authoritative guide to one of the most popular works of secular writing." Now retired, he created a new genre of fiction - Pulp Fantasy Noir - to exorcise the darker side of his good nature.

CONNECT
WEBSITE: https://AnniganCycle.com
FACEBOOK: https://www.facebook.com/noirrwmarcus/
TWITTER: @NoirRWMarcus
EMAIL: RWMarcus@yahoo.com

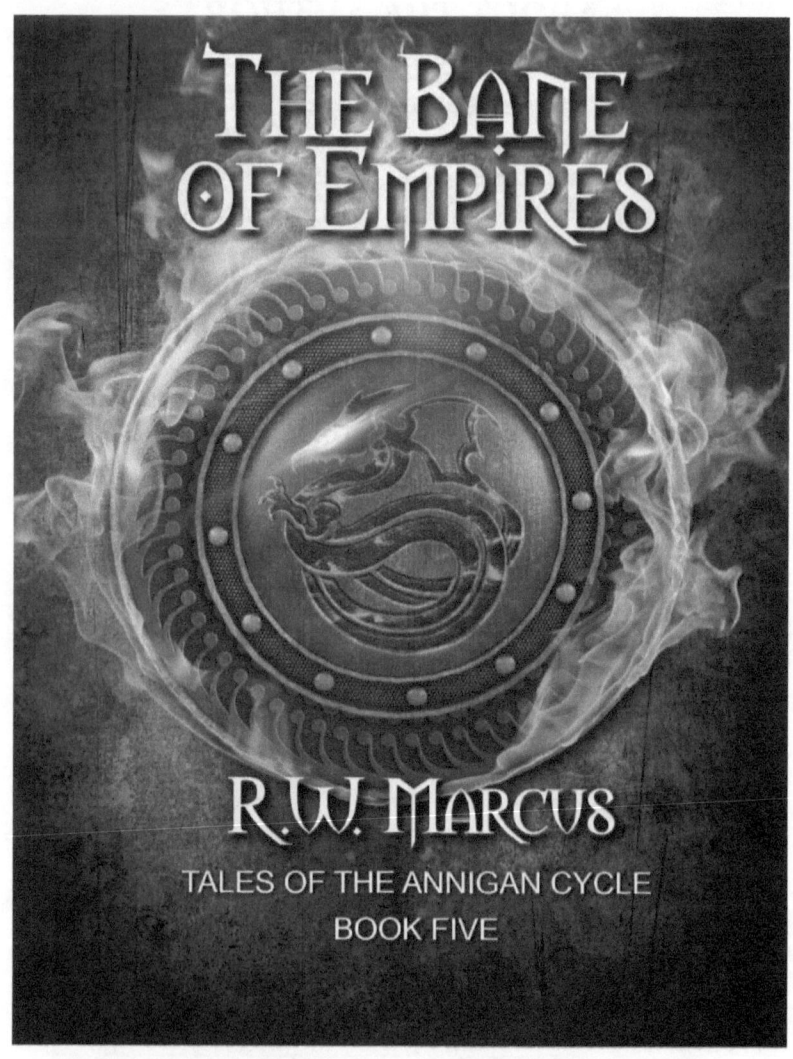

The BANE of EMPIRES
TALES OF THE ANNIGAN CYCLE
BOOK FIVE
AVAILABLE FROM LAUGHING BIRD PUBLISHING

www.ingramcontent.com/pod-product-compliance
Lightning Source LLC
Chambersburg PA
CBHW021958260626
47156CB00018B/1924